Wicked Lies

❦

Laura Renken

This is a work of fiction. Names, characters, places, and incidents either are the product of the author's imagination or are used fictitiously, and any resemblance to actual persons, living or dead, business establishments, events, or locales is entirely coincidental.

WICKED LIES

A Jove Book / published by arrangement with
the author

PRINTING HISTORY
Jove edition / November 2002

Copyright © 2002 by Laura Renken
Cover art by Don Case

Visit our website at
www.penguinputnam.com

ISBN: 0-515-13403-1

A JOVE BOOK®
Jove Books are published by The Berkley Publishing Group,
a division of Penguin Putnam Inc.,
375 Hudson Street, New York, New York 10014.
JOVE and the "J" design
are trademarks belonging to Penguin Putnam Inc.

PRINTED IN THE UNITED STATES OF AMERICA

10 9 8 7 6 5 4 3 2 1

For my husband, Thomas.
I love you.

Prologue

"They say no one comes out here after dark, my lord."

The somber words opened Julian's eyes. The sunlight had faded to dusk. Hunched on one knee, his elbow resting across his thigh, he lifted his head. His knee was damp where he knelt in the loam and dead leaves. Touching the headstone, he traced his half brother's name. The stone had been carved out of the finest white marble.

"You were at sea." His bespeckled solicitor stepped forward, his cocked hat crushed in his hands. "There's nothing you could have done, milord. You couldn't have known."

Julian plucked a flower from the mound and brought it to his nose. "What does a marble headstone cost, Robbie?"

"I don't know, milord. But it can't be cheap."

"Find out who purchased this stone."

Somewhere a tree branch scraped against a building. Julian stood. A gazebo drew his gaze. His cloak tangled in the sudden gust that lifted dead leaves around his boots.

"The townsfolk claim the place is haunted. Ghosts, Captain," his solicitor whispered. "Messy ghosts from the looks of this place."

Julian's gaze lifted to the house. Framed within a deep border of woods, the pillared monstrosity stood aloft the highest point on the James River, a faded remnant of misplaced wealth and shattered dreams, at home in the overgrown, weed-infested yard. Broken dormer windows looked out across the empty sky, void yet of stars. The house lay as dead as the dreams of the man who'd built it.

Anchored only in the shadows he'd sought so long to escape, Julian Reece Lambert was a man of two worlds, lost between both. He hated the darkness, but as much as he could not live within its embrace, he could not escape its grip tonight. He knew the dangers of hate, for the shadows behind a man's heart stole his soul as easily as his life.

"Find someone who will talk."

"Mum's the word, Captain. We risk much to do this on our own."

"I want a name, Robbie, not a magistrate's lies. Find someone who knows what happened."

"You cannot stay. I'm telling you, as your friend as well as your solicitor, it's not safe for you here."

Julian whirled on his heel, his knee-length boots making no sound as he strode out of the yard. "A name, Robbie."

His solicitor slapped the crushed tricorn back on his head and fell in beside him. They approached the sprawling oak where the horses were tethered. "But . . . who should I say is asking?"

"I have a cargo full of muskets." Julian swung into the saddle. Leather creaked beneath his weight. "Trade the price of the rifles and powder for the name of someone who knows what happened. I don't care what it costs."

His gaze lifted. He would set flame to that damn house before he ever set foot in it again. But before he left this town, he would know what happened the night his half brother was murdered.

"Tell them . . . Merlin sent you."

Chapter One

The fair arrived in Yorktown on September fifth every year for as along as Catherine Bellmay had lived in this tidewater community. Squeezing her eyes shut, she thrust out her chin and let the warmth touch her face. Her body moved in tune to the rhythm of dancing lutes and infectious laughter that surrounded her. Her artist's eye had memorized every vibrant detail of color. This was a special time of year, when the summer flowers bloomed amidst a scarlet countryside. When laughter intertwined with the winsome cries of the snowy white gulls that circled the river wharf. 'Twas a time for new beginnings. Perhaps peace would not be far behind.

"Look what you made me do!"

"No, I didn't."

A small body careened into Catherine's backside, and she stumbled forward. A little girl's wail made her cringe.

Her brother and sister exchanged blows.

Gritting her teeth, Catherine separated the twins. "We haven't been here an hour. Do you think the two of you might manage to last a little longer before you fight?"

Bright blue eyes peeped out at her from beneath a mop of blond curls so unlike her own sable tresses and dark eyes that she resembled more a Welsh nanny than their half sister.

Her sister's bottom lip trembled as the reason for their visit to the fair could no longer be avoided. "Are you going to murder Sally now?"

Catherine dropped her gaze to the pale pink pig sitting obedi-

ently at her heel, the only one of the trio who had behaved for the
hour trip into town.

This was the first time since she'd buried her husband four
months ago that the responsibility of filling her family's larder
weighed upon her shoulders. The thought of slaughtering Sally
churned her belly. But the task had to be done.

"Go." She opened her small reticule and handed each of them
a precious coin. "Both of you eat to your heart's content," she
called before they disappeared into the crowd, hoping they'd
both exhaust themselves before their trip home.

The crowd jostled her. Searching among the crush of people
for her errant sister Elizabeth, who'd clearly deserted her in the
face of Sally's demise, Catherine accepted that she would have to
endure the responsibility of killing their family pig alone. With a
sigh, she allowed her gaze to wander over the colorful booths
filled with ribbons and a bounty of rich cloth. She fingered her
simple brown linen skirt and the skimpy lace at her sleeve. Alas,
she was no spendthrift, but her coins were few, and she'd come
today for one purpose only. Resolutely, she turned her mind to
the grim task ahead.

Gripping the rope on the pig, Catherine shouldered through
the people, trailing Sally behind. In the center of town, the log
smokehouse loomed ominously before her. She fidgeted with the
frayed end of hemp and swallowed the ridiculous urge to burst
into tears.

Only a few short months ago, she'd lived in paradise. Now
her very survival was in jeopardy. At twenty-four years old, she'd
been left with the care of her family and loyal servants who had
followed her family since before her birth. The few who remained were too old to be hired elsewhere. They had nowhere to
go.

Gritting her teeth, Catherine knew she'd not be in this
predicament now if she'd been able to keep her newspaper alive.
She'd built the *Tidewater Clarion* into a rallying voice here: a
reckoning force within the political arena where words were
weapons of war used more effectively than muskets. Then a mob
of loyalists destroyed the press, just one day before her husband
died.

Even now, the memory of what happened jolted her. Unable
to fight the tightness in her chest, she closed her eyes, awaiting

the fear to pass through her. The past months had shattered more than a lifetime of dreams. They'd stolen her faith and destroyed her soul.

Moreover, her letters to Patrick's brother remained unanswered. But that hardly surprised her, considering his lordship never once even visited here. So she'd paid the price of his indifference. And now she was reduced to slaughtering the family pet for survival.

The muffled sound of the butcher's cleaver came from the square-built log hut directly in front of her and mingled with the smell of smoking ham. Across the dusty street, a line formed around a redbrick building where people waited to be served the finest honeyed cuisine this side of Williamsburg.

The thought of serving Sally up on a platter was enough to make her choke. Rocked by indecision, Catherine struggled desperately to reconcile the need to do her duty against the frivolous attachment she'd formed with a silly pig. Smoke steamed from pits buried in the earth. The surrounding heat curled the dark hair at her temples. Sally remained at her heel, a picture of domestic obedience. And a slow rage began to simmer. Men didn't suffer through antiquated emotions better suited to pampered women who could afford the luxury of whining.

Catherine drew in a deep breath. Squaring her shoulders, she headed toward the log smokehouse in search of the butcher.

"I should have known you couldn't go through with it." Elizabeth laughed. Catherine's cowardly sister wasted no time taunting her. The twins trailed behind them, kicking rocks and giggling.

With Sally loping happily at her heel, Catherine trudged up the crowded lane toward their wagon. The sun had set an hour ago. Elizabeth flounced in a circle around her, her cerulean skirts as ethereal as a beam of moonlight. "You have a soft heart after all, crusading sister of mine. Admit it." Lamplight from a nearby tavern flickered over the road, guiding their steps. "'Twas not a sword or a mighty quill in your hand tonight but that selfless beating heart you try to hide in your chest."

Catherine flung around, one hand on her hip. "I only know that not a one among us, including our dear brother, is responsible enough to manage our household. We cannot forever remain soft or shelter every cow and pig we have just because they have names."

Contrite, Elizabeth lowered her head. Pale blond hair caught in the breeze and flicked over her downcast profile as she seemed to study her bright blue slipper. The twins for once remained docile. Merrymaking filled the air as the evening's fireworks exploded and blossomed like rainbows over the sky. Guilt intruded when Catherine caught the twins' wondrous glances toward the display, and suddenly she wanted to hear their laughter again.

"Sally has been with us for years," Elizabeth said. "None of us wanted to see her killed. We weren't meaning to be cruel to you."

At seventeen years old, Elizabeth was on the threshold of womanhood, with a whole life before her. Hers was a world untarnished by deception. Catherine wanted more than anything to give her sister a season in Williamsburg, to shield her silver Camelot with a protective moat that would keep the world at bay. But their father had died two years ago, and her stepmother, who had raised Catherine since she was five, had never truly recovered in mind, much less body. Catherine had become their sole benefactor, attempting to manage their depleting wealth and their lives as best she could.

Somewhere thunder grumbled over the distant landscape, and Catherine shuddered against the encroaching darkness. "It smells like rain." She looked down the steep hill at the brightly lit taverns that lined Wharf Street. "Where's Daniel?"

Her wayward brother was wont to disappear like the rest of them, and today he'd succeeded. She'd not seen him since early afternoon.

Elizabeth stepped forward and took Sally's leash. "I'll stay with the twins. You'd best hurry and find him."

Catherine glanced up at the dark sky. Swinging her gaze up and down the crowded street, she blew a strand of dark hair out of her eyes. What Elizabeth didn't say was that this was the time of night when taverns filled with firebrand speechmakers and Tory hecklers, a stumping place for treason that too often brought the wrath of the king's soldiers down on them all.

As she hurried down the steep street, Catherine searched the doorways and grimy windows of the crowded inns and taverns for Daniel. A lone raindrop plopped on her forehead. Conscious of the approaching storm and lack of shelter for the night, she found another cause for haste.

Daniel was not to be found.

Worry crept over her. Soon, the fireworks display no longer lit the sky, signaling an end to the day's festivities. Children swarmed over the streets and filled the night with laughter as many families ventured back to their wagons or walked to their homes. Most of the people knew her by name and answered her greeting. Catherine owed her popularity to her work with the newspaper. Despite the cruel acts of a few, this was a decent town filled with good folk.

Going from block to block, Catherine reached Water Street. The air had taken on the stench of rot. Hugging her arms to her chest, she stopped across the street from the Red Lion Inn, away from the fanfare of rowdy patrons and anyone who might recognize her. Lantern lights illuminated the infamous tavern like some celestial palace, nothing that a good strike of flint wouldn't remedy. Horses stood at the hitching posts along both sides of the street.

At once, she straightened. Daniel Claremont stood at the far end of the wooden walkway. Papa's once-proud namesake leaned with both hands braced against the horse trough. Wet hair curled over his face and shoulders. His white lawn shirt was without a stock.

Lifting the hem of her skirts, she darted across the street. Mud sucked at her slippers.

When Daniel saw her, he straightened, but any attempt at sobriety was lost as he stumbled forward. "Ah, Big Sister." He swept his hat off and dipped into a mocking bow. "I should have known you'd rescue me from my wily ways."

Stains ruined his deep green jerkin and buff breeches. Her heart lurched with a sickening clarity. No amount of love or desperation could change her handsome brother or return the bond they'd once shared. She was helpless in the wake of his youthful defiance, helpless as she watched him throw away his talents. The path he'd walked since their father died would see him killed.

"Everyone is at the cart waiting." She beckoned him to follow with a touch. "I'll help you back."

"I know the way, Rina."

He staggered past her and tripped. Ignoring his protests, Catherine braced a shoulder beneath his arm. "Then maybe you should go in the right direction." He followed her hand left. "Our cart is that way."

A solid six inches taller than she, he outweighed her by three stone. Pushing against his weight, she struggled to stay balanced. They both went down into the mud.

Catherine sat back on her heels and slapped the grit from her hands. "Why couldn't you come today and, just once, not get drunk?"

"Don't give me your bloody lectures." His mouth tightened. He suddenly dropped his gaze to his scuffed hands. His beautiful slim hands that could wield a paintbrush or stick of charcoal with more talent than she could ever hope to possess. "Hell, Rina . . ." Struggling back to his feet, he offered his hand. "I'm sorry."

She scorned his aid and retrieved her balance without assistance. If she said anything else to him, they would only argue, as if they hadn't once been close, as if they were enemies.

She walked away from him, away from the drunken revelers and into the darkness. The ground smelled of manure and waste. Lifting her skirts, she edged past a pile of broken crates. Daniel followed, winded as he tried to keep up.

"I got a job, Rina."

"You already have a job," she snapped. "You're a fine artist. I won't let you throw that dream away."

Fumbling inside his jerkin, he removed a heavy leather pouch and dangled it before her nose. "Twenty pounds they paid me."

"Twenty!" She faced him. "That's . . ." Her eyes narrowed. "What job pays that kind of money?"

He tossed her the pouch. "All for a noble cause, sweet Rina. One dear to your own sweet heart." His boots crunched in the gravel as he swaggered past.

Her gaze lifted from the pouch clutched in her hands and landed with stricken uncertainty on his back. "No!" She choked on her whisper. Her heart leapt into her throat. "It's . . . them, isn't it?" She ran after him. "They've asked you to make a drop."

"And here, I'd thought you'd be so proud."

"Stop it!" His mockery cut into her heart. She grabbed his sleeve. "You promised to stay away from those men."

He whipped around. "I'm a man. It's time you trusted my decisions."

"Trust! This isn't about trusting yo—"

Daniel closed his hand over her mouth. It smelled of sour ale. She tried to pull away. His strength frightened her.

"Haven't you learned?" He wobbled as he pressed his face nearer to hers. "Those men don't play games. You either stand with them or against them. They told me to make a drop tonight. What did you expect me to say?"

A carriage rattled past. Daniel pushed her deeper into the shadows. Even in the darkness, she could feel the fear surrounding him. Despite his bluster and talk of patriotic duties, he was afraid.

No less frightened than she.

Clutching the pouch of money, Catherine swallowed the hard lump in her throat. But steel straightened her spine. "Why ask you? Have you considered that?" She wrapped Daniel's arm around her shoulder and helped him walk. They had to leave before the constable saw them loitering in the shadows.

"You're in no condition to ride tonight. They must know that."

"Rina . . ." Winded, Daniel leaned a hand against the redbrick wall that abutted the town's stable. He slumped against the building. "I have to do this. You know I do."

Her gaze swept his haggard face, sparsely covered in fuzz. "What are you delivering?" she quietly asked.

"Only a letter."

"For twenty pounds?"

His head lolled back. "I won't break the seal to find out."

Catherine managed to get her brother back to the cart. Sally came to attention at their approach. Tied to a metal ring on the side of the cart, the happy pig made a spectacle with her noisy greeting. Elizabeth rushed to help Catherine lift Daniel into the back of the cart, where he collapsed in a drunken heap. His legs dangled out the rear. The twins were asleep, curled in the straw near the front.

"Daniel . . ." Catherine shook him. "What else did they tell you?"

He rolled over and groaned. Catherine snatched up the tin bucket and walked across the street to the horse trough.

Elizabeth twisted her hands. "What's wrong, Rina?"

Catherine dumped the bucket of brackish water over her brother's obstinate head. He shot up, sputtering.

"Daniel Claremont. You talk to me!"

"Jeezus, Catherine!"

She grabbed his jerkin with both fists and gave him a furious shake. Thunder grumbled over the distant treetops, and she cast her gaze aloft to clash with the angry sky. "When is the drop scheduled?"

"Two . . . two hours before dawn." His voice was slurred. "The North Fork road between here and Williamsburg."

Catherine paled. "The North Fork road?" Her fingers tightened their grip on the thin cloth of his jerkin. Everything inside went still. That was the place Patrick was found dead. "Why . . . there?"

"My contact." Daniel's eyes drooped. "He . . . he wanted the meeting to take place there. That's all I was told."

"Your contact?" She met her sister's worried glance. "Who are you meeting, Daniel?"

Her brother didn't answer. Lurching forward, he hung his head over the wagon's lip and vomited.

A silver ribbon of light was all that remained of the moon as Catherine drew rein at the bottom of the rise. Thunder rolled over the angry sky, marking the approaching tempest with a fury that matched her pulse.

He was here. She could feel his presence. Felt it in the shudder down her spine as she turned her mount in a nervous circle to study the road from both directions. Her gloved hands tightened on the reins. She was mad to do this, insane to be here.

Her heart froze.

In front of her where the narrow dirt road melded with the darkness, the night had taken the shape of a man. He didn't move but stood before her, his feet slightly braced as if he rode the prow of a great ship. Embraced by wind and lightning, the shadows gave him wings for flight. Like her, he wore black, but it did not conceal his height nor the breadth of his shoulders. Beneath the windswept military cloak, a cutlass rode the sash of his waist. 'Twas not a gentleman's rapier he wore but a sheath of steel that lent to his reputation. A French cocked hat shrouded his eyes, but she could feel the burn of his gaze, shocking her into utter stillness.

To the Sons of Liberty, he was known only as Merlin. His exploits up north had been whispered among village gossips from Boston to the finest drawing rooms in Williamsburg. He was a hero to the fledgling Continental cause and an enemy of England. The price on his head could buy her an island in the West Indies, where she could run and never look back on a past she wished only to forget.

The gelding shifted and, after a moment's pause, Catherine kneed her mount forward. Though procedure dictated an exchange be made on foot, tonight she remained mounted. Perhaps 'twas the storm that plucked away a measure of her courage, or maybe sitting on the horse allowed her some advantage over this stranger's height, though she doubted it. He looked ruthlessly capable of taking what he wanted.

Yet he made no move to meet her halfway.

This man set his own rules. And he would play by no one else's.

But neither did she. Forcing her hands into fists to still their trembling, Catherine held her mount steady. She would go no farther. Let him come to her.

His cloak whipping around his powerful legs, the man considered her for a long space. The vague scent of cologne mixed with the rain-scented air and scrub pine that edged the road. A trimmed beard covered his lower features. Black breeches were tucked into knee-length boots, which only added to his formidable presence.

As she faced him equally, one question plagued her thoughts. What did someone of his repute want in this tidewater hamlet of Virginia?

"You are the courier they sent?" The barely polished timbre of his voice gave away a Northern drawl and something else borne of authority. He was not a man used to being challenged.

"I am."

His quiet oath touched her ears.

Edging her mount forward a conciliatory inch, she proceeded with the prescribed greeting, despite the fact that he'd already broken with protocol. They both had.

"Do you have a white rose for Guinevere?" she asked.

He laughed. "Only if one so comely has a kiss for Lancelot."

Catherine stiffened. He'd recognized a woman through her boyish disguise. No one had ever done that before.

"That's . . . not the correct response."

"Close enough, lady." His eyes scanned the road behind her. "You're not Daniel Claremont."

A skein of alarm stabbed her. That he should know her brother by name warned her an instant before he grabbed the bridle of her horse, preventing her from swinging away. "Who are you?" he demanded.

"You don't need to know."

"The devil I don't. I bought a meeting with Claremont. And lady . . ." He stepped closer. "You're not he."

A chill settled over her. Clearly, Daniel hadn't told her everything. But the reasons for his deceit made no sense and fanned an ember of doubt. "Are you here to make the exchange or not?"

"You tell me. Am I?"

Reaching inside her cloak, Catherine pulled out the sealed letter. "Is this what you came for?" she queried, snatching it just out of his grasp. "You go first."

For a moment, he didn't move, and her heart froze as she realized he could take the missive without her consent. Then his eyes moved leisurely over her body, lifting to pin hers with their glittering touch. The air surged, sucking the breath from her lungs. She could not breathe for the unexpected shiver that burned through her.

"What fool sent a woman into the night to do a man's job?"

Heat filled her cheeks. "Definitely not the same fool who sent a boor in a man's stead?" Her voice remained steady. Catherine had not survived in life because she was weak-kneed. "You get this . . ." She boldly flagged the paper. ". . . only after you speak."

He gently stroked the gelding's long nose. The wind caught his heavy cloak and the hint of a chuckle. "The muskets are hidden beneath the Low River wharf off the James." A sudden flash of lightning lifted his gaze heavenward. Her breath caught. The bright flickering light revealed the kind of decadent looks that annihilated feminine virtue with a single, solitary glance. His dark hair was bound in a queue.

"The muskets should remain visible as long as it doesn't rain too hard tonight. So I suggest they be fetched before the river rises." His gaze came back around and trapped her stare before she could cast her eyes elsewhere. Snatching the document from her grasp, he had the audacity to be amused. "You *will* remember that?"

"Oh . . . !"

He easily evaded her kick.

"Get your hands off this horse." Catherine drew her pistol from her belt and pointed it at his chest. The first drop of rain splattered on her nose. "Now."

Tucking the paper in his shirt, he kept his gaze on her face. There was something feral in the white flash of his smile. "Are your eyes as bright when you kiss a man as when you threaten to kill him?"

"I guarantee you'll never find out."

Catherine shoved the pistol in her waistband and whirled the gelding. The wind nearly took her hat. She kicked the horse into a gallop, furious that she had allowed the arrogant roué to provoke her.

She reached the top of the first knoll in the road when the crack of musket fire sounded from behind her. Her heart stopped. Bone-chilling fear iced her veins. That sounded like an ambush. Reining in her horse, Catherine snapped her gaze to the brow of the next rise.

Her heartbeat marked the frantic seconds as she searched the darkness below for the stranger. Brandishing her rapier, she swung the gelding around. Suddenly, hands were all over her, trying to rip her off the horse. Tearing blindly at the grasping fingers, she kicked a man in the face. With a cry, she whipped her blade over the soldiers' heads, slicing the tops of their hats. They stumbled back, nearly on top of each other. She spurred the gelding back down the road. Behind her, a musket fired. Another shot. She felt the solid whip against her cloak. Somehow, she lost her rapier as she clutched desperately to hold on to her mount. The stranger was gone. She knew that now as she reached the dip in the road only to confront more soldiers. She wheeled the gelding off the road.

Blinded by darkness, the horse stumbled down a steep bank and flung Catherine from its back. The scream died in her chest. She rolled end over end, like a barrel cascading down a waterfall.

Branches tore her hat and cloak off her battered body. She smashed into a bush and came to a painful stop against a fallen log. She didn't know how long she lay in the mud and rocks, sucking in every breath, heart pounding, fear eclipsing every thought. She tasted blood. Voices roused her. To be caught meant certain death.

Clawing at the dirt for purchase, she raised to her knees. Her horse had vanished in the woods behind her. An empty field lay to her right. She swung her gaze back to the road, looking for the rapier. Soldiers were hunting the brush for her.

That was when she saw the rider, a silhouette forged by lightning against the ebony sky. He sat atop his horse on the opposite knoll, where the soldiers had first appeared. Seized by the tempest, his cloak whipped around him, inseparable from the roiling power of the storm. He seemed to search the darkness, and she knew the instant his eyes touched her. She cried out softly, terrified that he would leave, terrified that he wouldn't. Her heart thundered. Her ribs ached. Checked by the rider's strength, the horse pranced in an angry circle. Then the beast reared as the rider sawed hard on the reins, turning the mount down the road toward her.

The sudden cry to arms rang out. Good God! He would go through the ranks of soldiers to reach her!

Two men broke rank and ran. Catherine staggered to her feet. She would not have him flayed to ribbons. Pray let him see her in the night. Catherine whirled on her heel and took off running across the field. The mud dragged at her boots. A voice heralded her escape, and soon she heard the slap of boots pursuing her. Her long braid coiled like an inky rope around her shoulders, not unlike the palpable horror of real hemp. Her feet tangled with bushes.

Swallowing a panicked sob, she flung her rain-whipped hair behind her and saw him only a moment before the thunder of his horse's hooves rose above the din of shouts and gunfire.

Two horses struck off the road behind him.

"Grab on," she heard him yell.

The hot reek of horseflesh permeated the rain-scented air as he ran the huge stallion beside her. Mud sprayed her soft leather boots. Bending low in the saddle, he held out his hand. Breath rasped from her lungs. She latched on to his powerful arm and, without breaking stride, he swung her effortlessly behind him.

"Why the hell did you come back?" The wind lashed the ruthless words from his lips.

"To . . . save you!"

He swore.

She would have pounded his back with frustration, so great was her fear and relief that both mingled to leave her bereft of everything but the instinct to survive. Fused against the security of his broad back, she clung to his chest with fingers of steel. The cloak did not hide the hard warmth of his back beneath his cheek or the braided coil of his muscles as he kicked the stallion into a run. Harnessing the power of the wind, the horse easily outdistanced their pursuers. Escape was as imminent as the distant sunrise. They crested a hill.

Catherine barely saw the canvas tents or the line of British soldiers perched on one knee in wait. She had no time to scream. The black horse reared and then went down in a hail of musket fire.

Chapter Two

The stallion's death screams knifed through Julian with an agony that sliced his gut. Long-armed bushes snagged at his cloak, tearing his sleeves and scratching his face. He'd seen the soldiers too late. Too late to save his horse or the girl clinging to his back. In the waning echo of gunshots, he hit the ground. For a heartbeat, the world faded to an awful pulse-pounding silence. He sucked in rain-dampened air and sweat and the crush of panic barely held in check. Distant shouts reared up and surrounded him like a slithering beast: the beast in the darkness, those forgotten nightmares and memories that took him to hell and back, that always came with fear.

Drawing his saber, he staggered to his feet. He'd survived these past years because he'd chosen the time and place to make a stand. And now a world of principles languished with his decision to drag his personal life before the altar of justice. His capture jeopardized all that he'd built.

He swept in a half circle to find the girl, his cloak whipping around his boots. Scattered voices lifted over the thrashing trees. Lighting flashed like silver veins across the black sky. His heart froze. Two men leaped at him. He ducked beneath the savage glint of a cutlass. Lantern light suddenly spilled around him to reveal the cocky grin of a black-bearded corporal, too cocksure in his stealth to heed caution. Julian slammed his saber up to counter the assault.

Behind Julian, more armed men wheezed up the hill, their heavy breathing measuring an incline that won him precious few seconds to escape. The instinct to survive shattered his numbed senses, returning life to his limbs in a thundering cadence of battle. Julian stepped behind his sword and drove the man backward with savage violence, like the beast in the darkness, a violence so portentous, he reined it in before he cleaved the man in half.

Blood pounding in his temples, he parried twice, then swung his fist, connecting with the corporal's jaw. The blow sent him sprawling backward into the second soldier carrying the lantern. The lamp burst against a rock. Julian kicked out, hit the man's belly, and watched him somersault down the hill into the others.

"Go!" The soft voice touched him, restoring a portion of his sanity. "Run before it's too late."

Julian swung around. He'd long since lost his hat, and his hair caught the wind. Searching the darkness, his gaze found the girl. She'd lifted on one elbow, her dark, muddy braid dangling like a frayed band of rope over her shoulder and, for a moment, he felt carved in stone. Her legs remained trapped beneath the horse with no hope in hell of fast escape.

The instant he formed the thought, he'd condemned himself. And at once, she made him furious. What the devil had she been thinking racing back down that hill in the first place like some vengeful She god? As if *he* needed rescuing.

Holding her liquid gaze, Julian lowered his saber. The soldiers were on him like dogs, ripping the weapon out of his gloved hand, leaving him to fate and a decision that was no longer his to make.

He might have laughed at his own absurdity had the irony not punched him first. For he was not a man prone to impulse or self-sacrifice, especially for a woman. Such futile nobility killed braver men than he. But something in that split second of decision had defeated him, something powerful in her enigmatic eyes that touched him in places he'd left to a long-ago past. Julian respected courage and, as misguided as hers was, he could not leave a defenseless woman to face a platoon of British soldiers alone.

The sharp jab of a pontoon brought him upright. A man stood at his back, ready to spear him at the slightest provocation.

Spurs clinked. "Well, well. Who 'ave we here?"

A bulky sergeant wearing the green uniform of a dragoon, and missing one button on his waistcoat, swaggered into the lantern light. The wind batted the horsehair crest on his helmet. His gloved hands held a quirt that he snapped against his thigh. Black boots encased thick calves. His white shoulder belt carried Julian's saber.

Julian lifted his gaze. The sergeant's cold gray eyes gloated, and Julian had to admire the man's nerve to parade before him like Jehovah's peacock. Except the brag went deeper than merely capturing a sword. Before Julian could respond to the sharp stab of unease, a loud scuffle behind the sergeant turned his attention.

"Don't you dare touch me! Let me go!"

A soldier dragged the girl, spitting like a bobcat, into the weak light. She looked like a volcanic eruption of ash and mud, a walking catastrophe, only her pride recognizable from the comely maid he'd glimpsed in the moonlight. Her loose black shirt and breeches fared no better than the rest of her. And there should have been nothing appealing about the little sand crab, yet Julian was conscious of a jolt all the same. Dangerous. Because it demanded action.

"Lookee here, men, what the storm dragged in." The undercurrent in the sergeant's voice pulled Julian's gaze around. "I be thinkin' we caught us a woman."

"Bastard!" She kicked out at her captor, a hairy brute of a man who lacked one top tooth. "Get your hands off me!"

"Or what?" the redcoat guffawed.

Balling up her fist, she smashed the man in the jaw before aiming a well-placed knee to the other man's crotch. The night erupted in chaos. Beside Julian, the sergeant yelled, "Grab her, ye fools! Or she'll get away."

Julian must have moved, because the pontoon dug deeper into his back. Two more men seized the girl's arms in a fierce battle to subdue her. And before Julian could revise his opinion of a woman who wasn't the least bit defenseless, she'd found the hilt of her captor's rapier and whipped it out of the scabbard, scattering a half dozen trained soldiers in the melee.

Quick fury flamed in the sergeant's eyes. In the end, the mud and a noticeable limp defeated her. She slipped and splattered in a puddle. Her grip on the sword vanished. Two men yanked her up.

At once, her eyes swung to his. "Why didn't you leave when you had the chance?" her voice accused. "You must be mad!"

Hell—his fists clenched—*she didn't know the half of it.*

"Aye," the sergeant slapped the quirt against his thigh, "we got us a true warrior in our midst."

Thrusting out her chin, the girl faced him with the impertinence of a nor'easter. "Better that than a Tory coward who attacks women."

The sergeant's hand rounded like an uncoiled spring. Julian caught the fist and checked the power behind the blow.

Shocked silence fell around the motley group. Even the girl froze. Only the storm remained a reckoning force as Julian's eyes locked on the sergeant's with bone-chilling clarity.

"You already ran us down and shot my horse." The wind snapped at his cloak. "Don't . . . make another mistake."

"Aren't you a regular white knight." The sergeant yanked his hand away. "We seen ye go back for her. Now look what it's got ye." He grabbed the girl by the braid. "You're under arrest."

Chains rattled, an insidious sound that warned Julian he'd underestimated this enemy with the foresight of a novice.

"Try escapin' with the twit beached to ye like an anchor."

Julian's eyes closed on the girl's pride-stricken face before the sergeant shoved her into his arms. The top of her head didn't reach his shoulders. Manacles on his ankle and wrist bound him to the girl. "Since when is a predawn tryst grounds for arrest, Sergeant?"

"Tryst?" A gloat of satisfaction marked his lips. "Ye don't think we went to all this trouble fer just anyone, do ye?"

Julian's eyes narrowed. "And what trouble is that?"

"I have a writ for the arrest of Merlin. And the promise of a rich bounty for bringin' ye in. Alive."

A drop of rain hit his eye. "Then you'll be a laughingstock. I am no magician."

"Merlin is a spy!"

The girl pressed against Julian as the sergeant stepped closer, a menacing specter in the sputtering lamplight. Julian edged her aside. "A fancy man with the ladies, too, I'll be wagerin', what with yer comely face and all."

The sergeant slammed his fist into Julian's midsection, doubling him over. He hit him again in the ribs already bruised when his horse went down, and Julian dropped to his knees onto the wet earth and grass, dragging the girl down with him.

"Stop it!" she screamed.

"Too bad you won't be nothin' any lady will want when I'm finished with ye."

Julian lifted his head. A lazy smiled turned the corners of his mouth. "You're very brave . . . with nine men to back you up. Is the lord governor hiring mercenaries now to torture civilians?"

"You ain't no civilian. This"—the sergeant stripped the letter out of Julian's cloak, the seal still intact—"this condemns ye."

Julian laughed. "Of what?" he rasped. "That letter is of no import to you or the British government."

"No?" Turning his back to Julian, he hunched beside the lantern light. "Think again."

An icy gnawing took hold of his gut. It started as a warning, then became alarm, until it blossomed into rage, a deep, gnarling fury that consumed every nerve, every fiber in his body. The sergeant took too long to read the one single name Julian knew should be written there, the one he'd paid dearly to get. It was a cost that clearly had yet to be paid in full.

The sergeant's head lifted, triumph glittering in his pale eyes. "The whore hangs at dawn 'less she signs a statement—" His soliloquy didn't end with the girl's startled outburst. "And you, Merlin, will be brought up before the magistrate on charges of treason." A thin white scar showed with his grin. "The governor will be pleased that we have stopped a plot to assassinate him."

"You're a damned liar—"

A boot slammed Julian in the ribs. The girl screamed. "I'll be presentin' this letter with the names of your accomplices." *Slam.* "Names that you have so personally supplied in your moment of weakness to save yourself." *Slam.* "The lot'll be arrested, poor buggers. All because of you."

"They won't . . . believe yo—"

Slam.

"The good folks 'ere don't know ye like they do in Boston where ye been more than a thorn in the king's ass in the past."

But Julian could scarcely listen. He gasped for breath, desperate to stave off the blackness. Bent over his knees, blood pounding in his skull, he raised his gaze to the letter dangling in the sergeant's hand.

A single name would not condemn him for anything, except maybe for his arrogance—arrogance in thinking he was so much smarter than his enemies. But this wasn't about treason. He knew that now, too late. He's stepped into a spider nest far beyond the ken of his brother's murder.

And as sure as God made sunlight, beautiful scrawls filled the flawless ivory vellum: a litany of condemnation that almost made him laugh out loud, so perfect was the gilded frame that would put a rope around his neck.

Julian shifted his gaze to impale the girl.

On her knees in the mud beside him, her eyes were wide with horror and almost innocent in their very treachery. She was shaking her head as if to deny the accusation in his eyes. Hatred welled. They'd done more than set him up to die. They made him a traitor to the rebel cause. She was part of this. Unwittingly captured, perhaps, but neck deep in the mire and mud all the same. She hadn't been riding back down that hill to save him; she'd been running for her worthless life.

Julian tried to shove her away, but the chains caught him and tumbled him facedown to the wet earth and mud, where he endured another kick. And for a nightmarish moment, he was home again on the coast of Cornwall. The darkness had become the beast. Rain slapped him in the face, pellets of wind-worried rain that began to fall. He would not give them the satisfaction of crying out.

He . . . would . . . not!

"I said I would bring ye in alive." The sergeant hastily handed the letter over to a blond-haired pole of a man, a courier perhaps, who spun smartly on his heel and left with two others.

Then he laughed. "But I didn't say you'd be standing."

Julian's head snapped back with the blow. The last thing he heard was the crash of thunder as the sky opened up.

Catherine came awake with a start. A frigid wind slithered beneath the tent and wound around her wet feet. She lay on her belly, her muddy cheek cradled by one arm. The smell of wet grass and pungent loam struck her nostrils, and her head lifted.

Every bone and muscle in her body ached. Even as she twisted at the sound of the groan beside her, the jangle of chains brought her up short, dropping her back into the nightmare that exhaustion had rendered oblique.

She'd slept! Her gaze sliced back and forth across the tent. Heart hammering, she lifted higher on one elbow. Dawn had come and gone, leaving a stingy scrap of gray light to mark its passing.

And no one had arrived to drag her away.

Water pooled beneath her. Outside, the storm had not loosened its grip. Rain pebbled against the tent, rocking the canvas like a giant, angry fist. Her hand was bruised from trying to escape the manacles. She shoved away the hot, wretched panic. Elizabeth and Daniel would know by now that something had gone wrong with the drop.

Edging around, she could move no more than the length of iron on her ankle and wrist allowed. Merlin faced her, his chained wrist dangling loosely over his waist. Catherine blinked back the horror that flooded her heart. Blood caked his temple where the sergeant had kicked him. A bloodstained cloth wound around his forehead and over his left eye. A thick lock of dark hair swept his brow with a vulnerability that belied his sense of helplessness and something else that lurked just beneath her ken.

Heat emanated from his body. Even unconscious, and unrecognizable from the man she'd briefly glimpsed before the storm, he was a formidable man with arms that stretched taut the heavy fabric of his military-style cloak. He was powerful enough to survive the grueling abuse the sergeant had heaped upon him.

For once in her life, Catherine didn't know what to do. Indecision paralyzed her. She could not move her arm to touch him, even when desperation cried out to shake him awake. He'd accused her of betrayal with eyes that had burned with rage.

Still, he was her only hope of getting out of here.

Then she froze.

His eyes were open, watching her. Her breath caught and clung like lichen in her throat. She didn't move. The current of air moved in his hair. And he turned his attention away from her to scan the tent. He rubbed his swollen temple.

"Where are we?"

His voice was a deep rasp. She knew it must hurt him to talk. "The sergeant brought us to their camp. Seven men are here."

"How long have I been out?"

"Hours." Her heart hammered. Maybe she'd misread him last night. He *had* to know that she'd been betrayed as well. Or rather Daniel. The letter had been meant for him to deliver. "The guard hasn't come back in here since the storm began. You've been unconscious."

He swung his gaze back around. And as if seeing her for the first time, his eyes honed on her face like a blade. Her heart leapt fearfully. The chains snapped taut a moment before he launched. Despite being injured, he was quick, slamming her back into the wet earth. She shrieked and swung her fist, only to find that hand captured, too.

"Who the hell are you, lady?"

He was pressing her down, his body hard upon hers; she could not pry her hands from his. Rocks dug into her hip. "Get . . . off me."

"Answer me. Who are you?"

"You have misjudged me. I swear!"

"Aye. Fatally, I'll wager." Eyes hardening, he lifted slightly and raked her body, as if she wore naught between them. Slowly he brought his gaze back to bear on hers. The contact jarred her. A powerful surge of danger shimmied over her, and suddenly she was aware of more than his body pressed against hers. Her heart thumped violently in her chest.

"Cry innocent all you will," he said, "but you will tell me who you are. Or by God . . . I don't care if you are a woman."

"'Twas a lie," she whispered. "All of it."

"Do tell, madam," he murmured thickly.

Her breathing was swift. "No." She shook her head. Her hair had unraveled from the braid and tangled around her head. "You don't understand. The letter I gave you was blank. Empty."

He didn't move, as if every muscle froze. "What do you mean?"

"I . . . looked. Before I came to you last night. I popped the seal. There was nothing written in that letter."

"The hell there wasn't."

"The sergeant switched it somehow. It would make sense, considering the extent someone went to set you up."

Silence.

"Can we get out of here now?"

For a moment, she allowed the hope that he believed her innocent. Heaven only knew they needed each other to escape.

"Did Daniel Claremont give you that letter?"

Her shock came out in a small gasp. In a rush, she turned her face away, only to find her chin snapped back and her eyes wide on Merlin's. He thought her brother guilty of being the traitor here!

And, at once, she remembered Merlin's words when she first confronted him on the road. He'd been expecting Daniel that night. But why? To demand an answer would give her away. And this man could destroy her family every bit as thoroughly as the British soldiers.

"Who gave you the letter then?" His voice was level.

Her teeth chattered from the cold. "I don't know where the letter came from. Now, will you get *off* me!"

His eyes hooded. Her heart pitched against her ribs. She wondered what happened to people who crossed him. Did they end up stretched out on stakes in a tide pool?

"We need each other," she warned him.

His blasphemous utterance scalded her ears. Sitting back on his calves, he touched his ribs. "I've never needed anyone in my life. I'm not starting with you."

She gave a yank to the fetters. "Do you always curse with the same ease that you threaten women?"

"When it suits me . . ." He wrapped a hand in the chains. "I'm capable of anything."

She held steadfast to her grip. "No doubt murder is your vested talent."

His gaze roamed her face. His cropped beard and the dirty cloth tied around his head gave him the look of a pirate. "Especially murder," he said succinctly, and she lost her grip on the chains. His mouth quirked at a corner. "Don't tempt me."

Catherine steeled herself against the effect he had on her. As if her life wasn't imperiled enough without this added insult. She should have found his repulsive lack of character detestable, and she couldn't understand why she didn't.

A gust of wind vibrated the tent. All business now, he surveyed the walls of their flimsy prison. The space was barely wide enough for three people to stand shoulder to shoulder. His gaze eased over to the tent flap. The heavy cloth remained tied against the storm.

"That's solid oilcloth. You won't get out that way. We need to dig. . . ."

Raising to his knees, he stroked the side of the tent as if testing the seams. Her gaze followed that hand.

"There is a tent on either side of us." A slight wobble in her voice betrayed her nerves. "The guard checks on us every half hour. I haven't seen him lately. He's probably basking in front of a fire to stay warm." She glared at Merlin's broad back. Did men never listen to sense? "You're wasting time." She tried to reason.

Her jaw tightened. He forced her to crawl with him through the mud to the back of the tent. "The horses are picketed near the creek, though I doubt they'd be there now in this storm. The woods are . . . north. That way"—she pointed left—"about a hundred yards. The trees are dense and will be our best hope of escape." He was deliberately ignoring anything she said. "Will you listen to me?"

He finally paused in his work. His head turned, and she saw an edge of impatience in his eyes, as if nothing she'd said was news to him. Then something else flashed in that moment as well, and for the first time, she felt a hint of his compassion.

A thunderclap made her flinch. "You won't get out tha—"

She stared in disbelief at the small knife that appeared in his gloved hand. "I keep it in my boot," he said.

"And you couldn't tell me this sooner?"

"You didn't ask."

Instantly, she wanted to hit him. She didn't deserve his enmity. She didn't deserve to be in this mud pit. She wanted to go home to the safety of her house, to her bed, with her tablets and pastels and the beautiful paints that colored her world. She wanted her pig. Not this uncouth barbarian!

She glared at the tent, unable to comprehend how the blade would slice through the canvas. "Your weapon is too small. It will never work."

Working a tiny hole through the canvas, he applied one eye. "Some men might take insult to that, sweet."

"Surely someone of your ill repute would carry a bigger blade that?"

He turned his head. His eyes were laughing at her, actually laughing. He'd thrown one side of his coat over his knee. Leather boots encased his muscled calves. "Never fear, sweet. The only weapon that counts is bigger by far."

With that, he sliced the knife down the tent, rending the canvas as easily as he might part someone's throat.

Chapter Three

Merlin's arm went over her shoulder. "We have to make the trees," he whispered urgently.

Catherine realized he couldn't stand straight. And in that split second where a heartbeat measured a man's life, she ran with all her strength, or tried to as the chains that bound their ankles tripped her. His cloak caught her legs. They hop-skipped like a three-legged circus horse across the open meadow. Her boots slapped in the mud.

"Faster! Blast you!"

With head bowed against the blinding rain, Catherine stumbled. "I'm trying!"

Merlin smacked knees-first into the mud, hurling her down with him. She hit the ground. His mouth tight with anguish, he braced his hands on this thighs and sucked in air.

Catherine heard yells above the rain. The sentry had hailed their escape. "Oh, God . . . get up!"

Wind battered her face. Rain slanted in gray sheets, melding with the horizon in a menacing inferno of swirling clouds. This was hell in its most terrifying moment, and she'd plunged into its depths.

He wasn't moving fast enough. "Get up!" She shoved her shoulder beneath his and pulled him to his feet. The soldiers had reached the edge of the encampment. "I will not let them hang us!"

Struggling to run, Merlin swore. They splashed through a swale. Together, they reached the woods. The limbs of a giant willow whipped her face, and then she and Merlin hit the creek. As they both looked up, a wall of roiling water caught them. Merlin's arm wrapped around her. His muscles clamped like an iron vise. The once tame creek had turned into a raging river and tore her feet out from beneath her as easily as if she were a sack of feathers. She clung to the shelter of his body like a lifeline, burying her face within the wet folds of his cloak. White water swirled around his hips, then his chest.

"Christ." His mouth pressed to her ear. "Can you swim?"

She didn't comprehend at first. He was trying to remove his cloak, its sodden weight dragging him down. Terror seized her. What woman knew how to swim? Then she was being swept along in the rapids, human flotsam caught up with other debris. Her wrist hit a rock outcropping. Icy water went into her nose. She was conscious of his arm still around her, holding her solid against his body. Even injured as he was, he kept her head above the water. She flattened against him. Muddy water sloshed in her mouth and stung her throat.

Soon she was aware of branches slapping her head. The creek had risen above its banks and raced level with low-hanging trees. She knew their only hope lay with her. With all her strength, she reached out her free hand and snagged a branch, then another, until one held her weight and stopped their mad flight.

"Let go!" She heard Merlin yell. Her heart beat in panic and exhaustion. Tears scalded her eyes. Somewhere in her brain, she knew he was standing in the water, the torrent rushing around him. His arm wrapped her waist. She felt his strong hand go over her fist. "It's all right. I've got you. You must . . . let go."

Squeezing her eyes shut, she shook her head. Nothing would be right again, she wanted to scream. Too many shadows haunted her. Too many people had betrayed her, as if she were nothing of import, as if she were naught but an expandable piece of flotsam to be sacrificed.

What had she ever done to hurt anyone, except to love blindly? Fate had taken away her rainbows and given her nothing back to hold on to. Except this branch!

"You must let go." Merlin's mouth grazed her ear. "Or I'll consummate our blossoming courtship here."

Opening her eyes, she laughed and cried at once. Water sloshed over her face, but Merlin held her gaze. "Trust me."

And she did. This stranger in the night, who had helped her when he could have ridden safely away. Who now paid dearly for his choice.

Her arm let loose its lifesaving grip.

Merlin held her safe, as he said he would. A promise kept. Somehow, he made it across the river. Her heart pounding in her chest, she collapsed beside him on the bank. Over the roar of water, she could hear his labored rasps but could do nothing as she sucked in life-giving air. Lying next to Merlin, with rain pounding her back, she wanted to thank him, anything to loosen the clamp of hysteria that tightened her throat.

She blinked to clear her vision. They were at the bottom of a sloping hill, easily seen by anyone who should emerge from the woods. No words passed between them, yet Merlin's gaze had gone in that direction, too. They both struggled to their feet. He leaned heavily on her, and she braced a shoulder beneath his. The grassy slope lent her no purchase. Their feet worked in tandem, two sides to a whole. It took both of them fighting the incline to finally reach the top of the hill. Then they were running free until the trees swallowed them.

Catherine followed Merlin's lead. In the woods, she lost direction. He seemed to know where he was going, as if guided by some internal compass that she lacked. They were miles outside of Williamsburg, nearer to the York River than the James.

Later, after they found shelter, Catherine helped Merlin cut the sodden cloak off the arm that held his chained to hers. He laid the mantle over low-hanging branches, a roof against the storm. Pine needles softened the ground. In the damp shadows, his breathing came to her. Mindful of his unwavering regard, she briskly rubbed her arms and listened to the rain drum against the trees outside.

His strength frightened her. It eased her guard. Once they escaped the soldiers, she had to escape him, too. He could never learn who she was. Not that she was anyone of prominence. Few people would miss her if she perished. But anonymity protected her family. And treason wasn't a charge anybody survived.

Yet Catherine was aware of another storm just beyond her ken. The one growing inside that had naught to do with politics and everything to do with the man beside her. Lifting her gaze, she studied him from beneath her lashes.

His black Holland shirt had torn across one shoulder. He'd lost the ties, and it gaped open to reveal his chest. A dark sprinkling of hair narrowed down his belly and disappeared in the waistband of his breeches. He was finely muscled in a way she'd not seen a man.

Her heart suddenly lurched. Purplish bruises marred his flesh. She leaned closer. Even in the shadows, the marks were visible splotches on his waist and ribs. "How can you breathe?" she asked, aghast, not realizing she'd spoken aloud.

"It's fortunate for you that I can."

She touched his waist, testing for blood. "And its fortunate for you I can help."

She met his eyes. They weren't cold like she'd expected. Neither were they warm, but somewhere in the middle, where the frost might melt if the sun came out.

Her breast bindings would suffice for a bandage. The cloth wrapped her torso four times and bound her tightly. Lifting on her knees, she shoved her hands beneath her shirt. Her dark hair hung in wet clumps to her hips and entangled her elbows. Reaching behind her, she stopped. Merlin's hand rested near her right breast. Her eyes snapped to his. One of his dark eyebrows raised. Chained to her as he was, she could hardly escape his scrutiny or his touch.

"Normally, I wouldn't question a woman's motives when she removes her clothes in my presence, but in your case, I'll make an exception. Exactly how do you intend to help?"

Despite her worldliness, heat burned her cheeks. "No doubt women remove their clothes for you often. You must be very busy fighting them off."

His lack of response annoyed her. And without admitting to an irrational rush of jealously, she shoved his hand off her, only to find the chains pulled taut. She could sense his silent laughter as if he'd guessed her struggle. Glaring at him, she almost didn't relinquish the muslin that bound her breasts. The man had an arrogant streak that touched her in all the wrong places. His other attributes were no less disturbing.

"You are a conceited knave. Do close your eyes at least."

Her joints were too stiff. She couldn't fight the wet muslin. Her upper arms began to burn with the struggle. Then his hand touched her back, snapping her erect. He no longer wore his gloves, and his fingers were callused against her skin. He held the knife.

"Allow me." His hot breath touched her cheek, and she suddenly remembered his bold words about the bigger of his weapons. "Are you sure you want to do this?" he asked.

Meeting his gaze, she nodded. "I am not so ponderous that I can't live without my . . . disguise. You need this more than I."

"Ponderous?" His slow chuckle shimmied over her like warm chocolate. "Have you any other surprises hidden beneath your clothes that I should be aware of?"

Her eyes went wide, then narrowed. "Nothing that your *weapon* could handle, I'm sure," she delivered smugly.

The lazy smile that drifted across his mouth did not reach his eyes. "Do you feel safe, sweet?"

Without awaiting her uncertain answer, he pressed her forward into his lap. One hand caught against his muscled thigh. Her head dipped to his waist. "You could be a little gentler," she rebuked.

"And you could have been a toothless old crone they chained to me. But I'm not that lucky."

With a flick of his knife, the binding came loose and released her breasts. She felt their weight, and her shirt tightened against her chest. Their eyes met. Ignoring the flutter in her stomach, she yanked the muslin out from beneath her shirt. Her wet clothes, sticking to her like a glove, gave no respite against the chill.

"Lift forward." Her voice suddenly sounded small beside him.

He did, and his bare chest touched her ear. His heartbeat was strong against her cheek. She proceeded to wrap the binding around his upper waist. He flinched slightly. She wondered if he had a broken rib. Possibly two. Never had she hated anyone more at that moment than the sergeant who did this to him.

But Merlin showed no other sign of pain as she edged the wet wrapping around his back. His flesh was warm and supple beneath her palms. A scar crisscrossed his left side, and she touched it lightly, caught by the anguish that filled her heart. Her father had possessed a similar scar from a shrapnel wound he'd received in battle. Only he'd lost a leg and, in way, his whole life.

Shaking her head, she let the pads of her fingers tarry a little longer on the cloth before tying the knot off with a pull of her teeth. Finished, she lifted her shin. She stilled to find him watching her. The flutter in her chest turned to pounding.

She'd heard once that if someone saved your life, your souls were forever linked in some indelible way. In the hours since he'd charged down that hill and plucked her out of the soldier's hands, he'd become a part of her in a way her husband never had.

"Thank you," she said for want of anything else to fill the discomfiting silence. Caught by something she didn't understand, she welcomed the cold brace of wind at her back. "Thank you for pulling me out of the water." It was a ridiculous statement, and the subtle laughter in his eyes told her so. "But then having me alive and walking is far easier than having to carry my dead body, isn't it?"

"You look light enough. I'd probably manage."

She could tell that he hadn't decided whether he trusted her, but something was happening between them, something strong that wound around them like the wind, as if the storm outside suddenly found a way into the shelter. She dropped her gaze. Her belly gnawed her ribs. Battered and hungry, she'd gone beyond the numbing shock of the past night. Her hands trembled, and she clasped them together.

"How far do you think we've come?" she quietly asked.

"A league maybe. Not much. The storm will keep any dogs at bay, at least for now. If we're lucky, the bastards will think we drowned."

"A league?" Only a tar used the term so freely, or a smuggler. Snippets of old gossip drifted back to her. She'd heard that he was from up north in the colonies. "Is that how you arrived here from Boston or wherever it is you hail from? On your ship?"

He sprawled back against a deadwood log. "My ship?"

She challenged his innocent regard. "The one that you use to smuggle brandy and an assortment of other goods that grace the tables of wealthy colonists. Or are you dealing in illegal muskets now?"

In the somber light, his eyes were half hidden beneath the bandage that wrapped his forehead, but she could feel his gaze touching her. "It seems we're each curious about the other."

"Was it a ruse?" She suddenly had to know. "The muskets?"

His gaze on her face told her the truth before he spoke the words. "They were where I told you they'd be."

Her confidence shattered. Her people had clearly betrayed him, people that she'd lived with for most of her life. No man deserved such betrayal or the beating the sergeant had given him.

And what of Daniel's life? Was he so easily expendable?

Hot tears burned her eyes. "I thought I was fighting for something good. Or I was at one time. Before . . ." Dragging her eyes away from his face, Catherine fidgeted with a pine needle. "I thought I knew everyone around here." Her finger traced a heart in the damp earth. "Papa, everyone called him the Colonel, he taught me to always have a plan. 'Know thy enemy,' he'd said, 'and you will always defeat him'. Of course, he was talking about chess."

His eyes had not moved from her face. She wondered if he cared that she had a life before yesterday or if he just waited for her to get to the point.

"Papa would be ashamed that I let myself walk into the trap I did." Her teeth had begun to chatter. "I didn't betray you. I swear."

His hand lifted to gently cup her chin. "Have you bothered to consider that you were never meant to come back?"

She hugged her arms to her chest.

"And you still cannot tell me who they are?"

He was an outsider here. She could tell him nothing. Nothing without betraying her family. Nothing without betraying Daniel. Merlin would never understand her need to protect her brother and family. He didn't know the men who claimed patriotic duty to the Sons of Liberty. He didn't know what they would do to her. No one could fight them. Hadn't he just seen that?

Finally, he looked away. "Go to sleep," he said after a long moment. "I'll take the first watch."

Swallowing the sudden lump in her throat, Catherine lay down on the cold ground. She curled into as small a ball as the chains allowed and surrendered to exhaustion. Her body shook.

Lying next to the dead log, Merlin wrapped her against him as if it were completely natural for him to shield her from the cold. The heat from his body warmed hers like a golden sunbeam. His steady heartbeat filled the palm of her hand. In the narrow space of their shelter, his presence surrounded her, separating her from the wind and rain and the soldiers who hunted them.

Desperately, she needed to sleep, to repair the ragged tear in

her emotions. With tears in her eyes, she watched the slow rise
and fall of his chest. She detected a hint of sage and spice in his
shirt, not what she'd expect on a seafaring smuggler. She'd
smelled less costly cologne on high-society popinjays who
soaked in French perfumes.

No, this was subtle, as if he'd bathed and hadn't completely
removed the remnants of his other life. A life he may never see
again. He lived in a kingdom of shadows, a spy and a smuggler,
who hid behind another identity. He was dangerous in more ways
than she could count, and he was her anchor in a world that had
deserted her.

Catherine squeezed her eyes tight but couldn't stop the hot
flow of tears. The braided tendons in his arm tightened beneath
her head and suddenly, he'd raised to his elbow above her. She
met the heat in his eyes and embraced the surge of feelings that
rose in her chest.

"I'm sorry," she choked. "I truly am."

The pressure had built up for months, and she'd held back for
too long trying to hide her fear from those who would destroy all
that she held dear and protected. A hand went to her head. Gently, he pressed her against the folds of his shirt, saying nothing as
he let her sob against his chest. She had no ken for this man's
way of life or the choices he'd made, except he was strong and
his arms wrapped her in security. He made her feel safe. And
alive in a way she'd never thought to feel again after her husband's betrayal.

Wild longing raced like a hot summer wind through her
blood. She was alive when she should have been dead. She
reached out to cup his bearded jaw, knowing that she should not
touch him, knowing what would happen inside if she did. She
raised above him, her wet eyes glimmering. Her damp hair
fanned his face. He had an odd look in his eyes, no longer
hooded. They encompassed her face.

Too long denied affection, she was beyond caring that she'd
run headlong into something she didn't understand. She desperately needed to feel alive again. Her lips touched his.

She felt his hesitation and knew a flash of uncertainty just before he pushed her mouth away. Her stomach kicked in warning
as he raked her face with eyes that burned all over her, whether
with animosity or something else, she couldn't tell, but his cal-

lused hand slid beneath her hair to splay her head, and he pulled her down to his mouth. Despite a slightly swollen bottom lip, his mouth was warm and pliant, growing bolder as he prowled through her senses. Then his tongue dipped into her mouth, and he was kissing her in earnest, deep and hard. A groan formed at the back of her throat. Her fingers curled into his shirt, testing the strength of the fabric with a tightfisted grip. Moving his thigh over hers, he turned her slowly back into the earth, deepening the kiss, taking more of her response, mastering her body with subtle warfare as if he conquered his foes the same way, one battle at a time.

The kiss went on and on. Her senses hummed. He tasted salty with her tears. Alive. Like the sea and the restless rain that beat at their door. Her fingers tangled in his thick, coarse hair. His hand traced the curve of her waist and splayed the soft mound of her breast. She forgot her fear and the threat that loomed over her life. She forgot reason and pride.

She forgot to breathe.

He slid his lips down the wet curve of her throat, unfastening her shirt as he moved lower in a gliding caress, tasting the pointed tips of her breasts, until she thought she'd die from the hot rush through her veins. Her hands were clumsy on his shirt, and finally he reared back to pull the cloth from his breeches. In the darkness their eyes met and held as if the storm and the entire world had faded to nothing.

And it had.

She glided on golden wings, drifting through reality like a storybook character seeking redemption in truth. He was her only light. No one else existed. No past. No future. There were no tomorrows or yesterdays, only now, and the heady sense that in some way, he, too, needed her.

He dipped his dark head, capturing her mouth in a kiss that melted the final remnants of reality. "Do you know what you're doing?" His raspy voice shivered over her lips.

She kissed him deeply, lost because he'd stopped, and she never wanted him to stop again. Who would know anyway what she asked of him? Who would censure her behavior? She would never see him again when this was over.

"I want this," she whispered against his corded throat where his pulse raced at the base of his neck, where she now suckled and tasted, ravenous with need. "I do." She gasped as he dipped his hot tongue into her ear. "Oh God . . . I do. Now."

From somewhere, a voice cried out through her shocking madness, but it was too late to reconcile the woman she was to what she was doing. She was no longer in control. Perhaps she never had been, for he moved purposefully over her like a man who knew his way with a woman.

His hand moved inside her breeches, and then he slid her pants down to her thighs. She lifted to accommodate the movement, anxious that he remove her breeches completely, knowing the chains around her ankle made that impossible. She wanted him deep inside her.

For Julian, her fire burned unchecked through is body, until everything burst with a blinding intensity that shut out the darkness. There was no foreplay, no gentleness in the mating of their mouths. She smelled of earth and sweat and faded lilacs, the perfume of the innocent, and for one moment, decency reared its symbolic head, denouncing him for a bastard, for taking advantage of her weakness, for wanting her as he did. But he'd known too many women over the years where his was another nameless face in a world that gave no quarter to the weak. He was a man too long denied tenderness to care.

He kissed her, dragging from her throat a groan that stirred the tempest inside, that banished his neglected conscience to the nether regions of his life where honor mattered.

His body moved over hers. She clung to him and drank from his mouth as he spread her thighs with a well-muscled knee, opening her to his sensual probe. She was wet and slick, and he entered her easily, gliding until she took all of him inside of her, until she could take no more. And his mouth found hers, savoring her cries. He wondered only briefly at her lack of virginity before the primal drive for release pulled him. He rocked against her with a violence that drove her backward. Her nails dug into his back.

Raising up on his hands, his muscles coiling in his shoulders, he looked into the dark, liquid pools of her eyes. Her wild hair fanned around her like an ebony halo. Their gazes locked, their breathing labored, she came to him, her keening cries a feral aphrodisiac seducing him. His fingers dug into the damp earth. Powerless to look away, he yielded to the groan that wrenched

his chest and surrendered the hot flood of his seed deep into her
body.

Something he didn't let happen with any woman.

Their breaths mingling in the darkness, she watched him still,
until the throbbing inside her stopped, until his heartbeat slowed,
until he could hold her gaze no more. Braced by his elbows to
keep his weight from hurting her, he finally collapsed beside her.

Catherine closed her eyes but couldn't sleep. Only the wind in
the trees announced the presence of another world outside their
humble, dilapidated domain. She could feel Merlin's wakeful-
ness as he stared at the cloaked branches above them. Water
dripped on her stomach. They'd dressed, and he hadn't spoken a
word. Not a single, solitary breath to convey his thoughts. He
wore his gloves again.

She lifted on her elbow, frightened by his silence, perhaps because it left her to battle her doubts alone. He'd taken her to
heaven and back with no more than a casual by your leave.

Quietly, he turned his head, and her breath caught in his gaze.
He could be a wealthy English lord for all the power that emanated from that look. His hooded eyes bore a hint of green behind the black pupils and the fringe of dark lashes. She wanted to
trace a finger along his sensual mouth to find the man she'd
kissed.

"Go to sleep," he said almost gently, as if he spoke to an errant child who needed to be told twice to go to bed.

She lay down with one hand pressed against her cheek, this
time alone, as he made no effort to touch her.

He didn't like her.

He'd already forgotten her.

And in that respect, he'd become no different than her husband.

Julian's whole body was taut and fit to break. He leaned an elbow
against a tree and glared at the single bright beam of sunlight that
penetrated the feeble canopy of trees overhead. "For Christ's
sake. I'm not looking."

"Don't you *dare* blaspheme in front of me, *Mr.* Merlin or
whatever your real name is. Not that I want to know."

Julian raised his eyes and shook his head in disbelief. Blackbirds circled around the treetops, their chatter loud and annoying, adding to the dull roar in his head.

"I can't do this. I can't."

"You can," he managed on a level exhale.

"Close your eyes!"

Having known women most of his life, Julian had learned the fine art of silent warfare. There was a time for a man to stand his ground. This was not it. His hand dangled loosely so as not to construe anything rudely overt. He looked anywhere but at the flustered girl beside him, the girl who only hours before burned naked in his arms. He shut his eyes to remove the vision.

"I swear if you look, I'll kick you in the shins. I will. Judas," she groaned through her teeth. Julian drummed his fingers on the rough tree bark. "I have never been more humiliated in my life. Ouch! There are stickers down here."

Patience was a virtue, as was restraint, and Julian exercised what remained of both with gritted teeth. Men just didn't suffer the same predilection as women when it came to attending to personal needs. There was no necessary in the woods. Only a wide-open sky and an abundance of trees that mocked your modesty with a thorny branch in your ass. A person just got used to the inconvenience.

But in truth, he understood her frustration. She was worn out and starved, her feet shriveled in squeaky boots that hadn't dried out yet. She'd not complained an inch during the miles they'd covered, determined to keep up with the unreasonable pace he'd set. That, despite his being a boorish ass since he'd dragged her out of sleep at the first break in the weather, wanting nothing more than to escape their cozy little tent and get back to his ship before it left the rendezvous point.

At least the sun was out, and the ache in his temples had not worsened. He readjusted the bandage.

"All right. I'm finished." Her small voice came to him.

He twisted around and let his shoulder rest against the tree. She struggled to tie her breeches. Her head barely reached his shoulders. Dark hair framed her face. All he could see was a slim nose and rose petal mouth pressed tight with frustration. He felt a grin form. Let her suffer the consequences of wearing breeches.

"I imagine this is all normal for you?" she fretted, yanking the ties into little bows.

He gave her a half-lidded look. "Define normal."

Tossing him a wrathful glare, she pulled past him, her thick, tangled hair bouncing against her bottom like a giant knot. "Don't you dare laugh. I'm just in the mood to punch you if you do."

Rolling his eyes, Julian let her huff ahead as far as their chains permitted before following. Allowing his gaze to travel over her backside, he took advantage of her temper to enjoy the view. The chit wasn't beautiful in the traditional sense. She was no blue-eyed Southern princess with cotton for brains. She wasn't remotely his type of bed warmer. Dark-haired, doe-eyed women reminded him of everything he'd left England to escape.

And she was guilty as sin. He couldn't let himself forget that, no matter the temptation she presented. She knew who gave her that blasted letter. Perhaps she hadn't betrayed him to the soldiers, but she knew who did and, by God, she wasn't going anywhere until she talked. Everything told him that the unnamed traitor was connected to his brother's death. If it were his last act in this life, Julian would hunt the murdering bastard down and break his neck.

"Do you know where we're going?" she suddenly asked. He'd noticed that about her. She asked a lot of questions.

Julian pretended to study the dome of blue overhead. He knew precisely the direction they were headed and expected to reach his ship by tomorrow, his prisoner in tow. "I have no idea. Why? Do you live around here?"

She made a rude noise and evaded the question. "Don't you have a wife or someone who worries about you when you're gone? Anyone?"

"Do *you?*" He tossed the question back.

She slowed to let him walk beside her and presented him with a grin. Julian felt a curious jolt.

"Are you asking if I'm married?"

Realizing the folly of his curiosity, he grew annoyed beneath her amused gaze. They straddled a rotten log in the path, and Julian sat abruptly, exhausted. His ribs ached like the blazes. Maintaining his persona beneath the bruises had grown more difficult. He startled when she put a hand on his swollen cheek.

"You're warm," she said, intruding where she didn't belong.

He removed her hand. "I'll live."

"Let me check your ribs."

She touched his shirt. He clasped her wrists. "I said I'll live." He raked her wounded gaze. "The bandage is fine. Really."

"Then we'll rest."

He stood. A chilly breeze tiptoed through the trees. Julian would miss his cloak tonight and regretted having left it behind. "It will be dark soon. We need to find something to eat."

"I'm too weak to travel." She sighed with all the melodrama of a bad actress, eyeing him from beneath her lashes. "Perhaps you should sit and enjoy the respite until I regain my wind."

He narrowed his eyes, knowing the gamut of her game. "We have one too many chiefs in this partnership, sweet."

She idly inspected the iron manacle around her wrist. "Is it because of what happened between us this morning? Is that why you've been so put out with me? I told you it meant nothing."

He looked away. "I haven't thought about it."

Christ, he'd thought of little else, and he didn't know why. Nor did he understand his resentment toward her.

"I was distraught," she said.

"And you've recovered with the wind full in your sails."

"And you're taking our tryst too seriously."

He almost choked on her brass. "That's usually my line."

Her dark, sultry eyes nailed him with a cheeky boldness that made her all the more interesting. "Frankly," she flicked a pine needle off her sleeve, "I don't know what came over me. I don't even like you. You haven't been the least bit kind." Her chest rose on a sigh. "So if you have women taking their clothes off for you, it's *not* because of your endearing personality."

Propping a foot on the log, he leaned a little close, and to his satisfaction, her eyes widened just a fraction. "Maybe it's not my endearing personality that attracts a woman."

"Posh!" She had the effrontery to laugh. "I've learned three things about you, Mr. Merlin, that contradict all your conceited blustering."

He lifted an amused brow and waited for her to continue.

"When those soldiers attacked you after your horse went down, you could have killed them, but you didn't, which tells me that you aren't a murderer. A cold-blooded one, anyway. Second, you didn't let that sergeant strike me, which tells me that despite everything else about you, you're decent to women."

"Indeed." He wanted to laugh.

"And finally," she announced with the supreme understatement of a naive romantic, "I don't sleep with men who aren't my husband. But this morning . . . well, I'm not sorry if you must know the truth. In a way you saved me, which almost makes you a gentleman."

Hell, it made him an idiot. And he'd be damned if he'd let her tell him his own mind. "Now let me tell you what *I've* learned, Miss Secret in Her Breeches." Julian leaned forward until she hit her back against a tree. "Just one point, so I'll be brief."

Her back stiffened, stretching the downy fabric of her shirt. The sensual motion spoke more of her innocence than a deliberate act to inflame him. She was trying to avoid him.

"And what have you learned, Mr. Merlin?"

He let his indolent gaze slide down her rounded body before bringing his full attention slowly back to her flushed face. "I've learned that you don't have the sense God gave a drowning rat or you wouldn't be here in the first place."

"A rat?"

"Aye, a drowned one to be exact." He slid a gloved finger beneath her chin. "And you know nothing about me, either. I didn't refrain from killing those British soldiers because a sudden surge of compassion overwhelmed me. If you kill a soldier, it follows you. They hunt you forever. Second, I didn't let that sergeant hit you, because at the time I thought we were on the same side. And finally . . ." Julian slowly and deliberately lifted her hand to his lips and couldn't resist the sudden urge to act obnoxious. He was as mercenary as they came, and the girl trod on perilous ground. "I'm no gentleman; thus I'm quick to remedy any preconceived notions you have in that direction and put an end to your girlish fantasies."

She tried to snatch away from his grip. "Get your hands off me."

"Really," his eyes narrowed with sudden predatory interest, "I rather thought you enjoyed the camaraderie."

She didn't want to hear it. But he gripped her chin anyway and turned her face to within a hairsbreadth of his. "You were wrong about something else, too." In the shadows of his beard, his teeth flashed white. "You have very ponderous breasts. The kind that fit into a man's hands with nothing left over to waste.

And unless you want me to demonstrate, I suggest you start walking."

Her temper flashed in her eyes, and he laughed at the ease that he could prick her facade. Just wait until she realized he was leading her to his ship.

She leapt up. "You're a bastard. You really are."

"You just keep remembering that, my anonymous rose, and maybe we'll both get out of this alive." Because he sure as hell wouldn't if he didn't haul his brain out from between his legs.

Furious, she ducked beneath his arm.

Julian's cocky expression vanished. His eyes narrowing, he followed, glad now for the distance that separated them. Only the crackling in the underbrush and the rattle of chains as they walked broke the stillness around them.

They traveled for the rest of the day in blessed silence until Julian began to doubt the forest would end. He had confidence enough to know he wasn't traveling in circles. The night fell upon the woods along with hunger and exhaustion. They drank from a creek and spent the night freezing in a briar patch. He knew he was in trouble the next morning when he could barely move. But he forced himself to plod on, if not for any reason but to match the girl's dogged stamina. The woods thinned. Dust motes frolicked in the beams of warm sunlight that splotched the ground.

Suddenly, she stopped. Julian snapped his head around to scan the woods. A squirrel skittered up an old loblolly pine. Then his nose caught the scent. The smell of apple pie permeated the woods.

"We must be near the main road." The girl's voice lit up like a silver sparkler, all glowing with a childlike excitement. He fought the impulse to gawk down at her. "There are farms up and down this road." She hurried past, dragging him forward. "That pie is mine. Even if I have to wedge it out of someone's mouth." Her bright laughter left him in awe. "I'll even share with you if you're nice."

He grabbed her shoulder, bringing her up short. "Listen."

She heard it, too. The sound of harnesses, the rattling of sabers. So close he could hear their horses breathe, and quietly he went to ground with the girl beneath his arm. His chained hand wedged beneath her warm body and the cooler loam below. A minute more, and they'd have run straight into the soldiers.

Julian continued to drink in the scent of apple pie, fused now with her fragrance. His groan of frustration mirrored hers but for a different reason. A laugh escaped between his teeth. Aye, 'twas the pied pie of Williamsburg, a sensual melody for the starving masses.

The bloody soldiers had gotten ahead of him. Again. And all he could focus on was the one soft breast that filled his palm. A sensual feast more appealing than apple pie. Closing his eyes in disgust, Julian realized he was doomed. The chains had to stay on until he reached the ship.

Chapter Four

While Catherine vigorously plotted ways to get close to the farmhouse, Merlin dozed. Or at least he seemed to for all the attention he paid to their surroundings. But another look at him told her he wasn't asleep, and as the soldiers moved from the house to the barn, he'd lifted his head. There were only three redcoats.

"Do you think that pie is still sitting on a windowsill?" Stealing that delicacy had become Catherine's sole goal in life. But the soldiers wouldn't leave. She flicked at a black beetle. "The rest of their platoon are probably searching the farms up and down this road," she added for want of hearing a voice. "Everyone will know we're criminals."

"Our chains will certainly be the first clue," he said without bothering to look at her.

She wanted to stick out her tongue at him. He lay on his belly, watching the scene at the farmhouse. Grudgingly, she noted the breadth of his shoulders and the way his arms strained against the cloth of his shirt. Her heart gave an odd jerk before she returned her focus to his face. One eye was covered by the dirty cloth that bound his head. His other eye was narrowed as if he were familiar with the hurry-up-and-wait routine. She followed his gaze. He'd picked out the high-roofed barn and corral where three drowsy horses stood over a feed bin. The farmhouse itself was a log structure that had been made of the pine trees that once dotted these fields. Merlin missed nothing, she realized and, as she peered more intently at his profile, she got the distinct impression that he hunted like this for a living. He had the long, lean patience of a cat.

With a sigh, she dropped her forehead into the dirt. Frankly, she'd hate being his enemy and pitied the fools who'd betrayed him.

"I'm fading as I speak." She rolled onto her back and glared at the wispy treetops fluttering in the breeze.

Even ignoring her, Merlin made her pulse flutter like those leaves, all trembly as if she were some moonstruck schoolgirl. She frowned at the ease with which he dominated her thoughts. What happened between them yesterday . . . well, it just happened.

Men forever bedded women without a second thought to anything but their pleasure. Her need had been no different. Merlin certainly had been accommodating enough with no second thoughts to hinder *his* conscience. Indeed, he hadn't willingly touched her since.

"It's hot." She whacked a mosquito. "In another few hours, I shall be naught but bones. You'll have to eat that pie for me."

Her nemesis suddenly laughed, a strange, comforting sound coming from such a stoic man. He shifted and grinned down at her. "Your sacrifice is duly noted."

"If you can wedge my shriveled limbs from the manacles, I release you from your responsibility to stay with me."

"My responsibility?"

Despite appearing feverish, his one eye twinkled as he looked down at her. She raised up on her elbows. "Isn't that what Guinevere said to Lancelot after he rescued her from the black knight?"

"I think you have the tales confused."

"Then Lancelot confronted the black knight while searching for the Holy Grail, perhaps." She flattened her palms in the dirt and leaned closer to whisper, "A mission. Much like yours. A secret quest. Only I'll wager yours isn't so divine."

His eyes went cooler. But his mood seemed to pass. "Lancelot did not confront the black knight. Nor was he worthy enough to seek the Holy Grail. A woman ruined him."

"Are you saying you're not worthy? Or that you blame women for your faults?"

His gaze grew lively. "I was under the impression that I had no faults."

"Posh." Offended by his sly prod, she lay back to rethink her strategy. "Your conceit far outreaches your minuscule nobility."

He chuckled, which annoyed her. Theirs was a contest of wits. An engagement of wills to trick the other into revealing something about himself. The winner escaped, identity intact.

The loser would not escape at all.

And Catherine didn't intend to lose, which is why she hadn't complained to find herself heading in a northerly direction, away from her home. Let him think she was helpless. As soon as her chains were off, she'd escape him before he could bat those dark, exquisite eyelashes and wonder what happened. Before she committed any more rash sins, that sent her to purgatory for feeble-mindedness.

Besides, she was confident in her ability to outmaneuver him.

"'Tis my favorite childhood tale," she said, deciding to chat over neutral territory. She caught a glimpse of a woodpecker. "Lancelot and Guinevere so in love and unable to reveal that love to the world. Theirs was a romance doomed from the start."

"You're a fan of tragedy?"

She twisted around to face him and saw that he fingered a long strand of her hair. She removed it from his hand. "'Twas only a tragedy because she loved two good men."

He sniffed in obvious disgust.

"What could be greater than love?"

"A man's duty to a higher cause."

"Then you, sir, are a man who has never loved."

He propped his head on his hand, and they faced each other. The heat from his body jostled her senses. "Love makes men weak," he pronounced, finding another wayward strand of her hair to torment.

She tugged the lock away. "Who says that?"

"Lancelot lost his ability to think rationally. He betrayed everything he believed in."

She tilted her chin in disdain. "*That* cannot be blamed on love. Give a man a twitching skirt and his brain ceases to function."

Her brief moment of triumph faded beneath the soft glitter in his eyes. "Twitching skirt, hell. You're wearing breeches. The whole British Navy has failed to capture me. One night with you, I not only get caught, but I get the blazes kicked out of me."

Sensing a deeper meaning hidden behind his words, she peered into his bruised face. His eye was still swollen. "But you've escaped now."

He'd recaptured a curl and brought it to his nose. "Have I?"

She breathed deeply to bridle her racing heart.

"I've always fancied blond hair myself. The kind that runs through a man's fingers like fine silk," he said casually, and she hung on his every word, secretly awaiting some revelation about his newfound passion for black hair. He was grinning when he met her eyes. "Yours needs a comb and a good pair of shears."

"You're impossible." Catherine snatched her hair away. "Do you know so many women then to play the roué with such ease, sir?"

He turned away to stare at the farmhouse. "At least I knew their names before I ravished them."

Narrowing her eyes, she sensed the invisible gauntlet he'd thrown, the subtle declaration of war.

She knew better than to think that Merlin wasn't a dangerous adversary. He made her irresponsible when she should be thinking about protecting her family, rather than kissing him. Again. She couldn't read him, but his unaffected expression, like his appearance, was surely an illusion, shrewdly crafted to deceive the enemy, and very clever at throwing her off guard. Hadn't she already made a bloody mess of her life by falling in love and marrying an alluring liar?

"The barn will have tools to remove these chains," she said without sounding too hopeful or despairing at once. A dog barked.

He watched the farmhouse.

"Well, I for one, intend to look," she added to the silence.

Looking past his hair ruffled by the breeze, she wanted to strip the bandage off his forehead to see his whole face in the daylight. To look into his eyes. But he seemed adept at keeping her away. He made it difficult not to feel intimidated. "If I didn't know better, I'd suspect that you wanted to keep these chains on."

Twisting slightly, he let his eyes roam over her. His sensuous mouth quirked at the corners. "Now, why would I want that?"

"So you can keep me prisoner. You're too weak to chase me down."

His eyes dropped to her mouth, and her heart stopped. She thought he was going to kiss her. "Trust me." He resettled his body next to hers. "I want out of these chains more than you do."

"Well, I don't trust you."

A shout from the farmhouse snapped Catherine around. Buried in the heat of Merlin's body, she watched the redcoats mount up. After the thunder of their exit, a growing din crescendoed in the woods as birds resumed their happy romp in the trees above them, as if the whole world had returned to normal without her.

She was safe, she told herself. The soldiers were gone.

So why did she suddenly feel like a lamb in the jaws of a wolf?

Julian stopped to grab his breath and flinched against the sharp stab of pain. He leaned his head back against the rough-hewn wood of the barn. If anyone had told him three days ago that today, he'd be wallowing in pig slop, chained to a rainbow from hell with apple pie smeared on her chin, he would have locked up the soothsayer for insanity and thrown away the key. As it was, his intrepid restraint dawdled ankle deep in mud and all manner of ghastly slime he didn't want to consider. Beside him, the girl's quiet laughter wound around him like the breeze.

He peered down at her and was caught by something unexpected. Her tumbleweed hair framed a piquant face more suitable to a child fresh out of bloomers than the woman who filled out those clothes. She bit into what remained of the stolen pie they'd pilfered from the trestle table out back of the house. She'd made an orgy out of the thing. He'd been lucky to get his share before a near encounter with one of the geese that roamed the farm sent them running into a hog pen. Fortunately for their well-being, the only resident was a small pig.

"What's so funny?" he demanded.

She swallowed. "Normally, I'd find these circumstances too much to bear," she whispered, as he shook clumps of mud off his once fine boots, "but fortunately for you, I have a deep affinity for pigs."

"Why doesn't that surprise me?" The maligned she-beast in

question snorted and rooted at his feet. He made an effort to edge the creature away.

"Don't bother," the girl chirped like a happy bird flapping her wings for show, "pigs have feelings. And obviously this one is attracted to you." Taking the last bite of pie, she peeked around the corner of the barn. She swallowed. "Don't move, and maybe she'll become bored with you." Her midnight eyes impishly raked him. "But then maybe not."

Julian gave the twit a flat smile. "You're enjoying yourself."

"If we wait around here long enough, they'll bring out a bucket of slop." She ran her hot little tongue over the crumbs on her lips. "Frankly, *I'd* enjoy the meal."

Julian rolled his eyes. She'd make a fine sailor with her lack of aversion to disgusting food.

Voices drifted from the field. Julian moved the girl aside and slipped a glance around the corner of the barn. A large hunting dog dashed through the family of geese, scattering the feathered flock in a cacophony of flapping wings and honks. Three men wearing baggy breeches and shirts lumbered into the yard, trailing their plow horse. But Julian was more worried about that spotted hound.

"Do you think they'll notice the missing pie?"

Pressed as she was between him and the barn, Julian could only glimpse the top of her dark head. She dipped a finger between her lips, and he looked away. "If we're lucky, they'll think the soldiers stole it. Come on. We're not safe with that dog around."

She seemed to know her way around a barn, so Julian let her lead. Their leg irons clumped in the mud. Despite his want to dislike her, he'd found her company interesting. More than that, she'd proved dependable, and surprisingly, he relied on her. A sobering notion, for her very unpredictability intrigued him as much as it reminded him that he didn't trust her. Unfortunately, she was about to learn that blood sport was his particular forté. He was not a man who played by the rules to get to the truth.

"It will be dark in an hour," she whispered.

Not soon enough. And he was relieved when they finally found an opening in the back of the barn to squeeze through. She slipped through the hole as the rumble of male voices faded out the front. The air was musty, filled with the scent of straw, and a beam of sunlight that attracted a swarm of gnats. Julian didn't like farms any more than he enjoyed laboring behind a plow. Give him a deck beneath his feet and an ocean beneath the stars any day.

"I think they're gone," the girl whispered. "We should hide in the root cellar. There will be food down there."

"No." He straightened. "No cellars."

He didn't want to be trapped without an exit.

Scavenging through expensive tools hanging on the walls, Julian lifted a spanner and shoved it into his empty scabbard sling. He had no intention of removing their wrist bracelets but he did need to get out of the leg irons. They made their way over the straw-covered ground so as not to startle the animals and send that hound to investigate. The girl stopped to soothe the two bay horses with infinite gentleness.

He watched her pat a black-and-white cow with fat pink udders. "We could have milk," she whispered excitedly.

"Christ." He tried not to puke at the thought. "Is food all you think about?"

She squeaked in delight and pulled him to the back of the barn. A barrel of apples sat against the far wall next to a scarred workbench. Fermenting bottles of cider lined the shelves, and a clay jug of what looked like whiskey sat on the edge of the bench. But something else caught his attention, tucked in the corner.

He lifted the small blue bottle. Pulling off the stopper, he brought it to his nose and winced. His gaze roamed the table. The vial sat out of sight of anyone who searched this barn.

He scraped a thumb through a wet puddle on the wooden table and, for the first time, looked around him. The two-story structure boasted a wall of shiny new harnesses. Despite outside appearances, this was no squalid dirt farmer who lived here. Those two bay horses alone cost a year's wage. Where would people like this get that kind of money?

"Do you know these people?" he asked.

Raising from her stoop, she juggled eight green apples. Her gaze went to the workbench.

"Not in your social circle of friends?" he asked.

Her proud chin lifted. "Since my father killed himself, not many people are."

Julian didn't know how to reply to that, and he set the vial back on the table.

"Sodium carbonate," she said, pointing to the shelf above his head. "A by-product of potash. The stuff with which you make soap. Whoever lives here, at least they're clean. Someone obviously likes soap."

Stacked three high, soap filled the shelf. "If they're part of that group around you, I doubt it."

Looping a finger around the oval handle of the jug of corn whiskey, he brought it to his nose. He swigged slowly at first, then drank a full swallow, swiping a hand across his mouth as he met her gaze. He didn't understand her need to protect these people. Her silence angered him. "One of those racehorses you befriended should meet our needs. We have to get these leg irons off first," he said.

Her sudden gleam of hope made him frown. Somewhere outside, a door opened, carrying the irate scream of an angry woman. Julian leaned a sore shoulder against the wood-framed window and eased the shutters wider. A pudgy, brown-haired woman squawked out the front door of the farmhouse, battering one of her overgrown sons with a broom. Julian scanned the house, looking particularly for the dog. Dusk streaked the sky with red. Soon, it would be dark again.

The girl sidled between him and the wall. "Do you think that woman blames him for the missing pie?"

She smelled of apple pie and crust, a delectable feminine fantasy, an annoying buzz in his head. He'd had enough of her chatter and her damn secrets. His chained hand pressed hers against the stone. "Get rid of those damn apples," he growled. "They're green as sin. They'll make you sick."

Her hands full, she wiggled to dislodge him. "Get away from me."

"When you drop those apples."

She turned to glare at him over her shoulder. Her hair tangled in his shirt. "I will not."

He buried his mouth against her neck and was rewarded with a gasp. An apple thumped to the ground.

"Stop."

He felt her back melt against his chest. Another apple dropped.

"Are you mad?" she whispered.

"Aye." He itched to run his tongue across that sugary mouth and taste that sweet confection on her tongue. "But not as mad as I'll be if you get sick on me."

"And how made will you be if I slam my elbow in your ribs?"

Julian eased himself to the floor. She dropped next to him, her cache of apples piled atop her lap like a child's treasure. His back pressed against the cool stone wall, he met the challenge in her midnight glare and felt a hot wave of desire drench him.

"You can't force me to throw these away just because you have something against apples."

"You're a bossy thing, aren't you?"

The jug of corn whiskey sat between them and, bold as brass, she swigged. She didn't even choke on the burn. "I'm not so little."

He tore the jug from her grasp. "Did your father really kill himself? Or did you just drive him to his grave?"

Pain flashed in the midnight depths of her eyes. He'd hurt her, and the darker satisfaction that should have been his never appeared.

He tossed her the spanner. It landed with a dull thump next to her thigh. "The peg will have to be driven out of each manacle on our ankles. I'm not much good at bending over that far, so you'll have to do it." His eyes closed. He was finding it increasingly difficult even to maintain a simple accent. He had to stay conscious before she worked her way up to the chains that bound their wrists. "Those men we saw will probably be preoccupied with supper for a while. But you'll have to listen for that hound."

"You're ill, aren't you?" she said.

"Don't overestimate your prowess, sweet. So far, we're still mostly on the same side. And I'm not that weak."

Except he was.

Catherine swiftly saddled one of the bays. Wind beat against the barn, a somber echo to her own heartbeat. She didn't dare light a lantern. She stopped to listen for sounds outside the barn, and her gaze slid to the back wall where she'd left Merlin.

Freedom lurked only a few feet away. She yanked the girth tighter on the saddle. Apples filled the saddlebags. Hands trembling, she leaned her forehead against the horses's neck, soothing his nervous temper with gentle words. She couldn't leave Merlin here and, in truth, the thought had only crossed her mind for a zealous second when she'd finally released the manacles. Fever burned his body. She knew he'd fought the effects of his beating for days, and sometime during the last few hours it took her to dislodge the locks, his body had succumbed to exhaustion.

Dark hair laying over one bruised cheek, his eyes closed, he was vulnerable to more than her gaze. The duty to protect him swelled and unfolded inside her like the wings of a dragon. She felt a need to repay him, to know the satisfaction that she had in some way saved his life, perhaps making them even.

But he would not allow her to leave when he was safe. It was this thought that drove her to saddle the horse with the need to vanish. That and the fact that she knew this place was dangerous. No ordinary farmer would have sodium carbonate lying around. This house belonged to someone in the Sons of Liberty.

Her shoulders slumped. She could not leave Merlin here.

Catherine turned to get him. And froze.

A man leaned a shoulder against the stall door, watching her. Wearing a brown homespun shirt and black baggy breeches, he chewed on a long piece of straw. "Stealing a horse is a crime, Catherine."

Oh, Lord in heaven! She knew this man!

They'd attended the same church for the past twelve years!

Moonlight lay a path at his feet, and she realized the barn door was open. "Danny never told us you were a thief." Jed Tomkins took the straw out of his mouth and stepped into the stall.

The horse tossed his head at the intrusion. Frightened as much by the man as she was by the horse, Catherine backed away.

"Are you the one those soldiers are looking for?" He made a production of looking around him. "What'd you do with that traitor you're supposed to be chained to?"

She dodged left. "I don't know what you're talking about."

"You know what I think?" Completely at ease with the game, he cornered her. "I think, yer a liar and a horse thief."

"Get away from me."

"You can tell me where he is, or I can call my four brothers, and we won't be askin' again till morning."

He leapt forward to grab her, and Catherine hit him in the jaw. "Bugger me." He staggered back. And before she could stop him, he tackled her in the hay. The horse reared. She hit the ground. He straddled her hips and caught her wrists. "I'd forgotten you was all fiery beneath all that ice." His mouth rasped over her ear. "Maybe I won't be callin' in my brothers after all."

Catherine couldn't scream. She clawed his face. Then the horse reared again. Front hooves flailed the air, landing where Catherine had been. She kept rolling until she hit the straw. Her hair tangled in dirty clumps around her face. She lifted her head, dazed. The high-strung horse pranced out of the stall. Jed Tomkins lay where he'd hit his head against the wall. A string of brown hair drooped in his eyes. She crawled to her knees, then stumbled to her feet.

Backing away, she rammed a fist into her mouth. The sound of barking dogs intruded. She chased the frightened stallion to the front of the barn, wrestling for control of his bridle.

"Shhh. It's all right. Oh, please . . ." She cooed over his sleek neck. "You must be quiet. You must!"

The horse pranced and stomped, but she held tight. A gloved hand came over her shoulder. Merlin stood behind her. He took hold of the horse's bridle. "Going someplace, Guinevere?" His voice was weak, but his eyes were hard as he turned to look down at her.

"We have to get out of here, now!" She mounted the horse.

Merlin's foot slipped in the stirrup. He climbed into the saddle behind her on the next try. Catherine kneed the horse, and they shot out through the barn door. The wind carried them into the darkness.

The dogs continued to trail them. Always at a distance, but close enough that Catherine couldn't slow to rest. She ached for the horse that carried the weight of two people. She ached for Merlin. But he'd regained his strength enough to take them through a swollen creek, walking the horse in the cooling water for at least two miles before leaving the creek. The reins looped in his fist, and without argument, she relinquished control.

Catherine dozed. She hadn't meant to fall asleep. When she awakened, a church bell pealed in the distance. Dawn had come. A low mist hugged the ground. She recognized the town she knew sat directly over the rise.

Merlin had brought her to within three miles of her home. The

York River was barely a stone's throw away. She could smell the brine that sometimes came when the bay was at low tide.

Sliding from the back of the horse, Merlin helped her down, and they drank from a spring. The grass was damp beneath her knees. Above them in the trees, a crow cawed, and the horse took off running, stirrups flopping. Catherine cried out.

"Let him go." Merlin leaned an elbow against his thigh. "We don't need him anymore."

Water droplets glittered in his tangled hair and beard. He sat back and let his gaze go over her. She tried to turn away. His hand caught her chin, and he looked at her mouth where she'd bitten her tongue during Jed Tomkin's attack. "What the hell happened to you back there?"

Catherine shook her head. "I was saddling the horse—"

"Deciding to leave me?"

"Yes!" She leaped to her feet. She'd been recognized by one of her own. Merlin would never let her go if he knew. The risk to him would be too great. "That crossed my mind numerous times!"

He was on his feet before she could turn and flee, his body standing before hers like a wall she couldn't breach, an impenetrable obstacle that stood between her and home, an object of doom.

He took her by the arms, but his grip did not hurt. Their eyes held and clashed. Then he suddenly wrapped her to him, and they stood in the wet mist, bound by invisible chains she didn't understand. The creek gurgled gently over rooks.

"I want to go home," she wept into his shirt.

"I know." His hand soothed her head.

"Don't you have a home? Someone who cares?"

His awful silence told her he didn't. And her grip on his shirt tightened. What kind of past created such solitude? How could he stand the isolation when she could barely imagine it herself? She loved her family, worried about their safety.

"Why did you let our horse go? Why?" she whispered, trying to fight him. Trying to pull away. "You can hardly walk."

"Neither can the horse—"

Running footsteps slapped against the creek. Three wild-looking men approached. Merlin laid a palm over her mouth, sealing her gasp. Armed with a brace of pistols, looking more like pirates than colonists, two of the men wore a sailor's flat-brimmed hat over shaggy blond hair and bell-bottom trousers rolled to the knees.

The taller man in the middle, dressed more conservatively in a leather jerkin, black breeches, and boots, stopped before them. His tawny hair curled over one eye. She pressed deeper into Merlin's arms as if that alone protected her from this man's piercing stare. His gaze suddenly shifted, and his grin was one of friendly relief.

"Christ, Reece. You look like hell."

"Glad to see you, too."

"The whole bloody countryside is crawling with soldiers. They've even searched the ships moored here at the docks." His blue eyes swept Catherine. "Obviously something went wrong with the drop."

The sudden reality of her predicament sent her heart racing into her throat. She wanted to fight. She couldn't breathe. The pressure on her chest increased. Somehow, Merlin had tricked her. Led her directly to his lair. And she'd let him. She clawed the hand on her mouth with both her hands. He wouldn't take her. He wouldn't!

Merlin's grip tightened. Her muffled cries went unanswered by the brutes that watched. Silver specks filled her eyes.

"I'm sorry." The whisper touched her cheek. "But I can't let you fight me on this or you'll get us all killed."

She heard the pain in his voice. Then she heard nothing at all.

Chapter Five

Catherine wrapped her fingers around the oval porthole that looked out across the river. Furious that she could not dislodge the window, she pressed her nose to the thick glass. Her hair hung dripping wet over her shoulders and left a puddle at her bare feet. Backing up a step, she hit the wooden hip tub that had been delivered compliments of the captain. Finally, she returned to the door.

"You're a bastard, Reece or Merlin or whatever your name is." She pounded the door. "You'll get nothing from me but a headache."

Wrapped in a white linen sheet, Catherine searched the room for weapons. She tore the straw mattress off the bunk. An innocent-looking ornate chest revealed a brazen cache of women's garments. She brought a chemise to her nose to test the scent and grimaced at the cheap perfume. To think she'd given herself to a man who serviced women with unquestionably bad morals.

Except who was she to cast stones? She'd sold herself for a night's comfort in a stranger's arms—and she'd not dismissed the unthinkable consequences of what she'd done in that glade with Reece.

Sitting down at the desk, she nibbled cheese, her finger drawing circles around the fruit next to it on the plate. She was scared. What would she do if Merlin decided to sail off with her into the sunset?

The renegade thought leaped out at her. She was shocked to find that despite everything, her mind still bent so precariously to the carnal memory of their time together. When she finished with her meal, the tray met the door in a furious clatter of pewter ware.

But by the time another day had passed, Catherine was ready to chat with the devil himself, if he'd just walk through the door. So she sat at the desk and remained quiet, hoping whomever it was who delivered her food would think her asleep. Within an hour, the door cracked open, and Catherine lifted her head.

The bald man stopped. His eyes widened as if she were about to leap at his throat. "Don't worry," she said. "I shan't kill you. You're not the one I'm angry with."

Behind him, the tall, blue-eyed pirate she'd first seen at the glade shoved the door open. Whisking the tray from the older man's hands, blue eyes dismissed the elder with a nod. His light brown hair was drawn back with a thong. He was a few years younger than Merlin.

"How are you doing?" he politely inquired. "I trust you've found these quarters to your liking."

His rakish smile was almost disarming and, reminded of her continued folly with pretty faces, Catherine stiffened. He moved into the room. "I see that you still haven't dressed. Did you not like your choice of attire?"

"I'll not wear the clothes of one of his floozies." She wagged a fierce finger at the ruby gown wadded up in a pile on the floor. "And you can tell your precious captain that I want my clothes back."

"I'm afraid that's impossible."

"But of course. The impossible is only possible if his highness dictates such miracles. Where is he hiding anyway?"

"He's been on his back since we boarded. His fever weakens him and makes him more prone to accepting the doctor's advice."

Feeling herself pale, she looked away from the man's scrutiny.

"The physician on board said he has two broken ribs. It's a wonder he lasted this long on his feet."

"When will you know if he'll be all right?"

"When he doesn't keel over and expire."

Her eyes narrowed but only because he made her grin. She refused to feel even a smidgen of kinship with this man, and especially to his awful captain.

"My name is Michael." A slight Irish brogue marked the introduction.

"Then you are not from these colonies?" she probed.

"We are all from the colonies." Setting the tray down, he picked at a juicy piece of fowl on her plate.

She slapped his hand away. "Why are we still at the docks?"

"The British won't let any merchant ships leave without a thorough search. We'd have difficulty explaining your presence. Especially if you were found gagged in the hold."

"Your wisdom astonishes me."

"Besides, we're awaiting word about a certain Daniel Claremont." His eyes found hers, "You wouldn't by chance know the chap?"

Her mouth went dry. "What . . . is your association with him?"

"None. We've never seen him before. But someone"— he waved a hand airily about him—"sent us out looking for him because of his potential involvement in a murder that happened some months ago that our wealthy client is interested in solving."

Catherine grabbed the bedsheet tighter around her and stood. *Patrick.*

This man was talking about her husband's murder. Everything suddenly made sense. Daniel was the only witness to the events that night Patrick had died, the weakest link in the chain that now wrapped around her throat in a conspiracy of lies. That was the connection between Merlin and her brother. That was why he'd been expecting Daniel Claremont that night.

A cold sweat formed on her spine. "How long have you known Merlin? I mean, the man you call Captain Reece?"

His smile boasted a mouthful of straight teeth "Six years. He took me off the gallows in Boston." He placed a hand on his heart. "I was a mere laddie and had stolen bread from the market."

"And I'm the Virgin Mary," she sniffed. So rumor was true. Merlin most likely hailed from Boston, which would explain his accent.

He picked a chunk of fowl from her plate and popped it in his mouth. "We're friends. As near to family as any we've got."

"You're fellow pirates, no doubt."

He looked offended. "More often than not, he works for someone else. Reece is very thorough in his profession."

"Does he know . . ." She turned to face the man, anxious to read his face. "Does he work for a Captain Julian Lambert?"

His expression vacillated slightly at the mention of that name.

The deck seemed to open beneath her feet. "He's put my family in great danger," she whispered. "I have to leave her at once."

"Your life is every bit in danger as Reece's."

"You don't understand." Dark hair spilled over her face. "You have to let me go before my family has to explain my absence."

He stood. "Eat your dinner, miss." He stepped around her.

"I won't." She sought to stop him from leaving. The door shut in her face. "Cowards!" she yelled. "Bring me my clothes!"

Catherine spun around. She leaned her back against the door, finally burying her face into her hands. "Damn you, Patrick Bellamy." She cursed her husband. Cursed him for getting her family involved with people who would as soon slit your throat as kiss you. Cursed him for taking risks, for dying, for not loving her enough.

She should have known Julian Lambert would turn up someday. The long-lost half brother, the blackguard who didn't care a whit for a brother who'd lived and breathed in his great brother's enormous shadow. The man who never showed for their wedding five months before or Patrick's funeral one month later.

The great Julian Lambert, coward that he was, had sent a mercenary to do his investigation. Now Merlin would pay with his life for his loyalty to a man who didn't deserve spit.

She collapsed on the bed. There was nowhere she could turn. She shut her eyes, hating her weakness, hating even more the urge to flee to Merlin for safekeeping. But Merlin's loyalty would be to himself first, then to Julian Lambert.

And by all accounts, Julian Lambert had no heart. Yet, even as powerful as he was, he wasn't strong enough to break the stranglehold of the men who used the rebel cause for their own gains. No one was.

Any man who ever tried, perished.

Julian was sitting at his desk when the door clicked open. He lifted his head and met his friend's somber gaze.

"Christ, Reece, you look at bad as you did two days ago."

Michael was the only person who called him by his middle name. Julian had upbraided him for calling him by any name at all in front of the girl, and now he felt like an ignoble ass for doing so.

"How is she?" He sloshed brandy into a glass.

"Furious." Michael shut the door behind him and leaned with his back against the latch. "And quite beautiful," he added offhandedly, lifting Julian's gaze from the rim of the glass. "I can understand why you've stayed away. She refused the dress."

"Did you think she wouldn't?"

"She thinks that you are this ship's captain." Michael laughed. "Little does she know who you really are."

Julian never could match Michael O'Hara's fatalistic optimism and certain by-blow cynicism that came from being raised an Irish bastard. Folding his arms across his chest, Julian leaned against the window bench. "What the hell is so funny?" he demanded.

"She asked if you worked for Julian Lambert."

Julian set down the empty glass in disgust. A clean bandage wrapped his head where the surgeon had placed seven stitches in his temple. One eyelid was now a pale purple and partially covered with the same bandage that wrapped his skull. He hurt to move, and his tender ribs did not lend themselves to breathing. Even the light hurt his head so he kept the room darker than he normally would have.

Michael pushed away from the door and walked to the desk. "Without mentioning names, I told her Merlin was seeking information about a certain murder. And she knew. She knew who I was talking about." Lifting the crystal stopper from the brandy bottle, he turned it over in his hands. "Patrick was probably neck deep in something illegal around here, and this girl is terrified to talk. She also made it clear that she held Julian Lambert in the same esteem as pond scum. Obviously, she's privy to local gossip. And I'm afraid Merlin rates only a little higher than pond paddies. So, whatever affection you hold for her, she doesn't return it—to either one of you."

Michael withdrew a missive from inside his waistcoat. "This came about five minutes ago. It's not what you wanted to hear."

His solicitor's seal was stamped in wax on the back. The contents had already been opened. Glaring at his friend, Julian flicked the missive. He put up with this kind of insubordinate behavior only from Michael. "Do I even need to read this?"

Michael sat on the edge of the desk and poured himself a glass of expensive brandy. "Daniel Claremont died two years ago. He commanded the Twenty-third Royal Welsh Fusiliers during the Seven Years War. He lost a leg at the Battle of Minden against the French. For his services, the king gave him title to a plot of land and the house where his family has been living for the past twelve years."

Julian braced his arms against the desk. "Then Claremont's name was a bloody ruse? A joke?"

"Reece . . . you need to return to your command. What's happening here is too big, especially now. You can barely walk. You're not thinking straight."

Julian's hands clenched into fists. A sudden desperation welled, an unfamiliar emotion that wrestled with his restraint. He'd never given up or quit anything in his life. The girl's silence condemned him. He wanted to shake her. Rattle her until sense spilled out of her ears. He knew nothing about her. Not one fragment of history to tell him who she was, where she came from.

"I won't let them win."

"Christ, Reece." Michael pulled him around. "I haven't seen you like this since—"

"You don't know anything, O'Hara." Julian flung away from the desk.

Michael was wrong. His obsession with the girl was nothing more than a need to see justice rendered.

Michael moved next to him beside the stern gallery window. His eyes followed the path of a gull as it settled somewhere above them on the masts. "I didn't think you dabbled with dark-eyed virgins."

"She's no bloody virgin," he threw out in anger.

"Really." A brow rose. "That wedding band you still wear would be hard to explain if adultery is suddenly your cup of tea. Assuming she's not just a whore."

Summarily disgusted with himself, Julian pulled away. He owed no explanation, no statement of reason to justify his silence concerning his personal life which, at the very least, wasn't anyone's business. He didn't ask for this girl's presence in his life.

But by God, he would take what she'd offered and more. He'd take his damn life back.

"She's dangerous to you, Reece. Let her go."

After Michael left the cabin, Julian dropped into the chair at the desk. He reached for the half-empty bottle of brandy and froze as his gaze slipped to the ring on his finger.

Aye, he still wore his wedding band. He'd built his wife a grand home off the James River where the sunrise burned the water bronze. Where darkness couldn't touch.

And yet for all his money, power, and status, he could not save the one person he'd loved most in his life.

Fighting to keep his hands steady, Julian sloshed brandy into his glass. His wife's death had taken everything in the world that had been his to give. Except his honor and a brother who'd give his life for him if Julian had ever asked. Now both had been stolen from him.

With one furious swallow, he downed the contents of the glass.

Now his future had dropped to hell in a basket, carried by one dark-haired, anonymous female that he hadn't wiped from his head since she'd brandished her saber and ridden through a bevy of soldiers to save him. A woman he didn't even know existed a week ago.

Clutching the sheet to her body, like a lady Thor ready for battle, Catherine stepped over the threshold into the captain's quarters. One glance behind told her Michael had managed to vanish. A lantern creaked with the ship's rhythm on the river.

Edging the heavy door wider, she stepped over the coaming into the room. Sandalwood assailed her senses. Her eyes went to the stern window. Fading sunlight reflected off the thick mullion glass casting the walls in a warm brilliance. It was the only light in the room. The door clicked shut behind her. Her heart raced with the flight of a hummingbird.

Reece stood next to the far edge of the window. His hair was neatly queued with a leather strap. A bandage wrapped his head. A trimmed beard covered his jaw. He wore a blue, loose-fitting shirt with billowed sleeves, and no gloves. Black breeches shaped his muscled thighs and tucked into knee-high boots that lent an inch to his already imposing height.

The room was even more uncompromising than the man but certainly less definitive. A narrow bunk sided up to a plank wall on one side of the chamber. Void of wrinkles or imperfection, a blanket hugged the bed. A pale gray shirt and brown homespun breeches lay atop an ivory counterpane. On the other wall sat a polished teak desk void of maps or charts. Only the leather-bound classics that filled the bookcase revealed any glimpse of his character.

When she blinked again, she found herself in Reece's gaze. It was all she could feel from him as he stood in the shadows. And suddenly Catherine was seized by the memory of those unfathomable eyes pressing into her that morning in the glade, when he'd taken her into his arms and made the world go away. The tightness in her chest increased. For a long time neither of them spoke. Her bare toes curled against the polished floor.

"You've been comfortable?"

"I want to go home."

"And where is home?"

Catherine remained by the door as he approached. Clutching her pitiful sheet tighter, and with her hair framing her torso, what started out a valiant protest to regain her clothes suddenly felt foolish in the wake of his surrounding presence.

She turned away. He pressed his palm against the door, blocking her flight. "Someone is bound to start looking for you. Start asking questions. A husband maybe?" His voice was hard against her cheek.

She'd given him everything this past week, endured personal intimacies that she'd never shared with anyone. She knew him better than her husband, yet she knew him not at all. Not on the outside anyway, the mask he showed to the world where a lifetime of walls concealed the man she'd briefly glimpsed beneath. She didn't even know what his face looked like beneath the shadows and the bruises.

"I hate you," she whispered, furious because he could control her with such ease.

"For what?" A finger tipped her chin. "For wanting the truth? For fighting to keep my honor and my life as one?"

"How much is Julian Lambert paying you for your loyalty?"

The question seemed to startle him. Clearly, he knew the name.

"Why?" The silky drawl touched her ear. "Are you wealthy?"

He'd bathed with sandalwood soap. He stood so close, the heat of his body was like an invisible aura around her. Yet he didn't touch her. "No," she whispered against the softness of his beard.

"Then what are you offering . . . for my loyalty? What do you have that the esteemed naval hero doesn't?" His mouth slid to the curve of her jaw and down her throat.

Desperately trying to avoid what she'd set in motion, she couldn't voice the words. The outright proposition. Her head fell back against the onslaught. "I didn't come here for . . . this."

"No?"

"Surely . . ." She strived for indifference. "Surely, your social life is filled with more ample . . . opportunities."

"My social life is not without its rewards." He caught his hands in her thick hair. The heady taste of brandy touched her lips. "But then, this isn't social. It's personal."

He would kiss her, and heaven help her, she'd let him.

"No!" Her breathy pronouncement stopped him.

She'd bargain away her body and her pride. Indeed, had already done so in a tormented moment of despair. But what did she know of this outlaw anyway? Merlin's reputation had been forged by drawing room gossip. What had rumor ever had to do with truth? He was a ruthless man who possessed an inordinate amount of arrogance to think he could kidnap her, who taunted her and made her life miserable. If she succumbed, he would devour what rationale remained to steer her through this disaster.

He lifted his head and blinked back a scowl. "You'll have to do better than this if you want my undying loyalty," he said. "I've seen more willing virgins in the front pew of St. Paul's in London."

"I . . ." She shoved against him. "I made an awful mistake—"

"Damn right. And not just one." His hand encircled the delicate length of her throat. "Have you ever felt a rope around your neck?"

"Of course not!" she rasped. "I'm not a criminal."

"You are to those English soldiers hunting you. I know that sergeant's ilk."

She probed his eyes cast in dark amber by the light. "You're one of them, aren't you? You're British."

His gaze narrowed on hers. "Aren't we all British?"

"No." Hot tears betrayed her courage. "I'm a Virginian."

She turned her face away and stared unseeing at the floor. Her hair fell over her chin. "Go back to where you came from," she pleaded, wanting to bury her face into the downy fabric of his shirt. "The sergeant will take that letter to the governor. Mayhaps, he already has. And more than irate soldiers will be hunting us both."

"I could protect you," he whispered in her hair.

"No one can."

"I can."

He was asking for her help, but she couldn't give it. He didn't know that Patrick's death had been one of many in this area.

Catherine wrapped her arms over her torso. A rector and his daughter had been murdered not far from this very place. She remembered the tragedy only too well. The man and his daughter were robbed and their carriage driven off the bluffs. The little girl had only been twelve. Catherine spent weeks investigating their murders, trying to find justice for a crime few seemed anxious to solve.

That's when she'd first discovered that the Sons of Liberty were somehow involved. Or at least the men who pillaged the roads called themselves that. For they weren't rebels. She'd discovered other things as well. Things that she wished she'd never learned. About her husband. About the kind of man she'd really married.

She'd also learned that there was danger in pursuing the truth. And months ago, she'd decided she would no longer risk the lives of her family. She'd given up her newspaper. She'd immersed herself in her drawings. She'd pruned fruit trees and baked pies for the money they brought into the family coffers. She had become a shadow so they would forget that she and her family ever existed.

Reece's shoulders blocked the dregs of dying sunlight. The white bandages that wrapped his chest stood out beneath his loose shirt. She wanted desperately to trust someone. She'd been alone for so long with nowhere to turn. But was the promise of vengeance by this man who masqueraded behind a noble cause enough to risk her family?

She turned away.

The pale flash of gold on his hand stopped her breath. He'd worn gloves before. She hadn't seen the ring until now. Her heart ceased to beat. And for the world, she couldn't make herself breathe.

Her eyes roamed his face. "You asked if I was married," she whispered, horrified to hear her voice crack. "But what about you, Captain Reece?" Taking his left hand, she lifted his fingers to the fading beam of light that sprinkled the polished floor. "Or do vows mean so little to all men?"

Dropping his hands, he stepped away from her.

"I don't know anything," she whispered, "and even if I did, I wouldn't tell you. You don't live here among us. You don't care about anything but your own brand of justice."

"You're mistaken."

"Am I, Captain Reece? Then prove it. Let me go."

For too many heartbeats to count, he held her gaze. "There are breeches, a shirt, and boots on the bed. The clothes belong to one of my crew. Michael will supply you with a hat and cloak."

He stopped short of swinging open the door. One hand bracing against the wall, he turned. "I trust you can find your way home."

Then he closed the door behind him.

And just like that, he'd closed the chapter in their lives.

Chapter Six

"She did as ye said she would, Reece," Michael stepped into the cabin and closed the door. "Are you sure we shouldn't have followed the lass? To see her home?"

Julian continued to stare out the stern gallery window. "A few hours ago you were touting my cruelty for holding her captive; now you're complaining about my neglect for setting her free?"

"That's not what I mean, and you know it. She's a woman. A comely one at that."

A pale line of gray edged the horizon. Holding a flask of French brandy in his hand, Julian swigged. The ache in his ribs had not subsided, even with laudanum. "She wields a cutlass as dangerously as any man and carries a right hook better than yours. The *lady* can take care of herself."

The ship creaked in the wake of another ship's passing. "And maybe you've just grown soft." Michael had the nerve to laugh. "I didn't expect that you'd let her go."

Julian turned to face him. Something had been bothering him for days now and, as he stared at the bottle of brandy, his mind lingered in distraction. "What do you know about sodium carbonate?"

Michael's interest seemed to go on alert. "It's a by-product of soap. It's used to make glass—"

"It's also a chemical dye that can be used to decipher invisible ink. She knew who lived at that house," he said half to himself.

Julian set down the bottle. "Before we leave on the tide, get a messenger to Robbie. I want to know who owns that farmstead where we took that fancy racing stud. I want to know everything about the Sons of Liberty in this area. Who their leader is. Who else besides Patrick has been killed in recent months."

"Then you think this whole affair goes beyond framing Merlin?"

"It certainly isn't the hell about politics, liberty, and happiness for all. This is about a few select thugs using the Sons of Liberty as a cover for malicious activity. Merlin stepped into the middle of something big. I intend to find out what."

The door shut solidly behind Michael. Julian dropped into the chair behind his desk. He blew out the lamp on the desk. For Julian Reece Lambert knew how to lose himself in the darkness and did so now. He'd known since the first time he'd ever run from his father's fist and learned how to fight against a thug's tyranny.

Find the leader, and the pyramid would crumble from within.

His gaze went to the window and stayed.

He wouldn't be going far.

Old scores aside, he would bury every last one of the men who'd betrayed him. Starting with the one who'd murdered his brother.

Somewhere between darkness and the dawn where dreams fused with reality, the day slowly awakened. A breeze carried the smell of brine. Catherine struggled up the steep, grassy path to reach the bluff overlooking the York River. She'd been running for the past hour, and she had long since removed the cloak. A costly item, she carried it with the knowledge that someone in her household could use such a garment in colder weather. For now, she needed to reach the shelter of the woods before daylight revealed her presence on the hill.

Bending with her palms flat against her thighs, she stopped to grab her breath. A rooster crowed from the Millers' farm beyond the grove of trees. Somehow, she'd made it this far without being seen. Beads of moisture coated the long grass and leaves with the promise of a humid day to come. The main road was just up ahead. Bright red seedpods from wild magnolias provided the only color in the weed-infested strip of land between the street and the bluff. Wiping her forehead, she turned to look back at the river below.

And her gaze froze.

Gold emblazoned the water and touched the high masts of the single ship that crept out of the river with the tide.

Merlin had kept his promise and let her go.

Shielding her eyes from the golden sunrise, Catherine watched the brilliant white sails open with the fragile grace of a bird's wings. Clearly, he'd made it past the British checkpoint.

The schooner began to heel over as she entered the bay. Without taking her eyes from the tall masts, Catherine ran along the ledge of the bluff until the path took her back into the woods. The wall of trees muffled her breathing as she hurried to a point where she could better view the ship. Emerging near the road that led down to Water Street, she looked once more toward the bay. Beneath a flawless blue sky, the ship had faded to a speck on the open seas.

As if she gazed at a painting, her memory framed the scene, its beauty eclipsed by the growing tightness in her chest. All around her, the woods awakened to a cacophony of life. And in that moment, she'd never felt more alone. Would he go back to Boston now? Ruined for what had happened here? To his wife and maybe his children?

Powerless to stop the rise of foolish ears, Catherine turned away from the river. Aided by guilt and her own cowardice, a monstrous sense of defeat overwhelmed her. She wiped her nose with the back of her hand and told herself again that she'd done what was best for everyone.

The clank of harnesses alerted her. The first soldier appeared over the narrow rise the same instant that her head snapped up.

Dropping to her knees, Catherine crawled into the long grass. Grasshoppers skittered in all directions. The cloak lay wadded beneath her, and she buried her face into its folds to shield her panicked breathing. The cloth smelled faintly of sandalwood and the sea, and other memories better left forgotten. She squeezed her eyes tight, waited a dozen heartbeats, then checked the road again. A platoon of soldiers, their heavy red coats barely visible through the trees, rattled past her hiding place and continued into town.

Gritting her teeth, Catherine groaned at her carelessness.

Finally, she stood. Why would soldiers come here to town?

Had there been another robbery or raid last night on one of the warehouses? Or were the soldiers still tracking Merlin?

Sprinting across the road, Catherine climbed the terraced hills, past the old abandoned Sunderland estate. Crossing Main Street, she followed the familiar path for another two miles before she crept into the grove of fruit trees Papa had planted ten years ago. A source of her family's income, jams and pies brought enough money to the family coffers to feed them for months.

She hunched beneath the branches and scanned the white frame house. Her home with its glazed sash windows stood at the top of a rise overlooking the York River. And her heart tripped.

No lack of whitewash could hide the intricate craftsmanship that had gone into building that house. The Colonel's pride. He'd always been so good with his hands. A faded white picket fence enclosed the main yard around the house where a profusion of cockscomb blossomed like tomorrow's sunrise. The woodshed, steepled icehouse, and root cellar were barely visible beyond the circular drive near the carriage entrance. Out the front door, a long green fairway slanted toward the bluff where the river was in full view.

Her gaze found the iron arbor just beneath her bedroom. She hadn't used that lattice since she and Elizabeth had snuck outside to stand nude in the rain. It had been so hot that night. That was before Papa died. Long before she'd met Patrick.

Smoke twined from the chimney in the white brick kitchen house to the side of the main house. Millie was awake. That would mean Millie's father, Samuel, was in the barn.

Nothing had changed in her absence.

Everything was as it should be.

Catherine drew in her breath and started to stand when she stopped. Shifting her attention, she scanned the yard.

No one ever got past Sally.

That bad pig was wont to linger in a hidden wallow or shadow and leap out at an unsuspecting person or horse, friend or foe. No one ever entered this property unannounced.

Fidgeting with the cloak, Catherine frowned. She didn't know why she put up with the pig except that Sally was worth any ten watchdogs at alerting the household to visitors. Sally might be pink and walk on four legs, but she was much like the loyal servants who remained at the house and, though she terrorized the neighbor's hounds, she kept the property clear of intruders.

But today, Catherine didn't want to be found. She didn't know what had occurred here during her absence or who might be watching the property. She wanted to creep into the house unannounced, crawl into bed, and pretend this last week had never happened.

Then she'd wring Daniel's neck, if that's what it took to reveal the traitor who'd given him the missive that night he was so drunk. Someone set him up, and she wanted to know why.

Brushing off her hands, Catherine dashed toward the house. No sooner had she stepped out of her shelter than a high-pitched squeal alerted her that she'd been discovered. Sally had been by the barn.

"Shush," Catherine hissed, frantically waving her hands. Casting her gaze toward the house, she took off for the arbor, her pace matched by the pig chasing her across the yard.

Catherine reached the waist-high fence first. One hand on top, she leapt the fragile slats and plummeted among the roses. A thorn scraped her hand. Squealing energetically, Sally poked her flat nose through the wobbly slats.

"Go away! Shoo!" Catherine whispered, worried that the picket fence would pitch to the ground. She put her hand on Sally's wet snout and tried to push her away. Sally's excitement could not be abated. "All right, you found me. I missed you, too. Have you been watching over everything?"

Sally nuzzled her head against the fence.

"You have to be quiet now. Shh."

Catherine glanced toward the house, then back at the barn. Samuel stood in the huge doorway, looking toward the house.

She dipped back into the bushes. She didn't want Samuel or Millie or any of the other servants involved in whatever might come out of this past week. She didn't know how much anyone knew about her absence from the house. There would be questions, but none she wanted to answer until she spoke to Elizabeth and Daniel. The less anyone knew of her association with Merlin, the safer for everyone.

Catherine scooted away from the fence, looked back at Sally, and fondly patted her nose. "Now go away before I decide to make a ham hock out of you." Then, keeping low, she darted to the arbor.

Once inside her room, among her familiar things, Catherine stripped off the clothes Reece had given her. Tucking them carefully between the mattress and the ropes beneath her bed, she slid into a clean shift. Too exhausted to think straight, she slumped on the edge of her bed and clawed her fingers through her braid. She should wash or comb her hair, but she didn't even have the energy to think. She should seek out Daniel. But she wouldn't. Not yet.

Instead, she curled into a ball on her side and, tucking her hands beneath her cheek on the pillow, stared out the window.

The breeze caught the wispy curtains. The smell of sandalwood permeated her fatigue and, remembering that she used scented sachets in her linen closet, she vowed to use vanilla forevermore.

Pounding on the door reverberated through the room. "Mrs. Bellamy?" A man's voice spoke from the hallway.

Catherine stuck her arms in a threadbare wrapper she yanked from her wardrobe. The cloth whirled, barely missing the vase of dried-out roses on her cherry-wood desk. She had no time to make herself decent.

"I don't know why the door is locked," her housekeeper's voice sounded panicked. "I'm tellin' ye, she's been ill, sir."

"Stand aside, Mrs. Halstead."

"Nay, ye cannot be beatin' down the door of a lady's bedroom."

Still half drugged with sleep, Catherine threw the latch and swung open the door as two uniformed soldiers spilled into the room, followed by her harried housekeeper. All eyes fell on her at once.

Catherine needed no acting skills to appear shocked by the invasion. Recognizing the shorter man, her face paled. He was the cruel sergeant who'd beaten Reece half to death. Her only consolation was that the ruddy sergeant appeared no less shocked to find someone present in the room. The last time he had seen her, it had been dark and she'd been covered in mud.

Shoving the hair out of her face, she lifted her gaze to the taller man who stood within the doorway. Lieutenant Ross had been sent from Williamsburg to investigate Patrick's death. He'd stayed to fill the customs agent's position and catch smugglers and tax evaders.

Elizabeth pushed between the men and gasped. "Catherine . . . oh my God! You're . . . conscious!"

She was dressed in pale white ruffles, a virginal Raphael masterpiece, as she burst into tears. Elizabeth more than anyone in this family had perfected the art of overacting. "We didn't know—" She whirled on the men. "Are you satisfied now, Lieutenant? Does she look like a highwayman or a seditious spy to you? Why look at her." She encompassed Catherine with her arm. "She looks awful. And if you're fortunate, you won't catch what she's had all week."

Even the hard-bitten soldiers behind him appeared reluctant to enter the room, so Catherine allowed her sister to console her.

"Lizzy," Catherine managed. "What's happening here?"

"I'll be gettin' some vittles and a pitcher of water, Mizz Catherine," Anna, her elderly housekeeper announced. A white mobcap covered a full head of hair that used to be as orange as fresh marmalade. Looking pointedly at the lieutenant, she sniffed. "I may be a half-senseless old woman, but I'd say yer the one what lacks common wits, comin' at this time of the morn' to beat on a respectable young lady's door. Who'd of fixed the latch, if ye'd have ripped it off?" She huffed out of the room.

"These men have been going over the countryside rounding up insurrectionists," Elizabeth announced. "Truly, they will have to round up half the county then, will they not?"

Catherine's hand shot out. "Elizabeth!"

"Where is your brother, Mrs. Bellamy?" Lieutenant Ross asked.

Elizabeth stiffened. "Where do you think he is? He's out carousing with his worthless friends. And being the lady I am, I will not subject myself to explaining what that means."

The lieutenant's gaze shifted with irritation to Elizabeth, who boldly returned his scrutiny. "Will you give me your word that your sister has been ill?"

"On a Bible I will," she avowed. "Cross my heart and hope to die. She's been demented. Bloody mad with grief, if you ask me. You know she lost her dear husband this year."

"I'm aware of the tragedy that has hit this family."

"Then you are also aware that my sister's brother-in-law is an important official. Julian Lambert is a captain in His Majesty's Royal Navy. The Earl of Blackmoor. The Colonel, our father, was also an honored soldier to the king."

"The Colonel was a bloomin' cripple. A drunkard," the sergeant scoffed. "No better than 'is own son—"

"Sergeant Masters?" Ross snapped. "I'll see you downstairs."

Catherine's gaze moved to the sergeant. The bastard had a name, and with his dark mustache and goatee, he looked like a gargoyle. Turning on his boot heel, he pushed out of the room. The lieutenant followed, leaving Catherine to Elizabeth's ministrations. The steps creaked as the other soldiers descended the stairs behind them.

Elizabeth's grip loosened. "What a toad."

"Are you finished?" Catherine disengaged her hands. "Demented, indeed. Are you *trying* to get me locked up?"

Plopping her slim hands on her hips, Elizabeth glared at Catherine. "Didn't you think to let anyone know that you were back? Your horse returned days ago."

"Where's Daniel?"

"They called a meeting two nights ago." Elizabeth lowered her voice. "And Daniel went."

Catherine shook her head and looked away. "Then he's a fool."

"Momma and the twins are downstairs. I had to force my way up here past those wretched pock-faced soldiers. Where have you been? The soldiers have been scouring the countryside for some highwayman named Merlin. We've been sick with worry for you."

"Highwayman!" Catherine choked.

"And that's not all," Elizabeth whispered. "The soldiers are not the only ones looking to hang the knave. It seems that he was captured and, to save his life, revealed the names of those who were in league with him. Your name was on that list."

Catherine paled. All of a sudden, everything became clear. Someone was trying to make him the scapegoat for the rash of robberies and murders that have been going on here.

"Excuse me, ladies."

Catherine and Elizabeth startled. The lieutenant stood in the doorway. His tricorn tucked beneath his arm, his cool gaze stilled on Catherine's face. She noted that the lieutenant was not any older than she. He had a square jaw, a clean-shaven face, and intelligent eyes that missed nothing. No man in Yorktown held more authority.

"May I have a word with Mrs. Bellamy?" he said without looking at Elizabeth, who bristled like an irate porcupine at the dismissal.

"It's all right," Catherine said before her sister could voice any further protest. "At least he asked."

"I'll be outside the door." With a worried glance at Catherine, Elizabeth swept out of the room in a cloud of white ruffles.

"You don't have a fondness for British soldiers?" he said after a few moments.

Catherine crossed her arm beneath her breasts and looked over his shoulder at the knothole in the wall. When she was a little girl, her father let her paint the walls lavender. She'd created lilacs from the ornate cornices. A yellow counterpane, also remnants of a happy childhood, and canopy graced the mahogany bedstead where a silken mosquito barrier draped in feminine eloquence. Anna was an expert seamstress and had taught her to sew. They'd made matching curtains and pillows. The room was a veritable sunbeam.

Her pastels littered the polished surface of the desk, and the lieutenant picked up the sketch of the house on the James River where Patrick had lived before they married. The house belonged to her brother-in-law. "Your sister is correct. Lord Blackmoor is in a position to help you legally," he said. "His ship has been deployed for eight months and is in Norfolk now on repairs—"

"I know where His Lordship is."

"Tell me, Mrs. Bellamy," he set down the pastels, "are you acquainted with a man named Merlin?"

Catherine met the lieutenant's eyes. "By all accounts he is a smuggler."

"A hanging offense."

"So is stealing food!"

Stony silence filled the narrow width between them, and Catherine's grip tightened on her wrapper, exposing the scratches she received when she'd leaped the fence earlier that morning. Curling her fingers into her palm, she resisted hiding her hand.

He walked to the crystal vase of dead roses on her desk and

fingered the dry petals. "When a man has no stake in the consequences of his actions, where is his courage?" Studying her, he
settled his tricorn on his head. "I recall at one time that you used
to have the courage for uncovering the truth. Whatever happened
to that woman, Mrs. Bellamy?"

Catherine's appalled gaze fell away.

The lieutenant turned and hesitated. Elizabeth stood in the
door. She looked stricken and, for an instant, regret flashed
across his face. He tipped his tricorn. "Good day, Miss Claremont. Oh, and by the by, Mrs. Bellamy, you should do something
about those scratches. They could become infected."

After Lieutenant Ross left, Catherine swung around to the
vase of roses. Her heart dropped into her stomach. Anna never
gave her roses without first plucking the thorns. Outside she
could hear the sergeant calling to mount up. Leather creaked in a
subversive sort of way that managed to undermine her confidence. She was trapped if the sergeant recognized her. Nor could
she dismiss the niggling certainty that Jed Tomkins knew her as
Merlin's accomplice. Yet he had said nothing.

Downstairs, Catherine could hear the twins laughing as they
raced up the stairs to her bedroom. Elizabeth's voice was a whisper. "Somebody gave Daniel that missive when he was drunk.
They must have known that he was in no condition to make a
drop that night."

Clutching her wrapper, Catherine turned and tried to focus on
Elizabeth's words. "What?"

"Have you thought . . . maybe it was *you* they wanted dead?"

Oblivious to the need to breathe, Catherine stared at her sister. Not once had she even considered herself the target.

Yet the shiver that raced down her spine bore the full measure
of Elizabeth's observation. Catherine knew she'd fallen out of
favor with certain people. She'd been investigating them when
her newspaper press was destroyed. Had she become a threat to
them?

Expendable?

Movement behind her lifted her gaze. With a squeal, the twins
barreled into her arms. Her stepmother entered behind the housekeeper as Anna brought in a tray of hot food. Millie carried water
and rags.

Catherine closed her eyes and let the soft bodies of her brother and sister warm her heart, a place that desperately needed tending. Brittany and Brian smelled of biscuits and honey.

Where had she gone so wrong with Daniel?

"Are you all better, Rina?" Little Brittany asked.

"We saw those soldiers," Brian chimed in when Catherine pulled back to look at them both. They still wore their nightclothes and caps. Their mouths were sticky. "Momma said that we couldn't talk or move or they'd shoot us. But I wasn't afraid!"

Brittany elbowed him. "You were, too."

"Rina?" Brian wrapped his arms around Catherine's waist. "Will that bad man make you go away like Uncle Patrick and Daniel?"

Catherine wiped the moisture from her little brother's face. "No one can make me go away. Not ever again."

These people were her family, and she loved them deeply. But could she betray Merlin to the lieutenant to protect them?

If Reece were smart, he'd never return. For without a doubt, Catherine realized that Patrick's death had only been the beginning.

Chapter Seven

Someone had been to Patrick's grave recently. The faint print, barely discernible after the heavy storm weeks ago, bore the depth of a man's weight, Catherine noticed as she finished pulling the weeds. Someone taller and heavier than Daniel. She stood and peered around the yard.

Yesterday, she'd ventured to the Sons of Liberty haunts east of Yorktown. An abandoned farm and various sorting sheds had shown no sign of use for months. Today, her search for Daniel took her south to the James River. Autumn had turned the foliage red and yellow. Branches crept toward the dome of blue overhead, reaching but never quite touching the sky.

Catherine looked at the once-proud three-story brick manse.

Hope Plantation.

'Twas a beautiful name for a house that nobody loved.

The last servant had left here shortly after Patrick's death, and rumors that the place was haunted had kept most vandalism at bay.

Her gaze touched the second gravestone in the neglected plot next to Patrick's, illegible now for the moss that grew within its marbled crevices. Catherine had been thirteen when she'd first heard of Julian Lambert. He'd been a hero of the Seven Years War, the catch for every mother's daughter from here to London. She didn't remember much about the woman Patrick's brother had taken for his bride, except that she'd been the belle of Virginia society. And a man known for his mercenary decision in battle had loved her so much that he'd built this home for her. She was five months along with child when she'd died.

Turning away, Catherine finished gathering the weeds and threw the plants in a ditch. Finally dusting off her hands on her breeches, she mounted the gray and, passing beneath the weathered arch that separated the yard from the road, she didn't look back. Once a month she made the trip out here, usually with Elizabeth and the twins in attendance for the daylong outing. Today, she'd come alone.

Necessity dictated certain matters be settled in her heart today; she'd finally dispensed with her chores to see it done.

Catherine trotted the horse downriver. Blackbirds filled treetops, their loud chatter preventing her from hearing anything beyond the shadows. Keeping to the trees, she periodically scanned the fields behind her. Since the sergeant had discovered her following him last week, he'd become a daily fixture in her life about as pleasant as a chamber pot. She had to be ever vigilant.

The lieutenant hadn't arrested anyone off the list the sergeant had handed over because the sadistic dolt couldn't provide the source of his information. A source that clearly didn't include Jed Tomkins, who had remained loyal to the code of silence. Bastard that he was. Once a member always a member. She'd wanted to laugh at the hypocrisy. Yet someone had fed the sergeant information about Daniel's rendezvous with Merlin.

Trailing the sergeant had interjected new purpose into her life. If she could find the man who gave him the information about the drop, she'd find the traitor who gave Daniel that letter. She'd followed Masters nightly to the tavern outside of town and paid the tavern maid a shilling only to discover that he had a penchant for strong rum.

Switching to a back trail, Catherine shifted directions. A chill hit her face. With the change of seasons, she wore woolen breeches and stockings beneath her boots. Merlin's cloak, heavier by far than her own, shielded her from the chill in the air.

Merlin had said the muskets were hidden beneath the Low River wharf off the James. She shoved the pistol in her belt. Dismounting, she found what remained of the narrow loading dock that once serviced the various plantations up and down the James. After so many weeks, she didn't know what she'd find. Her steps sounded flat on the rotting boards.

Unable to control the pounding of her heart, Catherine knelt and looked over the edge. The smell of decay assaulted her. With the drought this past summer, the river ran lower than usual, exposing most of the pilings beneath. At first, she didn't see the crate. Then the sun came out from behind a bank of clouds. The momentum of the storm weeks ago had wedged the wooden crate against the pilings. The box had splintered open, leaving muskets buried in the riverbed.

Catherine lowered her head. Finding nothing would have been proof that Merlin had been equally deceptive as those who'd betrayed him. Reece may not have had a stake in the affairs of this region, but he'd told the truth. And truth was everything to her.

Lowering herself from the dock, she set her pistol on a rock and made quick work of the muskets, breaking off the wheel locks, then swinging them into the river. No one around here would ever get their hands on those muskets or connect him to that drop.

Mud caking her hands and her boots, Catherine crawled out from beneath the docks and climbed the grassy berm. A flapping sounded. Blackbirds filled the sky, spiraling upward like an undulating arm. Catherine dropped onto her belly and primed her pistol. Her fingers trembled. Times had changed so drastically that the very neighbors who had mourned her father's passing and who had helped bury Patrick were now the same who'd betrayed her to the British authorities. Whoever waited out there was no friend.

Her gray went back to munching the grass. After a few minutes, Catherine mounted her horse. Reaching the next rise, she turned. No one appeared behind her. Still, she knew someone was there.

Watching.

And suddenly, for the first time in the months since Patrick's murder had stolen her hope and all of her dreams, something powerful stirred inside. There could be no yielding. Not to her fear. Not to the sergeant. Not to the thugs that reigned over this countryside.

She was finished running.

"With work, I think most of this press can be salvaged," Samuel announced days later.

Debris crunched beneath Catherine's feet as she ran her hand over the lever and splintered crossbars. Her heart ached. Only one essential part could not be rebuilt. She would need to import a new mechanism. That would take money. But this was a start.

"I'll need fresh lumber." Samuel lifted his mouth into a white grin. "But if anyone can do it, I can."

The boast was not without truth, and she returned his smile. Samuel performed miracles with his hands. He'd been responsible for building the Colonel's wooden leg after the war.

"Mizz Catherine?" Samuel's staid voice tamped her newfound eagerness. "You risk much in your attempt to repair this press."

She took his hands. "I understand if you don't want to do this."

"No, ma'am. No one calls old Samuel a coward."

She glanced at the black smudges on her hands. They smelled of printer's ink. Straightening, Catherine let the familiar sounds and smells of this place fill her memory. Light barely sifted through the cracks in the once picture-perfect, now boarded-up windows.

Upstairs, a family of black cats nested in what used to be a charming stationery shop she'd built above the pressroom. She'd specialized in drawing lilac letterheads, and the ladies in town had flocked to her store to buy her stationery. She didn't have to view the room to know that little of value remained. Yet, for too long, she'd avoided this place. No more, she vowed. No more apologies for the choices she'd made. No more regrets.

Not now and not all the next week as she, Samuel, and Elizabeth began renovating the building. To her disappointment, she discovered her printing plates gone. Her ink and tools had vanished as well. "Why would someone steal any of that?" Elizabeth asked on the way to the shop the next morning. Catherine only knew it was one more expense to add to her list. Samuel had left the house earlier with a wagon full of whitewash paint and would be at the shop waiting for her.

Catherine usually enjoyed the morning walks along the bluffs, but today she felt only relief when they finally reached town. She'd eaten something bad last night and almost didn't leave her bed this morning. "Oh, look!" Elizabeth clapped her hands.

Catherine's spirits lifted. The finest potted flowers in autumn bloom lined the cavalcade of greenery like colorful baubles among stone. Her artist's eye embraced the visual feast. "I want to buy a plant for Momma." Elizabeth stopped in front of a particularly festive bloom. "Everything is almost gone."

Forsaking the perfect white flower in full bloom, Catherine's gaze fell on the scrappy purple infestation beside it.

"The white will go with our parlor," Elizabeth was saying.

Catherine picked up the purple plant instead. She admired the canvas pot at arm's length and smiled. The plant was clearly a survivor. "But this one will still be alive next spring."

Eyeing the ugly flower, Elizabeth scoffed. "Prissy said that if you surround yourself with the mundane and boring, then that's all anyone will ever see of you."

"And of course, Prissy and her network of ring-tailed jackdaws knows all."

Elizabeth lifted her nose. "She received an invitation to the governor's ball next month. She was at the house this morning for a fitting of the new gown Anna is making for her. Bold as brass dancing about in her fancy new finery like she was royalty."

"Posh," Catherine said, "'tis hardly the end of the world that we didn't get invited to the ball this year."

"For you, maybe. You've already had one husband." Elizabeth's hand fluttered against her heart. "I, on the other hand, am doomed to live out my life in obscurity if I can't get to that ball."

Catherine managed not to roll her eyes. "Still," she returned her attention to her prize. "This is the plant that *I* want to buy."

"Since you are quickly becoming a consumer again, maybe now is the time to contact the elusive Lord Blackmoor about your newspaper. He loaned Patrick money before. Perhaps he will do the same for you."

Catherine bristled at the mere mention of her brother-in-law. And suddenly all of her failures the past year came back to slap her in the face. She was clearly a woman who straddled the fence between fading idealism and her personal war.

"I know you've written to his solicitor in Williamsburg. So it has crossed your mind to seek him out."

"Captain Lambert is too busy to allow for such triviality as correspondence to interfere with his daily life."

"Prissy quite confirmed that he is a snob."

"Who?"

"Captain Lambert, you ninny," Elizabeth commiserated on a sigh. "Prissy said his Lordship is corset-melting beautiful. All the girls are talking."

"Oh, for goodness sake." Catherine glared at her sister. "Prissy is sixteen. What does she know about Captain Lambert?"

"She attended the governor's reception in his honor last night. That's what she knows. All the wealthy Tory families were invited. He even arrived with a beautiful woman on his arm. So Prissy tells me."

"Prissy saw Lord Blackmoor in Williamsburg?"

"She said he's been in Norfolk over a month now. It seems his ship is being refitted. That means new line and sails—"

"Yes, I know what that means." Catherine cradled her plant on one arm. "Has he been to Patrick's graveside? Perhaps you've heard."

"Everyone knows he will not set foot near the manor house," Elizabeth flicked a leaf off her sleeve. "Perhaps our luckless hero is afraid of hosts as the rumor says."

Turning abruptly, Catherine set down the plant. Even if Julian Lambert might have been at sea since Patrick's death, that fact mattered little in defense of his character. 'Twas an insult to her sensibilities to be in the same vicinity with that particular loyalist who had so little regard for his family that he could not find his way home even now.

Elizabeth fell in beside her, her skirts stirring up a white puff of dust. " Seeing as how Lord Blackmoor is practically our relation, you should invite him to our home and introduce yourself. Prissy would be pea green with envy. 'Twould be a coup to snag him. It seems His Lordship is as popular as a sugar-coated apple."

"Aye, then maybe I should feed him to Sally." The thought had merit. "He's a scapegrace nobleman, and I don't care if his stepfather was lieutenant governor of Pennsylvania. Not once in the years that I knew Patrick did his brother come to visit."

"Rina," her sister pleaded, "you speak too loudly."

"Besides," Catherine's voice softened, "His Lordship would hardly come to our house. Our family is beneath his station."

"Papa was not an unimportant man."

Aware of how sensitive her sister was, Catherine bundled her in her free arm. "You should not worry so. You will have wrinkles before you are twenty. And then how will I find a husband for you?"

Elizabeth leaned against Catherine. "So much has happened. I do worry. Especially when you go off at night and follow that wretched sergeant. He doesn't like you, Rina—"

Catherine came to an abrupt halt in front of her shop. A notice of taxes due had been tacked to the door. Yanking off the parchment, she startled when spurs rattled on the walk. Sergeant Masters shoved off the corner of the building, his boots sounding hollow on the wooden boardwalk. Elizabeth sidled behind her sister in distress.

Catherine's heart raced, but knowing calm was her only defense, she met the sergeant's gaze without recoil. The moment this bastard had showed up with Lieutenant Ross, she'd known the folly of running from Reece. And with Daniel's abandonment, the realization that she now stood alone slapped at her with a fatal sense of desperation.

He stopped inches away. A dog barked down the street. "If I ever hear that you're following me again, princess, I'll nail more than a bloody tax writ to your door."

She opened the door to escape him, but he grabbed her arm. "I know who ye are, Mrs. Bellamy." His whisper touched her hair. "Why don't ye tell me where Merlin is? We'll split the bounty."

"Trust me," she rasped deliberately, turning slightly from the stink of his breath. Providence in heaven, 'twas her only concession to him, and still it was more than she could stomach. "If I knew where he was, I'd tell you, just so I could watch him kill you."

Elizabeth gasped. "Rina!"

The sergeant's nostrils flared, and Catherine thought he would strike her, when suddenly he stepped away. Two elderly ladies approached her on the walkway. "Are you all right, Catherine?" Eyeing the sergeant, the wife of the local jeweler patted Catherine's hand.

"Yes . . . everything is fine, thank you." Looking down at the placard in her hand, she ripped the notice into pieces and let the pieces flutter away in the wind. "perfectly fine."

"It's good to see you back here, Rina dear. We have missed your shop."

"Thank you, Mrs. Smith. It's good to be back." She nodded to both women as they bustled past.

"But for how long?" The sergeant took Elizabeth into his gaze. "Pretty things like you, left all unprotected by the menfolk here. A lot could happen."

Before Catherine could find her voice, Elizabeth dragged her inside the building. The bolt slammed down over the door. "Are you insane?" She shook Catherine. "Why do you rile him?"

Her furious gaze met Elizabeth's. "Don't ever do that again." But her knees were shaking when Catherine walked away.

Elizabeth was like a terrier with a bone when she latched on to an idea. And saving Catherine had become her mission. "Do you want to know what I heard this morning?" her sister whispered over Brittany's head the next Sunday at church.

Catherine hoped the narrow look she gave her sister would suffice to silence her. She didn't feel well and she wanted only to go home. Rain drummed against the colored glass and cast a dreary gray over the somber congregation, no happier for the fiery sermon coming from the pulpit. During the second hymn, Elizabeth had decided to start a dialogue.

Beside her, the twins squirmed. She'd strategically placed her youngest siblings away from one another and, guarded on either side by Elizabeth and her mother, they were rendered immobile. Anna filled out the rest of the pew that they'd occupied for the past twelve years. It was with much relief that the last hymn finally concluded.

"Guess who will be in Norfolk until January?" Elizabeth trailed her as they filed outside with the rest of the congregation.

Finally turning to face her sister, Catherine crossed her arms. "Will I need more than one guess?"

"Oh, you ninny. I'm thinking about *you*. Besides . . ." Elizabeth looked down. "I'm tired of being afraid. Who else do we have?"

"Mrs. Bellamy," a young voice startled her.

Catherine turned to find a youth Daniel's age. He wore brown homespun overalls and a red shirt, pressed for church. "My name is Ryan." He hastily removed his hat, and the wind buffeted his baby-fine hair. "I just wanted to thank you for your kindness last weekend."

Bells pealed from the steeple, and people milled in the yard. Catherine walked with him. "Ma, she's been in poor health, and she does love her preserves. I know you didn't have to make the trip to our farm yesterday. I just wanted you to know, is all."

Genuinely touched, Catherine thanked him. She and her stepmother had delivered jars to many families this past week. "You're Daniel's friend. From the Miller farm."

Ryan seemed pleased that she'd remember him. "I used to fish in that pond out back of your house." Crushing his hat in his hands, he shuffled his feet. "Da's been real angry. Some of us don't like what they tried to do to you. . . ."

His eyes widened, and Catherine saw him pale visibly. Alarmed, she swung her gaze over her shoulder. People milled around the steps, talking. No one seemed to be looking in her direction. She turned back, but Ryan had already walked into the crowd.

"That was strange," Elizabeth whispered from beside her.

"Get the twins in the wagon." Catherine cast around and found her mother in the crowd.

The sergeant wasn't among the parishioners when Catherine scanned the churchyard on their way out. "Don't ye be worryin' none about anything, Mizz Catherine," Samuel said, patting a lump beside him on the bench that appeared suspiciously like a pistol. "No one's going to be botherin' you while I'm around."

In her heart, she knew Samuel could not even shoot a turkey for dinner, much less a man. But he loved her enough to fight to keep her safe. "I hate this, Samuel, I really do," Catherine whispered. "I'm so sorry that I've brought this down on the family."

His teeth were stark against his dark complexion. "Don't you be thinking this is your fault, Mizz Catherine."

Although he didn't attend church, he wore his clean Sunday go-to-meeting red and white checkered shirt. A low-brimmed straw hat shadowed his brown eyes. Years before the Colonel had died, he'd given Samuel his freedom papers in reward for Samuel's service to him during the war. Samuel and Millie had stayed on when the money ran out, and Catherine didn't know what she'd do without them.

"It really is going to be a fine day," Catherine's stepmother breathed aloud after they'd been traveling in silence for a while. "Rain is good for the chrysanthemums. I think we are going to have a beautiful batch. I'm presenting the governor with another arrangement for the Autumn Harvest ball this year. What do you think?"

"Anna has been getting orders for gowns since July," Elizabeth said quietly. "The invitations have all gone out."

And none of them had been invited.

"Perhaps ours just has not arrived," her stepmother suggested.

The brisk wind had loosened her mother's bonnet. Blond hair peered out from beneath the rim, and Catherine didn't have the heart to remind her that they'd not been invited anywhere in years. Nothing would ever return to as it was before the Colonel died. Elizabeth now seemed aware of this as well. Her gaze had dropped to the hands folded in her lap.

"Mizz Catherine." Samuel's voice startled her. They were almost to the front entrance of their drive.

Sitting on a roan gelding in the middle of the road, Sergeant Masters watched their approach. If he expected her to stop the wagon, he'd be in for a surprise when she ordered Samuel to run him over.

"Faster," Catherine told her servant, forcing the sergeant to whip aside as the wagon rumbled past and sprayed mud on his breeches.

The sergeant galloped up to Catherine's side of the wagon. "Slow down." He tried to grab her arm and fell back. The sergeant made no pretense about the threat in his eyes. "Do it if you value your family's life, Mrs. Bellamy."

Catherine let Samuel slow the horses. Wind whipped the treetops. "What do you want now, Sergeant?"

"Oh?" He leered crudely at her breasts, before lifting his eyes to hers. "Your tongue someplace more interesting than your mouth."

Catherine gasped. That he would say something so base in front of the twins appalled her. She barely stopped Samuel from reaching for the pistol. The sergeant snapped his gaze to Samuel. But whatever was about to happen changed when the wagon plodded into their yard.

Clearly in hog heaven after lounging all morning in the mud, Sally was already halfway across the yard before the wagon stopped. Samuel pulled back on the reins of their horse. Used to Sally's greeting, the gray calmed easily with a touch. But the other horse reared and bucked like an exploding teakettle. The sergeant left the saddle. The twins, standing perched against the wagon rim, stared in awe as he hit the bushes. When he finally found purchase in the grass, he turned and glared directly into the bore of a pistol.

Catherine held the gun with both hands. She'd climbed down from the wagon. The wind billowed her skits. Elizabeth held Sally's rope collar. "How dare you come here and make threats to me." Catherine lowered the pistol to his heart. "Get off this property."

He slapped the mud off his breeches. For a terrible instant, Catherine thought that he would lunge for the pistol. Then his gaze fell on her terrified family, and something almost human flashed in his eyes. "Seems to me you should all be a little nicer."

Catherine didn't breathe until he mounted his horse and disappeared down the winding road. Lowering the pistol, she turned back to her family. Daniel stood on the porch.

Rifle in hand, he met her gaze from across the yard. He was tall and lanky, and ready to shoot the sergeant. His clothes were wrinkled as if he'd slept the last month in them.

"Elizabeth," she said, handing Samuel the pistol, "will you please get the twins upstairs and out of their damp clothes? Brew some willow bark tea." She ignored everyone's groan. "Anna, Momma will need your help."

The last person inside the house, Catherine went to the parlor. She grabbed the iron poker and stoked the fire. Closing the door, Daniel leaned against it. He'd set the long rifle against the wall. "How long has he been molesting you, Rina?" he asked.

"What difference does it make to you? Where have you been?"

"I found a job in Williamsburg," he said in answer to the accusation in her eyes. "We need the money, Rina."

Catherine set down the poker. "I see." He was such a liar. His statement settled the question whether or not he could be trusted.

Catherine let her eyes wander the familiar room. Except for the silver that had been sold this year, the room still bore her father's vision. He'd wanted to be accepted as a peer among Virginia's elite, and through the years, he had purchased the accoutrements to engage his children in the proper activities of other landed gentry.

Now draped in black, a pianoforte and harpsichord remained untouched since her father's death. Two tea tables and a red settee flanked by high-backed chairs sat on the fine Wilton carpet spread across the pine floor. With the thick red curtains drawn against the cold, the fire was the only light in the room.

"What are you involved in, Daniel?"

Pushing off the door, Daniel walked toward her. His brown hair had fallen from its queue and hung in strands around his face. "I'm sorry." With frightening restraint, he braced his palms against the fireplace mantel. His shoulders stretched the jacket Anna had tailored for him just last year. "It should have been me to go that night. It should never have been you. How . . . did you escape?"

"We ran—"

"Not the soldiers," he cut her off. "How did you escape Merlin?"

Her silence lifted his head, and he found her in the looking glass above the fireplace. "Did you think he wouldn't let me go after our own people betrayed him?" she challenged his expression.

"What's that supposed to mean?"

"I know what happens to dissenters in this organization. But Merlin was after *you* that night. Why, Daniel?"

"He was sent down here to investigate the Sons of Liberty."

"Because someone up North doesn't believe that Patrick's death was an accident? That a select few who masquerade as rebels down here are merely thieves and murderers?" She knew why Merlin had been here, and it wasn't the reasons Daniel gave her.

"No one wants to draw the British down on us," Daniel said.

"Oh, that's bloody rich. So, by discrediting Merlin, they discredit anything that he might say. And anyone else who has ever stood against the organization." Catherine could never fight that kind of power. "Who gave you the letter that night at the Red Lion?" She swiped her face with the heel of her hand. "Who all knew where I was supposed to be meeting Merlin that night?"

"I don't know."

She advanced a step. "Now that Patrick is dead, who is your illustrious leader that he would sell out all three of us? Patrick's lover? What do they have on you that would make you turn your back on your family and remain with them?"

"Christ almighty, Rina!" The firelight burned bright in his blue eyes. She'd never seen him like this. "I'm trying to keep you alive."

He pushed away her efforts to touch him and, striding to the wall, found the canvas tote that carried the new diagrams she'd drawn for her shop. Daniel crushed the papers in his fist. "And what are you doing now, Rina?" He dropped the drawings into the fire before Catherine could stop him. "Are you going to write more unfounded accusations? Get yourself killed finally?"

"Unfounded? Pray tell, brother, what is unfounded about the events of the past year? I won't sit around and do nothing."

"No, that's your whole problem. You never quit. You'll go on until you get me killed, too. Wasn't Patrick enough of a lesson?"

"What are you talking about?" she demanded, horrified.

"You really don't know, do you?" He laughed in disgust. "*You* killed your husband. You and your damn politics, your bloody causes. I wish to God that I'd never gotten involved with any of it."

"Daniel . . ."

He turned on his heel. His mother stood in the doorway, balancing a tray filled with a half-dozen fragile teacups, crumpets, and sugar.

Her faded blond hair was fastened at the back of her head and covered by a cap that matched her forest-green gown, an outdated dress belonging to another time in their lives. "I thought you might need some refreshment." She bustled. "Dinner will be served shortly."

"I'm not staying, Mother."

"But of course you are. Come, tell us about your job. We've missed you, haven't we, Rina?"

"Jeezuz, Mother. I'm not a baby anymore."

"Millie made crumpets." She smiled. "Sit down, both of you."

Daniel ran a furious hand through his stringy hair. "I've taken a room in Williamsburg. I only came home to tell you to stop looking for me." His eyes found Catherine's in a silent plea for understanding. "I have cut enough firewood to get you through the next few months . . ." His voice lowered. "For your own safety, leave everything alone."

The door slammed. Burying her face in her hands, Catherine fought the anger and frustration that sliced away the last remnant of her control. But anger didn't save her.

Almost two months had passed since Reece had left her. Months of forging ahead with her life. Of forgetting that night of the storm and his mouth on hers. But even if her heart had lied, her body had not.

Her courses were weeks late, and the telltale signs were as bold as bright orange script. Catherine Bellamy, the sainted wife, barely a widow, was going to have a smuggler's baby.

A man who was married.

Her pregnancy would tie her to Merlin forever.

It would tie her to the sergeant and a thousand other lies that condemned her as much as her own heart. And for the first time in her life, Catherine had no plan, no answers, and no way out. She couldn't tell her stepmother. Not yet, when she didn't understand everything herself.

"Shhh, child. Come here."

Catherine knelt beside her stepmother's chair and laid her cheek in her lap. The green cotton dress, faded by many beatings on the washboards, framed her cheek with softness. "Oh, Momma, I feel like I've done so many things wrong. I don't know where or how to start to make everything right again."

"Daniel will come back. Men have to find their own way." Her stepmother's frail hand cradled Catherine's head with affection. Her stepmother was the closest person to a mother figure that Catherine had ever known. "You've always made us proud, Rina. The Colonel told me only this morning how brave you are."

Catherine felt her eyes slide closed as disappointment overwhelmed her. Her stepmother was not well.

"He said that it is the Claremont way to stand tall."

"Momma . . ." She tried not to let defeat pull her down.

For once, she'd wanted someone stronger to lean on. She wanted to be a child again, where her biggest fear in life was getting restricted to her room for drawing on the parlor walls. For once, she'd wanted someone who could listen to *her*.

"It's all right," Catherine sighed instead. "I won't let anything happen to you."

"You think I'm a regular noodle, don't you?" A hand tenderly cupped Catherine's cheek, pulling her wet gaze around. "But I'm not."

"Papa is dead. He's gone."

"Perhaps to you, because he has hurt you as your Patrick did. He loved you, Rina."

"Patrick loved no one," she whispered. "Least of all me."

"The Colonel, Rina," her stepmother quietly said. "Your father loved you. He told me that you needed to go back to your dreams. Finish your fight."

Catherine felt her heart kick. "Papa said that? When?"

"Why only this morning. I heard him clear as sunlight. He said the words while I was helping Anna hem Prissy's new gown."

Catherine stood. 'Twas like her stepmother to romanticize the impossible. No one could hear the sunlight, or the flowers bloom, or the voices of dead people. Today it was Papa. Last month it was someone named Aunt Dorothy, who'd died a hundred years ago, then Beatrice, their old gardener. Once her stepmother had even quoted their old hound. But Catherine had dallied long enough in self-pity.

Catherine kissed her stepmother's cheek. "Tell Papa I'll try."

"He also said that you should trust him."

"Momma, I have to see Millie about supper tonight."

"He's a good man, Rina."

Catherine finally pulled away. Her taffeta dress rustled with her exasperation. "Who? Who is a good man?"

"Why the man with whom you're in love, dear."

Chapter Eight

"Reece—"

The door to Julian's cabin slammed shut. Michael stopped in his tracks. Glancing up, Julian flinched as the doctor continued to prod his rib cage. On deck, the wind hummed through the lines and rigging of the ship. Everything inside the cabin smelled of lemon oil and turpentine where the walls had been scrubbed for mold.

"Ah, sir." Michael gracefully recovered his aplomb as he set down a mail bundle on the cluttered desk below the stern galley window. "My lordship."

Julian tried not to smile at Michael's wretched subservience. He was certainly a better smuggler than he had ever been a naval officer.

"I met the governor's courier on the dock and thought I would venture on board to see you." Michael wagged a formal missive. "He wants his tea shipment. Yesterday."

Frowning, Julian snatched the missive. The seal had been broken. "He knows damn well this ship isn't fitted to sail anywhere."

"To that point, there are some disgruntled merchant captains who wish to speak to you as well."

After scanning the brief missive, Julian dropped the message on his desk. "Bloody hell, Higgins . . ." Julian gritted his teeth as the old man probed his ribs. "Do you think you could take care?"

"Pah!" The old doctor wagged a gnarled finger. "You can stand steadfast in the face of a full broadside and then wilt beneath a few broken ribs. It's a wonder you don't faint at the sight of blood."

Michael chuckled. "Now, wouldn't that be a sad sight, to see the Royal Navy's finest keel over in a swoon. Will he live?"

The doctor snapped his leather bag shut. "Might I suggest that next time you stay off a horse."

"Obviously he can't ride," Michael agreed.

"Listen to your man," the doctor shrugged into his coat. "Stick to what you know, my lord. You have great promise as a naval officer. And you'll probably live longer."

Eyeing Michael with deadly intent, Julian carefully tugged on his white shirt. "Don't you have to get back to your own ship?"

With a sly glance at Julian, Michael swung open the door and invited the doctor out. "That came in on the mail packet today." He pointed to the heap of unopened correspondence on the desk. "You're a popular man, Reece. You should hire another secretary. Boswell can hardly keep up. Oh," Michael's head popped back in, "you have a package from Williamsburg. I didn't get a chance to read it."

Julian suddenly forgot his annoyance at Michael. He'd patiently bided his time these past weeks awaiting Robbie's report.

A knock on the door sounded. People had been going in and out of the cabin all day. He should be used to the activity by now. While the ship underwent repairs, his men had been on leave. Daily reports were coming in about brawls and damages that needed to be paid. Yesterday, he'd restricted his crew to the ship until further notice.

The civilian captain of one of the merchant ships he'd escorted to Virginia entered. His cocked hat tucked beneath his arm, he wore a heavy cloak over buff breeches and the distinguishable blue frock jacket of a former naval petty officer. The stock reached his chin. "Captain Lambert?" He bowed slightly. "My lord."

Julian remained sitting. He worked on buttoning his shirt. His white periwig and the navy blue and gold-braided jacket of his rank lay across his bunk. The cuff flap bore one gold band. His bicorn hat remained on a hook beside his frock coat next to the door.

"We're leaving on the tide," the man said brusquely, taking in the cedar-planked room filled with shelves of books, disorganized to the point of chaos. "Headed south. Warmer clime. I don't have to worry about being shot at for delivering goods for half they're worth. No sir, I'm taking my cargo someplace else."

Julian buttoned the cuff on his sleeve. "Best of luck to you."

"Damn colonials don't know what's good for them."

Another knock sounded, and his steward entered. Julian finished with the captain and stood as the man left.

"Beggin' yer pardon, sir," his steward bowed slightly. "You're needed at a meeting in an hour. I've ordered a carriage to take you there from your ship."

With a frown, Julian turned his gaze on the stack of correspondence that Michael delivered.

"Sir." Boswell cleared his throat.

Julian looked up to see that his steward held out his uniform jacket. "I don't know what I'd do without you, Boswell." He stood and let Boswell slip on the jacket. His ribs still bore some tenderness.

"Weather is movin' in, sir. I hope the cold won't disturb your humors any. Seeing as how you're still recovering."

"Why, Boswell," he grinned at the flustered man, "I do believe you've been worried about me."

The gray-haired man sniffed. "Not at all, sir. You are perfectly capable of getting yourself killed whether I worry or not. Unlike you, I do not consider what you are doing wise."

Boswell had been in his family's employ since before Julian was born. The steward had stayed on after the old earl died and Julian's mother remarried Captain Tate Bellamy, moving from the rugged coast of Cornwall to Boston. Much later, Tate Bellamy would become lieutenant governor of Pennsylvania, but by then Julian had set his course.

He recalled the insecure boy he'd been, forever uncertain of his place in life. Boswell as much as Patrick's father had been Julian's mentor and, compared to the vermin his own father was, Tate Bellamy was the man Julian had always wanted as his sire. He'd envied Patrick the family that he'd had and the affection his mother had shown his youngest sibling. For no matter Julian's accomplishments, he was always the one outside the glass window looking into a world where he didn't belong, a world he'd wanted so much in which to participate.

But Boswell had never allowed him to wallow in self-pity.

He'd planted in Julian's mind a greater purpose, a need to be more than he was. At thirteen, Julian, the gawky little rich boy, joined the navy as a young midshipman on his stepfather's ship, *Excalibur*. For eight years, he'd worked his way up the ranks until he'd taken his first command at twenty-one. And in time, he'd returned to the colonies a man with an established naval career, where Boswell had stubbornly remained with him since. They'd been through hell and war together.

And worse.

The elderly steward knew that the current conflict in this British state weighed like granite in Julian's heart. He also knew Julian's inborn hatred of tyranny in any form. And the years had since tested his loyalties to a political system that sought to crush the fledgling colonies, a place that despite his heritage had rooted his heart to a land that gave so much more than a name or a title to a man.

His peers would call his conduct suicide, for the cause he'd become involved with would see him hanged for treason. But he believed to his core in the rightness of his actions. Until now.

Julian yanked the sleeves down his arms as Boswell applied the white periwig and dusted off the jacket. The wound on Julian's scalp had healed. The swelling on the side of his face had disappeared. His beard was gone now. His voice was different. The persona vanquished.

Nothing of Merlin remained.

Except the deep-down hatred for those who'd murdered his brother and set Merlin up to die.

Boswell stood back to admire his handiwork. "Perhaps you should consider remarrying, sir. Have a dozen children. You'd make some woman proud, if I can say so myself."

Julian's gaze fell on the narrow white band of flesh on his left ring finger. He'd removed the gold ring two days after returning to his ship here in Norfolk. Having learned long ago to keep his matrimonial philosophy to himself, he bent his attention to the mail. What a woman offered, he didn't need marriage to enjoy. And lately he hadn't even enjoyed that.

Something suddenly caught his attention and he checked his hand. A letter peeked from beneath the packet Robbie had sent. A knock sounded on the door.

"Sir," Boswell's voice pulled him around.

Impatient at yet another interruption, Julian turned, only to be brought up short. His heart slammed against his ribs.

Nothing could have prepared him for the sight that greeted his eyes, and if he'd not already been leaning with one hip to his desk, he would have sat.

Boswell had opened the door, and a woman stood framed in the entranceway of his cluttered cabin. Not just any woman. She was wearing a modest mauve and cream striped gown that clung to her breasts and waist like a pair of eager hands. The prim straw bonnet she wore rimmed her beautiful face in a perfect oval portrait of childlike innocence. Three capricious curls lay over her shoulder.

She'd pinned her long, dark hair into a respectable coif that did not fit his memory of her but that did things to his insides. Dangerous, reckless things. His gaze clung to her red mouth, then to her eyes. She was everything that he thought he'd forgotten, and only the certitude that he must be mistaken in her identity kept his jaw from dropping in disbelief. She was staring, too.

It was her attention that brought him up.

"Lord Blackmoor?" She tucked a wayward strand of hair behind one ear with a wariness and foresight to scout out her new surroundings despite her nervousness. Her presence of calm had the effect of dousing him with ice water.

"I'll see you on shore, my lord," Boswell said.

"Sir!" One of Julian's men stood behind the girl. He was a huge bear of a man, but the girl was not swayed to move out of his way. "My Lord," he squeezed forward, knocking her hat askew. "She came out to the ship before I could stop her. Insisted on seeing you. We had to bring her on board. I tried to explain protocol—"

"My servant is awaiting me on the docks," she announced.

"It seems that she didn't want to risk his life, sir. Or have him suddenly pressed into service. He's elderly, you see."

Julian lifted a brow. "Indeed."

"I had to hire a private ketch to bring me out here," she said. "It wasn't my intention to break any rules by coming on board. But you're a difficult man to see."

The wind buffeted the ship. The ship heeled slightly and pulled at her cables. Julian rode the movement easily. She did not. Her hand reached out to grip the first solid object she could grab, which happened to be poor Pulver. Pulver's hands on her waist kept her from falling.

"That's quite all right, Chief." Julian's gaze let go of Pulver's hands and slowly raised. "You may leave us."

"Aye, sir," he hastily complied.

The door slammed closed, and Julian faced the shadow in dreams, the dark-eyed nemesis that had haunted him for almost two months. Had she somehow learned who he was?

She was still struggling for balance but he made no effort to rescue her. Hell, she was the last person in the world who needed rescuing. "Is there something I can do for you, Miss . . ."

"Mrs.," she was quick to correct. "Mrs. Bellamy," she said.

Her hand bracing the shelf of a bookcase, she stood expectantly as he registered her name. "Mrs. Bellamy." He was still smiling, but his voice was no longer relaxed.

"Patrick's wife," she quietly said as if not comprehending his reaction. At the moment, he really did believe himself incapable of coherent thought. "We were married in York-Hampton church last May. Perhaps you haven't received my letters . . . the ones I mailed?"

How convenient that he had not.

Without answering yay or nay, he awaited her to go on, disappointed that she'd not been more clever with her disguise, or that she would try to pull another blanket over his eyes in such a disgusting fashion. Then he remembered her panic when Merlin had asked for her help. Her terror had been genuine. The threat to her life real. At least, he'd believed that. She was either the greatest liar in the world, or the grandfather of all coincidences had just dropped a big one on his shoulders.

Except, he knew for an absolute fact that Patrick had never married. Julian also knew the rumors of his wealth were drawing room fodder wherever he went. This girl associated with the same people who'd framed Merlin. He didn't put it past the whole sordid lot of murderers to try to scam him.

"Since you've gone to so much trouble to track me down, what can I do for you . . . *Mrs.* Bellamy?"

Some of the confidence left her face. "I thought we should meet. But since you seem busy . . ." Stepping forward, she presented him with a sheaf of papers, which he didn't bother to look at, but instead placed on the desk.

Fumbling through her reticule, she suddenly seemed unsure. "'Tis only a proposal. Of sorts. Nothing that I couldn't pay back. Nothing that you didn't already give me once before. I . . ." Watching her expression, he almost felt sorry for her.

Almost.

"I have my card."

After what seemed like hours of digging, she withdrew a lilac-rimmed card. The fingers that touched his trembled. He dropped his gaze to the flowery script: delicate and feminine like the curls that lay over her shoulder.

Catherine Renee Bellamy.

A sick feeling took hold.

"Before Patrick and I married, we were involved in a business venture. A lucrative one," she explained. "We owned the *Tidewater Clarion*. Perhaps you've heard?"

"And where was your father that he let a woman become business partners with anyone other than her husband?"

She thrust out her chin. "And where was yours that he allowed you to sail the seven seas without supervision? I happen to know you were barely thirteen when you left home."

He raised a brow, impressed that she would know that much about him. "I'm not a woman."

"And someone would have to be blind to mistake you for one." She turned and paced the few steps back to the door. The flare of her skirts emphasized her small waist. He'd wondered . . . when she'd left him . . .

"Yes, I'm a woman." She faced him with steadfastness. She went on to give him a detailed accounting of the *Tidewater Clarion* finances and something about a silly stationery shop. Clearly, she'd put a lot of work into this proposal. "And I understand that you might have doubts concerning my business abilities. But I guarantee I know how to run a business and turn a profit. I need the property where the building sits. Your name is on the deed, my lord."

"My name is on everything."

Her dusky eyes widened slightly. She seemed surprised that he would know that. "Nevertheless, I made the venture what it is."

"And what is it? It's nothing." He stood and walked around her to the door, where he leaned and crossed his arms. "My solicitor gave me the report over a month ago, and if I'm not mistaken, the funds to pay the taxes and repair that press are more than the building is worth. You'll be fortunate to find anyone willing to invest a single shilling. Especially since a mob destroyed the place."

"I'm aware of that, Lord Blackmoor. I was there."

Her voice held the same strength he saw in her face. "It's taken you a long time to come here and present this. Why now?"

Shifting awkwardly beneath his stare, she reached out to perch a hand on the bookcase and nearly tipped the stack of charts from their perch. "I'm sorry," she managed as he leapt forward to catch the expensive globe held in place by two metal brackets.

"Don't move," he said between his teeth. He saw that she tightened the reticule against her chest. Her hands were slender, the way he remembered, and he followed the length of the fine silk sleeve up the curve of her arm to find her watching him beneath the brim of her hat.

Julian welcomed the growing cloud of doubt in her eyes. His anger had grown, and he didn't understand its source, only that it was aimed solely at her and was probably the culmination of the frustration that had been eating his gut away. He wasn't ever supposed to see her again. Certainly not like this.

"This ship has been under repairs. I'd offer you a place to sit, but as you can see . . ." he swung his hand in a blatant invitation, "I only have a bunk at our disposal."

Her jaw dropped open. "Just who do you think you are?"

"Would you care for my full rank and title or merely my familial ties to Patrick?"

She took a step back.

"How much do you want, Mrs. Bellamy, if that's who you really are? To be honest, I wouldn't know. Perhaps Patrick's wedding announcement didn't make it to me or my solicitor. I don't know, but if this is some sort of joke, I'm not in the mood for humor, and I'll not hesitate having you arrested."

"You . . . hate me. Why?"

"Lady, I don't even know who the bloody deuce you are! But if I were a gambling man, I'd hazard a guess that you've come all this way from wherever for more than just money. Maybe to tell me that you have a passel of kids to support now that Patrick is dead or that you are a disgruntled employee who didn't get paid. Who knows?"

"Never mind," she whispered. "I should not have come here."

Her hand reached the door before he slammed it shut in her face. She whirled. Her bottom hit the floor. God in heaven, he wanted to rip that silly straw hat off her head and tangle his hands in her hair.

"Why did you come then?" His voice was quiet, barely controlled.

"I wanted . . ." Her eyes, as they drew around to his, were resolute. "I didn't know where else to go."

"Isn't this rather like jumping in bed with the enemy?"

"*Yes!*"

And it was in that emphatic word that doubt exploded inside Julian. If she were married to Patrick, it would make sense that she'd come to him if she were in trouble.

But why now? His ship had been in Norfolk for months.

He turned and walked beneath a low beam to the polished oak cabinet behind his desk. Withdrawing a crystal decanter, he managed to compose himself while he poured a dram of whiskey. Why did he suddenly feel as if he'd made the biggest tactical blunder of his life?

"As you can see by this place, I'm very busy. But I'll look over those papers when I have a chance." He lifted his gaze and perused her pale face over the rim of the glass. "Do you have a place to stay for tonight? It's a long way back to Yorktown."

"Not far enough from here." She swung open the door.

"Mrs. Bellamy!"

She spun around. Her eyes battle ready.

"If you are who you say you are . . ." *Jesus.* He didn't want to consider that. "I'll owe you an apology."

The door shut but did not slam. He wished it had.

Christ!

His whole body tense, he tipped back the whiskey and pondered the fury of his emotions. The movement of the solid deck beneath his feet was reassuring when nothing else at the moment was.

He also knew that the last ship for Yorktown sailed an hour ago.

Cursing, he sent Pulver to follow her. Then, drawn back to his cabin with a mixture of dread and urgency, he stared a long time at the papers on his desk before he finally sat down and started reading. The meeting could wait.

Dusk settled over the peninsula village in a gilded array of fiery clouds and a storm of personal frustration that grabbed Catherine by the throat and choked her. It wasn't enough that she'd failed in her quest or that her brother-in-law was everything wretchedly British she'd expected to find in a naval officer down to the strong scent of lemon oil and turpentine that still pervaded her senses. Two hours after missing the last ship to Yorktown, Catherine was no closer to finding a place to sleep for the night. In desperation, she'd come to what looked like the edge of town and paid the hostler a precious coin to give Samuel a cot to sleep on for the night.

The sound of the waves rolling onto the sand drew her gaze. She and Samuel had walked away from the shabby assortment of taverns that lined the water's edge, where ships bobbed like the skeletal remains of some mass burial. Lord Blackmoor's *Chimera*, with her graceful masts, not yet dressed in full seagoing rig, lay at anchor surrounded by lighters, ketches, and smaller schooners, almost obscuring her shoreline view. She'd seen Lord Blackmoor's infamous ship before when she'd visited Boston harbor two years ago. The Royal Navy's *Chimera* once served as the flagship to the British vice admiral himself. Blackmoor might be a naval hero, but he knew nothing about simple human compassion.

By the middle of June, she would have a child to support. She *had* to find a way to make everything work.

Lowering her hand, Catherine looked away from the bawdy houses and turned back to the inn where she could smell food cooking. She looked down at her beautiful dress, now covered with dust. Sand coated her cream slippers. The curls in her hair had slipped down her back.

She'd made such an effort to appear the refined lady today. She'd worn one of Anna's finest creations, made for a high-society belle who, after seeing the dress, decided that cream did not compliment her coloring. Not so on Catherine. But it hadn't mattered. Lord Blackmoor clearly judged her beneath his station. The instant she'd walked into his cabin, he'd looked at her with eyes that burned enmity and something she could not name. Eyes filled with no-nonsense British arrogance.

Her colonial pride had wanted to punch him in the nose.

Determined to eat before she passed out, Catherine climbed the stairs. A low roof covered the wide verandah. The door suddenly swung open, and two jaunty men in naval attire walked out, their laughter dying abruptly upon seeing her. A woman wearing a mobcap popped her head around the corner. The lacy handkerchief she'd been waving stopped. "Oh!" She gasped, and Catherine realized the woman was looking at someone down the stairs. "We've a wee bit of partying goin' on. 'Tis still early if ye be wishin' to join us, my lord."

Catherine spun around.

Lord Blackmoor stood in full military regalia, one booted foot planted on the bottom step. A military long cloak warded off the chill and fluttered at his calves. Holding her gaze, he then switched his attention to the two naval officers, who straightened briskly as Julian moved behind her. There was a feverish buzz of salutes and sirs before they swept down the stairs.

"I'm with her, Eve," Lord Blackmoor had the nerve to say, as if she somehow belonged to him.

"Aye, lovey," mobcap giggled at her, "'e's a fine one he is." She bobbed away, leaving Catherine alone with His Lordship. The wind swept through the treetops, stirring leaves and sand.

"Are you hungry?" he asked.

"You know her?"

Amusement fell over his mouth. "You'd be surprised who I know. Especially after spending time in one place."

"Which is uncommon for you, I imagine." A glance over his shoulder found two impressive men standing guard. She wondered if he expected to be attacked. "I missed the last ship to Yorktown," she said in explanation of her presence at a place like this. But that fact mattered little when she was so hungry that she could eat raw fish.

Touching her elbow, Lord Blackmoor shouldered open the door and stepped inside the smoky tavern. Warmth from his fingertips seeped through the fabric of her gown. Catherine walked into the smoke-filled room and met the stares of a dozen bristly patrons. Unconsciously, she sidled closer to the captain. "Is this place open for supper?" he asked aloud, and a tavern maid rushed forward.

"Aye, my lord." She bobbed a curtsy.

"A quiet corner will suit our needs."

Aware of her brother-in-law's presence behind her, Catherine accompanied the girl to a second room, where she sat them against the wall.

A taper centered on the table fluttered, and Catherine focused on the flame. The server came and, without asking what she wanted, Blackmoor ordered potato chowder, hot bread, and milk. Her lack of hold on her emotions tweaked her pride. Especially since he seemed to know her love for milk and took care to see that it was served fresh. But more than that, he ordered a meal for Samuel with the instructions that one of his men would deliver it to the stables. The serving girl left, and Catherine fell into the captain's gaze.

She'd been so convinced that she disliked everything about him, that just when she despised him the most, he went and ruined it all.

"Do not presume upon my good nature, Mrs. Catherine Renee Bellamy," he said as if he'd clearly read her charitable thoughts. "I'm not here because I'm convinced who you are."

"No?" She clasped her hands in her lap. "Yet you're here, nonetheless. Why is that?"

Leaning on his elbows, he bent forward but not so much that he encroached an inch into her space. His bicorn sat on the table next to his elbow. He wore a powdered wig tied back with a leather thong.

"How is it that someone who dresses the way you do can't afford the coins for a decent night's sleep or more than that rickety ketch that goes back and forth from here to Yorktown?"

"You're very knowledgeable about women's gowns."

"I've bought enough to know the difference between fine silk and cotton. What you're wearing cost some planter a month's wages, and I don't imagine that it was Patrick who paid that bill."

A hot blush crawled up her neck into her face. "No, it wasn't," she said, caring little what he construed. He was such an uncouth boor. "And I can pay for my own room and board. The problem was finding a place that would take Samuel. As for the ketch?

Unlike you, I don't have the Royal Navy at my disposal. I just wanted to get across the river. So if you've no more business—"

He tossed a sheaf on the tabletop. "You left that behind." His expression did not alter, but he spoke in an undertone. "Whoever drew this portraiture is very good."

Catherine tried to pretend the compliment didn't stir her. When she'd left home to come here, she'd done so with one express purpose. To take a stand. Putting back together a legitimate business had only been the start for her and the child she carried. She would rebuild her life from the dirt up and, in doing so, reap justice on those who threatened her: those who had killed Patrick and set her up to die.

"In truth, my brother is the talent in the family." She flicked the drawing. "The man's name is Sergeant Masters. The world would be better served without men such as he."

His expression had become careful. "What is he to you?"

"I have reason to believe that he might know something of Patrick's death or know others who do."

"Then, unlike the magistrate, who read over the case, you suspect my brother's death was not accidental?"

Catherine was very prudent in her response. "I wouldn't be surprised if you haven't already concluded that much. Maybe even *hired* men to do your investigation. You don't seem the type of person to take anything at face value. Clearly a sign of an unhappy childhood," she added.

Sitting back, he crossed his arms, clearly unimpressed with her sarcasm. "Has Masters hurt you?"

His concern was not the response she'd expected from him, and her expression reflected that surprise. Catherine glanced down at her hands in the shadows of the table. "I'm not afraid of him."

Except she was. But to admit that she knew what Sergeant Masters had done to Merlin was to practically confess to being Merlin's accomplice that night. In addition, there was the British ship moored in the river to consider. Lord Blackmoor was an officer of the crown. It was the dread of bringing down the authorities on innocent people for the crimes of a few that began to send doubt cascading through her.

"Has he, Catherine?"

The sound of her name on his lips brought her gaze up and

made her pause. Captain Lambert's attention had turned to his sleeve. He brushed at his cuff as if to rid it of lint. "Otherwise," he raised his gaze, "you have managed to confuse me," he said dismissively.

"I came here seeking partnership for the *Tidewater Clarion*, my lord. As for the other information . . . I felt that I owed you that much. No one will trust a British officer enough to tell you anything. You will not find out facts on your own."

"You've given me no facts."

"He's a British soldier. Surely it is an easy enough place for you to start an inquiry."

"Into what?" His shoulder shrugged. "What has Masters done?"

"He . . ." Her hands tightened in her lap. "He knows things. Someone is feeding him information that only a few are privy to."

"He's getting inside information, so to speak, on various illicit activities in the area, and you want me to do exactly what?" He braced an arm on the back of the bench. "Get rid of him for you?"

"Oh God," she swept the ceiling with her gaze. But it was true how she felt. "Now I'm conspiring to murder a man."

"So you're a true-blue, dyed-in-the-wool dissident?"

"No . . ." Lord, he'd have her condemning herself before the night was through. "Not anymore."

"Relax, Mrs. Bellamy. I'm not defending the man."

The server arrived and, smiling shyly at His Lordship, set down Catherine's dinner. Attempting to dismiss her brother-in-law, Catherine sipped her soup. His glower was gone. He looked preoccupied as he pondered the pine walls in the smoke-filled room, his gloved fingers drumming the back of the bench where he'd braced his arm. Her gaze encompassed the pull of his sleeve against the flex of his muscles. The midnight blue cloth of his uniform was rich.

Catherine finally gave her full attention to the hot soup. The bread was warm and heavenly, the milk delicious. For five minutes as she devoured her meal, she even forgot the imposing man sitting across the table. She didn't like him. There was something inherently dangerous and familiar about a man with too many facets to his personality. He reminded her of Patrick. And she decided then, that was why he seemed familiar to her.

Dabbing the crumbs from her mouth, Catherine folded the napkin flat and smoothed out the wrinkles before finally lifting her gaze. Lord Blackmoor was now watching her.

"Where did my brother meet you?" he quietly asked.

She sat straighter. Maybe it was the way he looked at her, as if he really did want to know, that kept her from pulling away.

"Two years ago, Patrick ran for the House of Burgesses and lost." She picked up a leaf that had fallen from her hat and studied its striated edges. "I met him at a . . . gathering soon after that. I was an unofficial apprentice at the local newspaper. Papa was a best friend of the owner. Patrick got involved with the business. He was as good a writer as he was a speaker. When the owner became ill, we had a chance to buy. Patrick came up with the financing, and we became business partners." His silence lifted her gaze. She brushed the leaf from the table. "Later, we married."

"How long have you lived in Yorktown?"

"Most of my life."

"Then you are familiar with the politics?"

"Enough to realize that you and I do not walk in the same circles, social or otherwise."

"Yet you married my brother."

"Patrick was different. He grew up in the colonies. You are nothing like him."

She finished her milk in silence and was relieved when he paid for the meal, especially after her boast that she could.

Outside, he took her elbow. "You're staying about a ten-minute walk down the road. The place is as respectable as it gets around here. I took the liberty to book you a room before coming here. My men have already taken your servant there. There's a building out back with bedding and cots where he can sleep."

Catherine didn't know what to say as he led her to the beach. The sand muted their steps. Lightning blinked in the distant clouds. "It has rained too much these past weeks," she said to no one in particular, certainly not to Lord Blackmoor, who seemed about as remote as the moon. It would be dark in an hour.

The sand dragged at her feet, and she stopped by a log that some recent storm had washed up on shore. Sitting to remove a pebble from her shoe, she looked up at her companion, his mind someplace far away, as his gaze came back around to hers.

She returned his stare. Turnabout was fair play, and if he was curious about her, she was certainly curious about him. "Will you be in this region much longer?" She stood and started walking.

"Not any longer than I have to be. I'll be attending the governor's ball in a few weeks. One of my civic responsibilities while here." He paused. "Will you be there?"

"Gracious no." Her voice faded in sudden embarrassment. That sounded pathetic. "In truth, I have no wish to attend."

"Because you don't dance?"

She lifted her nose. "I am an expert dancer, my lord."

"Indeed." His voice grinned.

Up ahead in a grove of trees, she could hear laughter. As Lord Blackmoor had promised, the two-story inn appeared respectable, with its whitewashed exterior that looked like moonlight in the trees, but as they drew nearer, she found herself reluctant to part.

"Frankly, I'd as soon not attend, myself." He smiled at that and conceded, "But alas, duty prevails."

Then their steps slowed and, just that fast, they were standing in the middle of a grove of trees looking at each other. Catherine felt her tongue stick to the roof of her mouth. "When I decided to come here today, I'd thought that somehow . . ."

Looking into his hooded eyes, she doubted that he'd ever allowed more than a handful of people into his life. Vaguely, she recalled that his mother had died years ago and that his stepfather had had a distinguished career in the Royal Navy. He'd passed away shortly after becoming Pennsylvania's lieutenant governor. Blackmoor had never visited there since. Of his real father, she knew nothing except that, for whatever reason, Patrick's brother had never returned to his estates in England. For all of his courage and willingness to face down foes, Captain Lambert spent a greater portion of life avoiding his own.

"There's still much I don't understand, Mrs. Bellamy."

"Then you believe me?"

"I don't know. I only know that I wasn't expecting you."

He said nothing else. And as she backed away, she didn't mention the papers she'd left with him. He did not attempt to stop her or to say good-bye. When she looked over her shoulder again, Lord Blackmoor was already gone.

• • •

Less than an hour later, Julian stepped into the cabin aboard Michael's ship. River charts covered the desk. With Julian off the schooner, Michael had returned to the main cabin. He looked up from the desk. Behind him the sun had set and turned the sea red. He and Michael had worked these waters for years. Because Julian spent so much time at sea, Michael had oft become Merlin's trusted go-between in this area. Michael knew these waters better than anyone did.

"Aren't you supposed to be at a staff meeting or something?"

"Patrick had a wife. Or she's a consummate good actress. Hell, I don't know." Julian paced. "She's been trying to get hold of me for months. I never received her letters. Nothing."

"She was here?" Michael's dark brows drew inward. "You were at sea for nine months. Ye can't be blamin' yourself you didn't know."

"Bloody hell." A deep sense of his own depravity began to take hold. "Why wouldn't Patrick tell anyone that he'd married?"

"Maybe there just wasn't time before he died."

Or maybe Michael was too kind to tell Julian that Patrick could be a bloody ass at times, that affection and tolerance had always tinted Julian's rosy vision of Patrick. But Michael didn't understand about Patrick. Since his first steps, Patrick had clung to Julian. Despite their seven-year age gap, they'd always been close.

Yet, he'd been excluded from a whole part of Patrick's life. And he didn't understand why.

"Why should ye be so upset, Reece?"

Julian lifted his gaze to find Michael watching him curiously. "Stay away from Yorktown. I don't want this ship recognized."

"Aye, whatever you think best."

Outside on the street, the brisk wind hit Julian in the face. He adjusted his bicorn. The narrow street was crowded, but he hardly noticed. His steward met him at the carriage.

"Cancel my appointments this week until I say otherwise," Julian said.

"But what about your dinner with Mistress Simms tonight?"

"Cancel it. Tell her I'll see her in Williamsburg."

"Sir?" At the sight of Julian's ill-tempered frown, his steward slumped back into the leather seats. "Yes, sir."

Julian turned toward the water, where seagulls bobbed like

snowy corks. Tossing up the collar of his cloak, he settled into its woolen warmth. His gaze encompassed the land that jutted out across the bay. Leaden clouds churned over the harbor where the remains of the day burned into the sea. He scanned the line of masts bobbing in the choppy water.

Pulling the full length of her cables, the *Chimera* rode each swell, her round lines a graceful contradiction to the power she wielded, a living testament that beauty could be deceptive.

And for the first time since his return to the colonies, something else eclipsed the hard knot of vengeance that drove his every waking moment since his lack of foresight dropped him into a nest of vipers. Vipers that had nothing to do with the rebel cause. Vipers that may include a dark-haired, dark-eyed Welsh beauty that had become as much his obsession as his hunt for Patrick's killers.

Julian's gaze fell on the crumpled card in his hand. Slowly, he brought the paper to his nose, the faint scent of lilac, reminiscent of a cold, rainy dawn.

Aye, the only thing worse than having slept with his brother's beautiful rebel widow was not forgetting her.

Shoving the card in his coat pocket, Julian walked down the busy street and hired a man to row him out to his ship.

Chapter Nine

Catherine and Samuel made it home safely. She'd taken a ketch to Hampton Roads early that morning and bought passage on the mail coach. She'd barely had the strength to climb the stairs to the house by the time they returned near midnight.

Skirting the edge of the road near a dilapidated farm shed, a remnant from the tobacco glory days, a shadow separated from the darkness and watched her go inside. Horse and rider remained frozen against the stygian backdrop of trees. A black cloak twined the figure in secrecy and draped the belly of the horse. Having followed her for hours, he remained where he was, watching the house. An hour passed, and the lights winked out inside the house as if it, too, was exhausted by the day's events and had to sleep. Then something spooked the horse, and the animal pranced sideways.

The dark-gloved hands swung the steed away and cantered down the road. Only when the house faded in the trees and dusty moonlight did he spur the horse into a gallop.

The night was young.

Julian rode into Williamsburg two days later. Arriving at Allison Simms's house, he slid out of the saddle, sprinted the porch stairs, and knocked on the door. Tucked back into the forest like a frothy white palace, her house bespoke the prosperity of her trade. Though it was nearly noon, he didn't expect her to be awake yet. Her butler opened the door.

"Good afternoon, Miles." Julian entered without an invitation, removing his cloak and laying it over the stair rail. "Is she alone?"

"Yes, my lord," he said to Julian's back. Julian knew the way well enough to Allison's room and took the stairs.

She'd been his wife's best friend a long time ago, when life promised the kind of dreams that came with youth. Back in August, Allison had been the one who had greeted him upon his arrival in Norfolk with the news of Patrick's death. Theirs had been a biddable relationship over the years, and he'd come to depend on her as much as he did Michael. Few people knew his identity as Merlin, and she was one. She was his contact here in this region with Robbie as their go-between.

With a yank, he opened the curtains and let the sunlight weep through the crystalline glass. "Get up, Allison," he said to the lump of expensive blue and white lace.

She flung the comforter off her shoulders and sat up, glaring sparks. "You look like how I feel," she snapped, clearly not in any benevolent mood. "Haggard."

"I haven't slept."

"Too much company at night?"

He ignored her sarcasm. "How hard will it be to secure a ball invitation?"

She fell back into her pillows. "They went out weeks ago. Besides, what good is that aristocratic title of yours if you can't secure one prized ball invitation?"

"Because this one will raise a few eyebrows. You're still seeing Dunmore's secretary. It won't take but a word from your beautiful lips to see it done."

She eyed him with studied interest. "Are you saying 'please'?"

The fluffy bedchamber was utterly silent as he recognized the blatant invitation in her eyes. Allison Simms was a beautiful woman, he considered as he sat back and lounged in the plush chair beside her bed. She could easily relieve his sexual tension and, instead of dwelling obsessively on his brother's widow, he could live to physical excess and die happily for the bliss right here and now.

"You're tempting, Allison." His voice was low, seductive. But it was dark cinnamon eyes, not blue, that stayed his lust. "And I'm truly sorry that I had to break our rendezvous in Norfolk."

With pouty lips, she lay back against the pillows, the invitation still open in her gaze. "Who is she?"

"Her name is Catherine Bellamy. She lives in Yorktown." Reluctantly supplying her card, he stood before Allison could register the full impact of her name. "And one other thing"—he tossed down the sketch of Sergeant Masters—"this man is also in Yorktown. Someone is feeding him information. It would behoove us all to find out who, before he disappears off the face of this earth."

Allison lifted her sultry gaze from the drawing and showed surprise. "Are you contemplating murder, my lord?"

Julian didn't bother to tell her he was capable of being a cold-hearted bastard, equal to that of Masters. Many a man had found that out the hard way. He was capable of anything when provoked.

And the whole bloody region had provoked him to do far more than murder! As he'd once told Catherine, this was personal, and his feelings were too heated to state just how personal everything had now become.

Catherine overslept her morning chores. For a second day. She dragged herself out of bed and dressed. With no explanation to excuse her tardiness, she gathered the new drawings she'd worked on late last night and walked downstairs for breakfast.

Johnnycakes and jam lined the breakfront. Passing on the food, she poured a cup of her stepmother's willow bark tea. "Are my wondrous eyes deceiving me?" Elizabeth observed as Catherine sat. Wearing a fawn-colored gown, clearly last year's fashion, her sister fairly burst out of the bodice as she leaned with her elbows on the table. "Methinks that you have slept in for a second day."

"Are you all right, dear?"

"I've had a lot on my mind, Momma," Catherine said.

She tested the scent of the vile tealike substance first before squeezing her eyes shut and drinking from the porcelain cup, hoping it would spark her drive to get moving. *Life must go on,* she told herself with more pragmatism than she'd had when she went to Norfolk.

Elizabeth's inquiring stare stopped her. The twins watched her, clearly curious to see if she might croak right over her plate.

Catherine detested the tea, so to consume it now claimed the attention of everyone at the breakfast table. Even Anna, standing with a hot platter of eggs in her hand, had stopped serving.

"I'll be glad when we can start drinking regular tea again," Catherine offered the silence.

Sipping her willow bark tea, her stepmother appeared detached, but Catherine knew it was an illusion. Indeed, she was unsure about everything except that, despite her stepmother's occasional odd behavior, her insight was nothing short of astonishing. And at the moment, she was reading Catherine to her soul.

"Have you heard from His Lordship, dear, since your return?" Her stepmother sipped her tea. "You've said little about your visit."

"Posh," Elizabeth delicately buttered her bread, "she's been a pill, Momma. I wouldn't be so diplomatic in my observation."

"Lord Blackmoor is busy with his ship." The words weren't a lie. She didn't expect to ever hear from her brother-in-law again.

Silverware clinked as the children eagerly consumed their eggs. She had to think of her baby now and what this pregnancy would do to her family. But twice Catherine had dreamed of Reece this week. She'd dreamed of a violent storm where Merlin shaped a man from the darkness: a man wearing the uniform of His Majesty's Royal Navy. He carried a large sword and lopped off her head for protecting Daniel.

Catherine had awakened with a strangled gasp.

In truth, she'd not had a decent night's sleep since her return from Norfolk.

But Catherine had other problems at the moment. She was determined that even though the *Tidewater Clarion* would be harder to revive, the Stationery Shoppe would survive, even if she didn't own the property outright. Last night, Samuel had started building shelves in what used to be the pressroom. And the new whitewash Elizabeth had applied to the front of the building last week gave their family project new energy. All they needed was a new front window.

The conversation at breakfast moved to the weather, and Catherine, who had worked on new stationery designs last night, started to excuse herself from the table when the topic changed to local events. Not just any events, either. "What attack?" Catherine asked her sister, her attention suddenly riveted.

"Someone raided the Tomkinses' farm."

"And you're only just now telling me this?"

Clearly pleased with the tidbit of gossip and the knowledge that she had discovered something so monumental before Catherine did, Elizabeth fluffed the lace on her bosom. "If you participated in the quilter's circle every once in a while, you'd hear a lot of things, sister of mine. Besides, I only just heard this news last night myself, seeing as how it's all been so hush-hush."

Catherine looked at the twins next to her and saw that they were hanging on Elizabeth's every word.

"Go play, you two." Her stepmother dabbed Brian's mouth with a napkin. "See if Millie has anything yet to feed Sally."

Excitement lit their blue eyes. They scooted off their chairs, and Catherine watched them race out of the room. "Dissension is buzzing through the local ranks here." Elizabeth's voice lowered. "No one knows who would dare trespass on the Tomkinses' farm. Why, just two weeks ago, their dogs nearly mauled poor Jeffrey Stanton to death. Jeffrey delivers eggs, you know. His only crime being that he took a shortcut across the Tomkinses' land."

"Barbarians, if ye be askin' me," Anna said, pouring more tea into Catherine's cup. "Fortunately, Jeffrey will be all right."

Catherine's heart raced. "Did anyone see who it was?"

"Not precisely."

"What do you mean, not precisely?"

"Well," her sister eagerly elaborated, "you know how Jed Tomkins's mother always likes to bake pies. It was near dawn. She was on the road gathering nuts when she saw this . . . this—"

"What?"

"This *shadow*. It had four feet and huge black wings." Elizabeth flapped her arms in demonstration. "She swears it flew away."

"Oh, good grief." Catherine let loose her breath. Her hopes dashed, she glared at her sister. It was most likely a traveler. He probably wore a cloak. It is nearly winter, after all. "You've missed your calling, Elizabeth. You should be an actress."

"Forsooth, sister of mine." Elizabeth patted her blond ringlets. "Would you have me ruin my reputation?"

"I think it's a lot of flapdoodle if ye be askin' my opinion," Anna said. "Frankly, I'm sick and tired of people sitting around this town doing nothing about the Tomkins and Sergeant Masters of this world. Good riddance to the lot of thugs."

Daniel's name remained conspicuously unspoken, but not for long, as her stepmother set down her tea. "Daniel is not one of them," she said with quiet determination, as if she'd read Catherine's thoughts.

"Anyway," Elizabeth was not to be interrupted. "That's not even the best part." She shoved aside her plate and leaned forward on her elbows. "It seems this has been going on for over a month. A few weeks ago, a coach was held up near North Fork. Before the robbers could count the loot, a highwayman robbed *them.* Imagine the nerve."

"You're serious." Now, this was clearly exciting news.

"Jed Tomkins showed up at the Red Lion and picked a fight with the Herring brothers. You know they were the ones who beat his horse last summer in the county race. Anyway, he accused the brothers of encroaching on his ground. They denied it, of course. And a huge fight ensued. The place is still closed to repair the damage."

"Truly." Catherine laughed.

"The lieutenant takes the threat seriously enough." Elizabeth said. "He thinks the scoundrel is Merlin."

The sound of an arriving horse and wagon interrupted Catherine's rebuttal. "Oh, my." Her stepmother stood and brushed the crumbs from her gray skirt. "Anna? Are you expecting more visitors?"

Catherine remained alone in the dining room.

Could Reece possibly have never left the area? Slipping her fingers around the tepid cup in her hands, she studied the brew. There were a hundred places to hide a ship. Catherine stood. As if in a daze, she followed the conversation to the front door.

Outside the house, Sally sat placidly at Samuel's feet as a man bent over the back of his cart. Elizabeth and Anna stood in the doorway, her stepmother on the porch.

She seemed to know the gentleman and greeted him warmly. Catherine had seen him often in the mercantile store where he worked as the town's postmaster. The store had been the center for mail delivery in town for years.

"This came late last night. From Williamsburg." The man, dressed smartly in a blue jerkin, bowed. "His Lordship wanted this to go to the lady of the house." A rare basket of fruit made its way into her stepmother's arms. "He wasn't specific which lady. Perhaps he didn't realize there is more than one."

"His Lordship?" Her stepmother laughed. " Whatever are you talking about, Frank?"

He fumbled in his jacket for a folded parchment. "It is an invitation to the Autumn Harvest ball," he said with some awe.

"A what?" Elizabeth snatched it up. "But it's only addressed to Catherine. Are you sure?"

"The courier was very specific, mum."

Catherine could almost hear the groan of disappointment emanating from her family's lips. The dialogue proclaiming the tardiness of the invitation, the lack of etiquette, an inability to create a proper gown in time. They thought the invitation wasted. Even the postal clerk knew how Catherine felt about this gathering of Virginia's elite. Was no part of her sacrosanct against scrutiny, public or otherwise?

"I'll go," she said, and she had to repeat the words again before conversation halted and all eyes turned on her standing behind them in the hallway. She regarded Anna with imperious delight. None of them had any clue the godsend she'd just been given. "Do we have the ability to make a gown in time?"

Anna hesitated but rose at once to the challenge. "Aye, mum."

"Then I'll go." Catherine snatched the invitation from Elizabeth, the hypocrisy of her stance clearly obvious. No longer could she be so totalitarian in her beliefs. No one would take her seriously. But that didn't matter. Reece's baby grew inside of her. She had to do what it took to locate him.

And that meant going directly through Captain Lambert. He'd hired Reece once to investigate Patrick's death. Surely, he would know where to find him now.

Catherine stood frozen before the looking glass.

"Are you nervous?" Elizabeth asked.

Her hand went to her stomach.

Anna had outdone herself.

Catherine wore a celestial blue satin gown with a white petticoat of the same smooth fabric. She touched her shoulders where the barest hint of flesh boasted her daring. A large Italian gauze handkerchief with border stripes of satin served as her décolletage. She touched her bodice. Her dark hair was dressed in detached curls, four of which fell on each side of her neck and were relieved behind a floating chignon. A pouf headdress composed of fashionable gauze finished the transformation. She touched her lips.

"Hold your head high, Rina," Anna reminded her. "There'll be no shamin' the Claremont name this night."

Catherine, Elizabeth, and Anna had ridden the mail coach from Yorktown yesterday and taken a room at one of the town's respectable inns. 'Twas common for events at the governor's palace to last two days or more. The city bustled with life and prosperity, and Catherine was in awe of the difference between the towns.

Sited at the end of a broad, imposing green, the governor's palace stood out like a warm, bejeweled beacon against the velvet sky. The elaborate gardens, falling terraces, and enclosed forecourt amplified genteel British authority. Heart racing, she scolded herself for her nervousness. She was on a mission tonight.

An hour after sunset, she descended the steps of the carriage.

"Your mum, my lady," the carriage attendant said, politely handing her the green canvas pot her stepmother had sent with her. A bright orange bow meticulously arranged topped off the gift.

She walked into the entrance hall, where the royal coat of arms and a wall of ornamental weaponry surrounded the long receiving line. Lord Blackmoor stood among the select group, tall and formal, a distinguished figure in his naval uniform and wig. Her heart began to hammer as she noticed that he'd paused slightly when he saw her. A butler suddenly appeared at her elbow.

"Madame." He took her cloak and invitation as another man politely removed the mum from her hands.

"It needs to be watered," she said quietly as the gathering crowd jostled her into the receiving line.

The other gifts people carried were nothing so insignificant as flowers, but knowing the love her stepmother had put into that plant, Catherine watched it leave, a little saddened that it would probably go unappreciated.

She met Lord Dunmore, Virginia's new governor. Walking

down the group of dignitaries, she greeted lords and ladies from places as far away as France, as well as the local elite. Lord Blackmoor's gaze lifted politely to hers. "Mrs. Catherine Renee Bellamy," he said her name as he brought her gloved hand to his lips with more zeal than any other gentleman had thus far. "Mums are my favorite plant."

Her lips parted. "Mine as well." She dipped slightly in a curtsy.

"I didn't think you'd come. The hour is late."

Glancing around to see if anyone had heard, she felt heat suffuse her limbs. She didn't tell him that she'd paced in her room until after the sun had left the sky. That he would note the hour surprised her. "I'm not so late," she graciously returned.

His gloved hand tightened on hers so she couldn't politely disengage. "I'm glad to see that you have stepped outside your political boundaries to enjoy the bounty of the approaching season. Your trip here was pleasant?"

"Yes." She tugged her hand. "Thank you for the invitation."

"You did say that you know how to dance?"

He was causing her to hold up the line. People were beginning to stare. "We peasants are a gifted lot, my lord," she chided behind a tight smile.

His gaze lowered to briefly touch her breasts. There was the merest indication of a bow and a distinctive sparkle in his eyes that even his staid demeanor could not hide. "In truth, madam, you wear your gifts well. You look very beautiful tonight."

Blushing hotly, she snatched her hand back. "Libertine," she whispered, and she thought he smiled at the dark look she shot him.

Flustered, she moved on, glancing surreptitiously back. But Lord Blackmoor had already dismissed her as he bowed over another lady's gloved hand, every inch the attentive naval officer.

While Catherine turned away, Julian watched her pass through a set of double doors into the lavishly decorated ballroom. He found himself impatiently trapped in the receiving line for another hour.

Catherine walked through the house, like a child, the act of sophistication lost in the realm of discovery. The scents of supper drifted from the cooking house. Strains of music came from the ballroom. She joined a group of ladies chatting about the latest fashions from France. Soon men claimed them for a waltz, and Catherine was left alone. A glance spotted the Earl of Blackmoor still in the crowded foyer. He was easily recognizable, his dark midnight blue and gray uniform setting him apart from the velvets and satins worn by the other men. She couldn't seem to keep her eyes from wandering back to him. Catherine walked out the doors that led to the governor's magnificent gardens.

"It's a beautiful night," Lieutenant Ross said as he handed her a cup of punch. "Did you come here alone?"

Catherine looked up into his eyes and smiled, pleased that someone had finally talked to her, even if it was he. "One of the allowances to being a widow," she said. "My reputation no longer hinges completely on social rules. Would you care to dance with me?" she said, aware that ladies of breeding would never stoop so low as to ask a gentleman to dance. But then she was no lady of breeding, she decided quite boldly. And no gentlemen were asking her to dance.

"I have not danced in a long time," he said evasively.

"We can talk about Elizabeth if you wish."

Taking her punch, he set the cups down on the stone embankment and led her into the ballroom. "She is not here. I've looked."

"I came here on an invitation from my brother-in-law," she clarified lest he deem her some sort of rebel spy.

"Ah, yes, the infamous Lord Blackmoor."

He whisked her around the room. Just beyond his shoulder, she no longer glimpsed her brother-in-law's uniform in the foyer, and her mood fell. "You say that as if you don't like him."

His grin was cautious. "One does not have an opinion about titled lords if one wishes to remain in the service of the crown. He is your husband's brother, I do believe."

"You know very well that he is."

"He didn't like the magistrate's report about his brother's death."

"A lot of us don't like the report, Lieutenant," she said coolly. "What did Lord Blackmoor do?"

"What could he do? Even titled lords can't bring back the dead. He went back to Norfolk. I haven't seen him again until now."

She sought to change the jarring subject. "Perhaps next time you pay a visit to my sister, you should change out of your uniform."

"I like my uniform, Mrs. Bellamy. Besides . . ." He perused her face. "Perhaps you're aware that my time has been taken up with new matters."

"For instance?"

"It's quite possible Merlin never left the area."

Her heart began to race. "Why would you think that?"

"A hunch, Mrs. Bellamy. And I think you know who he is."

For a few seconds, he must have seen her alarm. The music stopped. Smiling, she gently tugged her wrist from his grasp and stepped away. "I think supper is being served, Lieutenant." She nodded to the people filing into the dining area.

Recognizing the battle lines for what they were, Lieutenant Ross gallantly offered his arm. "Then may I escort you to supper?"

Her lashes swept her cheeks as she accepted his escort. But she would make sure she didn't talk to him again.

After six courses of supper, edgy and moody, Julian finally ended up in the men's drawing room discussing politics. The formal banquet had seated Julian and Catherine at the opposite ends of the long table. He would have to thank Allison for the consideration. Like a swaddled babe staring at a candied tit in the offing, he'd found himself unable to look away from Catherine's profile through most of the evening. He'd watched her dancing with the lieutenant and, as she'd laughed at something the young man to her left said, a gnawing irritation inside had begun to eclipse his restraint.

"More cognac?" Lord Dunmore asked, and Julian accepted the offer, realizing an argument had grown between the members present in the room.

Listening to the strains of the waltz filtering through the darkly paneled walls, Julian kept silent during most of the heated political debate over certain seditious members in the House of Burgesses, the ongoing tea embargo, and the current level of counterfeiting undermining Virginia's economy. His legs stretched out and crossed at the ankles, he noticed that Lord Dunmore had done much the same, and within a couple of hours only the two of them remained in the smoke-filled room.

On the outside, Lord Dunmore was a diplomat and a gentleman, but Julian knew from past experience that nothing stood in the way of his interests. And right now, the welfare of this region was his top concern, the golden carrot of economic prosperity and opportunity. John Murray, the fourth Earl of Dunmore, had only been in office a short while, which made him seriously motivated in his policies.

"They are getting the money for their weapons someplace," he was saying. "The *Chimera* can do the job that needs to be done here. Certain upstart rebels in Yorktown need a military presence."

"The fear of God and all that?" Julian no longer studied his cognac as he realized the conversation had shifted dramatically. Pitting the military might of the British Royal Navy against the local citizenry was not conducive to his goals to remain an obscure entity. "My ship isn't ready to sail, Excellency. We're still awaiting a requisition of supplies."

"Yorktown is a main port of entry for this colony. I have merchantmen that refuse to go there. And that is lost revenue. Last month, a warehouse filled with tobacco and lumber burned to the ground when someone got it into their heads to do away with the latest shipment of tea. You have a troop of loyal marines on board."

Julian sipped his drink, willing to listen.

"Lieutenant Ross is currently in Yorktown, but he is undermanned until I can get additional customs officers there. No one will take the job. You met him earlier, I do believe."

Julian had met the younger man in the receiving line tonight as well a month ago at the military reception given here in Julian's honor. He'd also watched him dancing with Catherine.

"The lieutenant is a good man in a tough job. I expect that you will give him your full support. Among his other duties, he's also been charged with bringing in a ring of thieves responsible for the rash of highway robberies in the area, the same area where your brother was killed. Lieutenant Ross has all of his available resources taxed and cannot give his full attention to customs problems."

Julian lifted a brow. "Won't my presence be contrary to good relations with the populace?"

"That's why I'll expect that you find a place in town to stay. Make yourself available to the local government. An ambassador of sorts to cool their tempers."

Julian half smiled to himself. Jailer was the more correct term. Except he had no desire to be thrust into the public eye. Tossing back the cognac, his expression gave him away.

"I'm not asking, Blackmoor," Dunmore politely reiterated.

Lord Dunmore's administrator approached from the corridor. Dressed in orange velvet and ivory satin breeches and waistcoat, he looked like a happy pumpkin, a perfect complement to the Autumn Harvest decorations in the corridor. "If you'll excuse me, Captain," Dunmore said. "I've been left with double duty as host and hostess. I expect that you will keep me apprised of your progress in Yorktown."

With typical British impassivity, Julian watched the arrogant bastard leave, his face expressionless as he tried to extract some sense from the orders he'd just been given. Containing his ire, he walked to the ballroom. Catherine was on the dance floor again, this time with some foppish swain.

"You've been glowering most of the evening like a possessive rooster," a woman's voice whispered coyly. She gathered his arm against her breasts. Allison Simms, resplendent in white satin, pulled him into the crowded ballroom. "You need to dance with me, or I'll be very jealous of your brother's beautiful widow."

Julian smiled tolerantly. "My heart belongs to you, Allison," he quipped as they swept into the room with the other dancers.

"So you've told me over the years." She laughed, but her blue eyes were serious as they studied him. "Tell me again how you discovered that your brother had a wife hidden away?"

"The story is long and very boring."

Her jaw set in a stubborn line. "You can be too ruthless, I think, with your usual single-minded determination. Why do I get the feeling the woman is in danger?"

"Because you are a woman of superb intuition, sweet."

And his chilly tone was more daunting than her lust. She sighed.

•   •   •

Giving up her vigilance over her brother-in-law, Catherine ended up at the whist table well into the early hours of the morning. She had enough money in the chips stacked in front of her to pay for a week's leisure at the inn. She was an utter genius at the game, she thought smugly, and the only one sitting at the table not in her cups. Across from her, she heard a voice as one of the table's players finally threw in his cards and stood. From the corner of her eye, she saw someone sit and take his place.

"Shall we cut?" she shoved the cards to the man on her right, took the cut, and began to deal, her hands freezing when her gaze came into contact with Lord Blackmoor's. By taking the seat across from hers, he had become her new partner.

"My lord." She nodded. Suddenly unable to dismiss any part of her awareness of his presence, she almost fumbled the deal. Flipping the final card faceup, she announced, "Hearts are trumps."

"I hope you know how to play as well as you deal," he said.

Her heart was beating fast. She held the cards close to her and stared hard at the suits. "Why is that, my lord?"

"There is something endearing about a smug woman. And I play to win, Mrs. Bellamy."

"Aye," the man on her left grumbled, "some of us can attest to that the last time we lost to him." He led with a knave of diamonds.

The play came around to her, and she lost. At the end of the third game, the other team had won the rubber and made much to do about the whole thing, celebrating with a glass of punch.

Holding her gaze, Blackmoor accepted the shuffle. She'd expected to find mockery in his eyes and instead recognized the faint glitter of battle in their depths. "Next time lead with the trump," he gently suggested. "Trust me to know how to follow."

She won the next game. Their gazes met again over the next deal, and suddenly they were on the same playing field. Aware of his voice, his nearness, everything else in the room had receded to his masculine presence. She answered him back with her own battle grin and promptly won the next two games. Catherine had a string of trumps that ended when Blackmoor took the final three for the game rubber, and two additional shillings.

Catherine's blood hummed. She was secretly pleased that she'd managed to hold up her end of their partnership. When the deal came back around to him, she watched his hands go over the cards as he dealt, his shoulders wide beneath the pull of his uniform jacket. She picked up her cards and regarded him over their tops. His warm gaze caressed hers as he laid out the trump, and again they played. A roguish grin tilted his lips. "Are you having a good time?"

She smiled over the low din of voices pressing down on her. "And you?" She laid out a knave of spades and scooped up her trump when all the cards were played. "I've not seen you except out on the dance floor." She raised her gaze. "You're very popular, my lord."

Blackmoor's eyes seemed to smile at her. "My apologies that I've neglected you. You haven't been bored, have you?"

Flustered by his seemingly bold perusal, she said, "You haven't neglected me, my lord."

He certainly had no responsibility toward her for anything, even if they were related by marriage. And certainly not with Mrs. Allison Simms clinging to his body like a wet leather glove. The widow was a known mistress to some of the most influential men in Virginia. What did Blackmoor have to do with her?

The two men to her right and left were currently engaged in their own social discourse and didn't appear to be listening. "How long do you plan on staying in Williamsburg?" she asked, suddenly annoyed for no reason at all.

"Are you interested in showing me the sights?" he asked, admiring her over his cards.

"Pray tell, what could I show you that would interest you?"

She could feel a strange heat run through her veins and into the pit of her stomach, before his gaze lowered back to the cards in his hands. "Yorktown, maybe. Perhaps all of the popular nightspots."

Laughter sounded from the other tables in the smoke-filled gaming room. "No," she said abruptly, suddenly frightened by more than her reaction to him. This was the first time he'd made any hint that he might actually be interested in the illicit activities there. Or that he knew that she was involved. Was the world his personal playground then? And he the player, that she hadn't even realized she was being manipulated? Maybe since Norfolk?

"You are a busy woman then?" he asked her.

They won another game rubber and the game point. But just

barely, no thanks to her. Gathering up her money, she replaced her reticule back in the pocket within her skirts and came to her feet. Everyone followed. "I've spent enough time in pleasant company. I think I shall leave while I'm still ahead. Good evening, gentlemen."

She made it as far as the ballroom when a hand pulled her around, and Blackmoor was suddenly standing beside her. "Talk to me," he said.

Someone bumped her, and he moved her against the wall. Intimately sheltered by his body, she had to tilt her head to look up at him. "Why have I been invited here tonight?" she asked.

"Because I wanted to see if you would come."

"Is Allison Simms your mistress?"

He pulled back to look at her, his expression bemused in the dull candlelight. "She was my wife's best friend. She and I have remained in contact. I visit her when I'm here."

A sophisticated woman like Allison Simms was completely at ease in the society of men. A little flattery could gain her the attentions of any man present. The woman wasn't good enough for Blackmoor.

Their eyes gently touched and, as if he'd read her mind, smiled. "It's not what you think."

With him standing so close, she was suddenly too warm. "You said that you'd owe me an apology once you were convinced that I spoke the truth in Norfolk," she reminded him. "Are you convinced?"

"As for how I treated you, you will appreciate my position," he said and leaned a shoulder against the wall. "Until two weeks ago, I didn't know you existed. It seems that Patrick failed to include me in his wedding plans. Or his life, for that matter. Or I would have seen you sooner. For that I apologize."

Catherine didn't know how to respond. Though barely discernible, his hurt made him vulnerable. They were family, on the same side, at least a little bit. "Apology accepted, my lord."

"Would you care to dance?" he queried in the dead space that followed as each of them tried to decide what to say next.

"Yes." She laid her hand in his.

Blackmoor walked her out onto the ballroom floor, his movements as bold as his persona and, captivated by his easy sensuality, she allowed herself to be swirled across the dance floor.

"We are nearly alone," he said.

Conscious of the heat of his hand through the layers of her ribbed bodice, she opened her eyes to see him gazing down at her face. It was impossible to ignore the feel of him as he brushed against her. "Why *did* you come here tonight?" he asked.

"To meet the new governor," she said, her music-laden senses pulling from those eyes the memory of her purpose. "And to see you, of course." She still had business to attend with him.

"And Lieutenant Ross? It looked as if you two are old friends." He swept her past another couple, her sapphire skirts whispering against his tall boots. "Don't think I haven't been watching you for most of the night," he said.

She studied a brass button on his coat, aware that they had attracted much attention in their trek across the polished floor. "It isn't as amiable as you think. If he could arrest me, he would."

"Arrest you?"

She raised her gaze. "And what of you, my lord? Have you ever done anything illegal in these climes?"

"I drink smuggled French brandy," he admitted with so much seriousness, Catherine had to look at him. "It is very good."

"Are you friends with smugglers then?"

He smiled down at her. "That answer could get me arrested."

"How easy is it to contact a smuggler . . . say if I wanted brandy?" She lowered her lashes.

"Do you drink brandy?"

She made a face.

"I thought not." His palm tightened on her waist, and they danced past a castle turret of straw that occupied one full corner of the ballroom. "Why do you have a wish to meet a smuggler? Does your life lack adequate excitement? Or is getting your newspaper destroyed by a mob not enough for you?"

"You can say that because you don't live here," she said, miffed by his reminder that he'd not responded to her proposal to make the paper viable again. "You live on your battleship and command a world of men to do your bidding. You don't care about the people here."

"Why do you say that?"

"Because you bask in the labors of other's sacrifices to get your brandy. You think it is all so simple. When I know it is not." Her passion surprised even her. "There is a man right now in

Yorktown quite adept at tweaking British noses. If you are not careful, you may not get any more brandy."

"Indeed." He had the audacity to look amused. "He is your hero? Your brandy smuggler?"

"Perhaps I wish to find him."

He twirled her around. "You're on dangerous ground, Mrs. Bellamy."

"Then you know him?" She held her breath. On some strange level, it felt perfectly safe for her to ask. "This . . . brandy smuggler?"

"Don't make the mistake of thinking that any man who lives in the shadows is nobler than he is. You don't want to know him."

"At least he has honor."

"For all the good honor does a man."

Her expression must have crumpled, because his mouth took on a wry twist. "I know many smugglers. There are probably dozens here tonight. Perhaps you will find the one you seek."

"Truly?" She looked around her, doubtful.

"I could even point out one or two Sons of Liberty members."

She checked his face to see if he might be joking. He was watching her. "Aren't you obligated to arrest them?" she asked.

"Sometimes just knowing the enemy is half the battle fought."

"But not a battle won, sir. Nor will military might defeat what is here." She touched her heart in a passionate statement of the political lines between them.

"We have digressed," he said, his manner no longer jovial. "I apologize if I've offended you with my observations."

Her undefined feelings about him concerned her. "You've not offended me."

"That's good, because I didn't want to give up this dance, not when I am finally free of my other duties."

To that point, she thought his hold tightened slightly. "You are a good diplomat, my lord?"

"Mostly I like to use my guns. Blow things up," he said, and she laughed.

With that thought, she allowed herself to relax and enjoy her powerful brother-in-law's company, more relaxed than she'd been in months. Their stances were clear, no pretenses, only a sense that, from now on, none of that mattered.

They ended up at the punch table and finally out in the quiet solitude of an approaching dawn, where sunlight had already relegated the shadows to their appropriate places. The dawn was spectacular.

"What is your estate like in England?" Catherine asked. They'd walked in the damp grass surrounding the gardens.

"The manor house burned to the ground when I was six. I don't remember it ever being beautiful. It always seemed terrifying to me."

Catherine paused. "Terrifying?" she asked him. "Why?"

He looked down at her. "Do we have to talk about me?"

"The past matters little to me. But you are a curiosity," she said, fingering the shiny leaves of a holly. "I want to know."

"Why?" His voice grumbled.

The morning light accentuated the planes of his face. "Because you won't tell me. Because I think a person's past is important."

He started walking. "I don't think about my life like that."

"What about your family?"

Lifting his gaze, he held hers the merest fraction of a second.

"I am pressing you too much," she said.

"Aye."

Catherine detected the undercurrent beneath his words. But he did not push her away. Instead, he walked. "My older brother died when I was five. He was the real heir to the Blackmoor title. My father never let me forget that. He blamed me for Raymond's death."

"At five?"

"Raymond was a year older, always sickly. I was too full of life to let that hinder me. I always thought if he just got up and moved around, he would feel better. One night, I talked him into going swimming in the creek. He caught lung fever and a week later was dead. My father never forgave me. If the estate hadn't been entailed, he would have tried to disinherit me. I wish he could have. As it was, my mother was hard-pressed to keep me alive after that." He stopped beside a brownstone retaining wall. She leaned with her back against the wall, her hands caressing the rough stone behind her.

"Six months later, my powerful, aristocratic father died in a drunken rampage after accidentally setting the manor on fire."

He leaned against his palm. "Now do you know me better than you did five minutes ago?"

"That's why you've never gone back there?"

Catherine stood arrested, as his gaze seemed to tenderly encompass her face. "I've rebuilt enough that the tenants have not been neglected through the years. For me, there isn't anything I want to go back to. My mother remarried Captain Bellamy less than a year after my older brother's death, and we left. I've lived most of my life here in the colonies or at sea."

"I was young when we sailed out of Liverpool." Her voice was quiet. Her heart raced in confusion. "I don't remember anything about England. Actually, I've only been out of this region once. And that was to go to Boston." She smiled. "I loved that busy seaport town."

Her eyes had not moved from his. And, as if in slow motion, she watched his gaze lower to her mouth. The breeze carried the scent of powder and warm wool.

A gardener was moving around below in the lower terrace. Catherine could hear him talking to someone else. She startled. Almost guiltily.

"It will be crowded out here soon," Blackmoor said.

Her response was muted beneath his disturbed regard. Nodding, she agreed that she needed to return to the inn.

And when he'd finally escorted her inside again, and the butler handed over her cloak to him, Catherine still did not understand what had just happened between them. Later, after the carriage brought her back to the inn and she'd undressed and slid beneath the covers, she stared at the timbered ceiling.

When she was a little girl, she'd oft ventured to the shores of the York River with her father to watch the wind ply the sails of the great ships that had traveled the world. With the stroke of her hand and her father's encouragement, she'd captured the long-ago images on paper. Drawing, like writing, had taught her purpose and the ability to overcome barriers with mere mind-set. It had also taught her about people. And as she'd stroked the paper with images of shadows and sunlight, she'd learned to recognize the quality of a man by his eyes. Eyes were truly the windows to a man's soul.

Captain Lambert's eyes, for one instant in the garden, had belonged to Patrick.

Maybe it was the way he moved in a crowd that bespoke a
man who cared not for the bounds or strictures that labeled a person. Or perhaps it was his height that exaggerated his persona, or
the way he could be nice when she'd least expected that had
thrown her so far off center.

And Patrick had oft spoken of his elusive brother. She'd
known Lord Blackmoor through gossip for over ten years. He
was as decorated a naval captain as any who served King George.
She estimated his age at thirty-two and, considering that he'd
been married before, he was no stranger to women. His character vagaries had probably endowed her imagination tonight with
a fuzzy feel that made him seem comfortable. But there was no
mistaking the clipped English of his class. And who could ignore
that kind of British arrogance?

God, what had she been thinking?

She'd almost kissed Patrick's brother! How insane was that!

He'd certainly been quick enough to stuff her in a carriage
and send her home after that, polite as he was.

Elizabeth turned over, her young expression eager as she re-
joined Catherine's lethargy with a sleepy sigh. "How was your
evening, sister of mine? Were you pleased?"

The imagined impression of Julian Lambert's lips still lingering on hers like fire, Catherine gently nodded. "I was pleased."

Chapter Ten

Julian left the Yule ball five minutes after Catherine. Too rest-less to sleep, too moody to socialize, he returned to his Fran-cis Street town house. The insanity of his actions in the garden struck him anew. Yet if he could have tasted the berry punch on her lips, he would have wanted much more against the stone wall where she stood.

If she had been some other woman than who she was.

Michael sat at the dining table over a soft-boiled egg, tapping the shell slightly, when Julian entered.

"You're back just in time," Michael cheerfully declared as the wind picked up and storm clouds chased the sunlight from the sky. "I'm getting ready to leave. But I wanted to drop that by." He nodded to the thin packet at the end of the table. "Robbie is still doing a full check. But that is what I found out, brief as it is."

Julian set his cloak and bicorn over the chair, his gaze on the packet. "I never doubted your abilities."

Michael took a bite of egg. "She lives with her mother and younger siblings south of Yorktown. The only men about the house are an eight-year-old and a servant named Samuel. No one visits. Patrick married her at York-Hampton Episcopal like she told 'ye. Robbie hasn't yet procured the certificate, but I talked to the man who married them. Once a month she goes to Hope Plantation, where Patrick is buried, and clears the site of weeds. Including Susan's," he added, as if testing Julian's re-sponse.

Except Julian already knew that somebody had been tending the site.

"I just returned from Robbie's office. Enclosed is the deed to the building and land where the *Tidewater Clarion* sits."

With that, Michael tended to breakfast, leaving Julian to thumb through the papers. "Thank you," Julian finally said.

"Did you stay the night at the ever-pleasant Mistress Simms's abode?" Michael asked. "Not that a gentleman tells."

"Or asks." Julian removed his gloves and wig. "I stayed at the ball."

"You?" Michael laughed, his shock evident.

Julian's gaze lifted to confront his friend's smile.

"I've never known ye to be staying at any social gathering past ten."

"I felt responsibility for Mrs. Bellamy."

"Aye, but not for Mistress Simms."

Julian slid the deed out from beneath the papers and, without comment, walked to the bureau where he pulled out a quill and ink.

Michael stood and, gathering up his jacket and gloves, talked amiably about the change of weather.

As he was about to leave, Michael found Julian in the drawing room, his legs stretched out in a cushioned chair. A glass of brandy in hand, he'd closed his eyes, and slept the sleep of the dead.

"Mind you, something important is happening," Elizabeth walked into the upstairs room at the shop, her footsteps hurried on the planked flooring. "I can feel it in my bones."

Working beneath the dormer window in bright sunlight, Catherine applied the last dollop of violet across a vivid sunset. Her new stationery designs dried in the caged warmth at her back.

Elizabeth stripped off her cloak. "People are up in arms."

"About what, now?" Catherine concentrated on a snippet of yellow, frowning at the sudden smear she'd just made.

She couldn't concentrate. Twice this week she'd sat down with her stepmother to talk about her pregnancy. Once, Elizabeth had been the recipient of her efforts. She struggled to make sense out of her strange feelings for her staid brother-in-law.

"Someone has rented out the huge Sunderland estate at the edge of town." Elizabeth laid her cloak over the desk chair. "Prissy told us this morning when she and her momma came to pick up her winter gowns. She saw people walking around the place."

Catherine lowered the brush.

The Sunderland mansion had always made Catherine a little sad because it's vacancy represented the dying town as a whole. With the failure of so many tobacco plantations, many people had left the county forever. But not just anyone could afford such a place.

A prickle of unease went up her spine. "Who?"

"Obviously someone with wealth." Elizabeth picked up her newest design. "Ships?" She raised her gaze as Catherine snatched the paper. "I thought our clientele was mostly women."

"It is. But don't you think lilacs get monotonous and boring after a while?"

Elizabeth narrowed her eyes as if to peer into Catherine's brain. "You haven't been acting normal since the ball. Prissy said that you and Lord Blackmoor created quite a stir dancing and carrying on until dawn."

"Carrying on?" Snapping the paints shut, Catherine was out of her chair. Downstairs, Samuel was installing new shelves, and the hammering had begun again. The noise vibrated through her skull. "Good grief, Elizabeth." She rolled her eyes as she took the stairs from the loft. "We danced a few waltzes."

And watched the sunrise.

And almost melded lips while walking in the secluded gardens.

Gritting her teeth, she picked up her pace. Even if she weren't carrying another man's child, she could not be responsive to *that* man of specific notoriety. His political agenda alone deterred regard, and if that wasn't enough, his relationship to Patrick clenched her opinion completely. They had nothing in common. And the one link that bound them together in a society that separated them by class and wealth would eventually tear them apart.

Yet she found herself thinking of him constantly.

Catherine came to an abrupt halt, her hand freezing on the

rail. Behind her, Elizabeth gasped. Samuel stood at the open door.

Jed Tomkins, looking absurd carrying a bouquet of half-dead flowers, entered, followed by his four brothers. Since the night in the barn, she'd only seen him a few times in church. His sudden appearance bode ill. "Mizz Catherine?" Samuel queried. "Do you want me to fetch the lieutenant?"

"Shut up, old man," Jed snapped. "We didn't come here to talk to the lieutenant."

Catherine bristled in sudden umbrage. "How *dare* you treat Samuel as if he were the interloper. State your business, Mr. Tomkins. Then leave." She regarded each man in turn.

All four men were brawny-shouldered duplicates of the other, with their long brown hair and brown eyes, brown shirts and breeches. At twenty-five, Jed was the eldest. He was also a bully. Her biggest mistake would be in turning the other cheek.

"You've been a haughty thorn in all our sides for too long, Catherine." Jed's gaze went over the room. "Some of us here in town have decided it's high time you remarry. You ain't been mournin' the loss of yer husband so much, so we figure it doesn't matter that a year ain't passed."

"By the town's decision, you mean, or yours?"

"I haven't said a word about findin' you in my barn, Catherine. That should count fer some consideration."

His brother snickered. "Since he woke up in the barn, he's been in love with ye, Mizz Catherine."

Jed cuffed his younger brother. "Maybe I like the kind of woman what can stand up for herself." His eyes leered. "No one's going to argue my decision. Danny boy can't control ye, but I can."

"Get out! All of you!"

Jed put out an arm to restrain his other siblings.

"Hell's bells." The middle sibling glowered. "I told you she weren't going to be cooperative. Even with those flowers Ma gave you."

"Jed said that she had fire," still another chuckled, and Catherine looked at them all in comical disbelief. Except this wasn't amusing, and her heart pounded against her ribs. He was serious!

Jed hadn't moved, and Catherine fought the urge to go back up the stairs. "Maybe she thinks that brother-in-law makes her something extra special," the youngest said slyly. "We'll see how uppity she is after we got that pantywaist Lambert strung up to a tree."

"Be my guest. All of you." She pushed through them and opened the door. "March over to Norfolk and give it your best try."

Jed's brother elbowed him. "She doesn't know." He smiled into her bewildered countenance. "Some newspaperwoman."

"What?" she asked, alarmed. "What don't I know?"

Jed dropped the flowers at her feet. "I've bided my time long enough, princess. After today, there won't be no more courtin'."

Catherine slammed the door behind him. Leaning against the solid portal, she wanted to scream.

Catherine left her mount in the woods, the night broken only by a blackbird's trill. No wind moved the trees. Fog lifted off the river. Her cloak dragged in the dry leaves. She whirled when she heard Elizabeth's approach, relieved when her sister appeared.

Carrying a watch lantern, she looked ethereal in the mist. "What have you found out?" Catherine asked.

"You risk your life if you go to the meeting tonight, Rina."

Behind her, Ryan Miller stepped into the clearing. Drawing off his tricorn when he saw her, he looked around at the trees as if to make sure they were alone. "I'm sorry, Mizz Catherine. Your sister is correct. It's too dangerous. You're not one of us anymore. Many already are believin' there's a traitor in the camp. Da sent me here to tell you to go home."

"Is it true?" she asked Ryan. "Is the governor sending a warship here? Do you know which one?"

"Rumor has it that it's the *Chimera*." Ryan's hands worked the rim of his tricorn, his eyes beseeching. "I shouldn't be here."

Catherine started her pacing again. "And will her captain be killed? Or merely strung up and tarred and feathered like that customs official last year?"

"That's Jed Tomkins talking—"

"Is Daniel involved?" Catherine would find out herself.

He blocked her path. "No one is planning anything tonight."

"I'm sure Lord Blackmoor didn't get where he is at without possessing some courage," Elizabeth told her as they walked away. "I don't know why you're getting yourself worked up, Rina."

Catherine didn't want Lord Blackmoor here. She'd prayed that he wouldn't be the one the governor sent.

Only God never listened to anything.

Three days later, Catherine was in the shop when she heard the commotion outside on the streets. The *Chimera* had been spotted.

Running down the stairs and out of the shop to the foggy bluffs, she watched the river with a score of other people. Faded sunlight blanketed the bay like an approaching winter frost. Catherine shivered in the chill. She didn't have to strain to hear the muffled sound of block and sheaves and, as she watched, a gust of wind seemed to dispense the mist.

A stab of incredulity joined the sudden race of fear that clenched her stomach as the *Chimera* sailed into full view of the town, the might of the British in all her staid glory.

Separated by more than size from the rank of sloops and fishing ketches that filled the river, the majestic three-masted frigate passed through the current with all the subtlety of a lion come to roost among sheep. Despite herself, Catherine's gaze was glued to the graceful beauty of the spectacle. Blue pennants rode the highest masts, the foremost being the red-and-gold Blackmoor crest riding aft of King George's imperial banner and flag of Britain. Finally, slipping in and out of wisps of fog, her masts disappeared.

"Perhaps Lord Blackmoor will tend to your request about the shop now that he is here." Elizabeth laid Catherine's cloak over her shoulders.

Yet, as Catherine stared at the approaching ship and remembered the man who captained her, the *Tidewater Clarion* ceased to concern her.

In the dying light of day, she knew a danger far greater than the brewing political turmoil that surrounded her. More dangerous even than the shimmering memory of Merlin's touch.

Captain Julian Lambert had finally come home.

And as she watched, the mist closed over the ship.

"Oh, milord!" A woman's shrill voice made Julian flinch. "Sally has never behaved so boldly before."

"I can walk, thank you, madam."

"I don't know what to say."

"Nothing!" Julian dusted off his sleeves. The door slammed behind him. "You don't need to say anything." Two children barreled past to take up a flanking position beside the thin blond woman wearing a blue silk dress. By the color and shape of her blue eyes, she looked to be their mother.

Plants cluttered the hallway. Readjusting his periwig, Julian straightened his uniform jacket and barely missed a hanging pot. Blossoms draped to the floor like a deranged bridal gown.

Aye, since his arrival to Yorktown, he'd debated coming to this place. Especially when his solicitor could have handled his business here. With the deed in his pocket, he stood there now feeling ridiculous. It was approaching dusk, and he had work to do at the ship.

"This is the Bellamy residence?" he asked, somewhat doubtful of his memory.

"Oh, please, milord. I mean," her nervous gaze dropped to his foot, "allow Anna to take a look at your foot. You could be hurt."

With her round, happy features and bright green dress, Anna looked like a plump leprechaun. He relieved his bicorn from her grasp before that, too, met with disaster. "Do you people always have a pig running free around your yard?"

"Sally is part of the family. She just has never come on the porch before. I don't know what got into her. Do you, Anna?"

"Sally likes him." The little girl giggled.

The two children continued to stare up at him in awe. "If Mrs. Bellamy isn't here, then perhaps it is better that I leave my card—"

"Nonsense, milord. She will be back shortly. . . ." The blond looked befuddled. "Where did she say she was going, Anna? She's been all aflustered since your ship came in, milord."

"Are you going to blow up our house?" the boy asked.

"Of course he isn't," the little girl scoffed. "*Are* you?"

"Rina says to stay away from the English soldiers because they are bad," the boy said. "Are you an English soldier?"

"He is a naval officer," their mother explained. "Captain Lambert is your uncle Patrick's brother."

The little girl's eyes widened in astonishment. "Rina said that you were even worser than the English soldiers."

Both children suddenly fell silent beneath his scrutiny.

"Go. The both of ye." The plump leprechaun shooed them both off. "Get Samuel over here to fix the porch."

The banshees raced down the hall. Anna fluttered her hands when the door slammed. "Little ones. They are a handful."

The blond straightened. "I'll have Millie fetch us some crumpets and my willow bark tea. We are not drinking East India tea. Catherine is adamant that we honor the embargo." Taking in his uniform, her eyes widened a fraction. "I . . ."

"Your tea would be refreshing, thank you."

"Anna, see to our guest. I will fetch the tea."

"When did you say she would return?" Julian asked Anna when they were alone. "Mrs. Bellamy," he patiently explained.

"Lately, our Catherine has spent a lot of time at the shop," Anna replied with an airy wave of her plump hand. "Especially since your arrival here in Yorktown. We never know when she will return."

Limping slightly, Julian followed her into the parlor. Aghast at the catastrophe that had hit the room, he froze in his tracks. Toy soldiers lined the floor at his feet and dangled from red thread hanging from the bookcases. Satins, silks, and half-made bodices draped the chairs and tables like a medical experiment gone awry. The scarlet curtains were open. All that remained of the day was a scrappy indigo halo that lingered over the treetops.

"We weren't expecting guests." Anna nervously scooped up cloth. "I fear I am the only decent seamstress in town. And it never hurts our coffers to bring in that little bit extra. We outfitted many a local lady for the celebration in Williamsburg two weeks ago."

Stepping over the toys, Julian perched on the settee, cautious not to impale himself on the scattered pincushions.

"The governor's ball?"

"You know him?"

"His cook makes the finest blackberry cheesecake." His gaze idled to the potted plants near the long window.

"We have a secret recipe, too," she whispered conspiratorially. "Pig dung. You should try it."

Speechless, Julian stared at her.

"Plants." She pointed to the potted shrubs as if he were daft. "We raise chrysanthemums. But this year we thought we'd have to eat Sally. That's why I've taken on extra clients. For the mums," she patiently reiterated.

Somehow, Julian resisted rubbing the ache in his temples.

"Catherine painted those. . . ." In a nonstop verbal marathon, the woman pointed out the various portraitures that stair-stepped up the nearby wall. "Except for the one of herself. Her brother painted that one only this year. Her father said that she and her brother had the talent of da Vinci. Do you know who da Vinci is?"

"Aye." He decided that she and Michael would get along famously. They both enjoyed hearing themselves talk. "I've heard of him. Your daughter is Catherine Bellamy then?"

"Not *my* daughter, sir. I am merely the housekeeper. Our Catherine is Mistress Claremont's stepdaughter."

Julian felt his heart pause. He turned his head. "Claremont?"

"Yes." Her face red from exertion, she laid the cloth in her arms over the nearest chair. "He died two years ago. We don't know what would have happened to us if not for our Catherine."

His gaze moved to the portrait of an older, distinguished man wearing the Welsh uniform of his regiment. A knot began to form in his gut. He suddenly stood. His tall black boots creaked with the sudden agitation of his movement.

The blond woman bustled in with a tray. "Millie is making crumpets. Do sit down. You must take the weight off your foot."

"Your name is Claremont?" he asked without turning away from the portrait.

"Why, yes," she said with obvious pride as she poured Julian a steaming cup of tea. "I'm Tabitha Claremont."

Taking the cup, Julian absently sipped.

"My Daniel commanded the Twenty-third Royal Welsh Fusiliers. Did you know him?"

He spewed the black tea back in the cup.

"Oh my." Rushing to set the teapot down on the tray, Tabitha touched his arm. "Are you all right? Did I make the tea too strong?"

Feeling the sudden twist in his stomach tighten, Julian pulled his gaze from the diminutive woman to the smaller portraitures of blond-haired imps until he stopped on the young man. Brown hair, once sun-washed blond, fringed the youth's blue eyes. "These are your other children?" His voice came out strained.

He hadn't thought to ask Michael that day on the ship if there might be another Claremont. A junior maybe.

"I have four children." The woman smiled from beside him. She pointed out each of them, giving histories and identities that he didn't care a fig to know.

Finally he could put a face to the elusive Daniel Claremont. And worse.

He'd done far worse than sleep with his brother's wife.

". . . Catherine is my stepdaughter," the woman was saying, "that is her father over there. The one you were looking at earlier."

Julian could not pull his gaze away from the last portraiture: a finely boned beauty tenderly painted by the artist. His gloved hand closed around the fragile teacup and saucer. He was acutely aware of his strength and the reality that he could crush that cup.

The vision fed his memory. Recklessly bathed in moonlight, her black hair swirled around her oval face like a midnight tempest. A pair of lips formed into a half-moon smile. The light from the lamp touched her dark eyes. Eyes that spoke to him in a seductive, familiar whisper.

Lying, deceitful eyes.

All along, she'd been protecting Daniel Claremont. How much time had he already lost because he thought the name a ruse!

"Bloody hell!"

He set the saucer and cup down on the table. China rattled with the force of his emotions.

"My lord," Mrs. Claremont sputtered. "Did we do something wrong?"

He narrowed his eyes but could not summon the words to reply. Were they really that blind to the truth? Or as stupid as they acted?

With a word to the governor, he could have them arrested, at the very least for seditious involvement with the Sons of Liberty, at the most for the cold-blooded murder of his brother.

"I'm quite fine, Mrs. Claremont." Walking to the door, he turned. "I'll leave my card, if I may." He didn't say more. He didn't trust the words that might betray him. Didn't trust himself.

His gaze went around the room. This wasn't the home of murderers. Hard work and love had gone into the creation of this room as well as the clothes that littered the furniture. The house was filled with living things: plants, paintings, laughing children.

Yet, as he made his way back through the cluttered hallway, one thought possessed Julian to the exclusion of all else. Catherine had lied to him about knowing Daniel Claremont from the beginning.

"Will you be in our town long?" Tabitha asked.

"No." His voice was flat. "I'm afraid my time here is limited."

Too limited, he thought, realizing how much time he'd already wasted searching shadowed corners for clues when Claremont had been beneath his nose the whole time. The two women dogging his heels barely missed slamming into him as he swung open the front door. A thin black man, hammer in hand, peered up from the bottom stair on the porch he was repairing. A watch lantern provided the only light. The air smelled damp with fog.

Julian's gaze swung to the hitching post and fell at once on the wonder pig sitting primly where his horse should have been.

"Oh my," Tabitha Claremont voiced with extreme understatement. The words bordered on panic. "Your horse is gone."

His jaw clamped shut.

"Oh my . . ." she gasped. "*Ohmyohmyohmy.*"

"Mrs. Claremont." He ushered her inside for fear that she'd faint. "I'll find my way home."

"But you cannot. Truly, my lord . . . There is no moon tonight." She blinked back tears and, for all of Julian's fury, he took pity on her. No woman could suffer so many blunders all in one evening and not be blackballed from the social scene for an eternity.

"The walk to town isn't that long. I'll make it," he said. "My horse will find his own way back."

Julian shut the door. Slowly exhaling, he turned his glare on the damn pig, and he knew a sudden appetizing urge for pork chops.

Chapter Eleven

Before Julian had limped a mile down the road, he sensed he was being followed. The foggy terrain amplified sound, and he moved over the slick ground to a better vantage point. The road was enclosed on one side by bushes and open to a slow-moving creek on the other.

The rider approached at a cautious lope, and Julian let a grim smile touch his mouth. A cloak wrapped the slim figure, covering her face but not her identity. Even if he didn't recognize the gray horse, he knew the rider intimately enough to momentarily forget that she'd barely been a widow when she'd slept with Merlin, that she'd lied about her brother, that her being out on this road was highly suspect, especially when he knew these woods crawled with thieves.

Without giving her the opportunity to bolt, Julian stepped out of the trees and yanked her off the saddle. She reacted at once. Twisting and screaming, she drove an elbow into his ribs. With an oath, he slipped and rolled with her fighting beneath him. Awareness of her roared through him hotter than black rum.

"You!" Her lungs heaved with the fight. "Get off me!"

She smelled of English nutmeg, and if she didn't cease her struggles, he'd put his tongue in her mouth and continue what they'd begun months ago. "You will understand that with the current turmoil I had no idea who might be following me. More than one man has been robbed of his goods and his life in the area."

"That naturally explains your wont to throw unsuspecting strangers off their horses and lie on them," she snapped.

"Naturally." Allowing his gaze to go over her mouth before returning to her furious eyes, he smiled. "I'm a cautious man. Especially when someone approaches me on a night like this."

"Get off me!" She renewed her struggle, bucking futilely.

Julian lifted his head. A moment ago, he thought he'd heard horses. A cursory glance around told him that the gray had wandered down the road. Curb chains rattled from his bit. The fog continued to thicken around them. He had to get to his men.

"Stay here," he ordered her.

With a smattering of dislodged leaves, he melded like a wraith to the shadows. Silence ensued. A racoon waddled across the path and scurried through the leaves down the hill.

Catherine came to her feet. "My Lord?" No response followed.

Moving forward, she conceded a few inches to the shadows. She possessed the acute impression of hazel eyes watching her back from the darkness. And an awful sense that she'd played out this scenario before plunged her into panic. There was no help for her pounding heart. "Are you still here? Say something."

Towing the reins of her horse, Captain Lambert moved into the fractured moonlight that crisscrossed the road. Tall, black boots hugged his calves. Anna was correct. A limp marked his step. In the shadows, his eyes were an inky jet. He looked at her a long moment before asking, "Did I hurt you?"

Catherine remembered her bruised backside and brushed off the leaves. "I'll live." Considering that *she'd* landed on him.

"Why the bloody hell are you out on a night like this?" The strength of his anger took her by surprise,

"Trying to find you. I had no idea you were prone to attacking people on the roads. Momma said that you'd been hurt. I brought you a horse."

He made a great pretense to look around her. "An invisible horse? Christ, why does that not surprise me?"

"Of course *not* an invisible horse."

"If you give me your mount, how are *you* going to get home?"

The faraway rumble of horses suddenly came to them both. Their eyes touched, and she read the accusation. Reaching into her saddlebag, Catherine withdrew a pistol. "Maybe I came after you because I don't want to see you killed," she said.

A brow lifted. "Do you think one pistol will be enough?"

Lord in heaven, he was an ass.

His hand wrapped around her arm. A slight incline took them over a ditch through branches and bushes. As the other horses neared, the gelding tossed his head. Captain Lambert soothed the horse. She lifted her gaze from the gloved hand that moved with gentle reassurance. For a jack-tar, her brother-in-law knew his way around a horse. His head moved slightly, and she suddenly found herself caught in his gaze. His heat wrapped around her.

But her instinct for survival warned that his reason for being in Yorktown did not bode well for her family. Where Patrick's death inadvertently brought her into Blackmoor's arena of warfare, Daniel's life kept her on guard. Indeed, why hadn't he *asked* her about Daniel? He'd been to her house. He must surely know the truth by now.

The ground vibrated beneath her feet. By strength of will, Captain Lambert kept the horse from bolting. Seven men on horseback and an empty wagon thundered past. In the shrouded darkness, she couldn't tell their identities. She could only pray Daniel wasn't with them.

Then the pounding in her ears dissipated. She spread the branches and looked out. Dust lingered where the horses had passed. In the silence that followed, she was aware that Patrick's brother continued to calm the nervous gelding.

"You're very good with animals." She came to stand beside the gray. "For a man of the sea."

"Anything can be tamed, Mrs. Bellamy," he said without looking at her. "Or brought around to my will. Given the right persuasion."

His eyes found hers.

"Are you threatening me?" She stared at him in disbelief.

"Those men were the second group of riders down this road tonight. Do you have anything to do with their sudden camaraderie?"

"Don't you think if I was one of them, I would have stepped out onto the road just now and waved my white flag?"

He snatched the pistol out of her hands, carefully, laying

down the hammer. "Perhaps you knew well enough what would happen if I was caught. Perhaps you don't have a stomach for murder."

"Give me back my pistol."

Shoving the pistol behind him in his waistband, he walked past her out of the bushes. He swung his gaze up and down the road.

"Is that why you came to my house? To interrogate my family because you think we're involved in something illegal?"

Leading the horse, he started walking. She glared at his broad back, trying not to admit that his attitude hurt. Especially since the governor's ball had left a profound impression of him on her mind. Captain Julian Lambert was typical of British gentry, so his arrogance shouldn't have bothered her. He was also a naval officer, so she wasn't surprised that he'd be alert to rebels, especially after what happened when a British customs schooner ran aground in Rhode Island a year before. Colonists had actually burned the ship. She was, however, interested in his reasons for coming all the way out to her house and what he might now know about her.

"Well?" she prompted when he didn't answer.

"Is it so abnormal that you would have a caller?"

"Only you, my lord."

Pine needles muffled the sounds of their steps. Something about him suddenly seemed vulnerable. Her gaze dropped to his limp. "What happened to your foot?" she asked. "No one told me exactly."

He yanked uneasily at his stock. For an instant, she didn't think he'd heard her question. "The bloody pig stepped on my toe," he said. "I'm afraid your porch didn't stand up to her weight."

Catherine choked. Since the worry of finding Blackmoor murdered on the road was over, the moment somehow seemed right to notice the staid captain's discomfort, and she suddenly laughed.

"Climb on. I'm not walking the rest of the way to town. Neither are you."

Catherine refused to budge. Maybe it was the past few months and her dementia over Reece that made Captain Lambert seem more than familiar, for it certainly wasn't his appearance. "Hold out your hands," she commanded. He looked at her as if she'd gone daft. "Please?"

He did as she asked. He wore gloves. Her hands felt small beside his. She wondered if he was as adept with a cutlass as he was at taming hard-to-manage horses. Catherine pressed the sensitive pads of her fingers against his, kneading his lower knuckles for a ring.

Nothing. Her throat tightened. For an instant, she'd been so sure that Merlin had somehow managed to pull a hoax on them all. What was she thinking, anyway? That he'd slipped beneath the staid British admiralty? That Merlin was really a lord and a decorated captain in His Majesty's Royal Navy? Or even that he'd stolen Julian Lambert's identity? God . . . she wanted to die of embarrassment.

Flustered by her forwardness and irrefutable idiocy, she met her brother-in-law's gaze. The lift of his brow did much to challenge her sobriety. Catherine waited for him to say something sarcastic.

She didn't wait long. "Where did my brother find you, exactly?"

Catherine wanted to kick him in the shins. Instead, she struggled to shove her foot into the stirrup. Her brother-in-law boosted her into the saddle and climbed behind her. "On second thought," he said against her hair, "where did he find your whole family?"

"You are very rude, my lord."

He was also warm. But it wasn't until her starchy brother-in-law squirmed away from her did she decide her pride wasn't worth freezing over. Feeling secure by his prudish reaction to her, she allowed herself to indulge in the comfort of his warm arms.

Perhaps she had overestimated his interest in Patrick's life. Maybe he hadn't hired Reece, like she had originally thought. With the exception of his earlier accusation, Blackmoor had yet to query her about his brother or the activities in this area. Unless he was saving that for the tribunal. And she didn't buy the balderdash that he'd visited her house on a social call.

But before she could interrogate him—or even decide how she could—the Sunderland estate appeared out of the fog like an overdressed lady at a barn dance. Mulberry trees framed the circular drive. The fragrant canopy of green did not draw her gaze from the imposing red brick and frame three-story house. Candlelight burned in each of the five upstairs windows. Two great chimneys braced each side of the house. Blackmoor climbed off the back of the horse as three men walked from the direction of the stables. While her brother-in-law instructed his groomsman, she noted on closer inspection that weeds had overgrown the garden.

Before she could protest, Blackmoor lifted her off the horse.

"I can't stay."

He placed his hand possessively beneath her elbow. Tall, imposing, and completely rude, he walked her up the steps to his house, slowing as one of his men told him that his horse had not yet returned. From the corner of her eye, Catherine caught other men ambling near the terrace. Certainly, His Lordship was taking no chances with his safety while he lived in Yorktown.

She squared her shoulders. "Captain—"

The door swung open, spilling warm light onto the marble steps. A tall, wiry man dressed in black appeared in the doorway.

"Sir . . ."

"Boswell, meet Catherine Bellamy, Patrick's long-lost wife." He brushed past the servant. "Mrs. Bellamy, meet Boswell, my steward."

Catherine barely had time to greet the man before Julian spoke to his servant. Gauzy spiderwebs laced the huge chandelier where six meager candles sputtered light. Sidling closer to her brother-in-law, she grimaced. There were probably huge spiders in this place.

"After you've settled her in, send two men to her house to let her family know that I'll return her as soon as the fog lifts."

Catherine yanked her arm from his grasp. "But that won't be until tomorrow."

"And tell my men to stay off the roads." His gaze dropped to hers. "As a gentleman, as your brother-in-law"—with a yank on his sleeve a lacy kerchief appeared—"I am responsible for your welfare."

"You are a knave, my lord. This is kidnapping."

He blotted at the pine sap on his gloves. The sticky residue stained his pristine uniform as well. "Because I refuse to let you out alone on a night like this?"

She crossed her arms beneath her breasts. "What do you plan on doing? About those men we saw tonight?"

"Have they broken the law? Do you know who they are?"

"They are Patrick's friends," she said, "which will never make them mine."

For a long time, he looked at her. Then his gaze found Boswell. "Take her upstairs."

"Yes, sir."

Blackmoor couldn't keep her prisoner. She'd climb out the bloody window.

Touching the banister, her hand came away with dust. Dust layered everything. Trudging up the stairs and down a long hallway, Catherine followed the silent Boswell up another flight of stairs.

"Does he think to lock me in tonight?" she asked when the manservant finally came to a halt in front of a sturdy oaken door. A cool, brine-scented draft wrapped around her.

"No, mum." He opened the door for her to enter.

Stepping inside the room, she wrapped her cloak around her body. A bed faced an open window. A wardrobe and secretary matched the cherry bedstead and nightstand where amber light flickered from a brass lamp. Old ivory curtains billowed slightly in the breeze.

"Then why is he putting me in the attic?"

"Guest rooms aren't ready, mum. I've only been here a few days. This is my room. The linens are fresh. The place is clean."

"I didn't mean to insult—"

"A pitcher of water and towels are on the commode behind that curtain. As is anything else you might be needing."

"Boswell?" she said as he turned to go. "How long have you known His Lordship?"

His gray eyes peered at her from beneath bushy gray brows. "I have served him since he was a lad in Cornwall."

Long, white hair reached his shoulders. A bulbous nose distinguished his narrow face. Catherine would have recognized this man easily if she'd seen him before. "Does he plan to stay long?"

Boswell's eyebrows lowered, and he suddenly reminded her of her old knuckle-cracking tutor. Catherine flinched guiltily. She'd overstepped the bounds of etiquette with her question. But for some reason, she didn't want this man to think her an uncouth colonial. She'd wanted only to gauge Lord Blackmoor's intentions.

Catherine suddenly realized that she was frightened.

"I will ask him. Thank you, Boswell." She smiled kindly.

He didn't like her; she could tell.

After he left, Catherine slumped against the door. She should have left Blackmoor on the road to fend for himself. Nothing good ever came out of being noble. The last time she'd tried to do something right, she'd ended up hunted and dragged around the countryside in chains for a week.

And pregnant!

Catherine opened the bedroom door and peered out. A single wall sconce lit the narrow hallway. The big house was eerily quiet. She exited the room and gritted her teeth when the floor creaked. Hurrying down the top flight of stairs, she reached the second-floor hallway. Beside her, a bedroom door stood ajar. A quick survey of the hallway emboldened her, and she crept forward to edge the door open.

A roaring fire in the stone hearth warmed the air. Pulled into the room by the warm glow, Catherine let her gaze wander in awe. Chinese hand-painted wallpaper framed the walls in a gilded production of exotic vines and flowers. Gathering closer to the rare artwork, she ran a hand along its design. She'd never seen its like anywhere. But it was the rococo bedstead half hidden beneath crimson and gold velvet hangings that dominated the room.

Her heartbeat quickened. Something about the earl of Blackmoor underscored the instinct to run. The threat stretched beyond fear for her brother's life in ways that she didn't understand.

Catherine spun to leave. And fell into Blackmoor's gaze. He leaned with his arms crossed in the doorway, watching her. "You are finding your way around my room all right? Perhaps I should have left my secret maps and papers out on the desk."

His inordinate self-possession made her wary. She pictured him on the deck of his warship, wearing the same captain's facade as he stared down his enemies, right before he blew them out of the water.

Snatching her cloak tighter about her, she dismissed all pretense of innocence and threw her crimes back at him. Clearly, he had been somewhere close, waiting for her to escape, to have snuck up on her at all. "Do you always spy on your guests?"

"One can never be too sure who is lurking around in my bedroom."

"No doubt you are plagued with women since your arrival."

His mouth softened in a way that she remembered from the ball. "Boswell said that you didn't like the attic room."

"There is nothing wrong with the room," she said quietly.

"Then can I get you anything before you go back upstairs?"

Garbed in a royal blue evening robe that hugged his broad shoulders and sashed his waist, he still wore the white wig. Like all men who dabbled in the English fashion plate, he probably shaved his head beneath. Normally, on any other man, the picture invoked was ludicrous. Not so on Lord Blackmoor.

A tall clock in the entryway began to chime. "I need to use the . . . necessary," she blurted out.

His eyes traveled over her, and she wondered at the private joke. Shoving off the wall, he led her downstairs to the expansive hallway. He stopped in front of a closet. "The room has been cleaned. There is a pitcher of water inside. A cloth is hanging on the wall for your convenience," he said as if he conferred with women on a daily basis about the proper science of using the necessary.

His hand went to the latch before hers. "Your cloak first."

Reluctantly, she parted with her wrap and dropped it on the floor at his feet. A corner of his mouth lifted. "I'll wait here . . . in case you should need help."

She slammed the door behind her. Once inside the closet, she rushed to the window. Gripping both hands on the sill, she glared out at the darkness. Even if she'd kept her cloak, the casement was too narrow to make an escape. Forsooth! The man left nothing to chance!

When she finally concluded her business, she splashed water on her face to calm her stomach. She found her jailer patiently awaiting her exit. "Are you hungry?" He no longer had her cloak.

"Is that what you ask all of your captives?"

Ignoring the barb, he shoved off the wall. She hastily followed. The elegant robe swirled around his ankles and, availed of this new view, she allowed her gaze to wander. Admittedly, he lacked nothing in the way of appearance from this side.

Snatching her gaze back, she glanced at the dusty brass wall sconces and cornices carved out of the high ceiling. "Don't British captains stay on their ships till death do you part, so to speak?"

"The governor thought it a sign of goodwill if I took a house in town while here."

"Naturally, with a troop of Royal Marines guarding the docks, Lord Dunmore would think that wise. Are all British officers so noble and accessible to the common masses?"

He stopped, and she nearly collided with his chest. "Perhaps you want to know my foot size? Or what flavor tooth powder I use?"

"Do you still think those men tonight were my friends?"

He didn't answer. Nor did he betray any inkling of his thoughts. Clearly, a tree stump was more forthcoming, so she shelved her interrogation for another time.

Noting that they'd entered the dining room, her interest heightened. She stopped when her gaze fell on a tray laden with warm pumpkin bread, fruit, and a glass of chilled milk. Her heart leapt and, pouncing on the milk, she could not contain the gasp of delight.

She swung to face him. "You have no idea how starved I am." The milk slid down her throat and left a delicious mustache when she was finished. Peering up at her brother-in-law, she licked the white stuff off her mouth. Her smile faded. He had already turned away.

"This room isn't ready to receive guests." He moved to the doorway, an invitation for her to leave. "You can take the food back upstairs. I'm sure you're tired."

Carefully, she set down the glass. Twelve empty chairs sat at attention around the long mahogany table. A large dusty candelabrum provided scant light. Still, as she looked around at the plush furniture and fine porcelain in the immense sideboard, she couldn't help but be impressed by the wealth displayed. Eating alone suddenly didn't appeal to her.

She picked at the bread. The heavenly slice melted on her tongue. "Is my horse being taken care of?"

"Stabled and fed."

Reluctantly, she wrapped the warm bread in her napkin, then wrapped her plate. "Very well." She walked across the dining room, only to stop before Blackmoor, who suddenly seemed disinclined to move out of her way. Beneath the robe, she glimpsed a sprinkling of dark hair where his collar opened at his neck.

"I'll return to my room," she said. "Only because I'm exhausted," she decided to add, lest he thought that he could keep her here against her will.

He barred her exit with his arm. Her eyes chased up to his. Except for their time together on the horse, it was the closest he'd come to touching her all evening. Her breasts brushed his arm and, without his uniform, she felt the hard muscles beneath his sleeve.

"I have just one question." He searched her eyes. "Did you love my brother?"

Catherine struggled to keep her breath even. She wanted to say no. But no anger jumped to her defense, only the truth. Patrick had been debonair and unafraid of anything. He'd given her back her life after her father died. He'd made her laugh with joy. He'd given her the newspaper because he'd believed in her talent; then he'd given her purpose and a reason to fight.

She nodded her head, aware that tears blurred her eyes. She was suddenly so tired of running from shame, of fighting for redemption, that she would not allow her brother-in-law to believe that they'd been less than a perfect couple.

"I loved him," she said quietly, "with all my heart."

For an instant, something showed in his eyes: pain, gratitude, maybe anger; she couldn't tell, nor did she understand. He raised his gaze to her hair. Then his arm dropped and he started to turn.

Catherine caught his robe, just above his heart. "Captain—"

Her touch jolted him. His gaze fell first on the curve of her hand, then raised slowly to her face. She pulled her hand back. "You're not what I expected when I went to Norfolk to find you."

"Indeed." He spun away.

"For instance"—she followed him down the long hall and up the stairs—"you were tolerant of Sally tonight."

"Because I didn't eat her? Don't think I've thrown out that option."

"Everyone says that you're a man who grants no quarter. Some have called you a pompous bastard. And not the fatherless kind." She nearly collided with his back when he stopped and turned. "You're very famous, my lord. As I can attest to by the attention you received in Williamsburg."

"I don't deny what I am, Mrs. Bellamy."

She clutched the plate. "They also claim that you're afraid of ghosts. That's why you haven't been back here in years."

"But you don't believe that."

Attempting to put space between them, she backed a step and hit the wall. A tangle of conflicting emotion tightened her stomach. "Any man who has stayed at sea as long as you have, only something powerful enough to eclipse your distaste for this place would bring you back here at all." Her voice held uncertainty. What did he know about her? And why had it taken so long for him to finally come here? "What say you to that, my lord?"

He trapped her between his arms, filling her senses with carnal heat. His gaze slid over her mouth to swim in her eyes. She blinked with sudden vigilance, and he seemed to welcome the shock in her eyes. Beside her, the door to his room swung ajar. "I'd say that if you follow me any farther, we'll end up in my bedroom again." He lowered his mouth to her hair. "I might not be able to restrain myself this time. Even if you do talk too much."

"Oh!" She pushed at him. "Perhaps I deserve the threat for prowling your room earlier," she conceded with amazing calm when her knees wanted to buckle. "But I know enough to recognize that a man who forgives an uncouth pig for stepping on his foot would not hurt a woman. Even if he did act the ass at our first meeting."

Amusement played at the corners of his beautiful mouth. But he pulled back slightly, and she could breathe again. "Don't depend on your woman's intuition to read my mind, Catherine. You'd lose."

She leveled a stare at him. "What made you finally decide that I spoke the truth about being married to your brother?"

"You purchased the granite headstone on Patrick's grave. Had I opened my mail sooner, I'd have seen the receipt my solicitor sent."

"Then you've been to the grave site?"

"Did you think I wouldn't go to the place where my own

brother was buried? You don't know me at all. And there's something else you need to know." His finger went beneath her chin. "I'm here to hang his murderer. My methods used to find the man will not be kind. They will not be gentle. But they will be precise, and anyone standing in my way will be a casualty."

He took the breath from her voice. The eyes that searched hers were deliberate. "You're either with me or against me."

For an unguarded heartbeat, she wanted to touch him. "I don't know who killed Patrick, I swear."

His expression loomed furious. "Someone with ties to one Daniel Claremont *junior* surely extols virtues at its highest plane. How fortunate that you failed to tell me in Norfolk of your family ties to a certain seedy element of this whole damn county."

"I told you that I had a brother. He's an artist." The wall at her back granted her no room. "I want Patrick's killer brought to justice, too. But after you hang the felon, what happens when you leave, Captain? This is my home. My family and I will still be here. Where will your sweeping justice be then?"

He dropped his arms but conceded little room for her to squeeze past him. "Then maybe you should move."

The olive branch she'd tried to extend snapped. "For an instant I thought that I'd misjudged you. I'm relieved to know which side we are both on." If she were evil, she'd step on his foot. But that would entail touching him. "Good night, Captain Lambert."

Her throat was suddenly tight. Then, gripping the plate to her chest, Catherine squeezed past. Julian crossed his arms, and even as he looked away, he fought the pull to follow her. To taste again the sweet magic she'd once presented him, the travesty of his position prickling like the proverbial thorn.

Aye, she was clever to read him so thoroughly. But his ghosts marked him well and good as a knave or a bastard as some would claim. For though she sensed many things about him, she didn't understand completely that which drove him now.

Upstairs, almost above his head, Catherine's door clicked shut. Movement in his bedroom pulled him around. Julian met Boswell's gaze and knew that his manservant had glimpsed the raw hunger in his eyes.

"Your uniform is cleaned, my lord," Boswell said to the silence.

"She knows who I am." Even to Julian, his voice sounded on edge and restless, a dangerous combination for a man who needed to keep his wits about him tonight. "Julian Lambert could be hidden beneath a pound of rice powder, and she would still guess the truth of it. She just hasn't pieced together the logic of it all, yet."

He shoved away from the wall and walked past Boswell into his bedroom. Stripping off the robe, he tossed it on the bed, furious that he'd allowed sentimentality to overrule innate sense. He should never have gone to that asylum she called a house in the first place!

"Any news from my men?"

"A Lieutenant Ross came by with a Sergeant Masters."

Boswell helped Julian shrug into his uniform jacket. "Masters?"

"Yes, sir, and I did some checking like you asked. He's been in this area for three months. He didn't even know Patrick."

"Maybe not. But he's getting his information from someone." The floor above him creaked. Boswell hesitated.

Julian turned his head. His servant's stoic composure fairly cracked for wont of not stumbling over his thoughts.

"I can handle Catherine Bellamy."

"Yes, my lord." Boswell stood back. "You want me to keep my mouth closed on the matter."

Drawing on his gloves, Julian could not summon the anger for a reprimand. "No," he strapped on his saber. "But I do want you to see her safely returned to her home the instant the fog lifts in the morning. She's not any safer here with me than out there."

He also knew that if he didn't stay away from her, she'd cost him his life. She was too bloody dangerous to his identity.

He couldn't gauge her character. Neither did he believe that her current loyalties to her brother gave her an open mind, and he resented her lies, no matter the rationale. His honor locked him in a cause that took no prisoners, including her.

And no matter the nights he'd spent thinking about her, he simply could not surrender the reality that she'd belonged to Patrick, palpable as his memory of her was.

Turning on his heel, Julian quit the room. "Tomorrow, contact my solicitor. Tell him Daniel Claremont is alive, after all."

At the bottom of the stairs, he paused long enough to swing his heavy cloak around his shoulders. His gaze found Boswell standing on the landing above him. "And I *want* him found."

Chapter Twelve

Thankful for the cover of darkness, Catherine switched to a back trail halfway home. Something terrible had happened to her last night. Nudging her gray, she continued on her way. She'd barely escaped Julian's manse. Boswell had seen her leave the yard. Let him report to His Lordship that she'd escaped. She didn't dare stay in that house until daylight. She'd had to leave! A chill hit her face, and she pulled her cloak tighter, narrowing her eyes to negotiate the path. Somewhere a horse snorted and, her heart racing, she reined in to gauge the direction.

Her breathing sounded staggered and erratic in the predawn mist. Another sound fell around her: the faint stir of bridle chains. The sound of horsemen.

Her nerves were too raw. Her stomach churned, and she closed her eyes to let the nausea pass. The roads crawled with soldiers. Why?

Dismounting near her stable, Catherine entered the yard and pressed against the side of the barn. Sally was nowhere. Her gaze tracked the silence to the house.

A hand covered over her mouth. Followed at once by a whisper that brushed her ear. "It's me, Rina. Don't fight."

Daniel!

Easing his hand away, he placed a finger on her lips and motioned with his hand that someone might be in the woods. She turned as he dropped a knife back in its sheath. The quick, proficient movement startled her. Her gaze shifted back to him.

A faint smile parted his lips. "I didn't know if it was you."

"And if it wasn't, would you have killed me?"

Eyes narrowing, he took the horse and pulled her into the stable. Sally fidgeted and squealed her disapproval at being tied. Catherine knelt beside the pig.

Movement just outside the rim of lantern light stopped her from asking why her brother was here. She and Daniel weren't alone. In the shadows, three men sat on barrels near the wall with muskets braced against their knees. One wore a bloodied bandage. Another, a makeshift sling. Two more men braced the wooden pilings against the door, and still another stood against the stall where Sally was locked and tied. All wore dark green or black. With their bearded countenances and expressions ravaged by exhaustion, most looked mean.

Her gaze fell on Ryan Miller, Daniel's friend. He sat slumped next to a bale of hay. Blood covered the front of his shirt.

"We walked into a trap," Daniel said. "Lambert was waiting for us at our rendezvous point. Two of our men were shot."

Catherine walked to the bucket where Samuel usually kept his drinking water. Sick to her stomach, she slipped a knife from the sheath on the wall and sliced off part of her petticoat. "Have you gone completely mad?" Panic underscored her voice. "Ryan needs medical attention. I'm no doctor."

Catherine knelt and opened Ryan's shirt. She removed the soiled rag someone had already placed there. A ragged tear in his flesh oozed blood. Her hand stilled. Catherine felt helpless. How did one dig a ball out of a man's chest? No one could survive such a wound.

Tears hampered her vision as she slowly met Ryan's gaze. Acceptance of that fatalistic reality resided in those once-youthful eyes. "I'll be all right, Mizz Bellamy."

"Where were you last night?" Daniel asked.

Her gaze fell on the shiny tips of her brother's new boots before rising to his face.

"Where were you?" he whispered, the plea in his voice evident as he reached out and pulled her up.

"I'll tell you where she was." Jed Tomkins approached. Taller than she was by at least a foot, he wore a torn homespun jacket and leather breeches that encased his thick thighs. "She was with that pansy ass Lord Blackmoor, that's where. I saw him with his bloomin' arm around her, taking her up the stairs to his house."

"Leave her alone," Ryan Miller rasped, and a few others leapt to her defense. "She wouldn't no more betray us than her own family."

"Isn't it possible that someone was smarter than you were for once?" Catherine challenged them all.

Tomkins snorted. "You gonna let her talk like that, Danny?"

"Why did you go to Lambert's house, Rina?" Daniel asked.

"Probably cried out everything, while he did all kinds of things to her," Tomkins sneered. "Every damn thing she knows. How else would he know where we'd be meetin'? Tell me that."

"I don't know, Jed. You're the one who gets the orders here."

"Your sister is a whore, Danny."

Daniel slammed Jed against the stall. Wood splintered. "So help me God. I'm sick of you maligning my sister. You have a grudge for whatever reason, take it up with me."

"She's a bloomin' liar. That's what she is."

Shoving him away, Daniel spun on the others. "There's a back path out of here. It leads to the bluff. Take it and get back to the horses before it gets any lighter outside. I'll stay with Ryan."

"You keep her out of my sight." Tomkins poked a finger at Daniel's chest. "I swear I ain't got a tolerant bone in my body for traitors."

After they left, Daniel met her gaze from across the shaky wisp of light that encircled them. Kneading the bloody rag, she stood stricken, unable to comprehend when the boy she'd known had changed into this man. "Tell me you didn't sleep with Lambert."

"How dare you!"

A terrible agony twisted her insides. Dropping to her knees, she dipped the bloody rag back into the water to hide her shaking. "Captain Lambert came here last night to visit," she said in his defense. Turning back to Ryan, she told Daniel that Sally ran off Captain Lambert's horse. "I didn't want him on the road, if you can understand that sentiment. After all, he's still Patrick's brother. I slept in the servant's room because it wasn't safe to return home." And because Julian wouldn't let her out of his sight. All along, he'd planned to lay a trap. He'd kept her at the house on purpose. "Who fired the first shot?"

Daniel didn't answer, and Catherine clenched her jaw.

"You fired on a troop of Royal Marines?"

"Did you think those men would just roll over and play dead?"

She found composure but little else to aid in her loyalties to her foolish sibling. Catherine pressed the rag against Ryan's chest. His skin was white against her bloodstained hands. "You've gone beyond politics, Daniel," she whispered. "Innocent people have already been killed."

"People have died. But they were rarely innocent of anything."

She sloshed the bloodied rag in the water. "God, I don't know you anymore."

"You mean you don't know yourself anymore. You're a hypocrite, Sister." A hand on her shoulder spun her around. "Who do you think has kept food on this family's table? Who do you think supplies Anna with her precious fabric to make her dresses and Momma with her absurd flower bulbs. You? Your silly drawings? That newspaper?"

"Daniel—"

"You and your precious morality don't keep the roof over the twins' heads. Or keep Sally alive come winter when the larder goes low." He dropped a pouch of coins at her feet. "Whether you like it or not, we're all in this together. Till the end."

"Danny . . ." Ryan's voice rasped. "Leave her be, will ye?"

Daniel dropped beside his friend. "We got ourselves in a mess now, huh, pal?" he said. "I don't know what to do here, Ryan."

"I ain't goin' to make it, am I? What will happen to Ma and Da?"

Catherine knew very well what happened to families accused of sedition. "Take the gray," she told her brother. "Get to the church and bring back Reverend Brown. Stay on the back trail."

He came to his feet. There was danger in being caught, and she knew what she was asking of him. He met Ryan's half-lidded gaze before nodding. She stopped him. "Don't come back here, Daniel. Leave the horse at the church."

His fiery eyes touched hers. But in that one brief moment, the gaze she touched belonged to the boy he once was. The one she'd taught to fish and mend breeches, though it was girl stuff he'd endured. She'd held him in her arms when they'd buried their father, and he'd been her anchor when Patrick swept into her life like a summer storm. Slowly, resentfully, she watched his expression change, and in her brother's stead was the man he'd now become.

Then he was gone.

"I put yer family in danger," Ryan whispered.

She laid her cloak on him, then rested his head in her lap. For a long time, Catherine stared at the bloody rag.

"It don't hurt so much anymore, Mizz Bellamy," he said. "I thought it would hurt more."

Her heart shuddered against her ribs. She tried to focus on the chill air or the pungent scent of straw, but her eyes strayed back to his face. "What were you doing last night?" she asked, suddenly desperate and furious. He would die, and for what? It had been folly to go up against the Royal Marines.

His pale lips broke into a boyish grin. "We were going to raid the stores. Only somehow they knew where we'd be meeting up."

Her eyes closed, and his body stiffened in response to her silent condemnation. "They don't have a right to break our spirit, Mizz Bellamy. That's what Pa says this fight is all about. A man has to stand up for something in this world."

"Everything has gotten out of hand, Ryan." The salt from her tears stung her cheeks, and she swiped the moisture aside.

"But we're on the same side again. Right, Mizz Bellamy?"

"We were always on the same side."

"You need to know that the rest of us never cottoned up to what they tried to do to you." Ryan's voice faded but not so much that Catherine hadn't heard the words or felt the burn of shock go through her. "The night Danny was so drunk, he'd have never let you go to Merlin . . . had he known . . ."

A cold hand of dread clutched her heart.

"Merlin . . . he found out about Danny and Patrick." Ryan clutched her sleeve. "Someone got real afraid."

Outside, a cock began to crow. "Why, Ryan? What happened? What happened between Daniel and Patrick?" she whispered.

"You . . ." A drop of blood beaded on the corner of his mouth. When he opened his eyes again, they were widely dilated. "Danny," he swallowed thickly. "Danny . . . he killed Patrick."

Icy shock gripped her heart. Her lungs refused to breathe and, for an instant, her heart ceased to beat. "They got . . . in a terrible argument," he rasped. "Danny . . . shot him."

Blood crashed through her veins. She smelled straw and aged leather and other barn scents. Familiar odors that should have wrapped her in security now only frightened her. Catherine raised her wet gaze to the rafters. Light crept between the wooden slats, and when she looked again at Ryan, brown hair fell over one staring eye.

He was dead.

Sally shifted and strained against her rope. Catherine finally eased Ryan's head off her lap. She couldn't stand at first. Her head ached with fear and hunger and a desolation she could not allow herself to feel. Soon Samuel would come to the barn to complete his chores. Her family was in danger. Ryan couldn't be found here.

She dragged his body into the horse's empty stall and covered him completely with her cloak. She said a prayer, too, because it was all she could remember of a faith that had abandoned her completely.

The reverend would arrive soon, and she needed to meet him in a clean dress. Somehow, they needed to hide Ryan from the authorities. How could anyone tell his parents that their only son was dead?

She should despise Julian Lambert.

But she didn't.

Maybe, in a way, she'd even helped bring him here.

Too numb to think, Catherine followed the well-worn path out of the stable to the house. Frost shimmered on the iron trellis. Wrapping her skirt around one arm, she climbed as she'd done a hundred times before. The feat was as automatic as breathing and didn't require any thought.

Later, she would let herself think. Think about Ryan's words, the accusation. A sob caught in her throat.

As was her custom, Elizabeth had left the window slightly open. Catherine climbed inside. Someone had placed a stand beneath the window. She flinched when a vase filled with flowers toppled to the floor. Roses. Staring at them spilled over her floor, she knelt and lifted one long stem to the light.

"Mrs. Bellamy."

Catherine spun. Heart pounding, she clenched the fist that held the rose to her chest. Lieutenant Ross, dressed splendidly in his scarlet uniform, stood as if he'd just risen half-asleep from the yellow damask chair. His tricorn sat on her bed. She saw his eyes take in the blood on her dress as he approached. But the brief instant of alarm passed when he realized the stains were not hers.

He lifted the frayed curtain edge, then met her gaze with something akin to disappointment. "You do understand that I have to arrest you this time?"

Samuel brought the cart to a grumbling halt in front of Captain Lambert's circular drive. Elizabeth swept her gaze over the large red brick manse before studying the road behind her. Her gaze dropped to her stepmother and pale siblings wrapped in blankets. Anna and Millie shared the second blanket. Tied to a tether, Sally rolled in the dirt, where a puddle of sunshine warmed the dirt road. She'd found the only warmth in all of Yorktown.

"Stay with the horse," Elizabeth instructed Samuel as he helped her down from the cart. The gray was acting skittish. "I don't think I could walk back to the house in these shoes."

Adjusting her bodice, she wobbled slightly in a pair of Catherine's high-heeled boots as she negotiated the path to the front door. The added height of her older sister's shoes was meant to give her confidence. Yet, once she reached the porch, Elizabeth stared at the solid door, made more impenetrable by apprehension than the fine oak that boasted sturdiness.

She turned back to her family. They watched her from the cart. The hedges had been cut to allow a full view of the river. Lord Blackmoor's ship lay claim to the glittery harbor, her three masts embracing the sky in a spiderweb of artistry, its webbed spars and leech lines in perfect symmetry to the blue horizon. A clever illusion if one considered the bold play of light and colors, a chimera.

An illusion. Because the ship really wasn't touching the sky.

The display was an effective show of power in a town that would prefer to slit the throat of a British naval officer. Especially after Ryan Miller's death. By allying herself with him, returning home was no longer an option.

Besides, their house was in shambles. After Lieutenant Ross took Catherine away, Sergeant Masters left no piece of furniture, closet, or crevice untouched in his search for contraband. Most of their winter stores had been stolen. Even the beautiful gowns Anna had been making for clients did not go untouched.

Elizabeth brushed her palms down her skirt. By heavens, she was seventeen years old! Her sister needed her.

Catherine had been charged with seditious activity. The kind of charges that hanged people. And if that didn't kill a person first, staying in the gaol surely would.

Elizabeth knew that Catherine had not been feeling well. Court cases were heard once a month. Being condemned to the gaol until January might mean certain death, especially if people thought she was a spy.

Her sister was in terrible trouble. And Lord Blackmoor was the only man powerful enough to help her.

Inside the house, a tall clock began striking the noon hour. Elizabeth turned and nearly screamed.

"May I be of service, mum?"

A white-haired man stood like a pillar of bleached salt in the doorway. His eyes took in her peacock gown, widening slightly as they came to rest on her hat. A fluffy yellow ostrich plume bobbed in the breeze, a carefree contradiction to her current state. Elizabeth swallowed as she asked to see Captain Lambert.

"Lord Blackmoor is not here," the servant said, correcting her social faux pas.

Her voice almost failed her. "But . . . he *has* to be."

The servant's doubtful eyes studied her, then lifted to encompass her family. "Is this about employment?"

She cleared the tears from her throat. "If this *was* about a job, could we await him inside until he returns? It's cold out here."

Glancing over her shoulder, he frowned. "He does not take in charity cases, mum."

Elizabeth lifted her chin. "Perhaps you could just tell me where to find him, and I'll talk to him myself."

His stiff brows gathered over the ridge of his bulbous nose. Uncertainly, she finally fumbled for her card. "Would you at least give His Lordship this?"

The servant read the card. "You are not Catherine Bellamy."

"I'm her sister, Elizabeth. Tell His Lordship. Tell him . . . that I didn't know where else to go."

His expression grew grave, but his eyes betrayed nothing as he started to close the door. Suddenly desperate that she not fail

Catherine, Elizabeth leaned closer. "Tell him they took her away a few days ago."

The door clicked shut in her face.

Elizabeth's shoulders sagged. She beheld the red brick face of the house, a world apart from hers, and somehow resisted pressing her face to the windows for a peek inside. She walked away, only to turn back before she reached the bottom. Every curtain was open to welcome the light. She hesitated when she saw Boswell standing in the doorway. He wore his cloak, the collar pulled high over his ears.

"If you've a mind to follow me, mum, I know where we might find His Lordship if he's returned."

Catherine nibbled one edge of the crust. Scraping off the green, fuzzy growth, she turned the bread over in the pale light and saw something move. With a cry, she dropped the chunk back into a bowl of gruel. Her body had given up everything she'd eaten since she'd been brought here.

"Lord." She lay comatose until a rat scurried across the floor beneath the cot. Drawing her legs up against her chest, Catherine sidled against the stone wall and buried her face against her knees.

The jailer had locked her in a cell no bigger than the width of a man's cot. Too furious to cry when the lieutenant handed her off, she now faced the wet chill with resounding desolation and hunger.

"Daniel," she whispered. Catherine waged a terrible and silent war where invisible bombs knocked fist-size holes in ideals that she'd stood behind for years. Her belief in all things had been buried in a graveyard of fallen principles. Now, as she glared in disgust at the worm-ridden food, she wondered how much longer she could remain defiant. And what of her family?

What would happen to them if she talked?

What would happen to her child if she didn't?

The door lock clicked. Her gaze snapped to the wooden portal that separated her cell from the rest of the gaol.

"You've a visitor." The possum-nosed guard stuck his head in long enough to hang another lamp on the hook beside the door.

"And you can tell Lieutenant Ross to go the devil. Along with the garbage you deem food." With what little strength remained, she hurled the bowl of inedible mash where it exploded in an obnoxious splash against the wall. "I have nothing else to say."

A shadow passed over the light as a man ducked through the doorway. Her breath left her lungs. Captain Lambert stood in the middle of the cell, unmoving, impenetrable, a British officer to his core. Shadows framed his shoulders and blocked his expression as he took in the room with one glance before settling his gaze on her.

"Stand in His Lordship's presence, ye little tart," the guard snarled and moved forward as if to drag her to her feet.

Blackmoor's gloved hand shot out. "Leave us," he ordered.

When her brother-in-law's gaze came back around, her heart gave a jolt. For a long time after the guard left, he remained as if he didn't dare move any closer to her.

"Are you all right?"

Catherine pulled her legs over the cot and sat on the edge. Dizziness followed the movement. "Why are you here, my lord?"

"It took me longer than expected to find you." He ignored her question. "Lieutenant Ross has you under tight security."

Contemplating the puddle of mash splattered over the door like some artistic attempt gone awry, he returned his gaze. "Have you eaten anything at all these last few days?"

A vision of grubs threatened to send her back over the rim of the cot. "I could never eat th-that—"

"You would in time if that's all that kept you from starving."

Studying his profile, she wondered how he could have been so sure of that. He wore his bicorn tucked beneath an arm, clearly necessary with the low ceiling. His white wig was queued back with a leather thong. When he turned, he caught her stare, and for a moment neither spoke. There was growing anger in his eyes.

With a twinge of apprehension, Catherine realized that Julian was reticent about nothing, even outright violence against her. Suddenly, the shadows seemed safer than this man. "Did you know the dead youth found in your barn?"

"Ryan Miller lived on a neighboring farm," she answered with an equal measure of reluctance and surrender only because she wanted her own questions answered. That and the fact that she'd do almost anything to get out of this place. "He and my brother were best friends." Her fingers brushed her neck. "What has happened to his family?"

"The farm was searched. The family arrested. They vanished last night while being transported to Williamsburg for detention."

The horror of his words struck the pit of her belly, and she was suddenly so scared she couldn't think straight. "My family—"

"They're staying at my house. Including that damn pig."

"You . . . would do that? For us?"

"Did you think I wouldn't come to your aid?"

Dropping her gaze to the tear in her dress, she didn't know what to think. She didn't know anyone anymore. Especially the minds of men, including Daniel. And her own husband who had led a double life beneath her very nose. And she was confused about her implacable brother-in-law. She wanted to be angry with Julian Lambert, not beholden. Not when their paths shot off in opposite directions. "I know that it cost you a fortune in bribes to get into this place," she said. "But I've already told the lieutenant everything I know about that night."

"I'm not the lieutenant."

"Nay, you're *worse,* my lord. I'm already in trouble because of you. It's not fitting for you to be here."

"No more fitting than your bent for traveling in the dark or your poor choice of company these past months. Why did you leave my house before Boswell could arrange to take you home?"

"I didn't want anyone to take me home."

"And does sheltering criminals go along with your independence?"

Catherine curled her fists into her skirts. "Ryan wasn't a criminal. He was good," she whispered.

"Just an apple-cheeked innocent who possessed no qualms about firing on a troop of Royal Marines? Was your brother with the men who were going to attack the warehouse? Is he pure and honest, too?"

Catherine's breath caught. She couldn't answer. Anything she said would incriminate her and, by God, Daniel would answer to her first before anyone else got hold of him.

Blackmoor kneeled on one knee beside her perch on the cot. "Then what about you?" Placing a finger alongside her cheek, he gently pulled her face around. The anger in his eyes was replaced by something else as he touched the blood on her skirts. "Catherine?"

He was too close. He smelled of crisp starch and wool and English imperialism. He was the man responsible for killing Ryan Miller. And hadn't she been a victim of the sergeant's brutality? She didn't want to see Julian Lambert in that wretched British uniform. She didn't want his gentleness.

She jerked away. "You should worry about yourself, my lord. I hardly consider the bowels of this gaol safe refuge for King George's mercenaries. What if they simply locked the door?"

His eyes roamed over her, and it took every ounce of will not to lay her palm over her breasts. "So, this isn't a war of politics but pride?" he asked lightly. "You don't like my company."

Her tangled hair fell over her face as she dismissed him to stare at the wall. He pulled her chin around. "If it makes you feel better, I don't like yours either at the moment. In case you haven't noticed, you smell like a barn. If we were locked in here together, one of us would expire from the effort it took to breathe."

The tension ebbed away. Despite herself, she felt the corners of her mouth lift. "Do you have something against barns?"

His wide shoulders shrugged. "The fragrance is nothing that a hot scrub in scented lye wouldn't cure. Would you like that? A bath?"

A jolt sent tears into her eyes. "Must you make everything sound simpler than it is?"

"It *is* simple. I'm taking you out of here. Mercenary that I am." He presented her a folded sheet of vellum. "Your release papers."

For a long time, she didn't respond. She couldn't. "I . . . don't understand. Lieutenant Ross—"

"—is away with other pressing matters at the moment. He wasn't there to argue your arrest. I was. I know you weren't part of that raid, Catherine."

Her hands tightened on the paper. "But only the governor has the power to drop charges of sedition."

Without denying the truth of her statement, he glanced around the cell before returning his attention to her. His gaze then slid down the curves of her bodice, touching her in places his eyes had no right to touch, before moving to her bare feet. She snatched down her skirt to conceal her grubby toes. "You have no shoes?" he asked.

She winced when she put pressure on her foot. Wiping her face with the heel of her hand, she knew that he was hiding something monumental here. And changing the subject wasn't going to erase the questions. Nothing was ever free. Hadn't life taught her that everything came with a price? For every rose, there were at least two thorns to draw blood.

"Let me see what you've done," he said.

"No—" She slapped his hands off her skirt, appalled that he would see her filthy feet. "It doesn't hurt."

"Catherine . . ." Removing his gloves, he regarded her efforts to push him away with a warning. "I know a little of medicine."

"I'll wager the moon you don't. What other excuse would you have to stick your hands beneath my skirts?"

Astonishment marked his aristocratic demeanor. But not as much as her own words had shocked her. To her surprise, he laughed.

The rich baritone voice rolled like warm marmalade over her nerves. Everything in her world stilled. She was aware of the scent of earth and straw and the taste of wonder on her lips. His eyes had lost their icy ferocity, their stoic command of the world eclipsed by the light of the lantern, and she met his gaze with sudden confusion.

He caressed her with his eyes. "Catherine, I'll only look at your foot," he promised. "My word as a gentleman."

"Are you a gentleman?"

A hand covered his heart. "My honor as a British officer then."

Hesitantly, she released her grip on her tattered hem.

"Does that mean you're not a gentleman?" she challenged.

His head bent as he eased her foot from beneath her skirts. "You have nothing to fear from me, Catherine."

Oh, God, she wanted so much to believe him.

The lump in her throat grew. She suddenly wanted to know this man whom Patrick idolized and hated at once. "What if the colonies go to war with England? Then would you give me cause to fear you?"

"Is that what you want? A war?"

Catherine thought about the young men in town. War had destroyed her father's life. And what of Julian Lambert on the deck of his ship? Facing the battle from the other side?

"How long have you been in service to King George?" she asked.

"Long enough to know that what's going on around here has very little to do with war or politics. And I think you know that."

Without waiting for her response, he ran a supple hand over the tender arch of her foot. As he bent, the uniform jacket pulled at the width of his shoulders. She remembered the feel of those muscled arms beneath his robe when he'd stopped her from leaving the dining room at his house. One hand clutching the papers to her chest, the other palm braced against the cot, she surrendered to his ministrations. His bare hands were warm against her flesh and disturbingly sensual as he traced the muscle along her calf. She flinched when his fingers touched a bruise.

He raised his gaze. And for an instant before his eyes hooded, his fingertips stilled, then slowly lowered her heel. "You haven't snapped any bones," he said, pulling her skirt down.

The papers in her hand grew heavy. "Why would the governor release me?" she asked.

With one knee in the dirt of the cell, he crossed his forearms against his thigh as he looked at her. "Because I asked him."

Suddenly, Catherine knew why Julian was here defending her in the face of authority when few others would dare. Because he loved his brother and would protect her as his family. Because Julian Lambert was honorable and decent in bone-deep ways that Patrick never was. Nor were Daniel and her father who, by their selfish actions, hurt those they supposedly loved most in the world.

"I'm sorry." She should not apologize. But she'd heard that two of his men had been wounded in the attack last week, a raid in which her brother had taken part.

"Why?" His boots creaked as he shifted to pick up his gloves.

"Because m-my shoes were stolen," she said irrationally. "And you have to carry me with your foot still sore from Sally."

His expression softened. "I'll manage." He slipped the gloves back on his hands, then settled his bicorn on his head. "Put your arms around my neck."

Tentatively, she stretched toward him. His gaze never leaving her face, he lifted her easily against him. Ducking with her out of the door, he carried her down a stone passageway, past other cells, then past the guards, who watched curiously but made no move to stop them as he climbed the narrow stairs. She felt like a broken doll and thoroughly humiliated in his arms. The tears gathered in her eyes before she could stop their fall.

"Why are you crying? Have I hurt you?"

She shook her head in despair. Upstairs in the main room, people stopped talking to gawk and make a pathway. Julian walked straight past them all. They reached the busy road, and his boots crunched against gravel. He was so calm about everything. About death and war. About carrying her in public when she was so filthy she could barely breathe in her own stench. He made her dizzy. Maybe he was used to women acting strangely in his arms. After all, he'd been married once. And rumor already placed him with a mistress.

"You'll have to forgive me." Wiping the back of her filthy hand indelicately across her wet nose, she sniffed. "I don't feel well."

"You mean it's not my earlier behavior that has you upset?"

For wont of any place to put her head, she rested her cheek against his shoulder. "No, not exactly." Her tired voice was muffled against the heavy wool jacket.

"Is that an apology?"

"No, not exactly."

She found herself liking him all over again as she had at the ball, and the urge to trust him pulled at her like a seductive whisper. But knowing her current state of vulnerability, she also knew her judgment had slipped away for a brief feminine sojourn in the land of whimsy. There were no such things as white knights and Camelot. Especially in the arms of an officer in His Majesty's Royal Navy.

The welcome rattle of a carriage broke the stillness that surrounded them. Julian turned with her in his arms. Four fine horses drew an equally impressive carriage. The driver greeted Julian as the carriage slowed to a grinding halt before them.

Catherine's disbelief marked her awe as she looked up at Julian.

His eyes smiled at her. "Did you think that I'd carry you all the way back to Yorktown? Food and drink are inside."

With dark blue lower quarters trimmed in gold, the carriage

tastefully displayed the wealth of its new owner. Two armed uniformed men rode in the driver's boot. The footman dropped to the ground to release the step and open the door. He stood back as Julian lifted her into the coach. The interior smelled of lemon oil. The leather seats were supple and rich beneath her palms.

She raised her gaze to find Julian standing with his palm braced on the door, watching her. Abruptly, as if suddenly annoyed, he straightened. "Someone will see to that foot tonight," he said.

"Thank you." Her fingers clasped her release papers to her chest. "I don't know how I'll ever repay you."

Julian shut the door and leaned into the window. He lifted one corner of his mouth. Ruthlessness had reared its head in a way he'd least expected, and it grabbed at him now with an intensity that clenched his fists. Catherine had no idea what he'd done to get her out of that gaol. "I'm of a mind we'll agree on something fair."

A curt order to the driver sent the carriage lurching forward. Catching herself from falling to the floor, Catherine pushed her head out the window, a tangle of midnight hair framing her beautiful face. A whip cracked. The carriage picked up speed.

Julian wondered how long it would take before she realized the carriage was not headed back to Yorktown.

Chapter Thirteen

Waiting until the carriage disappeared around the bend of oaks, Julian left Nicholson Street. A stiff breeze found its way beneath the lapel of his uniform. He lifted his gaze. Domed by a pewter sky, smoke curled from chimneys in a picture of innocent tranquillity. Unrest had heightened since the Miller family had vanished, their disappearance a point of dissension from here to Yorktown. With evening approaching and the town in a scrap, standing on the street corner in his uniform, he was about as inconspicuous as a bull's-eye on the side of a barn.

Julian walked past the square. He pulled his bicorn lower over his head. Catherine would have been better served had he gotten drunk when Elizabeth Claremont begged him for help instead of rushing off to Williamsburg to play the gallant.

At least he'd gotten her away from Lieutenant Ross.

Once out of town, the population thinned. Dead leaves crunched under his boots. The blacksmith stood at the door of the stables down at the end of the street, the last building before the forest engulfed the edge of town. Watching Julian's approach, he grabbed a filthy rag from the bench near the doorway and wiped his hands.

His hair was the color of burnt cornbread. He wore a red homespun shirt, and even in the chill, sweat stained him beneath his arms. Julian had known Joshua years before, when he worked in the stables at Hope Plantation on the James.

"Went right to the front shoe like ye told me," Joshua said, taking Julian to the last stall. He eyed Julian speculatively.

"Fixed the back one, too. He's been ridden hard to have those kinds of problems so soon after I sold him to ye, my lord."

Julian bent and checked each hoof for anything that might distinguish this horse from any other. "You did a fine job. I imagine I can trust you to take care of his needs during my stay here."

"Hear tell you got yourself a fine manor house in Yorktown."

"Only temporary, I assure you." Julian paid the blacksmith with a gold coin. "Will this do for upkeep?"

Pocketing the coin, the man's eyes lit. "Aye, milord. I like a man who can pay in gold. Even if he is a full-grown Tory." Shoving his hand into his grimy shirt, he withdrew a handful of Virginia Treasury notes. "Got this from a pair of farmers down your way who purchased a horse in my pasture yesterdee. Had them mixed in with the real thing. Ain't worth the paper they're written on. Don't know what this world's coming to, thievin' from the workin' man."

"Do you mind?" Julian nodded to the fifteen-pence notes, which the man handed over with no argument.

"I'd burn the notes before I had to explain them to the authorities. It's a death sentence to anyone what makes those." Joshua sniffed as Julian held one to the light. Black scrolls rimmed the edge, and together they pondered the script. "Takes an accomplished artist to do that," the man surmised.

"Williamsburg is full of accomplished artists, my friend. Go to any street corner and they're sitting with the poets."

"Keep 'em, if ye wish." Joshua's big hand swung to the blunderbuss leaning innocuously against the slatted wall near the front. "You can bet your royal blue finery that my Bess will deal with the sots if I see 'em again. The taller one was about as pleasant as a wasp sting."

Julian folded the notes into his jacket. "I'll be taking the bay gelding today." He patted the black stallion on the nose before turning to follow Joshua out of the stall.

"A man was hanging around here earlier." Joshua took Julian to the next stall where the bay munched hay. "An Irishman 'bout yer height. Guess he got bored of me staring holes in him."

"Thank you, Joshua. I'll saddle the horse myself."

"You?" Joshua appeared momentarily scandalized. "But milord—"

"I can saddle the horse, Joshua. Go tend your fire."

Julian remained at the stall door until the blacksmith disappeared outside. A glance up and down the long aisle told him he was alone. The scent of straw and manure assaulted him. Julian had just lain the blanket over the bay's back when he sensed the whisper of movement behind him. His leg shot out, and he tripped the intruder flat into the straw.

"Jeezus . . . Reece!"

Smiling down at Michael's grimace, Julian placed a boot on his chest. "An officer of the crown can't be too sure of the Irish, O'Hara. Especially a man who sneaks around in stables."

"Next time I'll wear a bloody cowbell. Will that suit ye?"

"No, it won't." Removing his boot from Michael's collarbone, Julian held out his gloved hand. "Why are you here?"

Michael brushed straw off his backside. With his brown woolen breeches and baggy shirt, he looked like a stable hand. "Did you know that you have a pig living in your stables? A bloody *pig*, Reece!"

Julian grabbed the saddle and set it atop the horse blanket. "I recommend that you stay out of her way."

Michael crossed his thick arms and leaned against the high slat of the stall. "Tell me that wasn't Patrick's long-suffering wife you just carried out of the gaol in front of God and everyone."

He yanked the girth tight. "Catherine is my business."

"Catherine is it now?"

Julian let his gaze roam up and down the long aisle before snapping back around to Michael. "Are you finished?"

Michael shoved off the stall. "Lieutenant Ross will be steamin' his breeches when he learns you've circumvented his authority. He's already boiling over the Millers' disappearance."

Julian kept his voice low. "By the time Ross spends days hunting me down, I'll be back in Williamsburg dining with the governor."

"Really?" Michael groused with surprising rancor. "You leave Norfolk, a man bent on finding justice, and little time left to see it done. Now you're carrying off the prime suspect?"

Crossing his wrists over the saddle, Julian drew in his breath.

"Isn't leaving your ship during a time of conflict an act of dereliction?" Michael asked.

"She's the only person who knows Merlin, and the lieutenant is all over her. She was with me the night the warehouse was attacked." He finally lifted his head. "Lieutenant Ross wants an informant. He's charged her with sedition and locked her up to cool her heels until her case is brought up before a magistrate. I'm not willing to feed her to the jackals for her brother's sins."

"It's out of character for you to make yourself so obvious."

But Michael must have recognized something on Julian's face, something that Julian couldn't see. A line that he'd suddenly crossed and knew instinctively that he now trod on fragile ground. He looked away. His frustration eased out on a sigh. "I'll contact you after I've safely moved the other cargo. They're very grateful, by the way. Give me a few days."

Julian slammed the stall door in Michael's path. Eye to eye, he bent a furtive brow. "You didn't spend all this time tracking me down so we could argue about Catherine and talk about the Millers," he said. "What did you want?"

Michael spat in the straw. Then, as if arriving at a decision, he yanked out a folded placard from his vest. "I pulled this off the marketplace wall in Jamestown."

Julian unfolded the wanted poster and froze. A wind gust rattled the stable, and he felt the ice clean to his bones.

"Someone has drawn a pretty good likeness of Merlin. There was a murder some months back in Yorktown. A rector and his daughter. Seems someone has now fingered Merlin for the deed, among his other crimes. A man would sell his own mother for that reward money."

Julian didn't reply, as dread stopped the breath in his lungs. "She's no traitor," he whispered.

"You're so sure of her. About everything?"

"No, I'm not sure of her!" Shoving the placard in his jacket, Julian braced his fists against the saddle. "Christ . . ." Lifting his head, Julian shoved away, but a cooler head prevailed long enough to consider that Michael meant only to protect him.

Except he didn't need protection. Not about this.

"As I live and breathe, O'Hara, I can't fault her principles for protecting her family. She's guilty as hell about many things, but murder isn't one of them." Julian stopped Michael midturn. "O'Hara, trust me to know what I'm doing."

"Trust?" Michael shook his head. "You've let this get personal. You can't decide if you're in love with her or if ye hate her.

The lieutenant knows she's her brother's weakest link. Don't let her be yours, too."

Without another word, Michael squeezed through a plank in the back of the stables and was gone.

Julian braced his hand on the stall. His fingers closing in a fist, he swore aloud.

Personal?

Aye, there were a hundred reasons never to go near Catherine again. Michael was right about his feelings. He didn't know if he wanted to make love to her or strangle the life out of her.

Or both.

But he could no more have left Catherine in that gaol than she could have left him that night in the stables after she'd unlocked their chains. The chains were invisible now but no less binding for the past they'd shared. And he was bone-deep certain of her character the moment she'd ridden hell for leather through the fog bank to reach him the other night.

The same way she'd done the first night he'd ever met her.

His decision today had nothing to do with nobility and everything to do with fair play. She'd run from Merlin full circle back into his arms.

And in that bit of irony, he figured he was about to even the tally between them. She owed him.

Aye, this was as personal as it gets.

Like the night they'd shared. Personal, like the fact that she'd belonged to Patrick. Or the beating he'd taken on her behalf because someone had set one or both of them up to die. For all his admirable talk about her character, he possessed no mercy in this present course. She was going to tell him everything about the men who'd ruthlessly framed him.

She just didn't know it yet.

Outside, a winter storm brewed. Permitting himself a small smile, Julian mounted the bay. The weather suited his mood.

At least the roads would be clear tonight.

Heart pounding, Catherine sat up in bed. With both hands braced on the mattress, she closed her eyes against the throb in her temples. Every muscle ached.

Confused by her lapse of memory, Catherine scraped a hand through her tangled hair, still damp from her bath. Her corset and chemise lay over the back of a nearby chair. The blanket smelled faintly of sunshine. She wore no other clothes beneath. She'd been ill when she'd arrived at the cottage, and she remembered nothing after she'd stepped out of the tub.

Good God, had she fainted?

She looked around the room. Hot water tins from her bath littered the floor. Someone had put her to bed.

A door stood ajar and, carefully, she waded through a narrow dressing room into a second bedroom a little larger than hers. A forest-green canopy bed backed against the wall next to where she stood. Matching curtains were closed to the storm outside.

Her bare feet chilled against the slatted floor, Catherine stared expectantly around the room. Nothing moved. A fire popped in the stone hearth where warmth mingled elusively with the scent of sandalwood and peat. The comforter fell off one shoulder. Finally, limping to the bedroom door, she edged it open.

"I wouldn't if I were you."

The sleepy voice spun her around. Heart pounding, she swung her gaze to the fireplace, to the high-backed leather chair set off in the shadows. Captain Lambert leaned forward into the firelight. Leather crackled with the movement.

"My Lord . . .

"Catherine."

For a long moment, silence hung in the air, suspended in the darkness between them. He wore his uniform, his coat carelessly unbuttoned as if he'd been sleeping. Firelight favored the pale gray breeches and waistcoat beneath his military jacket. Gone was the camaraderie they'd briefly shared earlier. Gone was the man who'd carried her to his carriage and solicitously administered to her ankle, the one who'd given her freedom.

"Somehow you always manage to end up in my chambers," he said, unfolding from his chair. "You should be in bed, Catherine."

She took a reflexive step away from him. The sudden movement brought him up short, and watching his eyes narrow perceptively on her face, she suddenly felt lost and furious at once. She didn't know which weighed her down more, only that her hands trembled.

Without asking, the one person she'd started to trust had spirited her off to a remote cottage in the middle of who knew where.

He was the British aristocrat, the fearless captain of his ship, and Catherine resented the ease with which he'd taken matters into his hands without so much as a by your leave, or a might I kidnap you *again,* Mrs. Bellamy?

She was glad he'd reminded her of his true fabric.

She didn't want to like him.

Didn't want to feel beholden or loyal to the Tory.

And by God, she'd declare war on him until he answered her questions.

But first she had to settle something else more pressing in her mind. "Who . . . put me to bed?"

He cocked an eyebrow, now devoid of powder and a sudden lack of patience. "Who do you think?"

Lord in heaven!

Heat crept into the roots of her wet hair and down her throat to boil in her stomach. "'Tis . . . unseemly, my lord, that . . ." She couldn't think. "Where are my clothes?"

"Your clothes have been burned. I'm particular about sharing my living quarters with lice."

Appalled at the insinuation that she'd share anything with Julian Lambert, including lice, Catherine failed to quash the sudden alarm. "That garment belonged to me. You had no right. No right at all," she said irrationally. Her head throbbed. But without clothes, she couldn't escape. She had to escape. Her eyes widened when she thought she saw him move. "Don't you dare come any closer!"

"Or what, Catherine?" He leaned one forearm against the canopy bedstead. "You can hardly stand as it is."

"You lied to me," she sidled toward the hall door, but he moved to block her escape.

"I took you out of that gaol. Where is the lie in that?"

"You're not the one standing here naked."

"Let me lay out your options." He stalked her backward, his gaze burning into hers. "You have one, to be exact, because in case you've forgotten, your own people have branded you a traitor. Be grateful I didn't leave you to the jackals you call friends."

"Grateful!"

Somehow, he'd closed the distance between them. Snatching the comforter to her chin, Catherine whirled. The fall of his steps sounded on the floor as she dashed through the dressing room.

She slammed her bedroom door only to find the tip of an expensive boot wedged in the doorway.

"Dammit, Catherine." He shoved. "Open the door."

Catherine stubbornly worked to keep her shoulder against the door. "For whatever nefarious purpose you have for keeping me captive, I refuse to cooperate. You lied to me!" Breathing hard, she pushed against his shove. But the effort was too much. She finally gave up the contest. When he fell into the room, she hurled a water tin at him.

"Catherine—" He batted the can away with his forearm; then he lunged as she swung her fist. A gasp underscored her shock. The blow knocked him squarely in the chin, and he sat abruptly in the chair, the twin of the one that sat beside her bed.

"Shit . . ." He sprawled backward, his wig slightly askew.

Catherine stood frozen, both her brows lifting in astonishment. "Did . . . I hurt you?"

"Aye." Testing his mouth for blood, he glared up at her. "You knocked my bloody tith loose."

Indecision momentarily rooted her. She fought the urge to kick him in the shins, too. But her foot ached, and now so did her hand. Hobbling to her nightstand, she retrieved a damp rag and offered it to him. "I'm sorry." She tried not to taunt him and found it impossible. "But 'tis nothing less than you deserve, my lord."

His gaze slowly lifting to hers, a hot dart of warning wiped the smile from her face. Before she could bolt, his hand shot out and yanked her sprawling across his lap. "Nefarious purpose?"

"Let go of me!"

"Then you aren't as angry that I brought you here to this place as you are that I saw you bare-ass naked. White as it was."

She gasped. His arms tightened around her, easily defeating her struggles. In her fight, the comforter fell away from her shoulders.

Her gaze shot to his, but whatever she'd thought to say was cut short when he pulled the blanket over her. A blush crawled up her face. "I do have my standards when it comes to ravishing women." He laid a cool palm across her brow. His mouth crooked into a half smile. "I prefer them to remember the deed come morning."

She slapped his hands away. "Don't you dare touch me.

You . . . you Judas!" Draped across his lap in an undignified heap, she shoved against him, but it was like pushing against oak. He'd braced an arm around her back and waited until she exhausted herself. Barely discernible over the masculine scent of wind and leather, his spicy shaving soap floated through her senses like the sweetest of pies.

"You didn't tell me your plans. Therefore, you were less than honest." She pressed a finger against one temple. "I thought . . ." Her emotions swung like a pendulum. In his arms, she felt too vulnerable as a sudden longing for security surged in her breast. "Lord, I don't know what I thought."

"I doubt it was flattering." He tilted her chin to study her eyes. Outside, the storm hammered the house. She sighed. "Of course it wasn't. You're a cad."

"Are you all right?" he asked, as if he didn't plan to use her to hunt down Daniel. Chatting as if he hadn't seen her naked as the day she was born when she could not tear the thought from her brain. Yet she found indignation no longer worked to rally her defenses. She liked the gentleness bestowed upon her.

"I feel like I'm going to throw up again," she said without raising her eyes to his. Her bare feet peeked out from beneath the comforter, and she wiggled her toes.

"You have a fever, similar to swamp fever." Wordlessly, he touched the bump on her forehead. She must have hit her head when she'd fainted. "It's common in people who've spent time in the gaol."

Her gaze pulled to the papers she'd tucked beneath the lamp beside her bed. They were still safe. "I won't go back to that wretched place."

"I know."

Closing her eyes, she burrowed into his woolen lapel before her eyes snapped open. "Are you telling me that I'm below your standards?" Her mouth challenged as if sexual sparring were her forte. She pushed up. "Lord above, men are such braggarts."

"You're exhausted." Standing, he lobbed her against the wall of his chest. "Mrs. Ericson gave you laudanum. Clearly, too much."

The edge of the comforter dragged on the floor. "You never smile except to laugh at me," she quietly accused.

He laid her among the pillows. "I'm not laughing at you."

"And don't coddle me."

"Aye, you don't deserve to be coddled." He handed her a cup of water as she struggled to sit. Her dark hair cascaded over her bare shoulders. "Three people were waiting to tell me that you were out of your head and threw your dinner fork at poor Mrs. Ericson."

Catherine choked. The tyrant who'd greeted her from the carriage walked around in the guise of a sweet old lady, but Catherine knew better. "I didn't know it was a fork. Besides," she exchanged the glass for the slice of bread he picked off the tray. "She nearly drowned me washing my hair. As for Grump and Grumpier," she chewed the bread crust, "the two men who brought me here, I get particularly testy when I'm being lied to. They refused to tell me where we were."

He bent her an amused brow. "Grump and Grumpier, as you refer to my footmen, are paid well to protect you, not dally in chitchat. As for Mrs. Ericson, you needed a bath." Dark lashes framed the lights dancing in his gaze. "I'd not have gone to all that trouble to get you out of the gaol only to let someone hurt you."

Numbly, she accepted the rest of the water to wash down the bread. She shoved aside the damp hair that fell in black tangles over her shoulders. "Where is this place?" she sleepily asked.

"Mrs. Ericson is my solicitor's sister," he said. "She's a widow. Occasionally, she takes in a boarder. And on other occasions, especially when I was coming from Norfolk, I've stayed the night here on my way to Williamsburg."

"You?" She peered over the glass at the less-than-luxurious accommodations, with the aged bedstead, pine dresser, and nightstand.

His expression unfathomable in the shadows, Julian Lambert leaned his palms against the canopy above his head. A lack of stock around his neck exposed the tanned column of his throat. "Is there anything else before I leave you to your rest?"

"Don't leave."

Had she said the words too quickly?

She looked up at him towering over her, the crackling light from the fireplace barely touching his eyes, and her stomach fluttered. She set down the empty glass on the tray before easing back to her pillows. "Are you sure my family is safe?"

"I suspect Boswell is lying in bed about now with a cold rag on his forehead, ready to shoot me."

She lifted her chin. "I admit we are a bit eccentric—"

His sudden smile rankled as much as it caught her off guard. Lord in heaven but he'd changed. "Only a bit?" he laughed.

Time seemed to slow to the barest tick of a clock, to the tiniest fraction of affection as she watched his expression soften on her wavering smile. Wind slashed the trees outside the window. Somewhere a branch cracked and splintered to the ground.

He moved to the window. His uniform coat opened. His waist was firm beneath the cream waistcoat. Her eyes followed him as he pulled aside the curtain to peer out.

"Shouldn't you be policing the citizens or something?"

He joined her then, stretching out his long legs as he sat on the chair. "Policing is Ross's job. Mine is to defend the coasts, or in this case, Virginia's commerce, which is why the governor put me in Yorktown. What more important job is there than seeing that His Majesty's goods are properly accounted for and taxed?"

"Important indeed. You must be very proud of your work."

He steepled his long fingers on his chest. "I'm good at what I do, Catherine. Never doubt that."

She narrowed her eyes on his and recognized the challenge for what it was. He had a reputation to merit his arrogance, she supposed. Men like him lived and breathed victory. He wore it in his stance, his uniform, and his very presence, which dominated the room.

Then she remembered that he'd fallen through the porch at her house while being chased by a pet pig. Her brother-in-law had been a good sport about the whole catastrophe, and he'd taken her family into his home when he could have turned them away. And despite knowing his motives for bringing her here to this cottage, she felt safer in his presence than she had anywhere else these past months.

Damn Daniel for tearing her heart out! Damn him for making her choose! "When you didn't show up after I arrived here, I thought—I thought you were dead someplace on the road," she said earnestly.

"Wouldn't my demise help your brother?" he said blandly.

"Don't say that." Conscious of the magnitude of her response, she looked away. "You have no right."

"Why not?"

"Because I thought that, despite everything, we could be friends."

Julian clasped his hands between his knees and looked at her. "What does that mean exactly? Friends, Catherine?"

"Friends. People with whom you spend time? Who laugh with you? People you *trust?*" She returned his stare, if only to deny that her once colored world had turned a messy gray. "If you share your passions with no one, what cause is worth fighting for, Captain?"

His face had become a mask as he looked at her. Just like that, he'd withdrawn from her, and she wondered why she should care.

Yet, in truth, she knew that Patrick's brother had always been an invisible force in her mind and 'twas not laudanum that influenced her thoughts now. "Did you know that I've seen you before?"

She stretched out her arm to touch his leg, and found her wrist captured. "Catherine," he stood, "you need to sleep. And so do I."

"From a distance, I saw you," she murmured. "I was in Boston the year your ship came with Admiral Lord Pentworth. Yours was his flagship. Patrick had taken Daniel and me up there in hopes of meeting you. It was before we'd married. He'd always talked of you."

"Two years ago? Patrick came to Boston?"

"Violence had put the British troops on alert, and you were too busy to leave the ship." Catherine seemed to study the hand that held her wrist. "We saw you from the docks . . . standing on the deck of your ship." Her sleepy voice sighed. "You were wearing a blue woolen frock with a cream lapel. Brass buttons caught in the sunlight."

His eyes were still locked with hers, and he could not form the words to reply. Turning her face away, she settled into her pillow.

"You were always there between us after that," she said.

"How so, Catherine?"

"Because his father loved you more than he did his own son." She drew in her breath and closed her eyes to sleep. "Because . . . you are honorable, Captain?"

•   •   •

"Are ye planning to sleep there all day, Captain?" Mrs. Ericson's voice drew Julian's gaze.

He'd been half asleep in the drawing room last night when she'd closed the curtains. Throwing more peat onto the fire, she beat the embers into submission.

Julian sat in the high-back chair, his legs stretched out. An empty snifter of brandy leaned over in his hand. The counterfeited bills lay in his lap as if staring at them gave him some insight or clue to their origin. Or whether or not they were even connected to the group of men he hunted. Or to Catherine. He'd not removed his uniform, and it draped his tall frame in disrepair. He needed a shave.

"I've laid out a dress for her. She was asking for you. Seemed important, but last I checked on her she was sound asleep."

Mrs. Ericson threw open the curtains. "The storm has left a bit of ice on the roads. 'Tis a shame if winter was to come early."

"Why is that?" he asked, not particularly caring about much as he closed his eyes against the piercing brightness.

"What lady wishes to travel with an icy draft up her skirts?"

At the moment, Julian could think of something else he'd rather find up a certain lady's skirts. Without glancing at Mrs. Ericson, he sat forward, nearer to the fire. "One of my men will take you to your daughter's house when the roads clear."

She sniffed, "I've left ye bread and porridge aplenty."

Julian lifted his gaze.

Aye, he was having a tug-of-war with his conscience and, by the look in the woman's brown eyes, she'd guessed as much.

Catherine did things to him. Things to his mind and his body that he understood only too well. She'd been oblivious to his arousal. He'd put her in bed last night to get her off his lap.

Under the blanket, her breasts had been full and firm, erotic as hell with just the right curves beneath his hand. His gut tightened, and it had nothing to do with fatigue or hunger, though he knew both had begun to take a toll on his faculties.

The conflict between them had turned away from Daniel Claremont, away from Patrick; he knew that now, just as he knew instinctively that he had hurt Catherine beyond repair by bringing her here.

The *honorable* Julian Reece Lambert, English aristocracy, smuggler, and now, according to the placard in his coat, murderer as well. Aye, he'd lived up to everyone's expectations well and good. He'd endangered a greater cause to take matters into his own hands.

He regretted the need to hurt Catherine.

He regretted that he hadn't put aside his work, shoved past the memories of this place, and spent time with Patrick.

Julian had never clapped Patrick on the back and told him how proud he'd been when his brother graduated from William and Mary. Never truly listened to his brother's dreams. Life had been too busy, too full of worldly importance.

And what of Catherine? Had she found herself impaled on the anointed political spike with nowhere to turn? The answer clearly justified her terror when faced with aiding Merlin.

Yet he had a feeling that, in her own courageous way, she'd waged her own war, a war she'd been fighting alone for too long. But by bringing her here, he'd destroyed her reputation. He risked making her an accessory to treason. And her people wouldn't trust her again.

One thing he knew for damn certain. He no longer regarded her as Patrick's wife. And that made him the biggest bastard of all.

Chapter Fourteen

Pounding on the door vibrated through the great manse. Elizabeth sat at the dinner table and lowered her fork. Stretching her neck, she watched Boswell leave the dining room where he'd been lording over them all as if they were his personal serfs. For a week, his glower had terrified the twins into docile submission. With his welcome absence, they started whispering. Her mother sat across from her. More alert than usual, she, too, had lowered her fork as voices rose in the main corridor. A moment later, Anna entered the dining room, her hands twisting her cleaning apron into a knot.

"Lieutenant Ross is here, mum," she told them all. "He is demanding to see Lord Blackmoor."

Elizabeth and her mother rose simultaneously. "Did you tell him that he isn't here?"

"Mr. Boswell has told him, mum. But there seems to be some disagreement as to his whereabouts. And that of Catherine's."

Lieutenant Ross straightened when Elizabeth and her mother swept into the entryway. A gust of wind hit the house. The huge chandelier trembled at its anchor two stories up. Despite his agitation, Lieutenant Ross had the manners beforehand to remove his tricorn and now held it beneath his arm. Elizabeth had once considered him quite handsome. But after he'd imprisoned her sister, he could be Michelangelo's *David*, for all the good it would do him. She'd not give him one minute more than necessary of her day.

"Mrs. Claremont," he bowed politely to her mother. His cool eyes reverted to her with barely a nod. "Miss Claremont."

Elizabeth bristled.

"What brings you out on this blustery day, Lieutenant Ross?" Elizabeth's mother asked, drawing everyone's gaze.

Lieutenant Ross straightened to attention. "It seems that while I've been preoccupied with local matters—"

"You mean the Millers' disappearance?" Elizabeth said, unable to help rubbing it into wounds she knew must smart.

Last Sunday's church service had hummed with gossip. Then two nights ago, the local magistrate's personal coach had been robbed, a man refuted to have on more than one occasion taken a bribe for his cooperation in certain legal matters. Already on the defensive since the attack on a group of Royal Marines left Ryan Miller dead, certain people had started to become afraid. Horrors! Elizabeth smiled to herself. In a matter of weeks, one man had accomplished more to undermine a particular faction of thugs than Lieutenant Ross and a platoon of redcoats had in six months.

"Lord Blackmoor took your sister out of Williamsburg five days ago," Lieutenant Ross informed her. "I will know where they've gone."

"Mayhap you should check with the governor. Doesn't it take a pardon to remove a charge of sedition from someone's head, even an unwarranted one at that?"

"Lord Dunmore has not been in residence nor will he be back for three more days."

Elizabeth's smug elation vanished.

"He has been in Maryland, Miss Claremont."

Captain Lambert had been furious when he'd discovered Catherine had been imprisoned. It had taken days of inquiries to secure her release. Would he dare have done something illegal to get her out of prison? "Are you telling us that you're here to arrest Catherine, should you see her again?"

"Perhaps, you will stay to dine, Lieutenant Ross?" Her mother graciously offered, breaking the unsettling deadlock. "It would not be difficult to add another plate."

Lieutenant Ross seemed as startled as Elizabeth by the invitation. Dressed in a green silk gown, her mother stood every inch the lady of this manor. "It's cold outside." She nodded graciously. "Will you not at least enjoy a hot meal? We may talk over dinner."

Clearly, the lieutenant was unused to being welcomed anywhere, and the brief glimpse of vulnerability did much to sink Elizabeth's posture. In truth, the weather was wretched.

"You have me at a disadvantage, Mrs. Claremont," he answered awkwardly. "I live with three men over the customs house. Needless to say, the cooking is lacking."

"Do you have family here, Lieutenant?" her mother asked as she offered the lieutenant her forearm.

"No, ma'am. My sisters live in England. . . ."

Elizabeth met Boswell's shocked gaze. Bewildered by the sudden change of events, she had no choice but to follow behind.

"Captain Lambert?"

Stooped over in the stall where he kept the bay gelding, Julian's hands stilled their busywork. He listened to her steps as she peeked inside the stables. Beside him, the big bay shifted nervously.

Julian had been awaiting the return of his men. Seeking some diversion to his restlessness, he'd come out here to groom his horse while she'd slept. In the cottage, the smell of bread baking drifted over the yard. Still holding the hoof pick in his hand, he lowered the gelding's front foot and straightened.

Catherine stood looking over her shoulder at the half-dozen kittens bounding after her in a flurry of fur and bobbing tails. Pale streamers of sunlight embraced the entry, where she bent to await their arrival. The faded primrose dress, a product of much washing and mending, was too big, even over the swell of her breasts. And as he listened to Catherine's sudden unguarded laughter, he felt a jolt so profound that it stopped his breath.

He would promise her those distantly fading stars if it meant she'd smile that smile for him, but in the end, Daniel Claremont would still be dead, and the stars weren't really his to give.

Finally, brushing off her hands, she stood and turned. Her hand went to her chest. "Holy mother! You scared the life out of me!"

The corners of his mouth lifted. Leaning against the warm barrel of the horse, he let his gaze go over more than her face. She wore no petticoat beneath the skirt. Sunlight coming into the stables from behind her limned her legs, and there raged within him the need to seek with his hands that which was so visible to his gaze. "I've never seen you looking more alive," he said.

"Anna will keel over in a faint when she sees me wearing this." She looked down at the purple bodice laced with patterns of yellow flowers more fitting for wallpaper and, holding out the skirts, surprised him with a sheepish grin. "This dress belonged to Mrs. Ericson's youngest daughter. She seemed so proud of it. I didn't have the heart to tell her it was probably better served as shelf lining."

The brisk chill had brought the apples to her cheeks and, setting down the hoof pick, he removed his cloak from the stall door.

"But it does have some artistic value," she was saying as she turned to and fro, "and it's not nearly as breezy as going naked."

The indecent word falling so casually from her lips checked her enthusiasm and humored him to the point of laughing. Her chin shot up. Their gazes held for a heartbeat, then two, before he laid his cloak over her shoulders. "Put it on," he said. "It's too cold for you out here. You've only just recovered your health."

She struggled to clasp the cloak, and she seemed small beneath its bulky weight. "You've recovered, as well, I see." Her eyes touched the slight bruise on his chin. "At least you've no missing teeth."

Although the cloak went just below his knees, it dragged the floor on her. Crossing his arms, he leaned against the outer stall door and watched her hands work to fasten the cloak. "Where did you learn to throw a punch like that?"

Her eyes were ablaze with sudden sparkle. "The first time a boy tried to kiss me, I ran away and cried my eyes out. Papa would have none of it. He told me Claremonts didn't run away, and if I was to defend myself that I needed to learn how to wield a fist. So he fashioned a punching bag out of grain in a sack and taught me how to hit. I was ten. Of course, it was shockingly improper."

"And you took your lessons seriously," he said, finally moving aside her awkward hands to fasten the cloak.

Catherine presented him her throat, handing him her trust as easily as she did her smile. "The second time Jed found me, I was squirrel hunting with Daniel. Jed was strutting for his friends, until I punched him in the nose. He never liked me after that."

"Jed Tomkins?" His hands lingered on her shoulders before he stepped back.

Wrinkling her nose, Catherine laughed. "He was eleven and about as bright as firelight on dirty glass, even back then." She studied the silver thread on her sleeve, then, drawing in her breath, she looked up. "Do you find me odd?" she asked.

"No." He held her liquid gaze.

Something in her eyes changed. He stared because he couldn't help looking, but to be caught so blatantly in the act startled him as much as it did her. Annoyed, he went back into the stall.

"This place looks deserted," she said, following him. "But I smelled bread cooking, so Mrs. Ericson must not be far. I'm ravenous."

He retreated to the stooll and surveyed her from over the back of the horse. "The bread is my doing."

"Yours?" She laughed as if she believed him incapable of common labors. In truth, there was a lot about him that was as common as the next man. "You can cook?"

"Actually, I do. Mrs. Ericson left to visit her daughter."

She glanced around suspiciously. "And Grump and Grumpier?"

Without taking his eyes from her, Julian ran a hand over the bay's withers. "Grump escorted Mrs. Ericson, and Grumpier is running an errand this morning. Aye," sensing her discord, he crossed his arms over the back of the horse, "We're alone."

He didn't tell her that they'd been alone for the past few days.

Contrary to expectations, she didn't bolt in indignation. She didn't call him names or demand to leave here at once. During the past week while she'd regained her strength, their tense banter had eased into a pleasant, sociable discourse that he'd actually looked forward to sharing over supper or breakfast. She'd beaten him at chess last night and gloated unmercifully. Julian liked her competitive spirit. He also liked to win as much as she did, which made the last few days challenging and daunting.

For the reality was that for the first time in his life, he hated the deception. Here in this cottage in the middle of a pine-scented forest more suited to a fairy tale, he wanted only to be himself while he was with her.

What a bloody novel approach to life!

No damn mask.

Julian sat on a stool. He'd give his men another few hours to return before he left her alone to run a perimeter check.

"Don't you have to return to your ship soon?"

"I do."

She took up a brush and began grooming his horse with long, slow strokes. Bending low over the horse's hoof with the pick, he could see her slippers from beneath her soiled hem.

"I would like to visit England, I think. Or India," she said. "You've been to all those places, haven't you?"

His hands paused in their work. There hadn't been much of the world he hadn't seen. And always, he came back here as if drawn by some rooted need. She brushed and stroked, and stroked and brushed with sudden energy. "What is it like? Out there on the ocean?"

"Cold. Wet." His hands dangled between his knees. "Beautiful. There are days where the ocean stretches into the sky, and it seems as if you're the only one in the world."

"Is that why you took to the sea? So you could be alone?"

He hesitated the merest fraction of a second. "Captain Bellamy introduced me to the sea. I think he believed that I needed focus."

"Patrick's father?" She moved the brush over the horse's neck. "You say that as if you admire him."

"Aye. He was a good man. His was my first ship: a ship of the line. Unfortunately, the *Excalibur* sank off the coast of France. I learned very fast how to swim, to speak French, and to survive."

Her hand against the bay's muzzle, she bent, and he was suddenly looking into her midnight eyes. "Your first ship was the *Excalibur*."

It was a statement, and Julian could almost hear her working things out in her head. *Excalibur* belonged to the world of Camelot. To Lancelot, Guinevere. And to Merlin. "The British Navy is fond of using fantasy to denote immortality in the eyes of our enemies," he managed casually. "Unhappily for many, in that case, it didn't work."

She was staring at him hard. "I see," she said almost to herself. "You must have hated the British for abandoning you."

He stepped past her to the rag draped over the stall, and he wiped the grit from his hands. "If not for Captain Bellamy, I would probably still be languishing in a French dungeon."

He slapped the rag down on the stall. "Do you think we can change the subject?"

"You're right." She set the brush on a ledge and followed him out of the stall. "I came out this morning to talk to you for a reason."

He could see the resolute set of her shoulders, traces of defiance in the face of some newfound determination. "I know you've had your own existence separate from our relationship to Patrick." Her chest rose and fell. "Away from the problems of everyday life here. Away from poverty or fear that someone would take away your house or a loved one. I only know that I'm tired of the dread and the constant need to be on guard. In truth, cowardice is crippling, especially when I cannot point the finger at others without first pointing it at myself. I don't want innocent people hurt."

"Innocent people have already been hurt, Catherine."

"Why haven't you interrogated me?"

He shut the stall door behind her and turned his head to look at her. And his eyes could not help but soften. "Did you kill Patrick?"

"No!"

"The rector and his little girl?" He slammed the latch closed. "Did you destroy your newspaper? Raid the warehouse? Are you involved with the men who call themselves Sons of Liberty?"

"Yes! Yes! Yes! Don't you understand? By being afraid, I've allowed bad people to take over my life."

"What more could you have done?"

She rubbed her temples, trying to make sense from her confusion. "I can no longer do nothing against these men who dare claim allegiance to the rebel cause. I want to do the right thing—"

His hand on her lips silenced her words. "Don't." Julian didn't know what he was doing. His gaze dropped to her mouth, and he saw her lips part. Up close, her misty eyes were rich with liquid sunlight as they found his. He could not name his mood or what drove him now. Except he wouldn't allow her to condemn herself. He'd brought her here while she was too ill to fight him, drugged her, and wooed her. Now he couldn't find it inside himself to betray her trust, when he'd already risked more than her life.

"I'm not your friend," he said, splaying his work-roughened hand over her cheek. "I'm not your ally. For that . . . I'm sorry."

His face was blurred through her tears. "You must despise me . . . for everything that has happened."

"Despise you?" His gaze searched the aged rafters before returning to her. "Aye, I despise your relationship to Daniel Claremont. I despise the course I find myself on. I despise that you were married to Patrick, and most of the memories of this place, and I stress, most because another part of me remembers more. Christ in heaven . . ." She felt his fingers press into the thick waves of her hair, closing possessively on her nape. "Have you ever wanted to grab the wind and, no matter how wrong it seems, never let go?"

Her heart hammered. She could not breathe. She could not look away. Something was happening between them, but she too was lost in her own reaction to take measure of his.

Then his mouth covered hers.

A shattering jolt stabbed her, parting her lips in a gasp. Heat infused her, exploded through her veins. Her hands, which had raised to push him away, clenched into tiny fists before opening against his chest, until she had no thought but the shameless taste of him in her mouth, no want but the feel of his arms around her. Then, with a groan that resonated against her palms, he was pressing her into the slatted barn door in earnest, his hardened body covering hers with a possessive urgency as powerful as her own. There was no tender melding of lips as his hand went boldly to her breast, the curve of her waist, her bottom, and lifted her against him. No gentle wooing of her soul as he plumbed the depths of her mouth.

Shivers raced down her spine. His skin smelled faintly of the sea, freedom, power, and a shimmering autumn morning, blurring reality in a once-tiny barren portion of her brain, as a vague awareness of his identity took shape. So very faint at first.

Inconceivable, because the very idea was impossible.

Yet she'd known. A part of her had known since the ball.

His stepfather's ship had been the *Excaliber*. Everything made sense.

His mouth slid to her throat, to the shell of her ear where he whispered her name again and again. Closing her eyes, she was torn, nay broken. Then her hands curled into fists, and she was suddenly fighting. Against her own weakness. Against him. Pushing him away. She felt the dawning of comprehension in his body, felt his arms loosen. Catherine tore herself free.

Breathing hard, now paralyzed, she met his gaze with dark, cutting eyes "'Tis impossible," she whispered.

His palm braced on the door and, as if he wrestled for control, he turned his hooded eyes onto her. Even now he held to the cloak of Lord Blackmoor. He was out of uniform. His shoulders pulled at the tailored silk shirt with an impatience that stretched the fabric.

She'd done far worse than melt like so much wax in his arms. Her chest rising and falling, she wiped the back of her hand across her mouth to rid herself of her own traitorous response. "You knew! In Norfolk, you knew who I was when I came to you."

The tension tightened his jaw. "What is it you want me to tell you?" His voice was tired, as if he were the one who'd suffered.

"The rumors of a highwayman were true. This place doesn't belong to your solicitor's sister. It belongs to you. This is where you've been working from in secret all these months! Coming from Norfolk—"

"This is where I come to escape my other duties."

"You mock my every word and throw my questions back in my face."

"When Lieutenant Ross or someone else asks you the same questions, Catherine, what can you tell them but the truth as you know it? A resemblance to someone does not guilt make."

All control deserted her. He was a man who spoke with such silver-tongued eloquence, she actually believed his sordid logic.

But who was Julian Lambert really? A British spy? A man on a mission of vengeance? Or a freebooter who made a profit at the ill fortune of others? Maybe all three.

Except, he was also the man who'd ridden through the soldiers to save her life. He was the lover in her dreams, the man who had carried her out of the gaol, and the father of her child.

Oh, Lord in heaven!

"I'm going to be sick."

And, before she could turn and flee outside, she threw up.

Catching herself against the door, she heaved on an empty stomach because she'd not yet eaten breakfast. She didn't care

that the arms that came around her belonged to Julian, only that
he'd had the intelligence to pull her to the trough and wash her
face and mouth out with cold rainwater.

"God, things can't get any worse."

"I have to admit," he said as he gently wiped her chin with the
lace on his sleeve, "I've never had this kind of effect on a woman
before."

She wanted to laugh, but mostly she wanted to wrap her hands
around his throat for thinking any act of kindness on his part
could make up for his subversion. "And you've had so many. I
forgot."

"You were wrong about me then. You're wrong now, Catherine."

Standing with his help, she looked up from beneath dark
lashes to find his expression filled with concern. Her stomach
fluttered, which she attributed to nausea.

"How long have you been like this?" he asked.

She reached her hand behind her to grab the fence. She didn't
want to depend on him, not for one ounce of her strength.
"Just . . . go away and leave me alone."

"That's exactly what I'm not going to do," he said into her
thick hair, pulling her against his body. "Lord, Catherine . . ."

She realized at the same instant Julian did that horses were in
the yard. Their bridle chains now loud in the silence, she felt Julian's body stiffen. With her in his arms, he turned his head. She
knew he'd left his pistol and saber in the stables, and panic grap-
pled with sudden relief.

"Daniel!" She cried out.

He and seven others sat astride their horses not twenty yards
away. Pushing abruptly out of Julian's arms, Catherine looked up
at her brother in disbelief. "What are you doing here?"

"What are *you* doing, Catherine?" her brother demanded.

Her brother's long hair was queued beneath a tricorn hat. He
wore a cloak and tall boots. The pistol in his hand nodded at Julian. "Back away from my sister before I blow your head off."

"Put the gun away," she whispered.

Three others had dismounted and held pistols at the ready.
She knew the men by name. Sons of farmers and gentry both.
The other three split and rushed into the house. The danger to Ju-
lian was real.

"You pull that trigger, and there will never be peace for our family. If the soldiers don't hunt you down, I swear I will."

The pistol lowered. "Rina—"

"I'm not going to let you ruin what freedom we have left because of some misplaced brotherly honor!"

"Freedom?" he scoffed, dropping from the saddle of his spotted mare. "Is that what His Majesty told you? Freedom to bear his bastards, maybe."

"Daniel!"

"Tell her, *my lord,*" Daniel demanded, lifting his gaze over her shoulder to impale Julian. "Tell her about her so-called freedom."

Julian's expression carefully blank, his eyes burned as they shifted to her. And something flickered.

"Tell her, Lambert. About her supposed pardon."

Catherine stared, utterly still, waiting for him to say something. One hand fisted against her burning stomach.

"What can I say?" He flashed her a smile that didn't nearly touch the ice in his eyes. "Lord Dunmore has been out of the area."

Daniel's voice fell over her. "After His Captainship finishes with you here, there's nothing to keep Lieutenant Ross from sending you back to prison. Isn't that so, Lambert?"

"You lied to me about the pardon, too?" An ache crushed her chest. "Providence above."

Still holding her piercing gaze, he aimed his next question at Daniel. "Where are my men?"

"You best hope that whatever task they're on will keep them busy. I'm taking my sister away from here where she'll be safe."

Safe? The very notion was ludicrous. She'd never be safe again!

Julian's brows furrowed as he continued to hold her gaze. "Don't go with them, Catherine."

She slapped him. Hard.

Whatever gentlemanly attributes she thought he'd ever possessed vanished in his eyes when he came back around to face her.

She could hardly breathe for the fury that pervaded every muscle, every nerve, and every thought in her body. He'd brought her here with the pretense to save her. Lied to her. There was no apology in his gaze. No plea for understanding. Only an ominous calm in his eyes as they burned into hers. He'd never deviated from his goal. He'd known who she was the instant she'd walked into his cabin on board his ship.

Everything made perfect sense. She'd been such a fool! All he'd wanted was Daniel and justice. It didn't matter how he got both.

One of the men led the bay gelding, now saddled, from the stables. High stepping in protest, the horse hauled at his reins.

"We gotta leave, Danny," the boy said, trying to gain control of the gelding.

"Where are you going to go, Catherine?"

Those who had raided the house returned with food wrapped in blankets. Daniel claimed her arm. "Take off your boots, *my lord.*"

The pistol aimed at his head did much to keep him obedient, but deceptively so, as he removed first one boot then the other. Hearing the drumbeat of her heart, she turned away with Daniel. Let Julian suffer the doubt that she would tell the world who he really was!

Daniel helped her mount the spotted mare, while he took Julian's spirited horse. "How did you find me?" she asked her brother.

"Did you think I couldn't? Or wouldn't?" Daniel pulled on the reins, swinging the bay around. "Chain his lordship to the fence."

Catherine snapped her gaze to the sturdy wooden fence. Her long hair caught the chilly breeze and whipped across her face. "Don't go soft on me now, Sister." Her brother bent across her saddle and eased the reins from her hands. "He's lucky I don't shoot him."

Chapter Fifteen

Oblivious to his surroundings, Julian strode to his waiting carriage, his seal emblazoned on the door and visible even from this distance. A ball of orange settled over the treetops announcing another night to come. He was too furious to take note. His long-awaited meeting with the governor had not gone as planned. Julian wasn't surprised by the thorough dressing down he'd received for leaving Yorktown.

And in view of the current conflict fronting Britain, without Lieutenant Ross dropping his charges. Lord Dunmore would not offer Catherine a pardon. That would set a poor example to others who would tread on British authority. Justice would be better served making Catherine an example. Lord Dunmore did, however, consider Julian's effort to defend his sister-in-law noble, before telling him to return to his ship. Two other merchant ships were due to arrive in the next few weeks, and he would be expected to maintain peace at all costs, doing a job that reminded him more and more of his divided loyalties. In addition, he'd turned over his house in Yorktown to a family that didn't belong to him, and waited word from Michael, who'd vanished too well with the Millers. All in all, a latrine smelled better than the current state of his personal affairs.

Julian started to cross the street, barely aware of the buggy that slowed. A high-stepping black mare pulled in front of him.

"Hello, Julian." The studied feminine voice brought him to a halt. "I'd heard that you were back in Williamsburg."

Stepping next to the carriage, his gaze went over the woman's half-moon bodice and ample cleavage before raising to the blue eyes he knew would be watching him. Allison Simms wore her body in public like a peacock wore feathers. All show, for he knew well enough her charms were not free to any man. The bottoms of her forest-green velvet slippers tapped on the floor of the carriage.

"Do you like?" Allison arced her arm over the plush leather seats, mostly for the benefit of those who listened. "It's imported from France. You know how I always insist on the best. Perhaps I can interest you in a drink at my place to change your mind about that special license you just paid me a fortune to obtain."

Julian leaned nearer and said through his teeth. "You never were one for proprieties, Allison."

"Don't be such a pompous ass, Julian," she whispered, handing over the document she'd been charged to obtain. "Especially when you know my improprieties so well." She lounged against the plush leather seats and observed him with open interest. "I understand you'll only be at the governor's disposal until the end of the month. Then you're shipping back to England. Maybe to face an admiralty board."

She laughed when he failed to be amused. "It pays to be the mistress of a powerful man. You should know there's nothing that goes on around here that I don't know. Including your little business meeting with the governor. *Tsk, tsk,*" she clucked. "I expected better than for you to involve yourself with the common classes."

"Yet, here I am speaking to you." He looked around in exaggeration. He was in no mood for her games. "Will that not be construed as a breach of conduct? Maybe I'll be further shunned."

Her lashes lifted to reveal liquid blue eyes bright with censure. "Might I be permitted to give you some advice? For the sake of our friendship." She reached a gloved hand to tap her driver. "Know who to trust, Julian. Then maybe you might live."

The carriage glided down the street to disappear into the crowd. Julian's gaze went to the sky, to the clouds that flattened over the horizon. Aye, loyalty and friendship were a leapfrog affair that had a way of burning him to death when he looked the other way.

Indeed, later, when Julian stood at the window in Catherine's room at the cottage, nothing was clear save the violence of his emotions. Michael should have checked in by now, but Julian could wait no longer. The cottage was dark when he'd walked through the rooms. With the exception of food and blankets, nothing had been stolen by Claremont's group.

Julian was dressed in black. Black boots beneath a black cloak. Standing with his hands clasped behind him, he continued to stare out the window. A silver prism of moonlight painted the floor a chalky white. For once, no lantern lit his quarters, and he felt the darkness in his blood as keenly as a man feels the heat of rum. A saber weighted the sling at his side.

He didn't know what Catherine would do. He hadn't wanted to see her hurt, but there was no denying she might not take his misplaced generosity in stride. He only knew that she was carrying his child, and all the rules had changed.

He turned on his heel. His cloak whirled around his calves. He descended the narrow stairs to the cellar. His saber scraped the stone walls. He lifted the tallow lantern from the hook on the wall and, holding the light above his head, scanned the low ceiling. The foundation of this house had been built a hundred years before, when Indian attacks ravaged families. An escape route behind the storage racks went directly to another stable down the hill. If the cottage were being watched, no one would see him leave. And tonight, he trusted no one.

He blew out the lantern.

The night was doomed to the ice and chill of an approaching winter when the darkly cloaked rider crested the hill. He rode a stallion black as the night and, like the darkness, the two blended with the churning sky. He'd traveled the low-lying riverbank of the York River, pausing at an abandoned farm, a barn that had recently been used. The rider thundered south to the caves he knew existed there, skirting an abandoned plantation that slept on the rise. Even the roads were empty of life, and by the time Julian finally reached the outskirts of Yorktown, the birds had begun to sing with the approaching dawn.

Watching the light of another day crest the trees, Catherine primed the pistol Daniel had given her. Her hands trembled. The moon could drop into the river, and she was too exhausted to care. She focused on her task and worked to resolve the tumult of her feelings. Fired by her fury at Julian, Catherine had spent two nights on the run before the cold, coupled with her recent illness, drained her stamina. Somehow, it had been different traipsing through the woods with Merlin.

The approaching sunrise provided welcome light beneath the canopy of pines, but she didn't feel more secure, even with the heavy weapon in hand. Especially since Daniel had ridden into Tomkins's rowdy group this morning.

Catherine sat back on her heels. With so many other people around, she and her brother had barely talked. But last night after they'd made camp, she'd demanded answers about Patrick.

"Ryan oughtn't to have told you anything." Only one other time had she ever seen tears in his eyes, and that was when they'd buried their father. "We had argued that night, yes," he admitted. "It was the night that mob had destroyed your paper. But I swear I didn't . . . *murder* Patrick. You have to believe that I didn't mean for it to happen." His voice barely above a whisper, his eyes never left her face as he accepted blame for her husband's death.

Daniel would hang for murder.

"You can leave here," she'd pleaded. "Surely, there are places where a man could disappear."

Without answering, he'd walked away from her. Something in his stance had told her then that he would not or could not run.

Aware of the low grumble of dialogue that excluded her, Catherine moved closer to the men gathered around a small fire. Daniel had stopped at this farm to retrieve a fresh horse, since hers had thrown a shoe. Most were angry with her brother for bringing her here. Now that she was sufficiently and publicly connected to Julian Lambert, anyone who might have been sympathetic to her before remained silent.

Dropping beside the creek, she scrubbed her face. She tried not to think of Julian chained to the fence or whether he'd escaped.

Or who he really was.

And at once all the past fury rose. She should have known that a man who hid behind the uniform of the Royal Navy would lie about everything else in his life. She'd believed in Merlin. He hadn't trusted her. They'd been to the devil and back fighting on the same side. But he'd not fought with her; his fight had been for himself.

"Someone has unsettled the masses." Daniel tied Julian's bay gelding to a tree branch and joined her at the creek. "I can't get another horse. We'll need to share. How are you feeling?"

Catherine clutched her skirt and cloak, dragging both up the hill. Leaves crunched beneath her feet. She told herself that she would not panic. That she could cope with the uncertainty of her future. Especially with a baby to consider. But she knew she needed to find a place to rest and a decent meal soon.

"Guess what I saw in Williamsburg yesterday?" Jed Tomkins lounged against the fence post, watching her from beneath his tricorn. Three of his brothers had walked to the edge of the yard. "I saw His Highness walking blissful as can be down Nicholson Street."

Catherine felt her breath catch. At least Julian was safe.

"Looked like His Lordship was back to business as usual with the ladies, from what I saw. Guess he doesn't much miss you."

Catherine slipped on the leaves. Daniel pulled her up the hill. "Is Jed Tomkins your leader now that Patrick is dead?" she asked.

Daniel took her to the horse. "He's not the leader of anything."

"I'd have finished the job on His Lordship," Tomkins scoffed at their backs. "Slit his bloomin' Tory throat."

"Maybe that's why you weren't invited along," someone said. Snickers followed the remark until Tomkins swung on his cohorts.

"Bugger you, Smitty." The fence creaked against Tomkins's weight. "He had no authority to go after that twit of a sister!"

Catherine stopped Daniel from launching across the yard. "Don't." She clasped his waist, holding him with gentle strength.

"My offer is still open for marriage." Tomkins laughed as he mounted. "Even if ye did let yourself get used." He and the others thundered past. "We'll be watching you, Danny." He chuckled, then amplified his threat with a crude *svvt-svvt* motion across his throat.

Catherine didn't know what possessed her. Suddenly all the fury of the past year clenched her fists. She picked up a rock and heaved it at Tomkins, hitting him square in the back of the head.

• • •

"My lord." Lieutenant Ross set aside a stack of papers.

Julian shut the door behind him. His military cloak swirling around his calves, he swept into the customs office on a blast of chilly air and shook the leaves from his shoulders.

Lieutenant Ross came to his feet. "I apologize that I wasn't here earlier when you came by."

Mildew assailed Julian's senses as he moved his gaze over the rickety bookshelves that lined the brick walls. Ross's desk was covered with books and papers overflowing in an office that lacked funding and personnel. "You've been as anxious to talk to me as I have you, so shall we dispense with the formalities?"

"Indeed." Ross motioned to the leather chair that looked as if it had been dragged out of the river. "Will you have a seat?"

Without removing his bicorn, Julian remained standing. He'd spent the last few days on board his ship. His requisitions that he'd made three months ago to finish refitting his ship had finally arrived. And typical of naval procedures, every damn thing took longer and was more formal than necessary. Yesterday he'd lost his temper with his crew. Last night he'd fallen asleep over supper.

Today, he was in no mood to be pandered.

"Then before we go on, I want you to know that I've filed this report with the governor." Ross dropped a packet of papers on the desk. "It's a list of grievances against you."

Julian walked to the desk and spread out the papers. Skimming the report, he found little to dispute. "Dereliction of duty is a serious offense," he said unimpressed, investing an annoyed air in his tone. The governor had already seen the report and dressed him down in full accord to the charges.

"You let Catherine Bellamy escape. She is a material witness to an important case. One that should mean much to you."

"I don't care what or who you found in her barn. She was with me the night Ryan Miller was killed and only just returned to her house. With the exception of her time spent at the gaol, she's been with me ever since my arrival here."

"I see."

"No, you don't see, Lieutenant." His steps harsh on the slatted floor, Julian moved to the desk's edge. "She's not part of your investigation, and I want the charges dropped against her."

"You of all people should understand my position." Ross shifted beneath Julian's gaze. "These are dangerous times, which call for extreme measures."

"Is that where the governor's dragoons fit?"

Ross's brows dropped over the ridge of his nose. "If you're referring to Sergeant Masters, I've relieved him of his duties here. He has been reassigned to gaol duty in Williamsburg," he said in an affronted tone. "Especially after he let the Millers escape. How well do you know your sister-in-law?" Ross suddenly asked.

The unexpected query threw Julian off his guard.

"I'm in charge of this investigation, my lord. It's my responsibility to ask. Won't you have a seat?"

Julian let his gaze go over the blond lieutenant. His tricorn sat on the corner of his crowded desk. The spit-and-polish uniform refined the image of a man who took his profession seriously. Julian almost felt sympathy for him because British autocracy was not friendly to the common man. Julian knew he could refuse to answer.

He withdrew to the window to look outside. Whitecaps dotted the river. "I know her enough."

"Did you know she left your brother five days after they'd wed?"

Julian's jaw tightened. "No." He turned.

"She'd been investigating the accident of a local rector and his young daughter. Their carriage went over the bluffs. During the course of Mrs. Bellamy's investigation into the rector's death, she'd learned that your brother was having an affair."

Julian's gaze came around.

"When Mrs. Bellamy connected the rector's death to those in the Sons of Liberty, she printed a story. A mob descended on her newspaper, nearly killing her and her brother."

The lieutenant suddenly appeared uneasy. "It was rumored that her husband had ordered the attack. Whoever killed your brother followed him to his mistress's house that night. Patrick Bellamy was found dead on the North Fork road hours later."

"Why the hell are you telling me this now?"

Ross sat on the corner of the desk. His hand absently moved aside the tricorn. "Because the Millers were found dead yesterday."

"What did you say?"

"That's where I've been. They were found on the North Fork road, the same place as your brother. It can't have been chance, which makes me suspect that the same person who killed Patrick killed the Millers. They'd not been dead long."

Julian wasn't listening. Catherine was somewhere out there, and Michael had been out of contact. Was he dead, too? Julian crossed to the back of the chair. "How many people know about this?"

"My guess is that the story is already in the *Virginia Gazette*." The lieutenant's soft-spoken words tore into Julian. "Mrs. Bellamy is at the very least a material witness to your brother's case. Her guilt is her loyalty to men like her brother. I think someone in that group killed the Millers to keep them quiet."

Until now, Julian had been adamant that Daniel Claremont was guilty as sin. He suddenly knew with fervent resolve that the young man who'd risked capture to ride to his sister's rescue was not the kind of man who would murder an old man and old woman. Certainly not the parents of his best friend. Which would make him innocent of Patrick's death.

The lieutenant leaned back on his palms. "Which brings me back to my original question. How well do you know Catherine Bellamy?"

"Enough to realize that something else entirely is going on in York County, Lieutenant," he shoved away from the chair, "and whatever it is, my brother was ten kinds of fool to be involved."

Minutes later, Julian swung himself back in the saddle and left the customs house. The Millers were dead. He'd forgotten to ask where the bodies had been taken. Somehow, it seemed important that they be cared for. Michael had disappeared.

His mind blank, almost reckless, Julian rode the length of the street before he realized that he'd galloped too far and reined in his horse. His gaze took in the simple shops, a tavern, the quiet solitude of the block, counter to the dangerous edge that gripped him, and some of his sanity returned. He urged the horse to a walk, the steady clip-clop loud against the peaceful surroundings.

People, dressed for the cooler weather, walked the street. Some men tipped their hats. A small child stood on the edge of the walk and watched him pass. He'd never ridden through Yorktown, and he did so now with his attention on these peoples' lives, so far separated from his world on the sea, a world fraught with battle.

Then he came to a stop.

For a long time, Julian did nothing. A low roof overhang shaded a window that shared space with the milliner. Inside, behind the glass panes, a mauve-and-cream striped gown graced the feminine display of ruffles and bonnets and the latest accessories from England. A cold breeze blew off the river below the town and, dismounting, he flipped up the collar of his cloak. His gaze scanned the quiet street before he turned and ducked through the door.

The two ladies behind the counter looked up from a case they were arranging as he shut the door. He seemed to fill the space of the narrow aisle, and he removed his bicorn.

"My lord." One hurried around the counter. Clasping her hands she asked, "W-what can we do for you?"

"Where did that dress in the window come from?"

The women exchanged glances. "Only yesterday Mistress Claremont brought it in to us."

Julian walked to the display and, fingering the cloth asked, "Claremont? Elizabeth?"

"I do believe she is staying in your home, my lord."

Julian knew very well that she was. She'd probably sold the dress because Catherine had asked her for funds, which meant they'd been in contact.

His gaze lifted to find the younger woman behind the counter, a blush high in her cheeks. A sparse array of colorful fabric lined the wall at her back. Clearly, this shop, like the town, had fallen on hard times. And as he'd ridden the length of the street, he'd realized that most people here remained upright. No wonder Catherine had been so intent on protecting them. It was too easy to blame everyone for the crimes of a few.

"Return the dress to my home." Reaching beneath his cloak, he withdrew bills, paying twice what he knew the dress to be worth. "The gown belongs to me and is not to be accepted for trade again."

"Yes, my lord."

Outside on the boardwalk, Julian let his gaze go up and down the street. A block down, two children played with a black kitten.

They looked up and saw him watching them. He recognized their small faces surrounded by a cloud of blond curls. The little girl wore a white apron over a pale blue dress. The boy wore a streak of mud on his chin. They came to their feet at his approach, their soulful eyes wide and, for the first time in his life, Julian felt like the enemy. A sign over the door read the *Tidewater Clarion*. He was standing in front of Catherine's shop. Hammering sounded from inside the building. Fresh-sawn wood and ink assailed his nostrils. A board covered what used to be a huge, square window.

"Are you going to make us leave now?" the little girl asked.

Lowering his gaze, it took Julian a moment to realize that she thought he was there to throw them out.

"Lizzy said that the English soldiers will make us leave."

"Why is that?" he asked.

"Because we haven't paid our taxes," the boy said.

"But I think Lieutenant Ross is nice," the girl surmised to the agreement of her sibling. "He ate supper with us."

"What are your names?" he quietly asked after a moment.

Elizabeth suddenly appeared in the doorway, flustered, her hair wilting around her face. The apron she wore hadn't protected her gown. White paint speckled her sleeves and cheeks, matching perfectly the white kerchief that bound her long, blond hair.

"I heard voices," she said as if in explanation to her rushed appearance at the door. The last person that she'd clearly expected to see was Lord Blackmoor in full naval regalia, standing with his hat in his hand on their doorstep. He'd not been back to the house since his return to Yorktown a few days before and had stayed on his ship.

"Their names are Brittany and Brian," she said.

"He's Brian," the little girl promptly clarified.

Despite himself, Julian felt the corners of his mouth tilt.

"Well," Elizabeth sighed when he looked up. "Would you like a tour? After all, except for the hard work that went into building this place, you own everything here. Come in. We don't bite." She grinned impishly at her siblings. "Do we?"

Laughing, they rushed past him into the building. "You don't like children, do you?" she said when he followed behind her.

He had to duck slightly beneath the door. Julian had never spent time around children. They were loud and messy, much like the dog Patrick had had when they were small. "Not particularly." His gaze went around the shop.

The floor was brick and crowded with bins of metal plates and blocks of wooden letters. The walls, also brick, were painted white and embellished with a flowery lavender border that was Catherine's particular trademark, which Elizabeth confirmed.

"In most towns, the printing office combines the functions of the newspaper, bookbindery, and a stationery store," she said, commencing her tour. "We have no working press, but we do have a stationery shop." Taking him to the back room, she introduced Samuel, who nodded in wariness as he straightened, hammer in hand. Then she took him up the narrow flight of wooden stairs. In the enclosed stairwell, his boots sounded heavy against the wooden steps. Fresh paint opened his senses. Elizabeth was babbling about the weather, the color of the walls, and an assortment of trivialities as the children shouldered past him to get upstairs first.

"They're not so bad. Children, I mean," she said, reading the expression on his face. "Do you have any?"

"No." Cautiously bending beneath the low overhang, Julian stepped into the attic room. It was warmer up here. And hazy.

"I apologize if I seem impertinent." Elizabeth studied him. "All we ever hear is the gossip. And of course, Rina's opinion."

New shelves lined the sloped walls. Curtains from a dormer window framed the blue sky like a happy rendition of one of Catherine's drawings. With his bicorn tucked beneath his arm, he walked to the counter and thumbed through the stationery designs before he let his gaze go back around to Elizabeth.

"Where is she?" he finally asked.

Downstairs, the bell on the door tinkled as someone entered the shop.

"She wouldn't let her family worry about her," he said.

Someone was downstairs talking to Samuel.

"I won't hurt her, Miss Claremont. She needs help."

"If you'll excuse me. We've had people coming in and out of here all day," she apologized, backing away nervously. "You may stay up here if you wish. Maybe you will buy something."

Before Julian could stop her, Elizabeth whirled for the stairs. With an oath, he turned back into the room, his gaze coming to rest on the twins. "Rina says it's bad to curse," the girl said frankly. The boy confirmed the words for the gospel it was.

Julian's eyes narrowed. Before he could gather his composure, a crash followed as if a bin had been dumped. He recognized the raised voice downstairs, and when he appeared on the stairs, his slow, distinct steps drew all eyes directly to him. One foot perched on the step above the other, he faced the room.

"Guvnor," Sergeant Masters said uneasily, easing his big hands off Elizabeth, who fell away at once and ran to the stairs. Samuel sat in the corner, nursing his lip.

There was a long pause and, replacing his bicorn on his head, Julian let his gaze calmly rake the room. "May I help you?"

"I didn't know the girl had company."

Biting back his rage, Julian descended the remaining stairs. He didn't expect to be recognized. The night of their original meeting had been black and rainy, and the sergeant had been too intent on breaking his ribs to take note of his physical appearance. Nothing about Julian paralleled Merlin except the contempt in his eyes, which he didn't bother to conceal.

"He's looking for Catherine," Elizabeth said weakly, rubbing her arm. "I tried to tell him that none of us knows where she is."

Behind Julian, wood creaked as the two children crept out of the attic room and sat on the top stair. Samuel watched him with scared eyes. "It seems we are at an impasse, Sergeant," Julian said neutrally, when every muscle in his body was primed to attack. "Catherine isn't here. And you're trespassing on my property."

"It's my duty to find the woman, my lord."

"Indeed." A dark brow lifted. "I was under the impression that you no longer work for Lieutenant Ross in this town."

"I don't. This is personal, my lord."

Bravado shadowed the man's eyes, but the sergeant kept his tongue in place until he flung open the door. The bell furiously tinkled. "Heard tell you got snookered by Danny boy, my lord. Lost your fine expensive boots and fancy horse, too."

"News travels fast." Julian smiled faintly.

"All fer lusting after your brother's wife." A terse laugh escaped. "It's all over town. Who hasn't been laughing hard?"

The door slammed on his chortle. Julian's jaw tightened, and with a great deal of effort, he turned his attention to the quiet sniffling. Elizabeth wiped the heel of her hand across her face. "Rina made a fool of him in front of the lieutenant. He hates her with a passion. He blames her for all that's happened to him since coming here."

Julian looked at Samuel. "Are you hurt?"

"No, sir. It will take more than that man's fist to hurt old Samuel."

"Stay inside, all of you."

Moments later, Julian leaned his shoulder against one of the roof supports and awaited the sergeant's appearance from the alley where he'd gone to relieve himself on the side of Catherine's shop. The fact that the sergeant was looking for Catherine meant two things: whoever framed Merlin didn't know where Catherine was, and whatever corruption brewed in this county, Catherine wasn't a part of it.

Wearing what was left of a soiled uniform, the sergeant was unaware of Julian as he stepped onto the boardwalk, hitching his pants. His hands froze on his waistband, leaving the flap gaping.

Only enormous self-control restrained Julian from killing him outright as he thought of Catherine these past months terrorized by this bastard. "Did I not make it clear that the outside of the building was mine as well?"

The sergeant blanched.

Julian smiled faintly, allowing the words to soak in. His next actions were so fast, the sergeant never had a chance to react. Julian slammed him against the side of the brick building and, squeezing an elbow against his windpipe, pressed his words as near as he could stand to the sergeant's ear.

The street plummeted into silence. "Allow me to rephrase my words, Sergeant . . . Masters is it?"

"Maybe," he squeaked, clawing at the arm choking off his breath.

"Well, Sergeant Maybe," Julian's voice lowered with pleasant intent. "Everything here belongs to me, including my sister-in-law and her family. If you go near any one of them again, I'll cut your spleen out and feed it to the fish. Do I make myself clear?"

Eyes protruding, he nodded and gasped for breath.

With that, Julian let his grip loosen and watched the sergeant sink into the mud.

•   •   •

Elizabeth stood at the top of the grand staircase, listening as the tall clock in the entryway struck eight times. Her hand rubbed the polished skirt of her dress. Tonight, she'd worn her finest gown, a sable cotton. In all of her seventeen years, she'd never experienced such an exhilarating rush as when she saw Lord Blackmoor drop the sergeant into the mud. Her heart fluttered at the mere visual marvel and fervent replay of that memory. His Lordship was surely the bravest of men.

Even if he was a scapegrace nobleman for ruining Rina.

Gripping the letter in her pocket, Elizabeth found her warrior resolve strengthened. Daniel was very firm in his instructions to her. Drawing in her breath, she glided down the wide stairway. Boswell exited the study as she reached the foyer. He stopped when he saw her, his bushy brows lifting slightly.

"Good evening, Boswell. Is Lord Blackmoor in there?"

"No, mum. He's in the dining room. It seems that mistress Anna and your mother have taken over his study during his absence."

Elizabeth kissed his weathered cheek. "Bless you, Boswell, for your patience."

He preened slightly. "And the twins?" Elizabeth realized that she hadn't heard them all evening. "Are they accounted for as well?"

"I believe they are also in the dining room."

Alarmed, Elizabeth straightened. "At this late hour? With His Lordship?"

"It's quite possible that His Lordship has served them up on a platter by now."

Elizabeth hurried down the hallway, her skirts swishing. Captain Lambert had moved back to the house, and she worried that someone would do something to get them all thrown out onto the street. Admittedly, she was frightened at the prospect of leaving here; but in truth, she knew that after tonight, it was probably inevitable.

Elizabeth stopped in the doorway. Silhouetted by glowing lamplight, Lord Blackmoor sat at the head of the long table, working. He seemed to be studying the charts spread before him. The light also revealed a snifter of brandy. He'd made no effort to be sociable tonight. He might be corset-melting beautiful, but he was about as far away as the stars. Yet, even as her mind absorbed whether or not to turn and run back upstairs, he lifted his head and checked her cowardice.

"Good evening, my lord." She smiled and waltzed into the room.

The twins sat at the other end of the table, and Elizabeth was shocked to see them there, alive and well. She hurried to their side and saw that someone had given them paper and charcoal. "I hope they haven't been a nuisance," she said earnestly.

Lord Blackmoor's gaze shifted to the twins. She thought amusement twinkled in his eyes. "They've been fine."

Elizabeth suddenly felt young and childish in this man's presence. "You gave them charcoal sticks. How clever."

His silence prompted a change of subject. "I wanted to thank you for what you did this afternoon for us."

"Sergeant Masters won't bother you again, Miss Claremont."

She clutched her hands together. When he saw that she wasn't going to leave, he set down the quill. His hand was a tanned contrast to the ruffle on his sleeve, and she followed the length of fine silk to find him watching her. Though he wore a white wig, he was no longer the British officer. It was as if a whole different persona filled his clothes now that he wasn't in uniform, a side that had nothing to do with the public image he portrayed.

"River charts." She bounced closer, observing his work. "Do you know that the York River is twenty-six miles in length? I'd heard that once. But then I suppose you already knew that." She looked down and saw that he'd been graphing anchorage points on the James River. The other maps were of the surrounding area and held similar marks.

He folded the charts. "Can I help you, Miss Claremont?"

"Was it true what Sergeant Masters said about you and my sister?"

Conscious of the subtle change in his expression, she didn't understand what had happened between Lord Blackmoor and her sister these past weeks, but she'd seen that same look on his face in the shop, and she knew that he loved Catherine.

"I do not wish her harm, Elizabeth."

She shoved her hand into the slit of her skirt and withdrew the single sheaf of paper. "This arrived for me earlier."

Chapter Sixteen

Catherine shoved the note beneath the tallow lantern on her nightstand and read its briefly scrawled words. She lifted her gaze to the sleepy-eyed woman dressed in a mobcap and simple cream linen dress. The reverend's wife was a kind, elderly lady who Catherine had known since she was a child. When she and Daniel had arrived on their doorstep days ago, Mrs. Brown and her husband had taken one look at her and pulled her inside. Without question, they'd given her a bed and food, caring naught that the soldiers had banged on their door later that day in search of her.

"Did Daniel say something was wrong?" Alarmed, Catherine threw her legs over the side of the mattress and sat up. Her window was cracked open slightly to the fresh air, and she braced herself against the chill.

"No, mum." The woman's kindly gray eyes reassured her. "He only said that he would be awaiting ye in the chapel."

"Thank you, Mrs. Brown. I'll be there as soon as I dress."

The elderly woman patted her cheek. "Everything will be all right, Catherine. You remember that, dear."

The door closed. A frown wrinkled Catherine's brow. She would have questioned the woman's odd words but for the sound of bridle chains that suddenly touched her ears.

She slipped from the bed to her window, where she pulled aside the curtains. Reverend Brown's stone house sat directly across the churchyard. Behind the steeple of the church, pale moonlight lay a sleepy carpet over the town cemetery. Headstones protruded from the uneven shadows. The barn sat back against the pine trees. She saw no movement in the frosty stillness.

The horse had probably been Daniel's. By the time Catherine rushed to dress and crossed the flagstones to the church, a full moon sat in a golden halo over the treetops. Something must have happened at home for Daniel to risk his life coming back here.

Heart racing, Catherine stopped within the main portal of the church. Her gasp turned her brother, who paced in front of the altar. Candles fluttered and twinkled on the main pulpit and shone from dozens of wall sconces around the chapel. Positive someone had died, she rushed to her sibling's side. "What has happened? Is Momma—?"

"Momma is fine," Daniel said, moving her to the solid oak door of a connecting chamber. "She's in the sacristy now with Elizabeth."

A fire glowed in the hearth, lending radiance and warmth to the room. Two high-back leather chairs edged the thin carpet and faced the desk. Congregating near the desk, her mother and sister stood beside Reverend Brown and his wife. Every eye lifted as the door clicked shut behind her.

"Sweetheart," her stepmother opened her arms.

Catherine's slippered feet carried her across the room into her stepmother's arms. "Momma, whatever are you doing here?"

"Did you think we would not be here for you?" She checked her for residual fever as Elizabeth flung herself into Catherine's arms.

"We've missed you, Rina. The horrors you've been through."

"Stop it, both of you." She separated herself from Elizabeth's arms. "I feel as if I'm at my own funeral. Why are all of you here?" She spun back to Daniel, who remained beside the door.

A stifled cry came from her lips. Sitting with his back straight in the wing chair, Julian wore no expression as his gaze held hers. A stark frisson spiraled deep into her belly. He was garbed in his uniform, his tall, broad-shouldered frame breathtakingly beautiful as he rose to his feet in front of her. Following his ascent, she found herself trapped in his dark gaze. Her head barely reached his shoulder. She hadn't seen him in over a week.

His very nearness seemed to steal the air from the room.

She fell back a step and hit the desk. "How . . . *could* you?" She aimed her fury at Daniel.

Daniel, her traitorous brother!

"How could I?" Daniel's voice was incredulous. "You spent the night in his house, Rina."

Reeling on her heel so fast, her skirts swirled around her legs, she strode a wide circle around her nemesis. By all that was sacred, she'd surrendered her flag for the last time. To any man.

Julian Lambert had lied about her pardon. Pretended friendship when she'd been so vulnerable. Purposely annihilated her reputation to force her dependence on him. He was naught but a skilled liar and deceiver, dishonorable to the core of his being.

So very like his damn brother!

"How *could* I?" Daniel stepped in front of her before she reached the door.

"Get out of my way." Her angry frown warned him to move.

Daniel backed a step. "You throw rocks at Jed Tomkins. You're wanted on charges of sedition. You're in trouble—"

"Because of you!" She poked her finger at him.

"Something I intend to correct tonight."

She'd been betrayed by her own flesh and blood. After everything she'd done for him. "How could you even risk your life to bring him here, Daniel? He'll have you hanged."

Elizabeth took her shoulders. "We captured him, Rina. He gave Danny his word—"

"His word!" Catherine pierced Julian with a deliberate stare to emphasize exactly how much she valued his so-called word.

With his arms crossed casually, he leaned against the desk, listening to their every utterance, his calm completely at odds with her tumult. He looked about as captured as an uncaged cat and as lily-white innocent as a rat. Daniel had been tricked. Sure as Providence had cursed her by bringing Julian Lambert here, Daniel would feel his wrath soon enough!

Reverend Brown cleared his throat. "Do you think we can proceed?"

Taking her anger up in aimless pacing, she gritted her jaw. "You don't have the authority to make me marry against my will, Daniel," she warned. "I'm almost twenty-five years old. I have my own authority to—"

"Aye," her brother mocked. "You can tell that to Lieutenant

Ross when he drags you back to that gaol. Tell him you have authority over your own life, and he's not allowed to arrest you," her brother said bluntly, his lack of patience now harboring anger. "I bought a special license. The money was more than enough to see to the legality of the arrangements."

"Rina," her mother turned her around. "He came of his own free will, and he will do what is right by you. He is a good man."

"Momma," she whispered against shoulders that suddenly embraced her. "You don't understand—"

How could she make her stepparent understand that Julian Lambert was dangerous to her? Dangerous to them all. Why was she the only one here who possessed any reason?

"Have you no ken of the child you carry, dear? Your future?"

Catherine jerked back. The quiet words had silenced the room as effectively as if her stepmother had just announced that she carried the plague. Unable to grab her breath, Catherine briskly wiped at her face with the back of her hand. Daniel and Elizabeth stared as if awaiting a vehement denial. Reverend and Mrs. Brown had paled considerably. A stolen glance at Julian revealed only hooded eyes and something she could not name.

Did he defy her to deny that he was the father?

When the baby arrived eight weeks before their supposed first encounter in Norfolk, would he dare claim the child even then?

A hot flush crawled up her neck. But instead of slinking off in shame, she stiffened her spine. She was aware of her stomach all aflutter and the desire that welled inside her when she looked at him, but it simply was not enough to forget that he'd tried to use her to get to Daniel, that he'd do anything to accomplish a goal he'd set. Vaguely, she'd wondered if he had even worried about her the slightest bit these past days. Or if he'd been as shanghaied as she.

Yet something in his unrelenting gaze told her that his passiveness was as much an illusion as his identity. He'd allowed her this tirade because he was patient, and maybe because he understood her anger and panic.

She would never love him.

He must know that.

Her shoulders surrendered a little more to the weight of reality, but her chin didn't drop. Anger burned in the back of her throat. What difference did it make if she never married for love again? Clearly, the first time had proved disastrous. Love did not mean happy ever after. At least her child would have a name, even if he had nothing else from his father.

Catherine looked down at her dress and knew a ridiculous urge to change into something beautiful, more fitting for a bride. Her rags were surely symbolic of her future, for money could not buy respect or trust.

But trust and love were feminine notions of little importance to men. In a few weeks, Julian would leave, maybe for another ten years.

Maybe forever.

"Catherine?"

She braced herself. Julian stood in front of her, a dark figure encased by shadows. She lifted her gaze past the shiny brass buttons on his uniform, past the breadth of his shoulders. Firelight flickered in his eyes. Eyes that were neither green nor brown. And she could not stop the seditious catch in her breath. His was not the presence of authority but of a man who, for one instant, one tiny instant, made the whole world go away.

"I don't do this lightly, Catherine." His voice carried to her.

Confused by the warmth she felt for him, she didn't hear Daniel at first. "Rina." He nudged her elbow, and she lowered her gaze to see Julian's hand extended.

He wore no gloves, no barrier to her gaze or to her touch. The vulnerability of that strong hand struck her and, suddenly unable to trust herself, she snatched her palm away.

"I won't do this." She backed two steps.

How could she? They could not make her do this awful thing. She would not sign the papers. It wouldn't be legal.

She watched numbly as his hand retracted. "We'll be married in the church," she heard Julian say.

And there, practically dragged out of the sacristy, she took her vows before God to honor and obey until death parted them. They exchanged no rings, and she didn't know why that loss should have bothered her, but tears gathered in her eyes. She stood arm to arm with him, kneeling when asked, standing when told. A hint of sandalwood touched her senses. His sleeve brushed hers. She'd memorized the slope of his shoulder, his chest, the angle of his jaw, traced that memory a thousand times in her head and in her heart. Every inch of her being came alive beside him. How could she have not known who he was when every nerve cried out in recognition?

Except, she had known. Pieces of Merlin had touched her, smoldered inside her and burned now. She was on fire for him.

Reverend Brown finished the ceremony by telling Julian that he could kiss the bride. Her pulse beat too fast. Her heart pounded like a battering ram against her ribs.

But he didn't kiss her.

Lifting her chin, she peered up at him through her lashes to assess if the ceremony were over.

Time seemed to stop.

He was watching her, the reflection of candlelight burning in his eyes, as if awaiting her to turn, and she suddenly felt tricked an instant before he covered her mouth with his. Outside, a gust of wind pushed ominously at the windows and smothered her gasp. Heat spiraled through her, paralyzing her for several seconds until she clamped her lips tight against the sensual invasion. His arm tightened around the small of her back, bringing her against his solid length. Her foot dug down on his. Harder.

Catherine fought the fleeting panic his touch aroused. She finally tore her mouth from his, her face aflame. "Don't . . ." She rasped. Blood thundered in her ears. "Don't kiss me again." Her arms remained trapped against the strength of his chest. Her words whispered to his ears alone.

"Indeed," amusement flavored the sarcasm in his eyes as he slid his lips over her temple in a parody of affection while taking all manner of liberties with his mouth. "Do you find my touch that offensive, sweet?" His whisper touched her cheek.

"I abhor it." She pressed harder on his boot.

"You have put me in a dilemma," he murmured in a silky undertone, nipping her ear. "So I'm never to touch you? Ever?"

A taper on the pulpit fluttered, and Catherine focused on the flame. Her heart raced. "Once has been enough for a lifetime."

"And you call *me* a liar." The almost feral heat of his whisper brushed her ear. "Be not misled by my complaisance, milady Guinevere." He chuckled with brittle humor, using the name he'd once given her in mockery. "You *will* be my wife in every way."

The reverend cleared his throat and, as if realizing they weren't alone, he finally loosened his hold. She broke away from him, but his hand was quick to pull her back to his side in what could only be construed as a loving embrace. His piercing gaze went at once to Daniel, who had yet to close his jaw.

If any one of her family doubted that Julian Lambert was every bit as ruthless and dangerous to them as she'd claimed, he'd certainly dispelled that notion tonight.

"The wedding is over," he said tersely. "My bargain is met. You have until you leave the grounds of this church. After that, our truce is off." Turning to her pale stepmother, he bowed slightly. "You and Elizabeth will stay and return with my *bride* and me in the morning. If the Reverend and Mrs. Brown don't have room, then we will stay at the inn down this road."

"My lord," Mrs. Brown gushed. "Our place is humble. But we would be honored by your presence."

Catherine listened in disbelief as everyone complied with His Lordship's orders. The palm splayed around the curve of her waist tightened. "And you, madam." Julian turned his attention to her. His eyes had softened to a challenge. "You have papers to sign."

"Well," Elizabeth clapped her hands to her chest, clearly the only one who didn't appreciate the tragedy of this whole circumstance. "Won't Prissy just eat her heart out now?"

Catherine could only roll her eyes and groan.

Julian stood at the sacristy window. Moonlight illuminated the sky and clung mercilessly to the cobwebs of doubt that had somehow entangled him. With his hands clenched behind his back, he watched the slim shadows of his wife and her family vanish into the reverend's stone house for safekeeping, felt her turn and look at him a moment before the door shut.

Catherine had the ability to make everything in his life more interesting. He liked that about her. Her take-no-prisoners attitude. Her willingness to stand up and fight, even if it was he she fought. Even hating him as she'd claimed, he'd seen her eyes in the church, seen her confusion and knew that she didn't despise him as much as she thought. The moment his lips had touched hers, they'd both known theirs would be no chaste marriage.

He wanted her. He wanted to be inside her.

He wanted to be on the same side again. But he knew that would never happen. As well suited as they were for one another, they were really never on the same side to begin with. Not in this.

Not when he would see Daniel Claremont tried for certain crimes.

His men would have snared Claremont by now, and feeling like a son of bitch didn't change the frustration gripping him. The one thing he hadn't planned on was his damn conscience.

His chest rose and fell and, giving himself a mental shake, he found Reverend Brown's reflection in the glass. No longer bent over the papers on his desk, he was watching Julian at the window.

"You didn't have to marry Catherine," the reverend said with interest. "Men of your stature do not usually align themselves to the common masses here. Will you be taking your bride back to England?"

Julian didn't know what he would do. He was fairly assured though, that Catherine would go nowhere with him.

But Reverend Brown was wrong about him if he thought Julian had been forced to marry Catherine. He'd known by Elizabeth's strange behavior that night that something was afoot. But he'd never dreamed when Daniel confronted him in his stables and demanded that he marry Catherine that Claremont had somehow conspired with fate and delivered to him something precious for the taking.

He had only to walk away from this fight, and Catherine would be his. But with the Millers dead, walking away was no longer an option. He needed Claremont.

He needed answers.

The papers safely tucked in his jacket, Julian slid on his gloves. "Did you know my brother?" His voice was quiet, uncertain.

"I married Patrick and Catherine." Clear blue eyes watched him back carefully. "Unlike what others have said, I considered him an effective leader here. I thought the man very much in love with his wife. And she with him. I truly do not understand everything that has happened, my lord, any more than I understand her willingness to lie with you and conceive a child."

The condescending remark rankled. "Then let me assure you it was willing, Reverend." He crossed the room. "On both our parts."

"Perhaps then you intend to be more honorable with your marriage vows than you were with your promise to her brother?"

Without comment, Julian swung open the door and shut it soundlessly behind him. Outside, the chill hit him. His heavy boots crunched in the grass, leaving prints beside those that had passed before his. Two men stood at attention in front of the stable door. Another two watched the woods behind the stable. Daniel sat inside, propped against the back wall, his hands bound behind him and his head resting on his knees. Julian shut the huge swinging door. Lantern light spilled a harsh glow over his haggard features.

"My lord," Claremont mocked, "will you hang me now from the rafters or await my family's presence in the morning to do the deed?"

Julian took his stance against the stall door that housed the bay gelding. Claremont's loyalty these past weeks to Catherine had impressed him. Twice, the young man had risked his life for his sister, which was why Julian hadn't hauled the young man up by the collar and slammed him against the back wall for his belligerence.

"You left out one option." Julian caressed the bay's forehead. "I could turn you over to Lieutenant Ross in exchange for Catherine."

"Or you could let him go on your word, my lord." Catherine's voice stiffened Julian's shoulders. Forcing himself to breathe, he turned to face his new bride and confronted a pistol.

In the semidarkness her liquid eyes were challenging. "I know my way around barns, Captain," she said with an air of smugness that at once raised more than the battle flag between them. "And I'm not so stupid to trust you at your word."

His eyes fully on hers, he raised a brow. "Do you really think waving that thing around is wise?"

"You don't deserve this, Daniel Claremont." She looked past Julian. "But I've come here to make sure this man honors his word."

A slow smile turned up one corner of Julian's mouth. She looked magnificent with her dark hair flowing around her near-perfect shoulders, the light from the lantern reflecting in her eyes. And getting an eyeful of her nipples pressed against the cloth of her dress, he took a step in front of Claremont. "You are not taking proper care of my child, madam, to be out here half naked in the cold," he remarked, suddenly annoyed that she wore no cloak.

"Get up, Daniel," she said without removing her eyes from his.

"Stay down, Claremont. If I have to chase you again, one of us might not live."

Daniel didn't move. "Forgive me if I don't applaud my choices."

Catherine set her teeth as if to prevent her jaw from clicking in the chill. "I knew you had no intention of honoring your word."

"I don't bargain with thieves, Catherine. Nor would I be talking to your brother now if I thought he were a cold-blooded murderer." Over his shoulder, he said, "You can't live your life running, Claremont. Believe me, I know."

"Rina," Daniel's voice was suddenly tired. "This whole thing is more complicated than you know." He sighed. "Put the pistol away before the thing goes off."

Julian's dark brow slashed up. "What an interesting prospect. Two dead husbands. Even I couldn't save you then."

"How dare you imply . . ." She looked desperately at her brother. "I won't let him bloody hang you!"

Behind her, Julian glimpsed one of his men in the shadows and realized her danger.

"Please . . . Captain—"

It was the way that she'd said both words together, her uncharacteristic humility that grabbed at his gut like long talons. He snatched the gun from her fists so fast, she didn't have time to blink before he tossed the pistol to his man standing in the shadows. "Give Claremont a blanket before he freezes to death out here."

Catherine ran to Claremont. Julian grabbed her hand and swung her around into his arms. "Say good night, sweet."

"Let go of me!"

He liked her family, and that put him at an unfair disadvantage, especially when the whole damn world had begun to collapse around his ears. But that "please" had come from lips he'd wanted to kiss since she'd walked into that sacristy and saw him sitting in the chair. Nay, even before that. He'd had enough of wanting and watching her; the next "please" out of those lips would come when he had her in bed beneath him. To hell with gentle persuasion.

She didn't like to lose. Well, neither the hell did he!

"You promised my brother that you would let him go!" Catherine dug her heels into the dirt and called him the worst name she could think of, before he threw her over his shoulder, kicking and shouting.

"Vile snake?" he laughed. "I should put you on my ship for a week if you wish to learn to curse properly."

"Hah!" Nearly in tears, she pushed down on his back and lifted her head. "Which ship, my lord? The HMS *River Rat*? I will be free of you, Reece. You won't do this. This marriage isn't legal. I am your brother's widow."

"Half brother, and this isn't England, sweet. The banns were posted last Sunday in Williamsburg. I received special dispensation from all the appropriate authorities there."

"Then you didn't even need Daniel's license. You had this planned!" Every step knocked air out of her. Her hair trailed down Julian's hips. He slammed open the back door to the reverend's house.

"Which room have you been staying in?"

"Put me down, you *bastard!*"

"Which room?" he asked again without breaking stride as he swept through the modest drawing room.

Catherine stared in disbelief at her mother and sister standing with Mrs. Brown in front of the hearth. A fire crackled behind them. The elderly woman pointed mutely to the last door down the hall.

Inside the room, Julian shut the door. "Take off your clothes, Catherine." He dropped her on the bed. Bed ropes groaned as she whipped around and came off the mattress on the other side and hit the wall. "I will not!"

Without removing his gaze from hers, Julian wedged a chair beneath the latch of the door.

"Where is your honor, Captain Lambert?"

Slipping off his stock, he walked around the bed. "Tucked away for the night in the stables. Along with my bay gelding, which your brother stole from me last week."

"You gave him your word he could leave this church safely."

"And he did. But take note, dearest wife." Julian deliberately removed his wig. "The stable is not on consecrated ground."

"I could see you hanged. I'll tell the whole world who you are."

"And who is that, sweet? Except the father of your child. The love of your life. We are partners in crime, wife."

Catherine could not respond. Not to his twisted logic. Not to his complete lack of atonement for all his sins. Not to anything.

The man who stood before her took the heated breath from her lungs. His dark hair fell in a queue down his back, and the sight of him sent a hot chill through her bones. Without his white wig, his jaw looked more pronounced, his lashes darker as they framed his glittering gaze. A gaze unmarred by swelling. The rich fabric of his uniform stretched taut over his shoulders and, mesmerized by the long fingers unhooking each brass button from its mooring, she lost herself in the swirling contradiction of her emotions. She watched his uniform jacket slide down his arms to the floor.

Enraged that he could have so little respect for her feelings or for her family, she snapped her eyes to his face to find his gaze boldly raking her. She had never seen such a reckless regard for his own life in him. "You are a rogue." She slid sideways along the wall.

"Nice only gets you killed, Catherine." He removed his waistcoat. Lantern light limned his powerful body beneath the white fabric of his shirt as he made quick work of those buttons as well. "No turning your cheek. Is that your adage?"

"It is if I don't want my throat cut."

Panic exploded inside her. Catherine refused to admit that he was right. Or that she and Daniel needed his help. Or that he made her so hot, she thought she'd die from bodily combustion.

Seeking refuge in the shadows, she wedged against the corner until she was trapped between the wall and her nightstand. "How did I miss seeing all of these sterling qualities of yours earlier?"

"Maybe you were admiring someplace lower than my heart, Catherine. Someplace no decent *widow* would be looking."

"That's not fair. You do me an injustice."

His shirt hung open. "Injustice?" He laughed, but his eyes were unrelenting. Pressing his palms to the wall, he trapped her between his arms and the impenetrable barrier of his chest. His shoulder muscles rippling with constraint, he looked too good not to breathe into her starved lungs.

He bent until his face was level with hers. "The truth is that I was with you that morning in the glade when you gave yourself to me. I didn't ask for that, but I took what you offered and, had I known who you were, I still would have taken you. You denied any knowledge of Daniel Claremont. I was with you in the stables the night when you tried to leave me. The British as well as your people want Merlin for being a traitor." He scraped his fingers into her hair. "Tell me where the injustice lies, Catherine."

He had been wronged from the very beginning. But so had she.

He pulled her against him. She balled her fists to keep from touching him. He didn't kiss her; instead, he whispered her name, willing her to open her eyes. She could feel his heart pounding against her chest. "Look at me, Catherine."

She opened her eyes. Wet with unshed tears, her gaze encompassed his. "I tried to do what was right." Her voice was distant. "Daniel told me I was meant to take that letter to you. Blackmail to keep him loyal. It didn't matter if I lived or died; Daniel would have gotten the point. He had other family to protect. As for Merlin, you were raising questions about Patrick. Questions no one wanted answered."

"Catherine—"

"Nor was I leaving you that night in the stables. Something happened. Jed Tomkins came in when I was saddling that horse. He . . . he attacked me in the stall. The horse escaped. That's why it looked as if I was leaving you."

"You kept silent about everything. Why?"

"My silence was never noble. I cannot condemn anyone in this organization without condemning my family or myself. That's why I could tell you nothing."

"Why hasn't Tomkins spoken out against you?"

Catherine shook her head. "You would have to know Jed. In his mind, I bested him in a fight. He would not want that to get out. Heaven forbid that I would ruin his reputation. And in his way, he also lives by that twisted code that keeps us all silent."

"I'm sorry," he said, and she lifted her eyes. He scraped his fingers into her hair. "I'm sorry I wasn't there for you that night in the stables. That I allowed you to leave my ship at all."

Despite her earlier determination to stay strong, she longed to touch him. "You've . . . not asked if the baby is yours."

His eyes softened possessively on hers. "The baby is mine."

"How can you be so sure about everything? So strong all the time?"

"Strong?" His lips smiled against her temple. "You make me weak, Catherine."

"I am no man's weakness. Certainly not yours."

He pulled back and placed his palm over her abdomen. Skeins of warmth enveloped her. "When all I think of is you and the baby you're carrying, your very presence weakens me." His lips brushed hers. "When I fall asleep over my veal cutlet. When I bribe an official of the crown to get you out of that gaol, when I threaten a king's soldier with imminent torture and death, I'd say I've sufficiently crossed the line from professional integrity to personal effrontery."

"You did all that?"

"Aye, I threatened to remove Sergeant Masters's spleen if he bothered you or your family again. I fear the whole town heard."

Catherine suddenly laughed and cried at once. "Did Elizabeth see that? Lud, no wonder she's half in love with you."

"What about you, Catherine?"

His gaze was earnest, and it stilled the breath in her lungs.

"I love no one."

He brushed the hair from her face, tilting her chin, and driving away her will.

"You play all of your parts so well," she whispered. "Merlin, a British spy, an officer in the navy. I don't know who you are. Tell me, Captain. Whose side are you on?"

"Ours," he breathed into her hair. "I'm no different than I was. Only your perception of me has changed."

She'd missed him so much; tears sprang to her eyes. Her perception of him had not changed. It had only expanded with reality. And the reality was that he lived by a different creed than she. He was still too much like the chameleon. And not knowing or understanding his loyalties, she wasn't convinced that he hadn't stooped so low that marrying her didn't fit into his plans. As ridiculous and childish as that sounded to her own thoughts, her heart would not let go of that fear. Yet another part leaped with the joy that he was here with her, wrapping his body around her as near to making love as she'd ever felt from a man.

Then he was kissing her, pushing his tongue past her lips, past her resistance, past her defenses, the throbbing, hungry need inside capitulating to want. But he could not conquer. She would not allow him to consume her. The bed frame was suddenly pressing against the back of her legs. "Don't fight me, Catherine," his whisper bade.

His hands were on her bottom, the small of her back, and she could feel him hard beneath his breeches as he pressed her against the bedstead. She didn't know when she'd stopped fighting him. Her hands crawled up his chest in a carnal tribute to her desire.

His fingers splayed her ribs, and she realized he'd released her bodice. Pure desire stole over her with the familiar exotic inhale of his scent. She no longer wore her gown. Lifting her to her toes, he filled his hot mouth with the tip of one breast and then the other, pulling away only to remove her lacy shift. He cupped her jaw and kissed her hard, pressing her down onto the white, downy comforter.

His hand moved between her thighs. The groan was hers. Everything felt sensitive and alive beneath his skilled hands. His lips touched her navel. He was between her legs, spreading her to his gaze. Then he was kissing her where his fingers had been, and only his firm grip on her hips anchored her to the bed.

She'd already given up too much to him. This was . . . somehow . . . wrong. His tongue seared her.

No one had ever done such a wicked thing.

Blood surged through her limbs, rushing to her loins. She grabbed his hair.

She was seconds from climaxing.

She tried to swear at him, but she gasped for breath instead, sinking into his touch, lost to the hot pressure of his tongue. She threw her head back. A cry tore from her throat, and everything shattered around her: her thoughts and breath, anger and panic. Nothing remained as it was.

He was suddenly above her, and she shut her eyes, tried to turn away. Except mercenary that he was, he waited. Waited until she'd settled back to awareness of him, and she was looking into his eyes, wondering what she had seen there an instant before his mouth found hers and he was pressing inside her. Filling her, and she was tasting herself on his lips. She returned the kiss, aware of the melody of his mouth on hers, her blood humming in her ears. His hands shifted beneath her bottom, no longer gentle or patient but demanding as he moved against her with a hunger that drove hers. She cried out softly, brought again to silken heights. He shuddered inside her, holding her fast, where they both drifted back to earth.

Her gaze shimmering with something she could not name, she looked up at him and suddenly knew that he was as lost as she.

Julian didn't sleep. And when he finally did, dawn awakened him. The smell of bread and cooking eggs filled the room. Catherine slept with her head nestled on his upper arm. His body should be sated but was not. So he turned his attention to Claremont, disturbed by something Catherine had said last night. He realized the niggling concern had been with him since she'd said the words.

"Daniel told me that I was meant to take that letter to you. Blackmail of sorts to keep him loyal."

Loyal to what?

He lifted a long lock of her silken hair. Why was Claremont so important to an organization that would send a woman out to die?

And, with sudden tenderness, he shifted his arm to bring her nearer. The movement stirred the scent of him on the sheets and between her legs. Then he wasn't thinking about anyone or anything outside this small room as he bent his lips over hers.

He loved her. Plain and simple.

Only nothing in life proved simple, and Catherine was anything but plain. He'd made love to her earlier, before the sun crested the trees. She'd been hot and tight, and amiable because she'd still been half asleep when he'd entered her. But she'd also been sore, and he had no wish to abuse her further. She would fight him this time. And he'd already been too hard on her this night. Yet he felt safe in the knowledge that she could not make love to him the way she had and feel nothing for him as she claimed.

Easing out of bed, Julian washed from the chilled pitcher of water on the commode. Looking outside at the barn framed in brilliant, frigid sunlight, he thought about Catherine's threat last night to tell the world his identity. He knew that she had every right to questions concerning Merlin. In truth, she would not like what he had to tell her. And he damn well wasn't prepared to offer his heart up to her on that silver platter of trust. Dressing in his uniform and boots, he reapplied his wig, then removed the chair from beneath the door before he turned again to the woman asleep in the bed.

Her eyes were open, but she shut them fast, which meant she probably couldn't wait for him to depart.

Julian stepped forward. And with a gallant "Good morning," he stripped the blankets from the bed. "Rise and shine, my lady Guinevere. The new day awaits."

Sputtering against the gust of cold air, Catherine sat straight up. Her black hair swirling around her face and shoulders framed her furious dark eyes. Eyes that had glittered in passion last night. "How dare you!"

Julian propped a boot on the bed and observed her with a gleam in his hungry gaze. "Maybe now that you're my wife, I will forbid you wearing clothes. I like you naked and pregnant."

"Don't think every night with you will be like the last one."

His mouth quirked upward in a caressing grin. "Words of endearment, sweet. A challenge that I cordially accept."

An errant missile smacked him in the face. Julian tossed her back the pillow and, smiling to himself, left the room.

Mrs. Brown and Elizabeth sat at the trestle table eating breakfast. A North Atlantic ice floe was warmer than the greeting he received as he entered the room. Studying the two, he poured coffee.

"You've been awake long?" he asked Elizabeth as he moved to the window and carefully pulled back the frilly curtains. He could make out the barn from this distance. His men sat on hay bales, hunkered over what looked like plates.

"She brought your men breakfast," Mrs. Brown said.

Julian's gaze shifted abruptly to Elizabeth. Her interest remained on her eggs. With an oath, he slammed the cup down and sprinted to the barn. At his approach, his men jumped to their feet. "He's still asleep, my lord." The youngest swallowed a mouthful of bread. The barn door was cracked open. Shoving it wide, Julian spied a rolled-up blanket lightly bunched in the shape of a body.

The young man sidled nearer. "Miss Claremont went in earlier and left her brother's breakfast beside him."

An empty plate sat near the roll. Julian stripped off the cover. Claremont had cut his ropes. Little Miss Actress had probably batted her blue eyes and smuggled the knife directly beneath his guards' noses. "Goddammit!" He threw down the blanket.

"Rina would wash out your mouth for that."

Julian whirled. Straw crunched beneath his boot.

Holding something half wadded in his fist, Daniel Claremont stood with his arms crossed against the last stall. "I thought about what you said last night. About not running any longer."

With a nod to his men, Julian dismissed those who stood in the doorway poised for battle. He faced Claremont after everyone left. The stable smelled musty and in need of a thorough mucking. "I can't promise that you won't still be hanged."

"You can promise the safekeeping of my family?"

"Are you coming to me for help?"

"Elizabeth brought this out with breakfast." He waggled the paper in his hand. "The *Virginia Gazette*."

Julian's hooded gaze fell over the main article. A wicked depiction of a highwayman cloaked in a flowing cape on a horse boasted the paper's flair for sensationalism. Below that was a caption accusing the miscreant of the Millers' murder.

"Rina's been fighting this fight alone for too long," Daniel said. "I want the bastards who killed Ryan's parents dead."

Chapter Seventeen

"The Millers were good people," Daniel said.

Standing in the corner of his ship's cabin on the *Chimera*, an arm leaning against the bookcase, Julian didn't move. His eyes were on Catherine. The *Virginia Gazette* trembled in her hands. The tattered headlines blared out at her but not as much as the bold depiction of the highwayman deemed guilty of the deed.

He'd not returned to his house in Yorktown. Instead, he'd sent Catherine's stepmother home in the carriage with a sobbing Elizabeth, and he had taken Daniel for safekeeping to his ship. Refusing to allow Daniel out of her sight, Catherine had accompanied them as they'd rowed out to the *Chimera* in rough seas.

Heavy afternoon sunlight spilled through the stern gallery windows. She stood with her slim back to the cabin. Even with the world of problems between them, it was impossible not to want her.

The tangled fall of her hair spilled around her waist like a dark, wintry cloud. Daylight accentuated the smooth curve of her jaw, emphasizing her profile. She looked at him and flushed as if startled to see him watching her so intently. He didn't say anything, and he might have been amused by her rising color if it wasn't important that she believe in him, at least in this. For even as he'd always done what he deemed right, regardless of diplomacy, he'd forgotten what it was like to have someone believe in him completely.

But the sweep of her eyelashes veiled dark eyes fraught with confusion, a look he'd seen that morning when he'd brought Daniel back from the barn. Glancing away, Julian didn't begrudge the staunch loyalty shared between his wife and her younger siblings. Indeed, he admired, even envied the trait. He wanted that part of her. But he would not tolerate any more disaffection from her or Elizabeth or Daniel. He only had one pair of eyes in his head.

"I don't even know where to begin," Daniel said.

Claremont sat at the desk, staring at his hands. A crystal decanter filled with brandy perched near the edge of the polished surface, and Julian poured two glasses. Liquid sloshed.

Lifting his gaze, Daniel looked up at him in surprise. "Take it," Julian urged. It was the least he owed Catherine's brother for bringing them all together in such a fitting fashion.

Claremont's hand encircled the glass. He looked at Julian, clear resolve in his eyes. "You swear she'll be cleared of everything?"

Catherine knelt beside her brother. "Why are you doing this?"

But her brother no longer looked at his sister. She swung her gaze to Julian, a somber entreaty in her eyes. But if his heart had grown soft, his gaze had not.

"Most of us here still believe in fighting the British," Daniel said firmly. "Radical as it seems, my lord, we don't want you here. In the beginning, we were all dedicated to that cause."

"Bloody politics aside, Claremont, I want your leader." Julian tipped the last of the brandy from his glass. "And I don't for one moment believe that Jed Tomkins is the brains in your group."

"I have rarely seen him. My guess is that he doesn't live in this area year round. Maybe he's a high government official. He knows too much not to be. The Tomkins farm is his conduit, so to speak. Now that Patrick is gone . . . our orders come from there."

"What happened, Claremont? Where did everything go wrong?"

Daniel exhaled. "Patrick knew how to lead us. There wasn't anything that went on around here that he didn't know. He'd joined forces with someone who knew the river tributaries. We were getting smuggled goods past British customs."

Catherine lifted her gaze to Julian's. She'd been an active part of that operation. But he could hardly find guilt in that.

"Then some among us took their patriotism too far. Some started robbing coaches of suspected loyalists. When people threatened to go to the authorities, the rector and his daughter were killed, and everything changed."

Catherine stood and went to the window. Julian forced himself to look at the glass in his hand as Daniel continued to speak.

"It was a botched robbery. Ryan was there. That bastard, Jed Tomkins shot the rector, even after he'd handed over his valuables. The horses became frightened, and the carriage went over the bluffs. No one could get the little girl out in time."

"God, Daniel." Catherine looked at the timbers in the ceiling.

"When something like that happens, we are all bound together by the crime, whether we will it or not. The secret became the glue that would keep us from hanging. Patrick tried to tell you that, Rina. By condemning the few, you condemned us all. Including yourself. But you wouldn't let it go."

"A little girl died. People had to know the truth."

"Or were you just so damn angry with Patrick because you'd discovered . . . other things? Where was your proof to print that Sons of Liberty story?"

"In his pockets, Daniel. I found the cross that belonged to the rector. In his pockets!"

"Then he took it away from Tomkins. Because he wasn't even there that night."

"What happened later?" Julian asked.

"After the mob smashed everything Rina had worked so hard to build, I'd wanted to kill him. I thought Patrick was the one who'd given the order to destroy the paper. I followed him that night—"

"To Allison Simms's house," Catherine quietly finished. Julian turned. Catherine faced him, her chin high, her eyes wet. "She's the one he'd been seeing regularly. That 'other thing' as you called it, Daniel, might not be important to men, but honesty means everything to me. I followed him after I found the cross." Heart pounding, Catherine turned her face away, suddenly feeling as if she were choking. They hadn't even been married a week. "We argued terribly. But it had nothing to do with my decision to print that article."

"That night, after the attack on the newspaper, he wasn't at Simm's house long." Her brother's voice reproached her, for she'd never allowed him to speak about Patrick's affair. "I'd never seen him so angry. Then I accused him of ordering the attack on you, and he hit me."

Daniel slouched back in the chair, raking his fingers through his hair. "Somehow, I got hold of his pistol. I don't know what I wanted to do. Take him to the authorities. We struggled. The pistol went off. The ball hit him in the thigh. I bandaged the wound with his vest. He told me that he didn't give the order to attack you. He was astounded that I would think that. He couldn't walk, so I left him near the road to get help. When Ryan and I returned with a wagon, I couldn't believe that he was dead. I couldn't."

"And the doctor declared it a self-inflicted accident," Julian said with apparent disgust.

"Ryan and I told him that we'd found Patrick dead." Daniel looked hard at Catherine. "Before I left him that night, he said that he was going to the authorities. He didn't care if everyone hanged for it."

A worn Turkish carpet muffled Catherine's steps. "Why didn't you tell me this sooner?"

"Ah, Christ, Rina—"

Catherine pressed the back of her hand to her mouth. "The night I took that letter from you in town. Did Jed Tomkins tell Sergeant Masters where I was supposed to be meeting Merlin?"

His gaze snapped to Julian before Catherine realized what she'd asked. She wasn't thinking clearly. But she was too desolate to take notice or to care any longer about the wretched secrets that bound her to silence.

Patrick and Daniel had fought because of her. Two lives destroyed. Because she'd printed that article connecting the little girl's death to the Sons of Liberty. Had she really been so wrong?

She swiped her face with the heel of her hand. "Captain Lambert knows about Merlin."

She sensed the confusion in Daniel's gaze as he shifted his attention back to her. "Tomkins and his brothers are cold-blooded murderers, Rina. But they do possess a certain code of honor treasured among thieves. If they wanted to accomplish a job, they would do it themselves. They tolerate me because I'm needed to the organization. And I stayed because they would kill you if I didn't."

She wanted to shake him. "Why are you are so important to the organization that they would keep you alive?"

Julian suddenly tossed down three Virginia currency notes. He stood beside her, his height lifting her gaze to his face. "Let me guess," he said sharply to Daniel. "Or be the bearer of real tidings here. Your weapons, the fancy horses. Everything is financed by that." He shoved the bills across the desk. "You're important to the sect because no one can create counterfeited currency with your artistic skill. Without you, the organization's financing would go down the river. All means, including the attempted murder of your sister, have been used to strong-arm you into remaining loyal to a bunch of murderers."

Catherine stared in disbelief at the currency. Her brother's blue eyes had shifted to her in regret. "I'm sorry, Rina."

She pressed a fist against her stomach. "Sorry?"

Why couldn't he have just told her the truth? Because she'd failed Patrick? Did Daniel also think her weak and spineless?

Maybe her loyalties had been too divided from the beginning. Maybe Patrick had seen that inside her, which told her why he had shut her out of the inner circle that surrounded him. Did she possess some character flaw then that she had become the means to destroy all those she loved?

"Well . . ." Snapping her gaze to Julian, she laughed past the hot band around her throat. He stood against the stern gallery window with his arms crossed, his long, muscular frame encased in his usual control. "All crimes are practically solved, my lord. The criminals in hand. You must be very happy with yourself."

He didn't reply. But a tic was clearly visible in his jaw.

Whirling back to Daniel, she was less kind. "It's amazing what honesty can accomplish, little brother of mine." She poked a finger at his shoulder, vaguely shocked to feel so much muscle beneath the brown homespun. "You had no right to play the martyr in this family. Because that's exactly what you did by letting them use me to get to you." Her voice dropped to a whisper. "I loved Patrick. You let me believe all those horrible things. You didn't even allow me the chance to mourn my own husband."

Her eyes lifted to Julian because she didn't know where else to turn with her anguish. She'd expected to see censure in his eyes and was struck instead by a flicker of compassion or anger. She couldn't fathom which when her emotions were in a state of chaos, but she was afraid of the strength in him. Afraid of vanishing completely in a world she no longer understood.

And suddenly her temper flared. He'd never stopped fighting for Patrick. She also knew that he was somehow a part of everything that had occurred here. Part of what happened to the Millers. Part of the reason Patrick had been so adamant to prove himself.

But he kept these things from her. Just like Patrick.

A knock sounded on the door. Catherine turned away to gather her composure. Her hair fell in waves over her shoulders. She hadn't even had time to pin her hair back this morning and cover it properly. In the jumbled mesh of her thoughts, she heard Julian tell Daniel that Lieutenant Ross had sent notice that he was on his way to the ship. She'd known Julian had summoned Ross earlier.

But now it was too real, too final. She reached out to catch her hand on the desk.

Julian was suddenly standing before her, taking her elbow and escorting her into the privacy of the corridor. Her heart quickened. She was vividly aware of his uniform. There were seamen nearby. She could hear murmurs through the slatted walls. Footsteps sounded on the deck above her. "I'm all right," she told him coolly.

He pressed her head against his chest, against the beat of his heart. The smell of brandy touched her senses. And the scent of wind and the river that came up through the moist planking of the ship.

"I'm putting you in another cabin. You can lie down while Ross is here." Anger laced his voice.

"Damn you." Her hands trembled so that she clutched them into fists. She would not touch him. "You can never just leave me be." The scent of him pervaded her senses. But she was not amenable to his possession in clear view of the British Navy. "I wish to go home."

He raised his head slightly and looked down at her, his eyes intense in the shadows. His arm was strong around her waist, but she would not yield to another protector. Especially not Julian.

God in heaven, she was in love with Patrick's brother when she should still be mourning her dead husband.

But Julian was her husband now.

She was pregnant with *his* child. Not Patrick's.

"Did you have anything to do with the Millers' death?"

"Christ . . . Catherine," he breathed against her hair. "What the hell do you think?"

The knot in her chest loosened a little. She'd had to know the answer. The whole world had flipped upside down, but she could not have gone on without knowing for sure.

"I'll send one of my men with you back to the carriage." He set her aside. "He'll see you safely home."

"Thank you." Beside her head, the tiny flame from the lantern wobbled as the ship pulled at her anchor cables.

He walked back inside his cabin and returned with her cloak. Without looking at the door as it shut behind him, she let him escort her on deck. She didn't want to say good-bye to Daniel. She couldn't.

Resting his hand possessively on the small of her back, Julian handed her over to one of his men on deck with the express orders that she not be let out of anyone's sight. The wind lifted her hair and slapped at her skirts. "Catherine?" His harsh voice turned her.

She mentally braced her heart even as she braced her hand on the rail to keep herself balanced with the ship's movement. His gaze was inscrutable.

"I hold you to our vows."

Catherine's breath seemed to stick in her lungs. Hearing those words brought back last night with a clarity that had been branded on her soul: the gentle—and not so gentle—way he had loved all of her. She had not meant to be so cruel down in the corridor, for he must also have feelings about his brother that needed tending.

The ship dipped slightly in a swell. She started to run back to him, but hands lifted her into the jolly boat, and she was suddenly sitting behind a brawny, red-haired man. A gust of sea spray washed over her. When she cleared the hair out of her eyes, Julian had already turned away to give the command to lower the jolly boat.

*   *   *   *

Watching the pulleys lower the longboat into the water, Julian told himself that her rejection was not worth the hurt. After Midshipman Pulver reached shore, Julian went below. He slammed the door to his cabin, surprised at the ill-restrained shock of his temper. Events had put him in the middle of something he didn't understand. Even within himself.

Claremont shoved away from the stern gallery window as if he'd been watching Julian's entry with uncertainty. Their gazes locked. "She was better off not mourning him," Daniel said.

"That wasn't your choice to make."

"One good deed does not make Patrick Bellamy a bloody hero. I don't care if he was your brother. He started the biggest counterfeiting ring in this colony. Had Rina known what her printing shop was a front for, she would be sitting here with me now, facing the possibility of execution." He crossed his arms and leaned against the bulkhead. "I know I'm not innocent of everything." Claremont's expression faltered before he glanced away in disgust. "I'd be lying if I told you I was. But for the record, I drew the line at murder."

"And still you'll be just as hanged. Counterfeiting is a death sentence. Even for someone with your high morals."

"Aye." A wry smile touched his lips. Julian had to respect his cocksure poise, for despite his brother-in-law's youth, his courage was not to be taken lightly. The ground Claremont trod equated to treason. "There is a certain amount of power achieved at defeating the redcoats. No matter how minuscule. Pardon the insult, my lord, but I didn't expect to be caught."

Julian scooped up the banknotes. He was suddenly furious.

He had nothing.

Not justice. Not the satisfaction that he should feel with the mystery of Patrick's death solved.

Nothing.

They couldn't even prosecute Jed Tomkins for the rector's murder without better evidence than hearsay testimony. "You do realize that an accusation of counterfeiting against Tomkins and the others condemns you as well?"

Claremont's brows lifted. His hand fidgeted with the newspaper that Catherine had dropped on the ledge below the window. "Why would you care what happens to me, my lord, if I'm guilty?"

Julian opened the cabinets on his bookcase and rummaged through papers. "I care what happens to Catherine and, right now, I want the man who set her up to die." He slammed a blank sheet of vellum on the desk. "Who gave you that letter Catherine took from you the night she went to meet Merlin?"

He met Claremont's gaze squarely and saw the younger man's eyes flicker with new interest. "She's told you everything?"

"I think that whoever gave you that letter also ordered the Millers killed."

Claremont stared at the depiction of the cloaked highwayman before dropping into the chair. For a long time, he didn't move.

"Ryan Miller's da wanted out," Claremont quietly said. He picked up the slender reed of charcoal and seemed to study the edge. "After what happened to Rina, he called a meeting and warned us of his plans. Some speculate that Ryan's death was convenient timing. My speculations are not nearly as generous. Jed Tomkins and his small group of thugs are responsible for the terror hereabouts. Someone is paying them to play God with our lives while collecting the bounty they steal. As if counterfeiting hasn't made us all rich."

Then his hands began to move.

"Why hasn't your family benefited from your endeavors?"

"We did, while Patrick was alive. But I couldn't do that to them. The money I gave them was real enough."

"Proceeds from the goods stolen from the warehouses?"

He grinned. "Aye but the tax man is the poorer for it."

Julian started to pour himself a glass of brandy but hesitated. He stood mesmerized as Claremont's strokes gave the paper life. Catherine had said he was good. He'd seen the young man's paintings on the walls in their house.

Finally turning, Julian braced his palms on the window and watched the clouds blow across the sky. On shore, Water Street bustled with wagons. Narrowing his eyes, he could see Lieutenant Ross making his way toward the waterfront. Julian spotted his scarlet uniform among the crowd and wondered at what point his own quest to destroy Claremont had lost all its urgency.

"It had been dark that night." Daniel tossed the drawing to the desk where it skated across the scarred surface. "He knew all the right words to say, and mine as well."

Julian caught the paper as it slid off the desk.

A stab of shock cut into his chest. If he breathed, he wasn't aware of any sound. He brought the drawing into the sunlight, his hand no longer steady.

"He had an unmistakable accent." Daniel sat back in the chair. "Just scarcely there. Scottish may—"

"Irish," Julian cut him off, sick to his gut. His voice was barely a whisper. The Millers had trusted him, and he'd willingly given them over to the hands of their murderer. "He's Irish."

With both hands braced on the walnut stand, Catherine awaited the nausea to pass. That morning had seen Catherine at church with her family. But by the time they'd finished their noon repast, she'd been unable to keep her eyes open. The growing shadows told her that she'd slept away the afternoon.

Finally, after splashing cold water on her face, she rinsed out her mouth and scrubbed her teeth with her finger. She slipped her stockinged feet into her shoes and arranged her thick hair beneath a mobcap. The long, oval looking glass stopped her. She wore her shift. Turning to the side, she pressed her hand against the flatness of her belly, then puffed the fabric slightly to view an imaginary rounded shape, hastily flattening the cloth at her foolishness.

Her gaze moved over the elegant room, appointed in rich mahogany furniture. Catherine slept in Julian's massive canopy bed, in his room with the Chinese watered-silk wallpaper.

He'd still not returned home. But Boswell told her stepmother last night at supper that Lord Blackmoor had left with Lieutenant Ross to escort Daniel to Williamsburg. Had the message been sent to her and merely been intercepted by Boswell? She didn't know.

Boswell also informed her that His Lordship had ordered that a lady's maid be hired. But Catherine had been raised with the ordinary people in this town, and already she felt displaced and presumptuous to think that he could hire a neighbor to be her lady's maid. Then, this morning, an additional dressmaker had arrived from Williamsburg and, with Anna, poked, pinned, and prodded every inch of her flesh!

If Julian thought to buy what he couldn't procure any other way, he knew nothing about her. And all the linen, Irish Holland,

and silk ordered for her and her family would not purchase her affection.

Opening the armoire, Catherine pulled out the gown she'd hung there to help ease the wrinkles. Someone had brought her personal effects from the other house. She'd just fastened on her stays when a door downstairs slammed. Catherine slipped into her gown.

The bedroom door burst open. Elizabeth's face was pale. Her eyes wide. Catherine's heart pitched. "What happened?"

"Oh, Rina," she burst into tears. "Someone threw a tomato at Momma today. A tomato!" she sobbed.

Catherine hurriedly finished with the buttons on her bodice. "Where is she?"

"I don't know. She didn't come inside."

Catherine had found her stepmother up before dawn yesterday, tending to the winter mulch on the front flowerbed. She'd created a small plot of Eden from the weed-infested memories of a bygone day.

"I don't like what is happening." Her sister wiped a gloved hand across her cheeks. "Momma always stays to socialize at church. She lives and breathes the smiles. Instead, today she came here and played cards with Boswell. I think that he is worried about her, too. He told me that I should take her out shopping for seeds. So I did. Some people hate us, Rina. And it's not just because of Daniel."

Catherine stared at her. "Where did you hear that?"

"I heard Prissy talking." Her sister's sniffles increased. "She said the most wretched, hurtful things. Lord Blackmoor visited Allison Simms in Williamsburg yesterday. People are snickering behind your back. Prissy is such a wretched gossip!"

Catherine's hands trembled as she laced the kerchief around her neck. She was already out the bedroom door with Elizabeth on her heels. "What do you expect from someone like Prissy? You ride in His Lordship's carriage, live at his big house. You've failed to display any restraint in your enthusiasm to outshow her in all ways."

"Why can't I enjoy the same things she does? Do I have to be beneath her for her to be my friend?"

"That's the problem, Elizabeth. You were never beneath her." They glided down the wide staircase. "I don't need her, and I told her that to her face. I don't care if she does belong to the gentry's upper class. She oughtn't be such a snob."

Catherine's stepmother was not at the garden. Nor was she in her bedroom or with the twins. "She isn't anywhere." Elizabeth ran up to her, breathless, after a search of the stables revealed their gray horse still there. Boswell and Anna stood on the hill that led back to the house. Clearly, their search had turned up nothing as well.

"Where is Sally?" Catherine asked.

Elizabeth looked around, her gaze touching on all the usual hiding places.

Catherine swept past her sister. "Momma must have left here on foot," she said when they entered the house. "Sally followed her. I want you to stay here with the twins."

"But where are you going? It's almost dark."

"My lady." One of Julian's burly guards stopped her at the front door as she threw on her cloak. "I can't let you leave here."

Catherine yanked up the hood on her cloak. "My stepmother is out there, and if you are of the mind to argue with me, let me warn you that *I* am of a bigger mind to punch something! And if that something happens to be you because you are foolish enough to brandish His Lordship's orders in my face one more time, then so be it."

Boswell was behind her, but she didn't care. Flinging open the door, she swept past the speechless guard and followed the path out of the yard. A stiff wind whipped up her skirt and cloak. Two maids beating a rug crossed themselves. Catherine didn't look at any of them. Hiking up her skirt, she left the yard, leaving guards rushing to follow behind. Less than a mile down the road, she heard the rumble of a carriage and was soon joined by two more uniformed men.

Fifteen minutes later, Catherine climbed out of the carriage and greeted a happy Sally at her house. She found her mother on her knees, digging up bulbs. For an instant, Catherine could go no farther than the white, dilapidated fence. Holes pockmarked the earth like some fearsome campaign had been waged there. Her stepmother's beautiful garden was filled with the dead remnants of her loving work and little else.

Samuel approached Catherine from where he'd been working in the stables. "I've been watching her, Mizz Catherine."

She squeezed Samuel's hand. "Thank you."

"She won't leave there. I figure the diggin' will do her good."

Catherine knelt and lay her cloak across her stepmother's shoulders. "Come inside, Momma. You'll catch a chill."

"I cannot bear to see them die, Rina," she said. "I need to take these bulbs inside to dry out for spring, or everything will rot."

Catherine's gaze fell on the tomato that stained her stepmother's once-pretty dress. Tears filled her eyes. "You should not have left town without letting any of us know."

"You want to see a beautiful garden again, don't you?"

"Yes, Momma. And it will be beautiful again."

She smiled a gentle smile. Mud soiled her knees and sleeves. "People are angry with your brother. They don't understand, do they?"

Catherine shook her head.

"I noticed that our house needs paint along the eaves. Daniel will have to tend to that when he returns."

Looking over her shoulder, Catherine wiped the loose hair from her face. She saw the guards standing ill at ease near the trellis. She motioned them over.

"I'm frightened for him." Her stepmother's hands stopped kneading the soft earth. Catherine knew she spoke of Daniel. "But I cannot deny that I'm proud of his decision. Captain Lambert will not allow anything to happen to him. You will see."

Catherine's stomach fell. How could she say that? When he was the one who brought Daniel back? Julian had accomplished what he'd set out to do. He was very clever at conquering the world.

Lucid eyes suddenly lifted to assess Catherine. "Why would he bother to send a message telling me that he is escorting Daniel to Williamsburg if he didn't care, Rina?"

"I . . . don't know," Catherine was ashamed to admit, but neither did she possess her stepmother's unerring insight or faith.

She only knew that Daniel might die now when men like Tomkins still roamed free. She looked up to see one of the guards standing at the edge of the garden. "Momma, this gentleman is going to take us back to Captain Lambert's house. You need to eat something."

She took Catherine's hands. "Will you see the rest of the bulbs brought in? Please? They must not be allowed to rot out here."

Gentle hands touched the frail shoulders as one of the young men helped her to her feet. "Please, Rina."

Catherine's gaze fell on the piles of bulbs. She glanced at the sky. The coral-darkened clouds hung over the edges of the fading day.

"Leave two men," she said to the guard. "Come back for me after you've taken her home."

"Yes, my lady." He bowed slightly.

A few minutes later, she heard the rattle of the carriage. She worked in the remainder of daylight to clear the bed of bulbs, laying them out on wooden shelves in the root cellar as her stepmother did every year that she'd remembered living here. Samuel put Sally to bed for the night in the stable and boiled water. He brought her out crackers and some of her stepmother's willow bark tea.

"His Lordship is a mighty fine man. Fair-minded," Samuel said after they'd talked awhile. "I'm not worried about you or your family with him around."

Catherine set the teacup on the counter. "You don't know him."

"A man's actions speaks the true words of his soul, Mizz Catherine. I know that he was mighty worried 'bout you when you were missing. I know that he's seen your stepmother cared for and would be disturbed to learn that he'd caused what happened to her today."

"Oh, Samuel." She braced her hands on the wooden shelf, suddenly very tired. "If only it were all that simple."

"You go inside and wash up, Mizz Catherine. I'll finish out here and bed down at the kitchen house tonight. Don't know where that carriage is. It should be here any moment."

Catherine went inside her house and washed. She lit the lamps downstairs. None of the rooms remained as Sergeant Masters had left them, and it looked as if someone had made an effort to clean the place. She wondered if Daniel had been staying here these past weeks. Upstairs in her bedroom, she pulled off the floorboard and removed a cherry-wood box.

She'd put the box there after Patrick had died and, opening the lid, let her gaze touch those trinkets that had once meant so much. A lump tightened her throat. She touched Patrick's wedding ring. She'd left her ring on his finger when she'd buried him.

In truth, she had much to resolve within herself, and her heart was one. She had not made peace with the role she'd played in Patrick's death nor with her marriage to Julian.

She lifted the necklace Patrick had given her on their wedding day. A small heart-shaped emerald dangled from the silver chain. Yet it wasn't Patrick's eyes she saw in those verdant points of light.

Julian had always been with her. From the first day she saw him across the water in Boston. He'd been wearing a beard then. She had not remembered that before now. Even then, he'd been secretly fighting for the rebel cause. She held the heart to her cheek.

"It belonged to our mother."

Julian's curt voice snapped her chin up. He leaned in the doorway. His shoulder pressed against the jamb, his expression hooded. He still wore his cloak and gloves as if he'd just arrived and didn't slow before climbing the stairs to her room. The autumn chill still clung to his presence. Hesitantly, she put down the box and stood. Her pulse took on a new rhythm with his presence.

"You're back."

His eyes hesitated on her face. Then, whatever she'd glimpsed vanished as he straightened. "Does that disappoint you?"

"No . . ."

"You should have returned with your mother," he said over her concern. "She's enjoying a warm meal at my home."

"I expect I'll be joining her soon."

"The carriage broke an axle on the way back here." His gaze went out the window, then again to the box at her feet, before he turned on his heel. "I'll tell the men that we'll be staying the night."

Catherine gathered up her treasures, reassembling everything in the box before putting it away. 'Twas almost as if he took offense at that which belonged to Patrick. She descended to the first floor.

Julian stood in the entryway. He looked up at her. He wore no wig, and the beginning of a beard marked his fatigue. His hands hesitated as he removed his gloves. He didn't say anything, and as she remained with her hand poised on the banister, she struggled to erect the needed internal walls. When he'd kissed her the night of their wedding, there had only been his heat, his presence, and those golden moments where he'd made her dream the impossible.

Now, he only looked remote and exhausted as if he carried a greater weight than the confusing hostility she saw in his eyes.

"Did Momma tell you what happened today?"

"Your mother is stronger than you think, Catherine."

Slipping out of his military cloak, he walked into the drawing room. Catherine moved into the arched doorway. A Venetian lamp stood on a spindle table between two wing chairs where he'd laid his cloak. Julian stood with his back to the room, his eyes cast outside as if he were standing in front of the stern gallery window on his ship. Moonlight spilled through two windows where the drapes had been drawn. What did he think about with only the sea and the sky as his world? And she was suddenly struck by a sense of his loneliness.

"When will Daniel be tried?" she quietly asked.

An amber flask half filled with whiskey perched on the polished surface of the bureau. Julian removed the plug with a pop and poured a glass. "I don't know. He hasn't been arraigned yet."

"Will you even be here?" she asked.

"Christ, Catherine. I'm really not in the mood for this."

"Be in the mood, Captain. We need to talk."

He favored her with a slow glance before setting the empty glass on the desk. Folding his arms across his chest, he leaned on the desk corner. "The *Chimera* leaves the end of the month. Another ship will replace mine until I return from England sometime in the summer."

Her breath faltered, a reaction to the knot that tightened inside her chest. She'd known that he was not staying here. But that was before he'd married her. "And the captain of this new ship . . . will also live in your house?"

"Not if he wants to remain alive." He observed her over the lip of his glass. "The house is yours. I signed the papers yesterday."

"Mine?" She blinked in disbelief.

"You're my wife. Did you think I'd leave you homeless?"

"I don't know what I thought."

"I live most of the year up and down these coasts. I have an estate in Cornwall, what's left of it after one of my father's tantrums burned Blackmoor Hall to the ground. The tenants seem to manage just fine without my presence. I have a town house in Williamsburg and one in London. A plantation on the James River. Or is what I have not good enough for you that you still need to be mooning over my brother?"

She stared, dumbstruck by his animosity.

"What are you doing out here? I come home, and Boswell tells me that you'd remained here, with only two damn men to protect you."

Heat rushed to her face. "Is this to be a way of life, my lord? Even after you leave? Momma needed help. I'm not going to remain tied up like some helpless Harriet jumping at shadows."

"You will as long as you carry my child. You want to be reckless with your life, I'll tie you up to the bloody bedpost if I have to."

Shocked by his anger, Catherine passed the oafish statement off to the effects of alcohol. "What's wrong with you?" she questioned as she considered him more thoroughly. "I thought you would be more content. Is vengeance not to your taste, my lord?"

"Here's to being trumped, my lady wife." Instead of pouring more whiskey, he merely tipped the bottle back and swigged. "No points for the good guys this year."

"Truly, Captain." She crossed her arms to keep her hands from trembling. "Self-pity is unlike you."

"My name is Julian." He advanced on her until she was forced to tip back her head. "Say my name, Catherine."

"You're drunk, Captain Lambert." She spun on her heel.

He grabbed her wrist. "Say it."

His chest beneath the heavy cloth of his jacket was hard against her palm. Unrelenting. And she was aware of the thud of his heart. "Reece." Her chin lifted. She'd wanted her tone to be commanding, but the name came out in a whisper. "Merlin. Tell me about Merlin."

"He's a bastard. A fool. Name your moniker. He's dead."

A trembling went through her. She'd never seen him like this, and his mood frightened her. Whatever had happened during the last few days had changed him. "He's *you.*"

His eyes burned into hers. "My name, Catherine. I want to hear my name on your lips."

"As I said." She jerked her hand free. "You're drunk."

Whiskey flask in hand, he toasted her with a mocking bow. "Not as much as I will be, sweet," he jeered after her.

That was Samuel's rotgut, home-brewed whiskey he drank. She had no doubt of his future level of intoxication. She stalked out of the drawing room and, taking the steps by twos, she stopped on the landing. He leaned against the doorjamb regarding her flight lazily.

Keeping her shoulders back, she slammed her bedroom door, fired with indignation that he should berate her when she'd done nothing wrong. And she would not apologize for coming after her stepmother.

"Your consideration is daunting, my love," he yelled up the stairs. "Is it that hard to say my goddamn name? Once?"

Her gaze speared the offending portal. Something inside her had dared confront his belligerence, when all she had to say was his name, and perhaps they might have found some middle ground to stand. But he was asking for her surrender when everything inside told her she could not. When he'd threatened to tie her to a bedpost.

"Arrogant oaf." She leaned her cheek on the smooth wood. Downstairs, she heard a door bang against the wall.

"And my conceit is laughable." Julian glared at the hole he'd just managed to put in the wall. "Shit," he swore to himself. His fist throbbed. But that ache was nothing compared to the one inside.

In his anger, he had only hurt himself.

Everything hurt.

He hadn't slept in days. He turned back into the room and stumbled. The liquid amber sloshed in the nearly empty container, and he held the flask aloft to the light, wondering vaguely what the hell kind of stuff this was to fox him so quickly.

He hadn't been drunk in so long that feeling the effects hit him now was something akin to jumping off a cliff without wings.

Flopping down on the settee, he wrenched off his boots and threw them against the chair. He hadn't meant to come to Catherine in this way. Or to behave in so obnoxious a manner. Yet he continued to do things that he'd never planned or meant to do around her.

He needed her tonight. But he knew now it wasn't going to happen. He'd swallowed his pride for the last time when he took the stairs to her room earlier, running after his own wife like some lovesick lamb because she didn't want to return to the home he'd given her. After everything else these past few days, he'd not been prepared to see her mooning over his brother's possessions. Standing in that doorway, he'd wanted to rip her memory of Patrick from her heart, from her body. He'd been jealous as hell, half aware that the reaction was symbolic of everything that was wrong in his life.

Except he was sick of Catherine's rejection. Sick of the shadows that loomed between them and in the crevices of his life. Sick of failure. And now, listening to her pacing the floor above his head, he was sick of feeling alone and damn unappreciated.

Stripping off his uniform jacket, he tossed it on the back of the settee over the lacy pillows piled there. "Maybe I wanted to do something noble at one time," he scoffed at the ceiling, unable to even remember why he'd ever gotten involved with the rebel cause. A gauzy string of spiderwebs clung to the lamp and cornices.

He was finished!

Let the admiralty take his bloody commission away, too. He'd done little in the past years to earn the right to be called a naval captain. Not when his heart no longer belonged to the crown.

He didn't know where that much-maligned organ lay at the moment, but it wasn't pumping in his empty chest.

Julian blew out the lamp. He lifted the whiskey bottle and swigged. Just once, he wanted to lose control.

Just once, he didn't want to care. Just bloody once, he wanted someone to care whether he lived or died.

Michael's betrayal had taken everything he had left inside. They'd been partners. His throat tightened. If Julian didn't hunt down his closest friend and kill him, then Michael would succeed in destroying him completely, as he'd destroyed countless others.

There had never been any friendship.

And in his ignorance, he had willingly allowed two innocent people to go to their deaths. The cold-blooded reality of it tore a fist-sized hole in his gut.

Christ . . . He sat on the settee and buried his face in his hands. It hurt to breathe. It hurt because he didn't know why—

He didn't know why Michael had turned on him.

Why?

Julian was unprepared for the arms that wrapped around him. Unprepared for the soothing voice that touched his hair. Her lips touched his mouth, his cheek. She pulled him gently to her breasts where he lay quietly in torment; his silent tears no longer silent.

Men didn't weep.

Men didn't show weakness.

Yesterday he'd watched an eighteen-year-old show more courage in the face of what awaited him at the end of a rope than most men show in a lifetime. Someone threw a tomato at a woman like Tabitha Claremont, who had raised children willing to stand on their principles when so many others were afraid to pull their heads from the sand.

After a while, when he realized he would not sob like a baby, that he actually did feel some release, he felt Catherine's palm slide over his brow. "I know this isn't because we argued." Her voice was so matter-of-fact and gentle at once that Julian laughed.

Christ, he actually laughed. He'd had his heart ripped out, and he laughed. "What are you? The court jester?"

"If I have to be." She touched her fingers to his brow. "Why didn't you tell me who you were sooner?"

"I'm still not sure that your knowing won't end up costing you your life. I've been careless since the moment I laid eyes on you."

"We're still not on the same side. Are we? Not entirely."

Dark curls slid from beneath a simple mobcap, and suddenly he was thinking about plowing his hands through those dark tresses. Then ruthless reality erased the fantasy. "You and I are a pair." He sat and leaned with his hands laced against the back of his head. Closing his eyes, he let the room swim around his head. "I'm drunk as hell. Anything I say you can't hold against me in the morning."

"You'll probably be sick as well. I may as well tell you that now. Samuel's whiskey is strong enough to preserve the dead."

"You know firsthand, do you?" He remembered the night in Jed Tomkins's barn when she drank from that jug.

"I told you before, I grew up on this homegrown stuff. Twice a year we have barn dances, and people come from miles around for the whiskey-tasting contest. Few people get past Samuel's."

Moonlight silhouetted the furniture in the room in a surreal tableau. He felt as if he were looking at the backside of his world. "So, what does someone around here win for making the most potent drink this side of hell?"

Her scent touched him with her shrug, all feminine and inviting, the warmth from her body reminding him that he was nearly undressed. "He doesn't win anything, I suppose." She shifted on the settee, and he turned his head to look at her. "Rather like Merlin. You were the one who rescued the Millers from the soldiers, weren't you?"

"Rescue?" He tightened his jaw and bent forward to rest his elbows on his knees. "I was the one who killed them."

"I . . . don't believe you," she murmured softly.

"Believe me." Leaning his head in his hands, he plowed his fingers through his hair. His shirt pulled at his shoulders. "I failed them; it's the same difference. They trusted me, and I gave them over to the hands of their murderer."

"I don't understand."

"The consensus had concluded that the corrupted Sons of Liberty leader here was a top official. Aye, he read my mail, and I let him. He was an efficient secretary. Which is probably why I never received anything from Patrick concerning your wedding. I was in Norfolk many times over the last few years and was informed that Patrick had gone to Richmond. After visiting three times and receiving the same answer, I assumed that I'd done something to anger him. So instead of pursuing the problem, I got angry."

"And he assumed that your life was too busy."

"O'Hara liked it here without my presence. He wanted that rift between Patrick and me. He perpetuated that tear with his lies."

She didn't reply at first. "You're talking about Michael, aren't you? You think he's the one who was working with Patrick here?"

"He was the one who gave your brother the letter that night, then proceeded to get him drunk enough he couldn't make the drop."

"He was your friend. I'm truly sorry, Julian. I really am."

Julian turned his head. He could only stare at her. He didn't know what he'd expected from her, but compassion for his loss was not one. Yet it was the one thing that he'd needed most. A part of him had tried to cling to the hope that Michael was innocent, that coincidence in circumstances could be explained. But he knew it could not, and he welcomed the moments that she'd let him grieve.

He focused on her face and realized something else. "I have a name at last. Praise the stars."

"You mock me again." She hit him with a lacy throw pillow.

He caught her hand. His eyes touched hers, unable to break the lingering essence of their touch.

For most of his life, he'd protected himself from his emotions. It had always been easier to run from the frailties of his heart than to confront his own vulnerability. He could sail a ship across the seas, stand at the helm in the face of a full broadside, smuggle goods and people past British customs, a task that would hang him for treason. But he had scant knowledge of life. Of babies and children. Pet pigs and kittens.

He reached across with his other hand to pull her into his lap. "I love you," he said against her lips.

Tears filled her eyes. "You're just drunk, Julian."

"Aye, that I am." His hand went to the full bounty of her breast, then to her abdomen, to the child that they'd made. Then he kissed her because he was too drunk to realize that he might have frightened her with the declaration or that she might not love him back. Or that all it would take for him to stay was for her to ask.

He wanted her with an urgency that was terrifying, explosive. And then he plunged his fingers into hair and did what he'd wanted to do since he'd found her upstairs weeping over his brother's memory.

Catherine stirred restlessly beneath his feverish hands as he took her to the floor. He wanted to possess her in the most elemental way. He wanted to be there, above her, watching her face. He wedged between her thighs and worked to free himself from his breeches. Then a modicum of rationality returned. Just barely.

"Am I hurting you?" he rasped in her ear.

"A little foreplay might help," she whispered breathlessly.

She had the power to shock him. He sat on his calves. She lay on the floor, her hair ebony blue in the moonlight. Willing as sin, her sensual regard affecting him as if she'd put her mouth and tongue all over him and not her eyes.

"Christ, Catherine. Foreplay will have to wait."

Chapter Eighteen

It was sultry beneath the covers as Catherine later snuggled in the crook of Julian's arm. They'd come to her room in the hours before dawn. His hand slid around her breast. "My son has made these very big. Have I told you that?"

The warm whisper of his breath against her nipple made her groan. "Many times tonight, my lord." She ran her fingers in his hair. "Is there naught else you think about?"

He turned her on her back and leaned on his elbow as he rested his other arm on her thigh. Moonlight banished the shadows on his face. "Not with you lying naked in bed beside me," he said.

She tilted her head back to look at him. His dark hair was tousled, and she brushed the strands from his face. "Julian?"

She'd wanted to ask him about his visit to Allison Simms while he'd been in Williamsburg. But the words would not form. Had he gone there to find out why Patrick had visited her that last night he was killed? Maybe Catherine didn't want to know what he'd found out.

His mouth nuzzled her neck, and she closed her eyes. "How is it that you can be who you are and still be Merlin? It is as if you are two different people."

"I was beaten black and blue during our first meeting." His fingers curled around her breast. "Or you probably would have recognized me in Norfolk."

"I don't know. You have that aristocratic behavior down to a convincing art, my lord." She held him off her, her hands firm against the rigid contours of his chest. Her arms tightened, for in riding alone against O'Hara, he took a dangerous risk with his life and the authorities. "Do you hate His Majesty, King George?"

His hand smoothed her hair. "Strange that I do not. Yet my loyalties here go against him." His chest rose and fell with his breath, his frustration evident. "But right now—hell, who was I to think that I had some God-given responsibility to save the world? Are Merlin's actions against God and country any worse than O'Hara's? My own arrogance has put me here."

"You asked me once if Merlin was my hero." She cupped his face between her palm. "Yes. And I won't let O'Hara make you doubt yourself. He won't beat you. He won't beat us."

"Don't, Catherine."

His lips pressed hard against hers as if he would squash the spark of his doubt. She could sense the tension inside him.

Absorbing his taste and the heat of his mouth, she longed to allay her apprehension for him. "Do you want to know more about me?" She shivered as his hand digressed with clear intent over her belly to her thighs. "I . . . have not talked . . ." A soft moan slipped from her lips.

"I already know everything about you," he murmured.

"Everything?" Her back arched. He bit the flesh behind her ear, his fingers deep inside her. "Are you still drunk?" she rasped.

"I haven't been drunk since the first time I made you come."

"God, Julian." The words were explicitly arousing and so intimate she almost climaxed against his hand. But he wouldn't let her. He kissed her, pressing her deeply into the mattress. Then her arms closed around him. "Julian . . ."

"No more talking." He spread her legs with his knee. "No more . . ."

He kissed her even as his powerful body plunged deep inside her, riding hers, gliding, taking, giving. She allowed herself the sheer pleasure of his body and met his movements, her panting cries filling the silent bedchamber, her arms tightening around his corded strength with a violent desperation as if she could will the sun not to rise. As if she could stay the course of time. She held on to his kiss, the soft cadence of his breath humming in her blood and storming her defenses. Recognizing when he joined in her shattering release, she was crying and didn't know why. He pulled back to see her tears.

It had been like this for most of the night. They'd make love. They'd talk and pretend that there were no shadows outside the walls of this room. Cradling her in the circle of his arms, he wiped the moisture from her face. "Am I that good? Or that bad, love?"

"I don't know," she sniffed, her eyes liquid as she realized that she'd just insulted him. "It's not you. It's me."

"Shhh." Pulling her closer, he let her weep against his chest.

The window was open. Samuel was moving around below in the yard. Catherine could hear him talking to Sally, who had come out of the barn, squealing. "It will be dawn soon," Julian whispered against her hair. "Go to sleep."

His arms tight around her, Julian watched Catherine drift to sleep. He wanted to protect her from hurt. From the uncertainty of tomorrow. She'd awakened something dormant inside of him. A need to belong to the world that he'd lost after he'd sailed away from this place so many years ago.

He'd barely embraced the thought when a knock sounded on the door downstairs. Extricating himself from Catherine's arms, he pulled on his breeches and boots, carelessly slipping on his shirt as he walked downstairs to open the door. Two men stood on the porch.

"This arrived at the ship, my lord," Pulver said, handing Julian a bottle of smuggled French brandy.

Julian peered at the flask as if this was some sort of joke, then realized it wasn't. A message was attached, and in finely scrawled script he read, "The next move is mine, you lucky bastard."

O'Hara!

This was all a contest to O'Hara. A huge chessboard. People's lives were naught but pieces in the game. And now, with Claremont's surrender, almost overnight Michael had become his foe, his enemy. One that knew everything about him, taking with him the secrets of their former friendship and all his vulnerabilities.

Ripping the note off the flask, Julian handed the brandy back to Pulver. "Dump it. On the road. There's a pink pig on these premises, and I don't want her getting drunk."

"Aye, sir." Pulver's expression was dubious.

After he left, Julian turned to the other man. Catherine had once dubbed him Grumpier. His name was Grimms. He wore the homespun attire of the locals, but Julian knew him to be a tough-as-oak rebel: a former British master sergeant, now an active member in the Sons of Liberty from west of here that Allison had sent to him after his arrival in Yorktown. Now, with the reality of O'Hara's defection also came the realization that he and Catherine were nearly alone.

Julian leaned with his back against the door and crossed his arms. "What happened after I left Williamsburg?"

"I tried to find you earlier."

"I had to take a little detour on the way here. Personal business," he said. Hell yes, it was. Allison Simms had owed him an explanation about Patrick's visit to her the night he died.

"Lieutenant Ross took the names Claremont supplied him and began a house-to-house search. Nine people were arrested on counterfeiting charges. The lead engraving plates were found exactly where Claremont said they'd be. Stolen contraband and newly purchased weapons were pulled from Tomkins's barn and three others. Jed Tomkins wasn't at home, but his brothers were. Most of the contraband is unaccounted for. Still, the night was considered a success."

Julian's mood took on an edge. "Claremont came through then."

"Aye, Ross should be a bloody hero now. Does anyone know how much of that information came from Merlin?"

No one would ever know. "Where was Masters the whole time?" Julian finally asked, letting his gaze come back around.

"Back in Williamsburg, my lord. His quest for fame and fortune was only slightly marred by Ross's recent feat. Sir," Pulver hesitated, "there's little left here for O'Hara. He'll be trying to gather what he has left so he can leave."

"Aye, but from where?" Julian ran a distracted hand through his hair. "I've dispatched notice to the *Swan* in Norfolk. No ship will leave the James River without being searched."

Turning, his temper checked by the need to think clearly, Julian walked into the dining room and lit the lamp. Outside, dawn was a distant tier of gray on the horizon. A few moments later, he pulled the land chart from his saddlebags. Since September, he'd scoured the area north along the York River in search of the main hideaway. Michael's schooner was somewhere on the James, most probably on one of the tributaries. But Julian had been on the ship enough to know that O'Hara's operation had to be land based. He and Patrick had been partners. O'Hara had moved the goods. But from where?

"Ross will have someone watching the Tomkinses' farm," he said.

"Will you tell the lieutenant that you think O'Hara killed the Millers?" Grimms inquired.

"As much as I want to help Ross, I have to find O'Hara first." Too much was at stake for him not to.

His palms pressed against the table; the low sound of his voice was as crisp and distinct as his eternal resolve. As weary as his heart. "From the very beginning, I've been as carefully manipulated as this town," he said aloud, then he lifted his head. "If you were playing chess, what would your next move be at this point?"

Grimms pulled his shoulders back. "Bishop to queen," he declared matter-of-factly as if the question had not been rhetorical. "Anything to leave the king exposed to attack." Observing Julian's stare, he grinned. "I'm an excellent chess player, my lord."

"Aye," Julian turned back to the chart. "I can see that."

"Then you think he targets your wife to get to you?"

"She is my vulnerability."

And killing Catherine would be like tearing the heart from his chest while it still beat. It would be like burying Susan all over again, and he was loath to surrender one ounce of his future to a thief and a murderer, a man who had once been his closest friend, who might have remained that way, had it not been for Claremont.

No longer seeing the chart spread before him, Julian thought of Claremont again. Patrick and the Millers were both found on North Fork road. Suddenly, Julian needed to see the physician's report on Patrick's death.

She dreamed of coffee. Deep-roasted coffee with hot bread and melted butter. The smells penetrated her dream and, from deep within her chest, she heard herself groan. Her arm went to the pillow beside hers. The place was empty. She pushed up on her

elbow, her sleepy gaze roaming the disheveled state of her bed.
She was naked beneath the covers. Movement in the chair beside
her bed turned her. Julian sat with his elbows on his knees, contemplating her over a steaming cup of coffee. He looked as if
he'd been there a long while. Their gazes touched, and a warm
hue crept into Catherine's face.

"Good morning," he said.

Clutching the covers to her breasts, she lay back in the feath-
ery softness of the pillow and smiled back at him. She saw that
he was dressed, and an ominous murmur in her heart slid beneath
her newfound happiness. His dark brown hair was meticulously
combed back into a queue, his face clean-shaven. His white uniform shirt was buttoned and tucked in his breeches, and while he
didn't say as much, Catherine knew he should not have stayed
here last night when he'd already been away from his ship for too
long.

"You never sleep, do you?"

He set down the steaming cup on the nightstand. "Rarely."
Bracing his knee on the bed, he leaned forward and pressed his
palms on either side of her head. "But then you don't make it
easy."

His mouth moved over hers, the seductive whisper of his lips
pulling a groan from deep within her chest, beckoning a love just
awakened. Her whole being throbbed. "Hmmm. I never dreamed
coffee could taste so good." Her pleasure vibrated against his lingering lips, and her eyes slowly opened.

She suddenly sat up, hair tumbling over her shoulders.
"Where did you get hot coffee? I am famished."

"Have you no faith in my ability to provide for you, sweet?"

Anna suddenly bustled through the open doorway, carrying a
handful of towels and a wrapper. "Breakfast is ready, my lord. A
bath is also being prepared." Smiling and in high spirits, Anna set
her armload down on the mattress and observed them both like a
contented leprechaun, her faded orange hair tucked loosely in a
mobcap. "Is there anything more I may get for you?"

"That will be all. Thank you, Anna," Julian said.

Anna smiled brightly at Catherine and shut the door on her
way out. Catherine's narrowed gaze came around. Julian
shrugged, unrepentant, and stood. "The carriage arrived an hour
ago. Anna and two other servants were inside, bearing the fruits

of their morning labor." She watched him move to the chair in front of the window. His uniform jacket had been aired and smoothed out. "Your sister is also downstairs." Pulling his jacket off the back of the chair, he slipped his arms into the sleeves. "You can tell her to stop hiding every time I walk into a room. I've decided not to beat her."

Catherine grinned. "That should inspire gratitude." Clutching the sheet, she pulled her legs over the bed. "Where are you going?"

"I have business to attend," he said, tying the neckcloth and stuffing it in his waistcoat.

He was already fading away from her, his persona changing into the British naval officer even as she watched. The chameleon to his core. Darkly remote, and a little frightening.

"Julian?"

She'd worked to gather the nerve to talk about his visit to Allison Simms. He turned, dressed and ready to leave. She sensed his mind preoccupied with what lay outside the room.

A knock sounded on the door. "My lord," Anna said from behind the portal. "Your men have brought your horse around."

Looking at Catherine, he slid his gloves on his hands. "I'm on my way down, Anna." Then to her, he said, "With your brother's help, most of the gang was rounded up last night. They're finished."

"Everyone?" Excitement jolted her heart. "Was anyone hurt?"

"Tomkins wasn't home when Ross came knocking. O'Hara is still at large. You'll not be on the road after dark, and never without an escort. Do you understand?"

She watched him button his jacket. "Where are you going?"

"Among other things, I need to speak to the town's physician about the report on Patrick."

She raised her eyebrows. "Is this about Daniel?"

"I'm not sure," he answered evasively.

"May I go with you?"

"I'm not shutting you out, Catherine," he said. "But I'm not sure what I'm looking for."

And just that fast, the discussion was over. He was going off to do something important and leaving her behind. Yet bound by her own pressing business, she didn't push the issue.

"May I go into town at least, my lord?"

He tugged her into his arms. "Yes."

Her arms closing around his neck, she pressed against him and cast him a sporting smile. "May I go to Williamsburg and purchase ten new gowns? A cloak with sable cuffs? Chocolate bonbons?"

His answering grin was white. "You may go anywhere you like as long as you travel in daylight."

Her teasing smile faded because she wanted only to stay with him. "Is this about Michael O'Hara?"

"Everything is about O'Hara."

She sat back on the mattress. "Will I see you tonight?"

"If I can't make it home, I'll send a note. Catherine . . ." He bent and kissed her. Moving his hands to her waist, he pulled her against him, and the sharp-edged danger still threatening them both faded to the miracle of last night.

When he released her, his eyes gently smiled down at her. "I have no regrets about last night," he said. "How I feel about you has not changed. I'm more than content that you are my wife."

Elizabeth was standing at the door, and he paused on the way out. Catherine heard him talking in the hall and Elizabeth's mumbled replies. When the door finally closed, Catherine sat looking at her sister, the emptiness in the room suddenly unbearable.

"Do you think he'll leave here after all of this is over?" she asked. "He's in the navy after all. How often do they come home? Catherine whatever are you doing? You can't—"

Catherine flung open her door. Wrapped in her sheet and nothing else, she flew down the stairs. Julian was standing at the front door. He looked up and saw her on the stairs. Without a word, she hurried down and flung herself in his arms. "I love you," she said against his mouth and kissed him hard. His arms, hesitant at first, wrapped around her. Heat rushed inside her, filled her veins. He had replaced the white wig on his head. Still, her fingers found purchase in the strands as she lifted on her toes.

When she pulled back, she touched his cheek. "I wanted you to know that before you left."

His gaze was tender and searching, nearly fathomless in its depths. "Indeed," he smiled back at her, even as he let his gaze drift downward to her breasts. "But before you make me embarrass myself in front of my men, I think you should know that we aren't alone."

Horrified, she started to spin when Julian moved her behind him. Two men stood ill at ease in the corridor. One she recognized from the cottage. Heat rushed into her face. Elizabeth had stopped midstride on the stairway. Julian opened the door and told the men to await him outside. Mortified, the sheet a thin barrier to her modesty, Catherine averted her gaze as they hurried out.

Humor tugging at the corners of his mouth, Julian tilted her chin with a gloved finger. "Next time, warn me if you plan on leaving your room undressed, and I'll arrange to be alone."

His relaxed camaraderie softened her embarrassment. "I will try to be more precise with my lust, sir."

"I'm not saying good-bye, Catherine."

He kissed her, taking her face between his hands, no longer holding sway to decorum or another's presence. He left her then before she could barely open her eyes. Catherine ran to the front parlor window and pulled aside the dusty drapes. He turned upon his black horse and found her in the window, his high-stepping mount pulling at the reins. Finally, swinging around, he rode out of the yard, the other men following behind.

Catherine raised her gloved hand to knock and hesitated. From inside the beautiful brick house, she could hear the tinkling glass and laughter. The plume in her cap swept below her chin. Staring at the cheerful wreath that decorated the front door, she brushed her hands across the smooth velvet of her riding skirt. She'd waited two days to make this trip. She would not back away now.

Straightening her spine, she knocked.

Yesterday, she'd tended to her shop, awaiting the right moment to make her move. She'd packed food and drink and, this morning at dawn, she had snuck out of the house and boarded the mail coach to Williamsburg, where she'd then bartered with a stubborn hostler to lease a horse—if one could call the swayback mare a horse. She'd left a message on her dresser with a notation to her stepmother that she'd be back before dark. Word would probably reach Julian, as soon as someone went upstairs and found her gone. He'd be furious, she considered. She'd violated his trust by riding here without a guard. But she knew no one in his employ would allow her to scandalize herself by coming here and, besides, she'd been well accompanied by seven other passengers. She fully intended to be back before dark.

The pine-laced air smelled rich with apple cider. Fidgeting with the muff, she turned to scan the well-manicured yard. For December, the weather was thankfully kind.

The door opened, and she turned abruptly to face a hawk-nosed butler. Dressed in black, he seemed momentarily astonished by her presence. "Would you care to come in, Lady Blackmoor?"

The use of the formal title caught her by surprise. Not only because it sounded surreal but because he obviously knew that she'd married Julian. Stepping into the house, she politely handed over her card. "I came to speak to Mrs. Simms, if you please."

People milled in the main room off the hallway. Festoons draped the doorways, and a beautiful Yule tree had been decorated for the occasion. "Who is it, Miles?" a feminine voice queried. Hasty footsteps sounded in the entryway, and Allison Simms appeared.

"She wishes to talk to you, madam."

With the exception of seeing her on Julian's arm at the governor's ball, Catherine had never been introduced to Mrs. Simms. Nor would she be, in polite company. Wearing a red satin gown, she was as beautiful as Catherine remembered: pale, exquisitely coifed hair, blue eyes, with perfectly straight teeth when she smiled. Catherine realized that the woman was holding out her hand in greeting.

"Come in," she graciously offered when Catherine took her hand.

"I'm afraid that I've disturbed your party."

"No, I'll wager you've just enlightened it. Does Julian know where you are?"

The use of her husband's name made her pause. "No, he does not."

"Please, won't you follow me so we can talk someplace private?"

Catherine handed her cloak and muff over to the butler. She smoothed her skirts. Without acknowledging the curious stares, she followed Allison Simms up the stairs to a bedroom parlor. The quaint yellow and bright blue interior greeted Catherine's perusal. Plush white chairs faced a fireplace. Allison directed her to a chair.

A table and crystal lamp sat between them. Allison arranged her skirts as she sat. "Mind you, I'm only talking to you because Julian said that you know who he is. I suppose that makes you one of us. Sisters, so to speak. I'll admit that I have not trusted you." She motioned to the servant. "Would you care for some refreshments?"

"If you have some crackers or bread, please," Catherine said, removing her gloves.

Allison looked at her, then lifted her lashes. "Some hot cider and cookies." Lowering her gaze, she smiled at Catherine. "It is the Yule season, after all."

The maid left the small parlor. The sounds of laughter filtered into the room before the door closed behind her. "They are probably putting down bets to see which one of us will walk out of here still standing." Allison laughed. "The mistress or the wife."

Catherine folded her hands in her lap to still their sudden trembling and regarded her hostess with a level gaze. "Mistress?"

"I'd assumed that you'd made your way here alone to ask if I am still seeing your husband?"

Catherine could not reply. She'd come seeking answers about Patrick. Not this. Her composure fell away to the sudden racing of her heart. Amid a hazy cloud, Catherine forgot her entire purpose for coming here. "And . . . are you?"

"It's no secret to those who are close to me," Allison stated matter-of-factly. "He bought me this place." Her arm did an arc around the room. "Many years ago, of course, but Julian felt obligated, I suppose. I helped him in his time of need."

"Indeed." She managed to remain aloof. Her whole body had gone numb. "How is it that you and my husband are so close?"

"His first wife, Susan, was my best friend. She and Julian met at the grand ball in Philadelphia hosted by the governor. Julian's stepfather had just been appointed lieutenant governor of Pennsylvania, so the whole family was out for the celebration. Julian was a dashing naval hero on leave from his duties to attend in his stepfather's honor. Susan was the belle of the ball." She brushed her skirt. "I suppose it was inevitable that he looked at no one else."

The servant entered the parlor, carrying a silver tray of dainty sugar cookies. Catherine graciously accepted a napkin and her cider. Afraid that her hands would betray her emotions, she stirred the cinnamon stick in her cider. The scented spices wafted over her. Allison waited for the servant to leave before resuming.

"Susan miscarried in her fifth month of a difficult pregnancy." She traced a finger along the rim of her cup before sipping. "Julian was gone when she went into labor. I never left her side during that month. He arrived from Norfolk too late."

Catherine wrapped her hands around the cup in her lap and despite herself continued to listen.

"I was in Philadelphia two years later when we met again," Allison said. "I was there for a Sons of Liberty gathering. Most of my family lives there, you see. Julian was there because Captain Bellamy was ill. It seemed we were always coming together when someone he loved died. Some time after Captain Bellamy passed away, I suggested that he send Patrick down here to the college of William and Mary. I then gradually introduced Julian to our cause."

"And what cause is that, Mrs. Simms?"

Allison set down her cup with a clink. "You don't even know what Julian does for us, do you?"

Uncertainty seized her. She knew Merlin did far more than smuggle expensive French brandy, or he would not be so infamous with such a high price on his head. But in truth, they'd not had the time to learn more about each other. "I know that he and Michael O'Hara have worked together here."

"Pah! That weasly ingrate." Allison brushed crumbs from her fingers. "After Julian bought O'Hara's commission out of the navy, O'Hara became the runner, and Julian became the supplier of goods. But that is only the front. We smuggle political prisoners out of the colonies. Julian finds ways to give people new lives someplace else. That's where he got the name Merlin. He could make people disappear."

Her heart pounded. Catherine had no idea the true extent of Julian's work. "And you were his contact here?"

"Word went through me, and I went through his solicitor. There are others like me in Boston, New York, and Philadelphia as well that Julian works with. All Sons of Liberty members. Loyal people. So, you see what has been happening in your area has distressed many of us. It was not our wish to bring the whole

British establishment down on us for the madness of a few. And now Julian jeopardizes everything."

Catherine set her cup down on the table. "You were never involved with Patrick, were you?" The whispered words were out before Catherine could stop them.

"Good heavens. We rarely even came into contact, except when there was information he needed to pass. He didn't even know about my relationship to Julian. Our last conversation, he threatened to kill me if I didn't reveal the name of the person who had ordered the attack on the *Tidewater Clarion*. But then he always had a temper."

Catherine pressed her fist against her stomach. She could not breathe. Patrick might have committed many crimes, but adultery was not one of them. God! she wanted to throw rocks at the sky. He'd never had an affair with Allison Simms. The irony that it had always been Julian struck her anew.

"If he never told you about his visits here, it was because for once he was protecting the organization. I didn't even know that he'd married. It appears that he was adamant about keeping you out of the family business. Integrity is its own handicap. That article you printed on the Sons of Liberty proved that much."

Catherine almost looked away. "Did Patrick know who Merlin was?"

"He knew. But there was a rift between the two. Still, when Patrick was killed, I didn't believe the magistrate's report that he'd accidentally shot himself. When Julian's ship arrived in Norfolk for repairs in August, I went there and told him."

"Why are you telling me this at all?" She could no longer pretend that she was unaffected by everything that she'd learned. "And don't feed me the balderdash that I'm one of you. I'm not. I don't know anything about what it is you people do."

"I'm telling you because what Julian does is bigger than you and me. He fancies himself in love with you. Maybe you remind him of Susan, I don't know. I only wish that I'd let Patrick's death lie."

"You couldn't any more than I could *not* write that article."

"Oh God!" Allison stared at the ceiling. "I can't believe you and I would be anything alike. I don't even want to like you. You stand behind your principles like some holier-than-thou princess, but you don't have the courage to fight for anything."

What Allison said was not true!

"Many people depend on Julian's aid. You cannot allow him to throw away what we have built. You are not worth his life."

Catherine felt her jaw slide open before she shut away her shock. Disoriented, she didn't know if she were angry or frightened.

"I must leave now," she whispered. "It's getting late."

"If you'll wait here, I have something that belongs to Julian." Allison stood and, as regally poised as ice, she returned from her bedroom with Julian's naval bicorn in her well-manicured hand. "He left this on his last visit."

If Allison wanted to shatter her, then the woman had truly succeeded on all fronts. Catherine took the bicorn, only because refusing it would have given Allison Simms the victory.

"Didn't you come in Julian's carriage?" Allison asked as they reached the door. Without answering, Catherine struggled with the frogs on her cloak. The woman stepped in front of her. "I had no idea you'd come here on horseback. You won't make it home before dark."

Catherine's chin went up at the worry in the other woman's voice. The drawing room had grown silent. "Good day, Mrs. Simms."

Miles had opened the door, and Catherine rushed down the steps.

Allison stood on the porch, her full skirts fluttering in the breeze. Feeling a quirk of conscience, she turned and looked at her other guests in the entryway. "What are you staring at!" she snapped.

Then, sweeping past them up the stairs to her bedroom, she summoned her butler. Scribbling out a note, she ordered him to send a courier to Julian. "Tell him that his bride was just here." She stopped him. "If he shows up tomorrow looking for all the world like he wants to throttle me, tell him I have a dreadful headache. I don't wish to be disturbed by anyone."

Unable to forget the stricken look in Catherine's midnight eyes, she dropped on the chair at her dresser. Dammit, she propped her chin on her hand. She shouldn't care a whit that she had hurt Catherine. The woman was clearly very much in love, and Allison remembered the look on Julian's face when he'd watched Catherine at the Governor's ball and knew that he had loved her even back then. He'd be furious that she'd implied things to Catherine that weren't true.

Allison sighed. In the looking glass framing her face, she turned slightly to better observe her profile. Why is it that God had gifted her with such incredible beauty, and the only men who wanted her were unworthy of the ground she walked on?

A chill breeze wrapped her ankles, and her gaze went to the window. The white drapes flowed softly into the room. Frowning, she could have sworn she'd shut her windows when the first guests had arrived that afternoon. Flinging back the drapes, she started to pull the windows closed, when she saw the muddy footprint on her braided rug. She stepped back. Directly into a man's body.

His whisper touched her cheek. "Checkmate, Mistress Simms."

Michael!

Before she could whirl, something snapped around her throat, choking off her scream. "Aye, the weasly ingrate. My poor little bitch." His lips caressed her temple. "Ye shouldn't have brought him back here, Allison. You've gone and ruined everything for me."

She clawed at the knotted braid crushing her windpipe.

"I tried to warn ye, Allison dear. I really did."

Chapter Nineteen

"Excuse me, Lord Blackmoor," the attendant's voice followed Julian's steps down the hallway. "But you can't go in there. He's busy."

A handful of papers balled in his fist, Julian swung open the door to the magistrate's chamber. Focusing his gaze on the white-wigged man scrambling off the settee, he shut the door in the attendant's face. "I hope I'm not disturbing your afternoon nap," Julian said.

"Lord Blackmoor." The ruddy-cheeked magistrate fumbled to straighten his robes. "Captain. What a pleasant surprise."

A woodstove in the corner belched out the only heat in the spartan room. Julian slammed the papers on the desk. "Why the hell didn't you make this report public?"

"I . . ." He sifted through the papers, confused. "This is the physician's report on your brother? Where did you get this?"

"Patrick didn't die by any gunshot wound. He was bloody strangled to death."

"The devil you say!" The man squinted at the papers, finally applying his spectacles to his nose. "You don't know that."

"The hell I don't. There were marks on his neck. Marks similar to those found on the Millers. Didn't anyone here bother to cross-check other records after the Millers were killed?"

The man shuffled through the papers, owl-eyed as he lifted his gaze. "You're the one who said Claremont did it, my lord. Claremont admitted as much to shooting him."

"Claremont didn't kill Patrick."

"Did the doctor hold to this opinion?"

"The marks were made by a braided strap, knotted at the front. Better to crush a man's windpipe. Death is quick but hardly painless. Aye, after comparing the cases, our conclusions are the same."

"What . . . what is it you want from me, my lord?"

"I want the murder charges against Claremont dismissed."

Julian turned, and stopped when he came face-to-face with Lieutenant Ross. Still wearing his cocked hat, he must have just arrived. The chill December wind had left his cheeks red. "You're a difficult man to track down these days," he told Julian.

"Not so difficult. I've been on my ship. In case you haven't noticed, my men are up and down the docks."

Julian walked past Ross and out the small building that served as the courthouse. He stood on the street. The midday sky was a vivid blue. Woodsmoke permeated the sea breeze. He'd just spent the last two days attempting to reconstruct Patrick's murder. Claremont's story hadn't resonated. Too much had remained unexplained. The gunshot wound to the leg, for instance, had not been more than a superficial injury. Patrick had been killed that night after Claremont left. And Julian held no doubt who was the murderer.

Across the street, an old, abandoned mercantile had drawn a crowd of hecklers. Lieutenant Ross joined him before he reached his horse. "I understand that you had trouble at one of the warehouses early yesterday morning," he said, eyeing the boisterous group behind them.

Julian turned up the collar on his coat and looked out over the distant river. "Fortunately, my men didn't shoot anyone. My guess is that a bunch of overzealous Red Lion patrons got drunk. I let them go. They're not connected to the men we're after."

Ross raised his brows inquiringly.

"Make no mistake, Lieutenant. The man who killed my brother is still out there. This fight is as much mine as yours." Julian mounted and swung the reins around. "Why didn't you tell me about the marks around Patrick's neck?"

"In my opinion, the marks were consistent with a struggle." Leather creaked as Ross mounted. "What makes you think Claremont didn't put them there?"

"If it weren't for similar marks found on the Millers, I wouldn't be questioning them now. Claremont is not their killer." Julian nudged his horse. Ross followed, and Julian slowed as they crossed Main Street. Catherine's shop was a block north.

A wagon rolled past, stirring up dust. Dismounting in front of the watchmaker's, who was also the town jeweler, he tied the reins to a post. He ascended to the boardwalk, his boot pausing on the stair. He saw that Lieutenant Ross had accompanied him to the store. He had a vague impression that the man lacked friends and wanted company as much as he wanted to talk business.

"Is there some reason you're following me all over town?"

Ross leaned with his arms crossed on the saddle, his pale wool breeches showing signs of a recent scrubbing. "I'd heard that you'd visited the physician. I was interested in your theory about the marks." He looked at the wooden sign swinging over the porch.

"I'm here to pick up something for my wife." Julian hadn't seen Catherine since he'd left her standing in the window of her house. He was anxious to dine with her tonight, alone, and in bed. The shop would close in a few minutes.

To his annoyance, Lieutenant Ross dismounted and followed him into the building. The two men filled the crowded space.

Ross whistled when the bespeckled man behind the counter displayed the wedding band Julian had purchased. "Very handsome."

Despite himself, he felt a keen sense of pride at the comment. Seven amethysts encircled a golden band. They were not expensive stones, but lilac seemed to be Catherine's favorite color, and Julian had wanted to make a band that held special meaning to her.

He raised the stones to the light and met Ross's gaze over the ring. "Do you think she'll like it?"

Lieutenant Ross laughed. "You're asking me? That ring probably cost more than I make in a year. Unless I bring in Merlin."

The statement gave Julian pause. "Haven't you done well enough breaking the back of that counterfeiting ring?"

"My job is hardly finished," Ross said, watching Julian. "The two are connected."

Julian handed the ring back to the old man, and he watched

the veined fingers carefully reinsert it back into the small wooden box. "Don't count on it."

"Indirectly, maybe, but connected nonetheless. I haven't pieced together everything. But then maybe the answer is in front of my nose, and I just have to look a little harder to see it."

Julian did not remove his gaze from Ross.

"I've been remiss in my congratulations on your nuptials." Ross reddened slightly, as if realizing he'd transgressed the bounds of propriety. "Since you seem to be the current head of the family, I didn't know if I should request your permission to court Elizabeth."

Julian raised a surprised brow. "Won't the fact that you wear that uniform interfere with any romantic aspirations? Especially considering Claremont's precarious position at the moment?"

"She doesn't seem to hold a grudge against you, my lord. Indeed, you're all she talks about."

"Your ring, my lord," the jeweler said, and handed Julian the small cherry-wood box. "Mizz Catherine will truly love the gift. Oh," he hastily said in afterthought as he bent below the counter. "Do give this to Boswell for me."

Julian hesitantly accepted the package. "He ordered toy soldiers for the young ones," the man explained. "A gift for Christmas, I believe. It seems they were accidentally melted when Boswell lit a fire in the hearth and didn't realize they'd been hidden in the ash."

"Good, God. The children?" Ross croaked.

"The soldiers, sir. Brian's were waiting to ambush Brittany's. I daresay, her soldiers won the war."

Julian's gaze rolled off Ross's with a half smile.

"Oh," the jeweler called as they reached the door. "And there's the dolls he ordered that I was supposed to pick up at the millinery, on the way over to your house tonight. Whist, my lord," he explained.

Julian was pulled slightly aback. "Whist? *Boswell?*" No more imposing snob ever walked the earth than his uppity steward.

"Tonight is our whist night," the jeweler explained, "but my wife is ill, and I won't be able to attend."

"The millinery?"

The jeweler looked momentarily horrified. "I'm not expectin' that you will run errands, my lord."

A half hour later, Julian emerged from the millinery smelling like rose water. Having just submitted to a swarm of fawning women, he silently arranged the sundry goods onto the back of his horse and wondered how a captain in the royal navy would look carrying these feminine accoutrements home. An elderly couple in a cart nodded to him as they rumbled past, and Julian's hands paused as his gaze lingered on the couple's progress down the street.

"The people here in town like you." Ross grinned, handing over the two large, frilly dolls Boswell had ordered for Brittany.

Julian looked over at him. Ross mounted. "You've married one of their own. They accept you here, my lord."

Julian remained silent a moment longer as he considered Ross's observation. The streets were busy, and he caught the laughter of a child. His eyes focused on the hands that had stilled their labors, and he wondered about the future of his own child.

He'd never felt so vulnerable and drawn to one thought, one vision, one need with sudden aching. And as he struggled with the choices he'd made, he found his cause had stirred a greater need inside him. How did a man retire from his whole life and simply become a husband and father?

Ross seemed to be waiting for Julian to finish securing the dolls when Julian looked up. "I don't know if I can do anything for Claremont," Ross said quietly. "By law, the penalty for counterfeiting and murder are the same. Dropping one charge does not take away the other. But I will see what can be done."

Julian stepped into the stirrup. A breeze lifted his cloak. He swung the reins away, then turned in a circle as he faced Ross. "I'm under duress to host a formal dinner on Saturday, two days hence. The mayor will be there. Consider yourself invited for Christmas turkey."

Surprise widened his eyes. "Thank you, my lord."

Julian swung his horse around and galloped up the street, leaving the younger man gaping at his back. Hell, a little benevolence never hurt. He stopped at Catherine's shop, only to find the door locked. Frowning, he looked at the boarded window, then backed a step to peer at the dormer above the roof overhang. It wasn't like her not to be here.

Julian mounted again and rode the quarter mile out of town to his house. The horse trotted up the circular drive, gravel crunching beneath his hooves. Handing the reins to one of his attendants, Julian took the stone stairs to the porch.

The door swung open and, removing his gloves, Julian swept past Boswell. "Where's Catherine?"

"I'm sorry, sir." Boswell remained in the entryway. Julian's hands froze over the clasps on his coat. "But it seems that Lady Catherine went to Williamsburg this morning. She has not returned."

Catherine's gaze darted between the trees where she'd just emerged from the woods. Moonlight barely penetrated the thick pine canopy. The last cart that she'd passed was a quarter mile back. Uneasy for the last few hours, she watched the shadows play on the road and felt the silence straining against the pale light that filtered through the splayed branches of pine. She'd skirted the main road and came out near a farm shed.

Since leaving Allison Simms's, her anger had given her strength and the impetus to drag her sore feet through the woods and walk home. Now all she wanted to do was sleep.

Behind her, she tugged the reins of her nag and, no longer able to persevere, grabbed her canvas bag and collapsed onto a log. Letting the night sounds fill her, she reached for the bladder of water she'd packed that morning, then finished the last remnants of cheese and bread. Her temper had brought her to this place. She should have ridden back to Williamsburg, surrendered the bag of bones the hostler called a horse, and waited for the public conveyance.

Using her hat to fan the swarm of insects from her face, she drifted onto her back and stared at the stars visible through the trees. Tears of exhaustion burned her eyelids. She'd thrown Julian's bicorn away. And now she regretted the impulse.

Her foot tapped the spongy earth. Uncertainty seized her.

Why couldn't he just have smuggled brandy? A simple act of defiance against the crown. Why did he have to be involved in something noble and important?

They'd had so little time to explore their future; she hadn't considered the past. Pride and anger clashed. How could she make Julian choose? Maybe she was a coward, as Allison had said.

Stirring restlessly, Catherine was haunted by visions of Julian with Allison. Swirling across the ballroom floor. In bed, limbs entwined.

"He left this on his last visit."

"We rarely even came into contact, except when there was information he needed to pass. He didn't even know about my relationship to Julian."

Shaking her head, she would not allow herself to take the entire blame over her failed marriage to Patrick. She'd endured deception and manipulation. She didn't care if he'd been protecting a hundred orphaned virgins. Lies had hurt her life.

Catherine?

She jerked awake.

Her eyes were wide as she tried to gauge her surroundings; she blinked back sleep and realized she'd been dreaming. The air had grown cold. Heart pounding, she swung her gaze around the wooded copse again. Only silence answered her gaze. Every muscle ached. She looked at the sky to ascertain the time and realized she'd been asleep for at least a pair of hours. Her horse—

Lord, her horse was gone!

Grabbing the canvas tote, Catherine stumbled out of the woods to the road. The moon hung like a huge watch lantern in the sky. She sliced her gaze up and down the road. Empty.

Behind her, a bird flapped through the trees. She peered into the shadows. For the first time that day, a thread of real fear snaked through her. Without taking her eyes from the woods, she knelt and, scooping up a handful of rocks shoved them into her saddlebags. Wild dogs sometimes roamed these woods. She would smash anything across the head that came within striking distance.

Catherine walked at a fast pace, listening to the night sounds. Wrapped in her cloak, she slowed only as the trees thinned into an open field. A ribbon of moonlight marked where the road cut a narrow swath through the meadow below. She stood at the top of a hill.

The sound of bridle chains touched her ears.

Catherine's horse was below. Dragging its reins, the mare was enjoying a meal of dry grass. At least the horse had the good sense to go in the right direction. With a triumphant prayer of relief, she laughed aloud and started to pick her way down the hill, when the faint whinny of another horse suddenly stopped her cold.

She froze.

Pulse thundering in her ears, even as she sought a place to hide, a cloaked rider crested the opposite hill.

"OhGodohGod," she whispered.

He remained nearly motionless, a dark ebony silhouette against the huge moon that filled the sky. She sensed him scanning the open terrain. A brooding restlessness, held in check by the reins tightly clenched in his gloved hands. She didn't breathe. Or move.

What if he wasn't Julian?

What if he was?

Either way, a sense of peril pervaded every nerve in her body as she felt his gaze scanning the meadow. In seconds, he was bound to discover her on the hillside.

Though Julian had never shown violent tendencies toward her, no doubt he would throttle her tonight.

Except what right did he have to lord over her? She'd been riding these roads alone for years as a courier to the Sons of Liberty. She bristled, aware that she was thinking irrationally but unable to stop the downward spiral. And splinter by splinter, as the wall of her defenses crumbled, so did she. He may be a hero to the fledgling continental cause, but to her—to her he was naught but a rogue and a libertine!

Then her horse whinnied, and all hope of escaping undetected vanished. She watched the other horse rear, pawing the sky as its rider hauled hard on the reins. Catherine made a split-second decision. Julian or nay, on the ground she was defenseless. Lifting her skirts in one fist, hauling her bag with the other, she scrabbled down the hill. Rocks rolled and clicked. The rider saw her almost at once and kicked the horse into a run. Panic drove her faster. Heedless of crevices that would turn a careless ankle, she reached the field in a full run. The thundering hooves bore down on her.

She was nearly to her horse when the other horse skidded to a prancing halt in front of her.

Too winded to stare in anything but disbelief, Catherine met Julian's furious eyes. His cloak flowing around him, he swung a leg over the saddle. "What the hell are you doing?"

"Stay away from me!"

He ducked as she swung her saddlebags. Then he bore down on her.

Sidestepping him, she dashed around him to reach her horse. On some elemental level, she knew her confusion and rage was about more than resentfulness over another woman, but the one was easier to latch onto than the deeper choices of sacrifice and nobility. She wanted him to go away and leave her alone in peace.

Julian lifted her, fighting, into his arms.

"Let go of me!"

"What is wrong with you, Catherine?"

"You never told me about Allison Simms!"

She swung her fist, and her momentum carried her around until he held her crushed against his chest. "Is that where you went today? Jeezus, Catherine—"

"You bought her that house. She was your mistress. You are business partners, comrades in arms. Lovers."

She struggled violently. It was a storm, a tempest that had come upon her that embodied every ounce of fear in her life.

Yet, even as she condemned Julian, the rational side of her argued that he'd had a life before she knew him. And while she was fending off Sergeant Masters and Tomkins, coping with a pregnancy, and trying to rebuild her entire world, the rational part of her brain again told her that the fault was hers for sending him away in the first place. Except it was entirely unfortunate that the rational side of her brain no longer existed!

Then she stopped fighting. Her eyes flashed.

Julian was laughing!

His breath misted in the air.

"Ah, my beautiful wife." Her lashes swept up in disbelief, and he dared kiss her nose. His cloak enfolded her. "How it warms my heart to see you jealous. If I wanted Allison, I'd have married her years ago. She is a good friend, Catherine. Nothing more."

"She's in love with you."

"Allison loves the romance of Merlin. I'm merely the object of her affection while in town." He smiled down at her. "I thought I was the only one struck by that nasty, green-eyed monster."

Heart pounding against her ribs, pressed to his body as she was, Catherine stilled. "What are you talking about?"

"I have been jealous of my brother since I discovered who you were. Jealous that he touched you. Jealous that he had you first." He laughed. Her hair had fallen down and draped his arm. "I loaned the money to Allison to purchase her house after her husband died. She's not been my mistress since you came into my life, Catherine. But I can hardly apologize for anything that went on before. She does not promote saintly thoughts in any normal male."

"Oh!" She tried to kick him through her skirts. "Let go!"

"No." His arms tightened, their corded strength pinning her against him. "You left today with no regard to your safety. I'm furious with you, Catherine. I swear now that I've finally found you, I want to shake you until your teeth rattle."

She turned her chin. "I meant to be home before dark."

His hand dipped possessively to their child. "Naturally, that makes up for the risk you took for him as well."

Her eyes faltered beneath the anger in his. Her bottom lip quivered. If he made her cry, she'd hit him. "I know women who plow the fields in their ninth month of pregnancy," she snapped defensively. "My own stepmother carried twins and walked the two miles to town twice weekly."

His hand moved upward to her chin. "That's not the kind of danger I'm talking about, and you know it."

Catherine yielded slightly to his warmth and strength. She wanted to remain angry with him over his past dalliance with Allison Simms, but she didn't have it in her any longer to be jealous when he held her in his arms.

"Do you believe that I love only you?" he asked.

And she lifted her eyes. He'd made no effort at a disguise. His dark hair was queued back with a leather thong. A white shirt laced over his chest. Black breeches tucked into boots. He was not a highwayman. He was not Merlin. No powerful lord or naval captain. Only Julian. It was as if he'd left the house today with no more thought than to find her safe.

And she did believe that he loved her, as she loved him.

Gradually, she surrendered a smile. "Only if I don't have to walk all the way home," she whispered. "My feet are terribly sore."

"How sure?" His voice was husky.

"You will probably have to carry me in your lap." She lifted on her toes. His face was rough against her lips. "Especially since I've missed you terribly."

His eyes grew serious. "Swear you will never leave the house again unescorted. Don't make me worry about you, Catherine."

She was sorry that she had. "I swear."

Then his grin grew wolfish, sending myriad colorful shivers all over her. His eyes nodded to the horse. "Do you think us capable of such daring?"

She was never destined to answer, as his mouth descended on hers, hot and honeyed, his tongue dipped between her lips. His hands firm on her waist, he pulled her against him and, wrapped in moonlight beneath the velvet sky, she believed anything possible.

Even *that!*

Catherine awakened on Christmas morn in Julian's bed to a roaring fire in the hearth. Last night after decorating the tree with her family, she'd no longer been able to await Julian and had gone to bed, only to have him awaken her in the night.

He was like ice, as if he'd been riding the night. His mouth moved hungrily over her neck. "I've missed you."

She turned into his arms. "You've been gone from your ship all day. Is aught amiss?"

He rose above her, his shoulder rippling. "For once I can say all went well." His voice was husky and in such good spirits that Catherine lingered in his kiss. When his hands moved down her hips, over her bottom, soon the physical needs of her love joined his. He moved inside her, his softly whispered words a caress to her ear, and smelling faintly of drink. She gave herself to him without restraint.

When she opened her eyes again, the room was resplendent with sunshine. The drapes on the bed were drawn. Julian was on his side, his dark hand propped beneath his head, watching her. The shadow of a beard darkened his jaw.

"Good morning," he said.

There was something so utterly disarming about the way he said those two words that put all of her irrational fears to rest. A palm-sized box lay between them, but so conscious of his handsome face, the breadth of his shoulders, it took her a minute to realize that he was waiting for her to notice his gift. With a delightful cry, she sat up, sending the sheets to her waist.

Sunlight captured the amethyst stones of the ring within. Gasping in disbelief, she lifted her gaze and found his eyes intent on her expression. "It is truly beautiful," she breathed as he slid the ring on her finger. "Purple is my favorite color."

His fingers, suddenly so unsure, hovered over her hand. "I feel as if I'm asking you to marry me all over again."

She smiled into his eyes. "Is that so, my lord." She observed the glittering stones with an imperious tilt of her hand. "Except, I don't recall you asking the first time."

His mouth quirked wickedly. "The bun was already cooking, sweet. We didn't have time to negotiate the specifics."

"Oh," she smacked a pillow over his head. "How do you manage to appear proper in public when you are so wicked beneath?"

Grabbing the pillow, he demonstrated his state of mind with a lusty grin. "I am only wicked with you."

His lips were on hers, disarming the pillow from her grip, where she dropped it to wrap her arms around him. She floated to the blankets in a hot current of air. When he pulled back, her expression fell. "I fear that I have nothing so grand to give you."

His hands boldly framing the place where their babe grew, he planted a kiss below her navel. "I want the portrait from your wall."

"You do?"

"She is the woman I remember the first night I ever saw you."

"I was supposed to be a man," she corrected him.

"Like hell," he laughed.

Growing serious, she pushed up on her elbows. "Do you think that I am some holier-than-thou princess without the courage to fight for anything?"

"Why would you think that?" Brushing the hair from her face, he looked at her intently. "Allison has filled your head."

Her eyes embraced his. "I don't want you to quit."

There was a moment's pause as the silence took on a life of its own. "Your sacrifice is daunting, sweet." Throwing the covers back, he swung out of bed. "But I don't need your permission."

Firelight delineated the bronze textures of flesh and sinew that formed his body as he walked naked to the commode. His erection stood taut, out of a cloud of dark hair, yet his mood had evaporated like so much mist.

"I didn't mean to imply that you did." She sat on the edge of the bed. The intensity of his anger had caught her off guard.

She opened her mouth to speak but inspected a feather that had floated to her knee. She wanted him inside her, not acting like she'd stepped on his little toe. "Where did you go yesterday?"

Water splashed as he cleaned the razor. "I went to Williamsburg. To return that nag you called a horse and to see your brother." His hand paused midstroke. He looked over his shoulder at her. "There's a chance that I can arrange a visit for your family."

"Why . . . would you do this for him? For us?"

"Because I actually care, Catherine." He wiped a towel over his face. "I like him. I like your stepmother and siblings. I even talked to that damn pig last night when I came in. Christ," he raised his glare to the ceiling. "Who talks to a pig? Do you know what that makes me?" he challenged. "Bloody crazy as your family."

"Where are you going?" she finally asked.

He stuck his legs into a pair of breeches. "This is Christmas. My men are far enough away from home without having to suffer through another shipboard meal. I'm arranging for Boswell to deliver turkey, yams, and bread pudding."

She jumped out of bed.

"Where are *you* going?"

"With you."

A brow lifted as he raked his eyes down her body. "Should I wrap you up first, Catherine?"

"Oh!" She'd forgotten how absolutely arrogant he could be. "I'm your wife, *Lord* Blackmoor, and if you are doing something charitable, then I wish to do my part as well. In fact, we're married now, and I expect to be included in all parts of your life. Starting today."

"Actually, I'm impressed that you've rallied the resources for the festivities this evening." He threw open the doors to the armoire. "I didn't think you could. No, I take it back. There's nothing I haven't seen you *not* do. I was hoping the kitchen would blow up, and today would be canceled."

She braced herself in front of the armoire. "You're scared."

He pressed a palm near her head. "Damn right. This is all new to me, Catherine. Today isn't about politics or war strategies. It's about family and friends. I don't know these people."

Catherine now understood. Everything made sense. His mood. His anger. He wanted to remain here. He wanted to be a part of something he didn't understand. And it scared him to death to be so vulnerable.

"Come to church with us this morning. Please." She picked a feather off his hair, then wrapped her arms around him because she wanted so much to hear the beat of his heart. "We can forget about Michael O'Hara. Forget all the ugliness."

"Christ, Catherine. I wish I could."

"Boswell brought a tree in last night. Join us downstairs."

He rested his chin atop her head and in his way apologized for his behavior. "Do you think anyone will mistake me for an ass?"

"I won't tell, if you don't," she said, suddenly intensively aware that she was deliriously happy.

A knock sounded on the door. "It's me, my lord," Boswell said, his tone anxious. "Lieutenant Ross is downstairs to see you."

Julian's lips paused over hers. "Tell him, I'll be down later."

"I think you best come now, my lord."

Chapter Twenty

"You can't let them take you, Julian. You didn't do anything!"

"Catherine—"

"I won't let them do this."

"Did you go to Allison Simms's house, yesterday, my lord?" Lieutenant Ross asked.

"Everyone already knows that he did," Sergeant Masters scoffed. "There are witnesses."

"Isn't it true that you attempted to get into the house to see her?" the magistrate's voice interceded. "That on more than one occasion, you've ignored her servants and gone straight to her room, even while she was still abed? Did you try to see her yesterday after the woman had a confrontation with your wife?"

Catherine gasped. "'Twas no confrontation—"

"I did." It was all Julian could say in a room crowded with soldiers and his own guard who had followed them from his house to the magistrate's office. Then, to Catherine, his eyes desperately apologized for the lie he had told her that morning when he told her he hadn't gone to Williamsburg yesterday to talk to Allison. He'd gone to see Claremont as he'd said, but Allison had required a needed visit as well. Except her servants had said that she'd locked her door the night before and refused all visitors—especially him.

"She was still in bed," he told Ross.

"At three o'clock in the afternoon?" The magistrate observed the report. "And this didn't concern you?"

Julian turned his gaze on the man. "I am not familiar with

Mrs. Simms's sleeping habits. My call there was not of a social nature."

"She was found stuffed beneath her bed last night. There was a footprint in her room beside the window. The intruder had come in from the back. Was Mrs. Simms your mistress?" the magistrate asked.

Lieutenant Ross spoke before Julian responded to the urge to grab the man. "That is uncalled for, sir," Ross said.

Catherine held tight to Julian.

"No," he said, adamant. "She was not my mistress."

The magistrate shuffled the papers Masters had brought with him from Williamsburg. "Her servants say differently." Looking over the rim of his spectacles, he pursed his lips. "They say that you bought her the house she lived in. Let me rephrase the question then, my lord. Have you had carnal relations with Allison Simms? Have you, my lord?" he asked again when Julian didn't answer.

Julian's expression grew more furious.

Masters's triumphant sneer turned to Catherine. "Well, my lady." Masters observed the two of them. "His silence speaks for him." He laughed.

"Enough, Sergeant." Lieutenant Ross came to his feet. "Why would a man knock on the door and then crawl through the window to murder the woman after a dozen witnesses have seen him? You haven't the evidence to arrest him. I want this proceeding halted."

"This says differently, sir." Masters flagged the arrest warrant he'd brought with him from Williamsburg. "This says I take His Lordship back. Let the authorities there decide."

Julian turned to Catherine. "Go home," he quietly said. "There's nothing more you can do here."

"This is my fault. I should never have gone—"

Julian tipped her chin, her distress so evident that he crooked a grin. "This is not your fault." He nodded to his men standing ill at ease near the length of bookcases. "My men still need their Christmas turkey. Go help Boswell." She was shaking her head, her eyes wide with unshed tears. He caught her chin. "Don't leave the protection of those two men. Not for one moment, do you understand?"

"How can you think about me at a time like this? When you are the one they wish to charge with murder?"

Julian spoke over her shoulder to the men. "Find Grimms. Tell him what has happened. I want him at the house until my return."

Catherine threw herself against him.

"I didn't kill Allison," he said softly. "I swear."

"I know that."

"Then go," he whispered against her hair, aware that every damn eye in the room watched. He kept his arms lose, but restraint was thinning. "Please."

She brushed his cheek with her softly gloved hand. "I know that she was your friend. And I'm sorry."

Christ . . . His arms tightened.

Then, despite reasoning, he crushed his lips to hers, demanding, searing as violently as the explosive tension that rushed like fire through his veins, opening her mouth to his possession. She stood on her toes and pressed against his body, tightening her fists in the woolen fabric of his uniform.

"Enough!" Masters barked; then, in deference to Lieutenant Ross, he added, "I need to get him back to face the charges, sir."

Julian pulled away and, despite the uncertainty ahead and the presence of those in the room, he winked in affection, an enticing promise that said in more than words that all would be well. "Go home. Eat lots of turkey for my son. I'll return tomorrow."

She watched Julian's tall form leave behind two soldiers. Her mouth throbbed, his taste still lingering as if to remind her of his presence. Despite his orders, she gathered her skirts and hurried down the narrow hall, finally to shove through the doors. Surrounded by a dome of blue sky so bright her eyes ached, she reached the street to see him mount. Masters sauntered past her, pausing on the stair as he faced her. The plume on his hat whipped in the wind.

"Seems this scene is familiar, my lady." He caressed a strand of her flyaway hair.

Catherine jerked away from the stench of his breath, horrified that people might have overheard. She didn't allow herself to look at Julian and only prayed that he hadn't seen Masters, more frightened by what he might do to defend her than she was of the sergeant.

"Mount up, Masters," Lieutenant Ross snapped from atop his heavy bay mount across the street. Horses milled nearby. Bridle chains rattled. The sergeant stepped into the saddle and gave the order to pull out, sending a dozen soldiers and civilians who had traveled from Williamsburg thundering down the dusty streets.

The cold wind hit her in the face, and she pulled her cloak tighter. The last to leave, Lieutenant Ross reined his horse around, his gloved hands tightly clenching the reins to keep his mount in check. "I will see that he gets back here all right."

And in that moment, Lieutenant Ross, former adversary, had won her undying respect, her loyalty, and Elizabeth's hand in marriage, as far as she was concerned.

Somehow, Catherine made it through the day. She'd helped Boswell deliver the food to the *Chimera*, the excitement so high on board that she'd wished food enough to share with the other British ships that were anchored here away from home. Catherine wondered how many Christmases Julian had spent away at sea in his lifetime.

She could endure one night if she only knew that he was safe.

Under guard that entire day, she was reminded of Julian's fear for her security and the extent to which he had gone to see her safe. She'd been an idiot to travel to Allison Simms's house, even in the mail coach surrounded by other people. Certainly one for leaving unattended. Her hand drifted to her cheek, and she tossed in bed, remembering the touch against her cheek. Her name whispered . . .

Catherine's eyes flew open.

The room was dark and cold. Wind pounded on the house. She sat up in bed. She'd left her window cracked to the fresh air, and the fire had died to a soft glow. Outside, Sally raised a racket, then stopped as Catherine recognized Samuel's voice.

Catherine shoved aside the covers. Her gaze went around the shadowy crevices in her room. Swinging her legs over the side of the bed, she checked the priming on the pistol she kept inside her nightstand, and her gaze fell on her ring finger. "Oh, Julian, would that you had not gone to Allison's."

Finally, she padded to the window where she pulled aside the drapes. Sally had quieted, and her heart ceased its frantic race as the moon came out from behind the clouds. The distant river glittered. The *Chimera* bobbed peacefully at her anchor cables, a scene so starkly beautiful, Catherine found the contrast to her emotions painful. Turning back, she sighed, for she found no comfort in this room or its emptiness, yet, in truth, she was not alone.

She'd grown to love this baby inside her with a strange sort of helpless desperation that she felt for its father. What had gone before in her life was no more. Patrick was buried. In her mind and in her heart. She had been given a second chance at life and would not see it stolen another time.

Slipping into her wrapper, she tucked the pistol in her pocket and quietly padded downstairs. No one came in from outside. A fire crackled in the drawing room. She pushed open the door. Boswell sat in an overstuffed chair, a book in hand, reading by lamplight. The twins were asleep over a battlefield of soldiers.

"Pardon, my lady." He came to his feet. "They were having so much fun, I didn't think you'd mind this one time."

She took his hands and smiled. "I'm sorry that I left dinner early tonight." She looked around the room, touching her gaze on the furnishings. She remembered when dust had covered everything. "Can we talk?" She sat on the striped settee across from the chair. "I feel I'm in need of reassurance. It's cold outside, and all I can think of is that he might be without blankets."

Boswell sat beside her. The fire in the hearth warmed the room. "Rest assured His Lordship is not without blankets. Short of threatening to tear down the place, I imagine he is worried for you."

Finding it difficult to speak, she cast around for her voice. "You and I didn't get off to a good start, did we?"

"Quite the contrary." He grinned. "I thought you were quite brave, but foolhardy to ride out into a foggy night thinking that His Lordship needed saving. I think he was very touched by the gesture."

"You joke as if you have never feared for his safety."

His grizzled face sobered. "If you have known him as long as I, you would realize that he fears very little except his own heart."

"I once accused him of avoiding his wife's graveside because he was afraid of ghosts," she said. "He fairly throttled me. But for the life of me, I have not gone out there since October. I feel as if the very trees have eyes."

Boswell seemed to consider this news. "Have you told His Lordship that?"

"That ghosts haunt the place?" She laughed at her own childishness. "Perhaps it is time to open the house again. Exorcise the ghosts. His past and my present. 'Tis a beautiful house."

"I don't know that he will, my lady. *She* is buried there."

Catherine brushed at the lace on her sleeve. "Do you think Captain Lambert will be here when our baby is born in June?"

"I know that he's not so attached to his other life that he would not move heaven and earth to make it happen if he could."

Warmth filled her. "Truly?" She laughed. "That is your opinion?"

"He's not spoken of this himself?"

"I fear he must think me slightly hero addlepated and in love with the *romance* of Merlin. I would have him never take chances again with his life. But then I'm selfishly in love and wish a father for my child." Her eyes touched his. "I don't want to replace his first wife. I just want him to love me as much."

Boswell didn't reply. She didn't really expect him to, his loyalty was to Julian first, after all, but she'd needed desperately to talk to someone, and he didn't seem to mind the intrusion.

"I fear I've been naught but a weepy-eyed child lately." She laughed. An inhale returned her gaze to her sleeve. "Do you really believe that everything will be all right?"

"Circumstantial evidence will not hold him," Boswell reassured her, "especially someone of his peerage. But this is Christmas week, and as such he will probably remain incarcerated until a magistrate can be found to revoke that arrest warrant."

"He has hired the best council for Daniel. Perhaps he will need to do so for himself."

Brittany suddenly stirred and sat up. "Rina," she murmured.

Catherine knelt beside her sister. "Come, sleepyhead." She pulled her sister to her feet. "Your soldiers will still be here tomorrow. It's time for you to sleep in your own bed."

"I will put Master Brian to bed," Boswell said from behind her.

Catherine turned. "Thank you," she said. "For everything."

"Take a lamp," he said, pointing to the dainty table where one burned brightly.

After Catherine tucked her little sister in bed, she looked in on her mother, then closing her door, padded on silent steps down the long corridor back to the room that she shared with Julian.

Shutting the door behind her, she set the lamp on her dresser, glad for the light. She removed the pistol from her wrapper, then laid the garment over the back of a chair. She went to the window, weary and miserable, where she pressed her forehead against the glass. A biting cold wind whistled through the pane. Tomorrow, she would go into Williamsburg and see for herself what was happening with Julian.

Her eyes raised to her reflection in the glass, then lifted to a place over her shoulder. Her heart froze in terror.

"You should learn to close your window, Mrs. Bellamy. Or is it Lady Blackmoor now?"

She whirled.

Standing so near she could almost touch him, Michael O'Hara observed her casually. "We are at a standstill, colleen." He grinned leisurely as his eyes raked her lack of attire. "Do ye scream and risk the wee ones before help arrives? Or do ye come with me?"

Her gaze went to her pistol. "You harm me, there will be no corner on this earth for you to hide. He'll find you. He will!"

"He won't even know you're gone, colleen. He's ruined. They'll hang him high and good. I've seen to that. When I finish here, Reece will regret that bloody righteous arrogance that ever made him think that he could beat me." He lunged at her.

She shoved against him and dashed for the bed. The blood drummed in her ears. Michael's arms came around her, and they crashed to the floor. She fought him in earnest now, tried to pound the floor.

He flipped her on her back, his eyes glittering above hers. Her nightrail was gathered above her waist. God, he would rape and kill her, and Julian would find her, here in the bedroom they'd shared.

As if reading her mind, Michael's lips split into a leer just before his mouth crushed hers. She pummeled his head and shoulders. His hands went over her breasts, down the curve of her waist, over her belly, where he suddenly stopped and pulled back to look down at his hands. "No wonder he's been so protective of ye."

"Bastard!" She gasped for breath, opening her mouth to scream.

She didn't see his fist. Only felt him hit her jaw.

"Ye needn't worry, colleen. It's not rape ye need to fear."

"You could break the glass and escape, my lord," Claremont said. "No one is out there to stop you."

Julian's height allowed him the advantage of looking out the window across Market Square. The icy breath of an approaching storm whispered through the narrow casement. An uneasy feeling gripped him.

Still dressed in what remained of his naval uniform, he'd been brought to the courthouse for James City County and placed in the chambers separated from the commons. His gaze swung around the holding room with little patience left for the legal machinations of this county. Paneled walls, chairs, and a commode made up the furnishings. Claremont was already there, having arrived earlier from the gaol. Julian should not have been here at all.

Dammit, he shoved away from the wall.

He knelt before Claremont and examined the purple swelling around his eye before he spoke. "What are you doing here?"

The chains rattled in disgust. "Masters thinks that I know things about you, my lord. He actually believes that you killed Allison Simms. We argued the point."

A chill crept down Julian's spine. He'd seen Allison's body, dressed for burial tomorrow morning, and a cold rage still lingered at the brutality of her murder. "So you took a beating."

"They wanted to know about your whereabouts the week the Millers were killed. And your relationship to your brother."

One elbow braced across his knee, Julian shook his head in disbelief. Claremont's eyes were watchful. "No one is saying, but I think they are going to accuse you of being Merlin or some such notorious highwayman type, though I don't see how. Masters seems to think that by virtue of your marriage to my sister, you must be guilty of something. Masters has a vendetta against you, my lord."

"Do you know how he gets his information?"

"Masters is an English pig very good at extracting intelligence from anyone. Problem is, he doesn't much care who his sources are." Claremont's head turned. Someone was approaching.

Instantly alert, Julian stood as Ross entered. Sergeant Masters and three others followed. Masters carried leg shackles.

"Your solicitor is still in chambers." Fury laced Ross's voice, and almost an apology. "They are incarcerating you, my lord. There's nothing more that can be done until you are tried in three weeks. The magistrate is charging you with murder."

"Christ," Julian growled in amazement, "this whole incident is goddamn unbelievable. On what evidence?"

"This bag was found in your stables."

Julian recognized the tote as the one Catherine had carried the night he found her returning from Allison's. Ross carefully up-ended the bag over a chair, sending rocks, a wedge of uneaten cheese, and what looked like a knotted leather strap to the bunk. Something like a fist slammed into his gut.

"It's possible this weapon was used to kill three people," Ross said. "And it's in your possession, my lord."

"A charge like that won't stick." But Julian was no longer sure of anything. Tension arced through him. It went through his muscles and every nerve like a violent current of electricity.

O'Hara must have followed Catherine that night she left Allison's. Which meant Allison was probably dead before Catherine left the yard. Which meant O'Hara had gotten close enough to Catherine after that, and had wanted Julian to know.

"Catherine had that bag the night she visited Allison Simms." He raked a palm across his face. Ross had walked to the window across the room to stare out. "It's been in the stables since."

"Maybe a ghost put that strap in there," Masters whispered.

Some of the fever left Julian's eyes but only for the breath of time it took to focus on Masters. "Ghosts?" he said as if suddenly struck dumb and enlightened at once by something Catherine had once said. Something that had been in front of his face the whole time.

"Boo!" Masters rattled the chains. "*Now* who's going to be ripping out my spleen?"

Julian's hand snaked out and, before Masters could gasp, he'd wrapped his fist in the sergeant's stock. "How much is he paying you, you slimy worm?" Julian hissed.

"I know your dirty secret," Masters rasped. "They got evidence against you. You're never walking out of here."

Two guards had come running forward and now wrestled to free the sergeant. Hands pried at Julian's grip. "Let him go," Ross ordered.

"If I ever suspect that you're involved in what is happening, I swear the world won't be big enough for you to hide in, you bastard."

Thrashing wildly, Masters choked for air. Julian was heedless of them all. A red haze had pierced his skull. He didn't give a toad's ass if one more murder charge was added to the others. But the sergeant had done Julian one favor tonight.

For he now knew where Michael O'Hara was.

He knew to the core of his being where O'Hara had been hiding. And why not? The irony was so beautiful he would have laughed if not suddenly possessed by the bloodlust to commit outright murder.

Yelling in the corridor had grown, as panicked voices trailed up and down the hall. A third guard ran forward. Someone finally tore Julian's grip away, and while three people held his arms, another finished shackling his ankles.

Masters stumbled back and hit the wall. His opaque eyes wide with shock, he gasped for air. The guards edged back. Jerking his uniform tunic over his paunch, Masters pushed through the throng of men in a rapid thud of feet. Julian grabbed for each breath.

"Hell, Captain." Claremont hadn't moved from his place on the floor. "That outburst should inspire confidence in your plea."

Ross had gathered up the tote bag of evidence and now stood at the door. His eyes, filled with neither censure nor apology, watched him as if some part understood the desperation in his outburst but the other part, the man bound by duty, did not.

"Someone will be here in a few minutes, my lord. You will be under house arrest until the trial." He took Claremont into his gaze. "You'll be taken back to the gaol." With a flick of his gloved hand, he motioned the guard to open the door. It grated closed.

"Is it true then?" Claremont rose slowly to his feet. "Masters's dirty little secret about you? Are you Merlin?"

Behind him through the window, Julian saw that it had begun

to rain. In another hour, he guessed it would turn to snow. "This isn't the time, Claremont." He moved awkwardly to the door to listen.

"No? When is a convenient time? After you leave my sister pregnant with your child? And I have to hunt you down for being the lying bastard your brother was? Or will she bury you, too?"

Julian shifted his gaze to confront Claremont's. He didn't have time to pick through the hostility in Claremont's voice. Any conjecture the younger man drew from the accusations against him or what he'd revealed no longer mattered.

Finally, satisfied that the corridor outside was empty, he dropped to the floor and released his shackles, wondering how long before Masters realized that the key was missing from his belt.

Chapter Twenty-one

When Daniel caught up to Julian, he had already reached his town house and emptied his chests. "You're leaving here, tonight," Julian told him, throwing a bundle of garments in his direction.

Clothes lay strewn over the floor. Julian's uniform was piled on the bed. He'd changed into a woolen waistcoat and breeches more fitting for the weather. More fitting for the night A heavy cloak encased him like a shadow. With precious little time, he'd scavenged for a chart and, laying it flat out on the table, he hastily lit a lamp.

Hope Plantation.

It would be no easy task by any road to get there and, with the approaching storm, he would not make it tonight.

His palms grew moist on the polished table surface, and he lowered his head. A long saber hung from a sash around his waist. He thought of Catherine and the child they had coming into the world. The baby would be born the end of June. And for a heartbeat, his mind lingered uncertainly over his future. Delegating his emotions to the back of his mind, he could not allow himself the luxury of doubt. Yet, as his gaze went over the chart, a vague sense of helplessness gathered like a knot inside him.

He blew out the lamp and, for the second time that night, thought of Allison and the brutality of her death. It no longer mattered that Julian be the one to hunt O'Hara down. Only that he was caught. Now. The imperative need overriding all else with as much improvidence as a comet crossing the sky and divining one's future.

"You don't even know if O'Hara is at Hope Plantation." Still winded after running the whole way from the courthouse, Daniel bent over the last clip on his belt.

"It doesn't matter; you're getting the hell out of this place. I've given you the name of Allison's contact in Norfolk County."

And for a long stretch of furious silence, Julian contemplated a host of uncertainties in his plan. He rolled up the chart, hesitating only as he thought of Catherine, confident that his men would let no one near her. When he finally looked up, Claremont had not moved.

"I'm going with you." His blue eyes were stubborn behind the bruises on his face.

"Like hell you are." Julian shoved a pistol in his braces, gathered up what food remained in the house, and slipped out the back.

"His name is O'Hara. Michael O'Hara."

Lieutenant Ross spun, his hands no longer working the cinch on the saddle. Julian stooped on his haunches inside the stall away from anyone watching the front. A lantern on the wall spilled light over the black cloak pooled at his boots. His saber scraped the floor.

Ross was alone in the stables, for the moment anyway. Julian knew where he'd be because they'd boarded their horses in the same place when they'd arrived in Williamsburg.

"Every able body in Williamsburg is out looking for you."

"But not you."

Ross leaned an elbow on the saddle. "Is Claremont with you?"

"Would you be, if you were going to be hanged next week?" Impatient, Julian suddenly wanted only to get on the road. "Tonight is your lucky night, Lieutenant. I'm doing you a favor." He withdrew the placard Daniel had drawn, pausing for a moment as he contemplated one last time his actions, and what tonight would probably cost him.

"This man is the leader of the counterfeiting ring you broke last week. He killed Patrick and the Millers to keep them quiet."

He handed up the placard. "I have reason to suspect he is holed up at Hope Plantation. That he has been for some time."

Ross took the drawing. "How do you know this?"

"I became personally involved here after I started investigating Patrick's death." Julian picked up a piece of straw from the floor and studied the frayed end. "I had the unfortunate circumstance upon my arrival to find myself thrown into a game of cat and mouse. Or chess, as he would like to think we're playing," he said neutrally. "If I go tomorrow and if my guess is right, I am one man."

"So, the invincible Lord Blackmoor is mortal after all?" Ross said with appropriate deference to a man who had slipped his shackles and walked out of a well-guarded courthouse in defiance of them all. Who could probably break his neck if provoked. Who was risking his future by coming to him now.

Ross tucked the placard into his tunic. "If you had waited two or three days, your solicitor would have gotten you out with only a small scandal in your wake."

"I don't have days to play around with the legal system."

"What about Allison Simms?"

"She was my contact here." Julian's gaze lifted. "I've known her for years. She was a friend."

The silence that followed was broken only by the muted voices of guards outside in the street. Julian stood to look over the stall.

"They will have gone to your town house by now," Ross said. "I doubt they'll last much longer in the cold."

Julian turned. "After tomorrow, if you still believe me guilty of any crimes, I'll hand myself over to you."

Ross dragged his gaze away and bent his attention to his hands crossed on the saddle. "You do realize that you've just shot your naval career all to hell?" he said.

"Aye," despite himself, Julian grinned. "I was retiring from the life anyway."

Ross seemed to consider this. "And Claremont?"

Julian slipped out of the stall. "Claremont who?" he called over his shoulder.

"He confessed in front of the magistrate to being Merlin."

Brows arched, Julian stepped back into the lantern light.

"Aye." Ross leaned on the stall door. "God as his witness,

when the sergeant tried to accuse you, Claremont told Masters and the magistrate that he was the infamous highwayman, smuggler, pirate of all trades."

"Naturally, that would have made him fourteen when he smuggled his first case of brandy."

"You left home at thirteen. It happens."

"Christ," Julian's cloak swirled around his calves, "does the whole bloody world know everything about me?"

He slipped out the side door and stood in the darkness as his gaze went around the copse. The bitter wind swept through the trees and tore at his cloak. Restless energy surged through him. His sense of purpose, now strong within his chest, would not be checked. Not by the storm. Not by doubt or the road he found himself on now. There was no going back. He had to find O'Hara.

With gloved fingers, Julian worked a woolen scarf over his hair and ears. Swirling flakes of snow danced in the currents. Claremont waited in the trees, his expression defiant, when Julian found him a few moments later. Not used to being disobeyed, Julian was already walking past the younger man toward where the horses pulled at their tethers. "I thought I told you to get the hell out of here."

Daniel shoved off the tree. "You need me, my lord."

Battling the frigid wind, Julian grabbed at the reins and flung himself into the saddle. "You and I are destined for a long talk, Mr. Claremont." He bent over and adjusted the stirrups.

"Where are we going, my lord?" Daniel mounted.

"Tomorrow *you're* leaving." Julian swung the horse around. "But for now, I have a cottage south of here. It will do for tonight."

"Yes," the younger man's voice grinned, "I remember the place."

Julian only hoped no one else did. He paused and waited for Claremont to catch up to him. "How is it you found me that day?"

"I followed you from the gaol," he said over the wind. "I saw you take Rina out. Then I went back to get help to rescue my sister." For a moment, they rode side by side. "Do you think she's safe?"

A chill passed down his spine. As the miles passed, Julian

could not allow himself to think of Catherine. Getting word to her was impossible. At the moment, it was all he could do to stay alive.

Julian reached the cottage and, dragging Claremont half frozen from his mount, lit a fire in the hearth. By morning, the storm had blown past and left a pristine layer of white over the trees and the ground, which by midmorning had melted to slush. Julian took the long rifle down from its slot over the hearth, packed a knapsack with charges and balls, another with food. Strapping on his cutlass, he left the cottage, only to find Claremont awaiting him in the stables.

This time Julian gave up attempting to talk sense into his new-found family member. The horses were already saddled and packed with supplies. Julian stepped into the stirrup. "She will not forgive me if I let them hang you," he said flatly, swinging his leg over the horse. His cloak swirled around his legs.

"Rest assured, my lord. I will forgive myself even less."

They traveled fast, resting their mounts once before reaching the outskirts of Hope Plantation by late afternoon. Julian dismounted and, tying off the horses, walked through the surrounding woodlands until he reached the river. Carrying the rifle, he knelt in the long tufts of wet grass. He could see the house through the bare trees on the distant rise. Sunlight bathed the walls in gold, the perception of warmth a stark contrast to the wintry chill that ravaged the surrounding countryside. Voices came over the ridge.

Ross had not arrived with his men. A deer bolted through the tangled wood. Julian slid to the ridge. A ship lay in plain sight below on the river. A bonfire crackled and burned on the shore, sending sparks floating high into the sky. Laughter carried to where Julian and Claremont lay.

"They're leaving tonight," Daniel said. "How did you know?"

Julian didn't reply. His senses attuned, he searched the ridge for the watch. Mostly he searched for the man he had come to kill.

"I told you to watch her." Michael tossed Catherine on to the bed, knocking the air from her lungs. Before she could scramble away, he grabbed her wrist, crushing it in his grip.

"Let go of me!" Catherine kicked out and tried to bite him.

She'd come to an hour before Michael had ridden with her onto the grounds of Hope Plantation. A ride that had taken the night to get here. Jed and three other men had ridden with him, ice frozen on their beards when they'd arrived midmorning. Wearing woolen stockings and wrapped in a cloak and a thick down blanket, the barrier still had not been enough to keep the cold away. Michael had carried her to this room, half frozen from the elements.

But she would not stay.

She would not be used to defeat Julian!

Michael had caught her on the long, winding staircase.

"I thought she was asleep," Jed said. "I swear."

"She's not to be trusted. Do ye see my eye? It will be bloody black and blue, and I have you to thank, ye bloomin' halfwit!"

"You oughtn't be talking that way to me."

"Maybe you don't want to work for me." Michael withdrew his pistol. "Maybe we can just bloody sever our arrangement now."

"No!" she screamed. "Don't kill him because of me. Please."

"Indeed," Michael smirked. "You are fond of Jed here. I think he's fond of you, colleen."

"I would not have him shot between the eyes!"

Michael set down the pistol. The corners of his mouth tightened. She pounded him with her fists. He grabbed each of her wrists, binding them to the back of the thick oaken headboard with wet leather strips. Her back pressed against the oaken swirls. There was no comfort, not even a pillow to ease the pain against her shoulders.

"Bastard! Why are you doing this?"

"A diversion, my love. You will see." He solicitously covered her as he pulled back to survey his handiwork. She still only wore her nightrail, and her show of bravery was starting to crumble.

"You'll never get out of here. Julian will have contacted other ships by now. The British navy will be watching the river."

His thumb caressed her swollen lip. "Your concern for my welfare is touching." Turning to Jed, he said on the way out, "Gag her. I don't want to hear her screams."

The tone of those horrible words sent a chill down Catherine's spine. She had to think of her child. She could not allow Michael to destroy her. She had to find a way to warn Julian where Michael was.

"Why did you stop him?" Jed asked, drawing her gaze.

Catherine's eyes burned as she found Jed standing beside the bed, a rag in hand. He wore a heavy sleeveless waistcoat over a checkered shirt. "May I have something to drink?" she whispered.

He looked around him. His gaze told her what she could obviously discern for herself. "You shouldn't have tried to escape. Maybe I could have gotten something for you."

"Hasn't there been enough killing? You've lost everything because of that man. And now he seeks to harm the one I love most in this world. Do you think me wrong to fight for that?"

"He's made me rich."

"You have nothing. Your family is in jail. You will be running from the authorities the rest of your life. Aye, you have riches because that man out there has allowed you to think so."

Rag in his hand, he knelt over her. "I'm not going to listen to you."

"Let me go, Jed. Please," she whispered desperately, prepared to do or say anything to save her child. To save Julian. "He's not one of us. He didn't grow up around here. You and I did. He doesn't know about loyalty the way we do."

"Loyalty?" he mocked. "Yer brother betrayed us all."

"But I didn't, did I, Jed? I never said anything to anyone about you. And you never said anything about finding me in your barn. That counts for something. Don't you think?"

"We could go away together," Jed said. "O'Hara says yer husband isn't comin' back."

Catherine closed her eyes. Her heart would burst. She had to get away. From the look of the draped furniture and the lack of footprints in the dust, no one ventured here. "I will do anything, Jed. I beg you." She opened her eyes. "Just let me go."

Something passed across his features. Something as close to feeling as a man like him might show. "He told me to gag you." But Jed gave her a pillow for her back before he applied the gag to her swollen mouth, then bound it with a strap of leather.

The realization that she could suffocate on her own tears and panic nearly choked her. Her hair spilled over her face. Then, taking the lamp, Jed exited the room, leaving her in the frigid shadows without so much as a lifeline of hope.

She pulled and fought her restraints, finally exhausting her struggle. She'd been tied to the middle of a massive four-poster bed, it's floral canopy and velvet drapes pulled back to allow her full view of the river. The snow had stopped that morning. A huge bonfire lit the shore, leaping with glowing arrogance toward the sky. An eerie glimmer shone through the frozen trees. She could see a ship. Men were loading crates into the hold.

Tears gathering in her eyes, she looked around the room where Michael had dragged her.

This was the master bedroom. Julian had once slept here. He'd slept in this bed with his first wife. This room had been theirs, she realized. She had probably died here.

And in that fatal moment, Catherine knew that Michael intended her to die in the same place. The bitter irony of it hit her in the chest with the force of a kick. Her death would strike at the heart of Julian. He would never know what happened to her. Never know that she had been brought here. So, even if he defeated Michael, Julian would still lose.

Finally, she leaned back against the headboard. The distant fire burned hotter and brighter. After a full day of sheer emotional and physical exhaustion, she could not stay her eyes from closing.

But she had to. If she slept, she may never awaken again.

The sun continued across the sky. With its gradual descent, some of the ice began to return to the room. The bonds on her wrists tightened and, in the end, it was the horrible pain that kept her awake. No one came with food or drink. No one came to the house at all. The day grew colder, and when she opened her eyes to peer from swollen lids, she saw that it had grown darker, that the clouds had taken away the sunlight.

The wind whistled through the empty house. Then the door closed with an audible click. And somewhere she heard someone scream.

Screams of panic sent the camp into chaos. Julian watched from his perch on the ridge. He'd fired the first shot into the watch, standing just outside the burning pyre on the beach.

Somewhere farther down the beach, more guns fired. Powder

smoke drifted and mingled with the dying bonfire. Julian didn't know how many men in Michael's crew truly knew of O'Hara's betrayal, which made him reluctant to fire on anyone who didn't look as if he might fire first on one of Ross's men. Surprisingly, most dove into the frigid water from the ship's deck rather than face the prospect of capture. Others laid down their weapons, while another dozen shadows scrambled up the rocky ledge, only to be corralled by the men who stood behind Julian. He'd remained on the hill for one purpose, his eyes narrowing on the disorder below. Daniel shoved the rifle back into his hands and, raising it, he took aim at the shooter sniping from the top castle platform on the ship. A puff of smoke, and the explosion sounded. The rifle bucked, and the man tumbled to the deck.

"There, my lord!" Claremont pointed over the storage sheds.

Four men had broken through Ross's flank and now scrambled up the hill. Each man carried torches, and even as Julian watched, a storage shed went up in flames. Julian recognized O'Hara among the escaping thieves. Since Ross's arrival, Julian had lost sight of the man.

Raising the rifle that Daniel had shoved back into his hands, Julian took aim. From the beach, horses had broken down the corral and stumbled up the incline into his line of fire. Julian stood. His heart hammered in his chest and, even for all his driving fury, six years of friendship froze his finger on the trigger. Shooting any man in the back reeked of cowardice, and Michael had been like a brother. But a man didn't waste honor on dishonorable men if he wanted to survive. He'd learned that much fighting almost two decades of wars.

He sighted down the rifle, following Michael as he and two others broke off from the main swarm. O'Hara reached the first terrace. With an oath, Julian watched Michael hit the copse of trees.

He tossed the rifle to Daniel.

Oblivious to the chaos, Julian ran across the ridge, measuring his pace against the darkness now that he was away from the fire. Then watching his prey near the house atop the hill, he was suddenly running full out, recklessly leaping boulders and fallen trees. A horse galloped past, its rider intent on escape. Julian pulled him off and, grabbing at the reins, swung into the saddle. The horse reared, leaping off into a run. The tree line loomed. Julian dipped low to prevent a branch from knocking him off the saddle; then he bore down on O'Hara, gobbling up the distance in a thunder of hooves.

Michael had reached the house. Torch in hand, he seemed to be fighting someone. Metal hissed as Julian withdrew his cutlass. The wind whipped past his face. He leapt the fence.

As if sensing the horse bearing down on him, Michael spun. He carried a torch in one hand and a pistol in the other.

"You don't mean it, O'Hara," Tomkins said, backing away.

"Do it!" he yelled at Tomkins.

Legs braced, O'Hara flung the torch toward the house. "You're a bloody fool, Reece," he laughed as Julian reined in the horse. Clots of dirt scattered over the ground. "Do it, Tomkins!"

Holding the reins of the horse, Julian lifted his gaze to the house. Breath steamed from his mouth. His mount pranced a circle as Julian continued to hold tight to his grip.

"Give it up, O'Hara," Julian said. "You're beaten."

"I have to admit, Reece, my friend, I didn't figure you would call in the cavalry. You've surprised me." Julian saw a pistol in O'Hara's hand. "Well, I have a surprise for you. Do it, Tomkins!"

That Tomkins faced a pistol rather than torch the house brought Julian's gaze back around. He hauled hard on the reins, and the dark horse reared up on its haunches, pawing at the air as Julian searched the windows. He could smell burning wood. Someone had already lit the back side of the dwelling. But the house seemed to fight the vicious attack. Flames licked at the gazebo.

Aye, his heart and his life had once been here.

But no more.

"Bloody damn fool." O'Hara fired, hitting Tomkins in the chest.

The force of the charge threw Tomkins backward against the white column. He fell hard. The torch slid across the porch, rolling to a stop near the open door. Something caught and sputtered to life.

Julian swung his leg over the saddle, his cloak flowing with his motion around his calves. Sword drawn, he didn't wait to mince words with O'Hara. He slashed down on Michael's blade. Metal rang and clashed with the force of each blow. They battled around the clearing. Neither man was a novice; both had wielded

their sabers against powerful foes. Someone rushed him from behind, and Julian ducked, swinging his cutlass and fatally slashing
the attacker.

"You're a bastard, O'Hara." Julian hissed between each
breath, raising his cutlass to fend off Michael's blow. But his defense was late, and a slash opened the flesh on his upper arm.
Every nerve and muscle tensed with the blinding shock of pain.

"Aye, that I am, friend." His chest heaved with the exertion.
"You have no idea . . . how much."

Desperately marshaling every ounce of strength, Julian
pressed Michael. Blood made his grip on the cutlass slippery.

He'd wanted to ask Michael why. But he knew he was no less
barbaric in the way he had lived his life the last ten years. He
wanted none of that now. He wanted only peace.

'Twas ironic that he had to kill a man to find that peace.

Behind him, the flames had caught, licking and consuming the
house with a ferocious hunger that singed Julian's hair. Vaguely,
he realized the fighting at the river had stopped.

They broke apart. The heat was unbearable. O'Hara's eyes
glinted savage. "Have ye wondered . . . where your wife is,
Reece?"

Julian started. They stalked each other in a circle. "It won't
work, O'Hara." But the words had stolen beneath his guard. And
a prickle of unease began to gnaw. "It's over."

With a surge of force, Michael pushed him backward. And
then Julian sidestepped O'Hara's sword and his own sank deep.
Fatally. Neither man moved. O'Hara fell against him, his hand
gripping Julian's injured arm. "It . . . was always about . . . you,
Reece." Michael was breathing hard. "No one could ever beat
ye." He sank to his knees. "Until now."

With that, he flipped something round, a flash of metal, and
Julian snatched it from the air. His palm slowly opened.

Catherine's wedding ring.

And then he knew.

He knew.

God in heaven, he knew why Jed Tomkins had hesitated to
torch the house. He knew what Michael had done to get Julian
out of Yorktown, away from Catherine. He knew that in
Michael's mind, if the game were over for one, it would be over
for all.

Julian's gaze lifted to the inferno. Rage and fear and agony built and choked him. The house was already fully ablaze. Flames climbed high into the black sky, choking the heavens. He dropped his sword. Took two steps and started to run. Hands grabbed his arms.

He fought them wildly. Three men dragged him back. Glass began to shatter as windows exploded all over the house.

"Let me go!" He choked for breath. "She's in there!"

"You can't go in there, man!" Ross held him, fighting like a wild man, his arms shaking with the force it took to keep Julian from running head-on into the blazing inferno. "It's too damn late!"

Julian stared in horror at the wall of flame. He could no longer look without shading his eyes. Everything burned. Beside the house, flames raced up trees. Ross was moving everyone back to the trees.

"It was to be a beacon. A diversion," Ross said to someone, probably Claremont. "So he could get out of here."

Michael had been left where he'd died. If Julian could have killed him a thousand times more, it would not lessen the knot of agony and rage inside.

He could remain here no longer. Ignoring Ross and Claremont, he sought only to run. He reached a horse. And then he stopped. For climbing up the ridge from the river 'twas surely a ghost.

She wore white. Her silken hair, dark as night, bathed her shoulders like the velvet sky filled with a thousand stars. He stood unmoving. Only when he threw aside the reins and leapt down the hill did she lift up her gown and run toward him.

Julian swept her into his arms, heedless of the blood that he got on her nightrail. "It was Jed," she whispered. "I couldn't warn you that I was safe."

He knew that Tomkins could not have survived long with the wound in his chest. The only reality was that she lived. That they were both alive, that her arms held him as though she feared that he might somehow slip away.

Chapter Twenty-two

Catherine sat at her desk in the shop. Bent over a drawing, she didn't hear the door downstairs open. When she glanced up, Julian stood in the room, and her heart lurched. Dressed in his full uniform, she knew that he was leaving now. She'd come here to her shop because she could not bear to see him go.

It had been almost a month since Hope Plantation had burned to the ground. He'd been back and forth to Williamsburg with a number of loose ends that needed tying, including testimony against Sergeant Masters for misconduct. Lieutenant Ross for his part had received a commendation, but alas, was no further in the door with Elizabeth than he had been. Her sister was too much of a free spirit perhaps to tie herself to a man, especially a British officer, no matter how dashing. But Catherine had grown fond of him and welcomed his frequent visits to the shop.

Julian had seen that Daniel safely vanished amidst rumor that her brother had been the notorious Merlin. But Daniel had been adamant about retaining his newfound reputation. And who was Julian to argue the illogic of it all?

They'd said their good-byes last night. "I wanted to give you this before I leave." He held out a document.

Catherine read the parchment he gave her, and her eyes lifted in wonder. "This deed is dated the day after the ball."

"I'd intended to give it to you the night I went to your house."

She stepped into his arms. "Why can't you stay?"

He leaned against her. "One cannot walk away from the Royal

Navy." And his hand went to her abdomen. "Do you believe me when I say that I'll return?"

But as Catherine watched the *Chimera* sail away that blustery day in January, she thought her heart would die.

The months crawled past, and winter eased into spring much too slowly. Catherine's first run of the newspaper was a success. Elizabeth took on the task of reporter. They'd hired two apprentices who, as Catherine's time approached, gradually ran the business.

In March, the Virginia House of Burgesses had appointed an eleven-member committee to communicate with other colonies. In May, The Tea Act had taken affect. Here in Yorktown, there was only a sense of waiting, for surely nothing more could touch their peace.

Her labor pains started the first day of summer, while she was with her stepmother finishing the final touches of the nursery, and her daughter was born seventeen hours later, a red-faced screaming banshee that Catherine thought the most beautiful child put on this earth. As she held Bethany Faye Lambert, though she knew everything around her was changing, a new passion had taken hold.

By August, the weather had grown hot, and Catherine had begun to leave her window open to the balmy breeze. It had taken her months to get over the fear of leaving her windows open again, and tonight when she awoke to Sally's squealing, she came out of bed, her heart racing in her chest. She heard the rumble of a fast approaching horse and a man's voice as Samuel spoke to someone who had just arrived.

A voice she recognized.

A beautiful voice.

Catherine tossed back the covers. Julian was already at the bottom of the stairs when she reached the landing. And they both came to a stop. He no longer wore his uniform but a simple frock coat of royal blue. His hair seemed almost black; his hazel eyes aglitter. A memory invaded of another day, when she'd seen him atop the ridge, and his eyes had found her alive.

They met in the middle of the stairs, halfway up and halfway down, and she flung herself laughing in his arms.

"I'm free," he murmured in her hair. "I'm finally free."

"No, my lord." She kissed him deeply. "You shall not get off that easily. You have a family, and I shall never let you go again."

"Where is she?"

And when Catherine took him to their bedroom, and Julian held his daughter for the first time, he knew that he'd finally come home.

About the Author

Multipublished author, **Laura Renken,** is a romance industry RIO Dorothy Parker Award, Bookseller's Best, Golden Heart & Maggie finalist, and a winner of the prestigious Holt Medallion for her novels. She is a wordsmith, a creater of dreams, and a passionate believer in happy endings. A product of thirteen schools and twenty-two moves stretching across the United States and Europe, she is a self-proclaimed gypsy, whose passion for writing developed at an early age while living overseas where she acquired an appreciation for historical intrigue. She graduated with a degree in criminal justice from the University of Oklahoma. Laura lives near Chicago with her husband, a retired Marine Corps fighter pilot, where she now writes fulltime. You can visit her website at: http://www.laurarenken.com.

SEDUCTION ROMANCE

*Prepare to be seduced...by the sexy
new romance series from Jove!*

Brand-new, full-length, one-night-stand-alone
novels featuring the most seductive heroes in the
history of love....

❑ **HEART OF A WARRIOR**
by Betty Davidson   0-515-13101-6

❑ **NIGHT SHADOW**
by Laura Renken   0-515-13155-5

❑ **TOUCHED BY FIRE**
by Kathleen O'Reilly   0-515-13240-3

❑ **DANGER'S PROMISE**
by Marliss Moon   0-515-13275-6

AVAILABLE WHEREVER BOOKS ARE SOLD OR
TO ORDER CALL:

1-800-788-6262